GUARDIAN

DAUGHTERS OF LILITH:
BOOK 4

Jennifer Quintenz

SECRET TREE PRESS

Copyright © 2016 Jennifer Quintenz
Cover design by Jennifer Quintenz

All rights reserved. This book or any portion thereof may not be reproduced or used in any manner whatsoever without the express written permission of the publisher except for the use of brief quotations in a book review.

Printed in the United States of America

First Printing, September 13, 2016

ISBN-13: 978-0-9915222-1-7
ISBN-10: 0-9915222-1-4

Secret Tree Press
www.JenniferQuintenz.com

PUBLISHER'S NOTE: This is a work of fiction. Names, characters, businesses, places, and events are either the product of the author's imagination or used in a fictitious manner, and any resemblance to actual persons, living or dead, business establishments, events, or locales, is entirely coincidental.

Please purchase only authorized electronic editions, and do not participate in or encourage piracy of copyrighted materials. Your support of the author's rights is appreciated.

*To James, I'm so glad to be
on this journey with you.*

Contents

Acknowledgments	i
Chapter 1	1
Chapter 2	11
Chapter 3	27
Chapter 4	47
Chapter 5	63
Chapter 6	81
Chapter 7	95
Chapter 8	105
Chapter 9	119
Chapter 10	131
Chapter 11	145
Chapter 12	153
Chapter 13	169
Chapter 14	189
Chapter 15	205
Chapter 16	219
Chapter 17	239
Chapter 18	251
Chapter 19	265
Chapter 20	271
Chapter 21	281
Epilogue	289
A Note From The Author	295
About The Author	297

ACKNOWLEDGMENTS

With book four, I once again have to thank my family for their unflagging support—my husband, James, in particular for riding this rollercoaster by my side. He is an amazing wrangler of pre-schoolers, and no one makes a better turkey burger. Did I mention he brews his own beer?

I'm blessed to have a sister who shares my love of reading, doesn't mind me picking her brain about plot lines and character arcs, and who generously donates her time for reading outlines and drafts even though she's got two full time jobs and two little kids of her own.

I'm also indebted to a bevy of talented friends for their notes and feedback on outlines and drafts. Bethany, Josh, Manda, Marc & David, Barbara, and Dot—thank you for sharing your insights and chasing down those pesky typos that seem so good at slipping past me.

To the whole gang, these books would be so much less without you. Thank you, from the bottom of my heart.

*For we do not wrestle against flesh and blood,
but against the rulers, against the authorities,
against the cosmic powers over this present darkness,
against the spiritual forces of evil in the heavenly places.*

- Ephesians 6:12

1

The last of Hale's ashes hung suspended in the air, stirred by a subtle wind. Tiny glimmering motes swirled against the backdrop of a breathtaking valley, but its beauty left me numb.

How could this be the only thing left? Hale had seemed so substantial in life, so unstoppable. He'd been full of confidence and power, humor and compassion. And now... How could these ashes be all that was left of such a great man?

Juniper laced the air with its spicy scent, mingling with the musky smell of earth still damp with morning dew. The rising sun felt warm on my face, but it did nothing to thaw the ice beneath my heart.

Grief can be exhausting. Hale had played a huge role in my life over the last two years. He'd helped shape the person I was becoming. He'd shown me that it's not who or what you are that matters, it's what you do that counts. Even now, I felt the urge to seek him out in the crowd, to draw strength from his reassuring presence. Only he wasn't here, and he wasn't coming back. I looked around at our small gathering and saw the weight of Hale's absence pressing down on each of us. Gretchen and Matthew stood close together, their bodies hunched with an unspoken pain. Thane's face was a stony mask. Only his eyes, red rimmed and swollen, gave voice to the sorrow within. And Dad, Dad looked down at the empty vase in his hands with a look so lost I had to tear my eyes away. Lucas must have sensed my anguish. I felt his fingers tighten around my hand. I turned to him. His eyes were bright with unshed tears. I felt a sharp stinging in the bridge of my nose. Another tear escaped, tracing its way down my cheek before I brushed it off with the back of my hand. Beyond us, Cassie and Royal stood with their heads bowed. After two years of trying to keep my friends separate from my destiny, it was clear they were now inescapably entangled in it. I let out a soft sigh. I couldn't stomach the guilt, not now. Not on top of this grief.

There was nothing left to say. What Hale had meant to us couldn't be articulated. Thane had spoken the customary words, words I had heard at other Guardsmen's funerals. Words about sacrifice, and valor. But those words were incapable of summing up his life.

And so we stood here in silence as dawn flooded the mountains with the light of a new day. All around us, nature awoke. We could hear it in the happy chattering of meadowlarks, the buzzing of bees, the rustle of lizards snaking their way through the high desert scrub brush. But underneath it all, was the profound silence of death.

I heard footsteps on the path behind us and turned. Karayan approached. A fist tightened around my heart. In her hands, Karayan held a wreath of tenderly braided bluebells. Even wracked with grief, Karayan was beautiful. The wind teased a few honey blond locks away from her face. She knelt at the edge of the cliff and laid her wreath on the ground.

Something within me broke, and I turned my face into Lucas's shoulder. His hands came up around me, caught me in a tight embrace. I felt his heartbeat against my cheek. He was here. He was alive. And I was so grateful. Somehow, Lucas had emerged unscathed from the ordeal in the mines. What I had taken from him should have rendered him a shadow of himself. Should have marked the beginning of the end of his life. And yet, miraculously, he had survived whole. If not for that miracle, I would be Karayan, laying a wreath on the cold earth for Lucas.

And then I felt it again—the inky smudge of her presence. The demon who'd attacked Lucas had left something of herself behind, like a toxic spill over his spirit. Elyia. My skin crawled in response. I pulled away from Lucas quickly.

"We should give her some privacy," I said, hoping to disguise the reason I'd jerked out of his embrace. Lucas nodded, but his eyes were troubled. We withdrew leaving Karayan alone with her grief. After a time, the others joined us, until Karayan was the last of us still standing at the edge of the cliff.

Thane was the first to speak. "Someone needs to call Clay."

"Could we just…" Gretchen swallowed hard. "It hasn't even been three days since…" She didn't have to finish the sentence. Three days since the slaughter in the mines. Three days since Seth had snapped Hale's neck with no more effort than it would have taken to break a toy.

Thane drew himself up. His voice was cold, tight with fury. "You think I don't know that? I've served beside him longer than any of the rest of you. Do not make the mistake of thinking I'm unaffected by…" Thane cleared his throat, struggling to contain his emotions. "We are close to the end of this war. And we are perilously close to losing. Terence Clay is our last, best hope."

Dad glanced at me, and then turned to Thane. "I'll make the call." He strode off back toward his truck. Thane followed him, and I saw them put their heads together. Whatever they were talking about, their voices were too low to carry.

Cassie and Royal joined Lucas and me at the edge of the trail. Cassie's eyes were wide with empathy. Royal put an arm around her shoulders, then glanced at me. "How are you doing, Braedyn?"

"No matter what I do, we keep losing ground." My voice sounded hollow, even to me.

"It's not all on you, Braedyn." Lucas studied me. I could see the worry in his eyes.

"Yeah. You've done some stuff right," Royal said. "If it weren't for you, I'd be dead." He gave me a lopsided smile.

I dropped my head, studying gravel at my feet, but I nodded. Royal was alive. It seemed a small victory given everything we had lost. But it was a victory I clung to. A victory I wouldn't trade, even if losing Royal had meant ending Seth.

"We're going to wait by the car." Royal's eyes shifted back to Karayan, still kneeling at the edge of the cliff. "Take as long as you need."

I watched Cassie and Royal walking back to his little two-seater. Lucas put an arm around my shoulders. My body went rigid again.

He withdrew his arm as if scalded. "I'm sorry."

"No, I just… You startled me." I forced a smile for his benefit, but I saw the look in his eyes. He wasn't fooled.

"That's not what I mean." Lucas eyed me with a look of deep self-loathing. "Braedyn…"

"I should check on Dad." I tried to move away from him, but Lucas caught my arm, stopping me gently.

"When are we going to talk about this?" His voice was low and husky. "Every time I touch you… it's her, isn't it? Hale said something… back when we were protecting Derek. Something about how another Lilitu wouldn't attack him now, because…" Lucas frowned, dredging up the old memory. "Because one had already marked him."

I couldn't meet his eyes. I heard Lucas draw in a shaky breath.

"What did he mean? What's wrong with me?"

I opened my mouth, meaning to ease his fears. But the words wouldn't come. Lucas misunderstood my hesitation.

"Braedyn, I wouldn't blame you if you couldn't stand to be in the same room with me. What I did… what I did…" He balled his fists and shoved them into his pockets. He cleared his throat, unable to meet my gaze. "Just tell me if it's over between us."

"No." It came out more forcefully than I had intended. Lucas's eyes settled on my face once more, drinking in my every movement. "No. Don't even think that."

"But she… she marked me. That's why you can't stand being close to me. Isn't it?"

I dropped my eyes.

"Braedyn."

"Yes. She marked you." I felt my throat constricting. The rage threatened to choke me. Elyia had done this. Elyia, who hated me for some secret reason of her own. This was her idea of revenge. She had taken the one night Lucas and I might have had together. She had taken him. But deeper than that rage I felt for Elyia, was a troubling anger at Lucas. How could he have slept with her? How could he have mistaken her for me? He'd explained it, and I knew he held himself accountable—hated himself—for the mistake. Still, that didn't change the fact that he had given Elyia something precious. And now he had been damaged, and there was no undoing that damage. Not ever. If he spent another night with a Lilitu, any Lilitu, he would become a thrall.

I shivered, because even that wasn't the worst of it. After Elyia had taken him… I felt my eyes swimming with a new wave of grief. We had been trapped in the mines together. Seth was on the verge of re-awakening Lilith. And I had had to choose. Attack Lucas for the strength I'd need to stop Seth, knowing it would likely turn Lucas into a thrall, or let Seth sacrifice Royal to bring Lilith back into the world.

So I'd done it. I'd let the Lilitu part of myself feed off of Lucas's already diminished vitality. And… it had felt fantastic. I couldn't stop thinking about it. I couldn't stop thinking about taking even more. Just being this close to Lucas was intoxicating. How could I tell him this? How could I tell him what I felt for him now was even more intense than before? The answer was clear: I couldn't. Lucas could never know this aspect of me, this predator inside, hungry for another taste.

These two feelings, revulsion and desire, warred inside of me. Lucas seemed to sense the conflict. He bit the side of his lip, considering me for a long moment.

"I have no right to ask for your forgiveness. I get that. But…"

"You don't have to ask." This time, the smile I gave him—though watery—was genuine. But it didn't last long. "Lucas, she was gunning for me. What she did to you, it wasn't about you. If anything, what she did to you is my fault."

"Don't." He shook his head in frustration. "Braedyn. Don't do that."

"We have to find a way forward."

"No fresh starts…" Lucas spoke so softly I almost didn't catch the words.

"Lucas?"

Lucas looked up at me, a fragile hope edging into his eyes. "We've been through too much, too much to let one horrible mistake destroy us. If you are still willing to give us a chance… Maybe we need a symbol. Something to remind us of everything we've been through, everything we've survived. Something to help us make things right again."

"A symbol?" I glanced away. "I think we'd need a lot more than a symbol to make things right again." When I said it, I was thinking of the Guard, the Seal… But that's not how Lucas took it. His shoulders hunched. He nodded, avoiding my eyes. I felt a wash of regret. "Wait, I didn't… that came out wrong." I tried to catch his eye.

"We should catch up to the others." Lucas gestured.

I followed his gaze. Most everyone else was heading back down the gravel path toward the Lookout Point parking lot. Suddenly, it felt too real. Hale's memorial was over. Now, suddenly, we had to find a way to live without him. I wasn't ready. I wasn't ready to say goodbye.

I felt my mouth go dry. "You go. I'll be there in a minute." The view from Lookout Point stretched across Puerto Escondido, all the way to the western horizon. With the sun at my back, my shadow stretched to the drop-off of the cliff and disappeared over the edge.

If I hadn't been looking at it, I might never have seen her.

"Lilitu!" Adrenaline shot through my system. My scream cut through the morning silence like a shot, alerting the Guard to her presence.

The strange Lilitu spun and fled along the mountain's ridge, dodging into a copse of scrubby pine trees. I leapt after her without hesitation. It felt good to have a clear goal. It felt good to have an enemy to fight.

She was fast. Her feet picked a path through the trees with agile grace. I heard the Guard behind us, giving chase. But they were human. They couldn't keep up. After several minutes, we'd left them far behind.

Paranoia drove me. My muscles strained, my lungs burned, my eyes watered. I refused to let her escape. I couldn't shake the feeling that this was another message from Elyia. We'd lost Hale along with close to 60 soldiers in the mines. Why else would a strange Lilitu show up at Hale's funeral? Why else if not to gloat?

I burst through the edge of a line of trees that had obscured my path. Ahead, a steep ravine split the cliffside. I saw it too late to change course. I skidded to a stop half a beat too late. My left foot slid past the edge of the cliff, over into the open air above a hundred-foot drop.

Someone caught me by the scruff of my shirt and yanked me back. For an instant, I was too shaken to do more than stare. Her wide eyes were framed with thick dark lashes, and wild, curly dark hair spilled over her shoulders. Something pricked in the back of my mind, but I shoved it aside. A murderous rage rose in the back of my throat. How easy it would be to spin her around, kick her over the side…

The Lilitu saw the change in my face. She launched herself at me, driving me back into the trunk of a tree, pinning me against the rough bark. But Hale had trained us for this. I kicked out, planting my foot in her stomach and shoving with all my strength. The tree at my back became an ally, something strong to brace myself against.

Surprised, the Lilitu released me. The force of the kick was enough to send her careening, off-balance, toward the cliff. She gave a strangled half-cry of fear, coming to rest at the very edge. She eyed the drop at her feet.

I didn't wait for her to regain her composure. I circled toward her, looking for an opening, meaning to send her plummeting to her death. She turned to face me. But the look on her face stopped me cold.

"I'm not here to fight." The Lilitu held up her hands, fingers splayed, looking for all the world like a helpless victim. "Please. Please. I need your help."

"What kind of idiot do you think I am?" My voice was harsh, hardened by the grief of the last few days. "You saw me with the Guard. I'm one of them. Why would I help a demon like you?"

"You're Braedyn Murphy." She licked her lips, her eyes darting over my shoulder. We both knew we didn't have much time before the others caught up with us.

"Why are you here? Who are you working with? Did Elyia send you?" I took a step toward her.

The strange Lilitu flinched at my approach, but she didn't take her eyes off me. "Who? No. No, I came of my own volition. I came to find you. Please, you may be the only one who can help—"

"Braedyn? Braedyn, where are you?" My dad's voice cut through the forest. The Lilitu before me jerked at the sound.

"This way!" I kept my eyes on the beautiful demon. There was nowhere for her to run. The same thought seemed to cross her mind.

"I'm sorry. This was a mistake. Please, let me go. You will never see me again, I promise." Her hands shook slightly. "I'll leave you alone. Just please, please let me go."

"And why would I do that?" I took another step forward. "We've lost too much as it is. We can't afford to leave any enemies on the battlefield. You certainly haven't."

She edged back, but there wasn't any more room to retreat. We heard the sound of gravel cascading down the face of the mountain. Her eyes closed briefly. "This isn't my war," she whispered. "I am not your enemy. If you believe nothing else I say, believe that."

"Braedyn?!" Dad burst through the tree line behind us. I turned at the sound of his voice. His eyes found me, and something in his face eased. He clutched his daggers in his hands, ready for a fight. His eyes searched the landscape beyond me.

I turned back to the Lilitu—only she was gone. I stepped forward, shaken. The edge of the cliff dropped down below my feet, sweeping away from the mountain hundreds of feet below. I looked up at the side of the mountain. Was there a flash of movement? If so, she was already beyond our reach. For today, not forever. Steely determination settled in my stomach.

"What did you see?" Dad joined me at the edge of the cliff. Grim concern clouded his eyes.

"A Lilitu." I met his eyes. "She knew my name. She asked for my help."

Dad's face grew troubled. "Help? With what?"

"She took off before we got that far." I nudged a fist-sized rock over the edge of the cliff with my toe. It plummeted, glancing off the cliff face a few times before clattering to a stop on the rocky floor below. One thing was for sure, the Lilitu had not gone over the edge. Not even a demon could survive a fall like that.

"All right. We should get back to the others." Dad sheathed his daggers. He dropped an arm around my shoulders, pulling me back from the edge of the cliff. "You'll tell me if you ever see this Lilitu again." It wasn't a question, but I nodded. Dad let out a breath. "Okay. Time to go home."

It's strange, how tragedy can make even familiar places seem alien. My room, which had been my haven for years, seemed cold and uninviting that night. It was as though Hale's death had cast a shadow that reached into every place of comfort and drained them of warmth. I looked out my window, and saw the lights gleaming in Lucas's room. He wouldn't sleep there tonight. He might not sleep there ever again. It was the room in which Elyia had attacked him. But it still held his clothes, his things. There were eight rooms on the second floor of their house. Eight small rooms, meant to house soldiers. One week ago every one of them had been filled, most with two or more soldiers on bunk beds and cots. Tonight, only three of the rooms were occupied.

I turned away from the window. The day caught up with me in an instant. My limbs felt suddenly leaden, heavy and useless. I didn't have the energy to do more than strip off my jeans before crawling into bed.

It took almost no effort to step into the dream. My garden. My garden of black roses. Draining Lucas of his vitality had also drained my roses of the last of their crimson hue. I couldn't dwell on what that might mean for my future. But I refused to give into despair. Until I had spoken with Sansenoy, I wasn't ready to believe that I had forfeited the opportunity to become human.

It had been three nights since Hale's death—three nights since Elyia had attacked Lucas. And each night, as I lay down to sleep, I resolved to do whatever I could to find her and make her pay. The pool rose out of the ground at my feet. Within it, I saw a swirling scatter of stars that signified the sleeping minds of all of humankind. Scattered among them, Lilitu dreams gleamed with a faint blue halo. It was one of these I searched for now.

I let my mind focus on Elyia's face. Her beautiful features, her long straight brown hair, her lithe frame. She could have been my double, on the outside at least. But within Elyia there was a potent hatred for mankind, and an even more bitter hatred for me. The dream rose like a glimmering ember from the surface of the pool, responding to my summons. And yet, I could not sense Elyia inside. The dream was shielded. I had tried for three nights in a row to break through the shield guarding her sleeping mind. For three nights in a row, I had failed. I set myself to work. But no matter how I approached it, the shield was slick, impenetrable. There was no chink in the armor, no loose thread to pull. Whoever had crafted the shield had done impeccable work.

Frustration swelled within me. Frustration and despair. I knew—just as I felt drawn to Lucas, hungry for another taste of his spirit—Elyia would feel the compulsion to return and drain him again. We had each staked our claim to him. We had each marked him, drawing our claws along the tender skin of his back, leaving a network of fine scars in our wake. It was a contest between us now; only one of us would walk away victorious, with Lucas as our prize. Some part of me was bent on defending my territory. The thought made me sick to my stomach.

I redoubled my efforts trying to break through the shield. Elyia was a living threat. As long as she drew breath, Lucas was in peril. And so, as long as she drew breath, I would spend my nights throwing myself against her shield.

Time passes differently in the dream. I sensed the world outside growing light, and a new swell of despair flooded through me. Soon it would be time to join the waking world, which meant Elyia had another day to walk among us. I returned to my garden. The feeling of failure dogged me as I turned to the sea of ebony flowers. I reached out and plucked one of the roses. The stem snapped off in my hand, and I saw beneath its black skin, the heart of the stem was a vibrant green.

Something like hope flared inside my heart. But it was tempered with the knowledge that, if I had not already crossed the line, I stood on a knife's edge. This garden was a constant reminder to me. I could not afford to make even one more mistake.

2

The summer became an exercise in recovery. It took us weeks to adjust to life after Hale's death. Walking into the Guard's house, part of me still expected to see Hale emerging from the kitchen, or studying some old tome with Thane in the office. The ghost of his memory was an ever-present specter. And yet, somehow, we found a way to move on, to make peace with that ghost. Well, most of us.

Karayan cloistered herself in her room for weeks, coming out only to eat, and even then only every few days. I left her alone for the rest of June, but as July passed week by week, I took to hovering outside her door. Occasionally, I would knock. Less occasionally, she would respond. By the time August arrived, I realized her grief was not a passing affliction.

On one of the rare occasions she let me into her room, we spent the long afternoon talking. Something within her seemed to have broken, and I wasn't sure there would be any fixing it. But when she confided to me that she had no fight left in her, I felt the chill settle in my chest.

"Don't say that. We need you, Karayan." I reached for her hand, but she pulled it away before our fingers connected. "I need you."

Karayan only nodded, noncommittal. I felt her sorrow almost palpably, as though it were a third presence in the room. It shadowed her, stealing each moment of joy before she had a chance to experience it. Siphoning away the pleasure she used to take in simple things. Dad's cooking. Family movie night. Teasing Lucas and me. It scared me, how absolutely Hale's death had gutted her.

Unfortunately, Karayan wasn't the only thing I had to worry about. After the massacre of the Guard and the ritual to reawaken Lilith, things seemed unusually calm, like the temporary peace within the eye of a hurricane. Knowing chaos and destruction lie just outside that calm, how can you relax? As the summer drew to a close, I was getting used to living with the idea that Lilith might actually return. That the final battle everyone kept talking about was on our doorstep at last. It was an odd feeling, made odder by the lack of any movement from the Lilitu forces. What were they waiting for?

Other things were harder to get used to. The last night of summer, the Guard—what remained of us—gathered together to eat at our house. Dad had gone all out. He'd spent the weekend cooking green chile stew, homemade tortillas, chicken enchiladas… and Hale's favorite: stuffed sopapillas smothered in cheese and green chile sauce.

The aromas filled our house, savory enough that even Karayan emerged from her room for dinner. Despite the feast, the mood at the table was reserved. After dinner, Lucas and I cleared the table and retreated into the kitchen to do the dishes. Lucas washed, I dried. We fell into an easy rhythm; this was something we'd gotten used to doing together. But when we both reached for the same dish and our hands brushed, I flinched. Lucas froze. After a moment, he set his washrag down and turned to face me.

"It's been two months." There was a new tension in his eyes. It was like a knife in my gut to see how scared and hurt he was. "Am I going crazy, or do things seem to be getting worse between us?"

"It's getting worse," I forced myself to meet his gaze, "but not the way you think. I feel you like the pull of gravity. We have a connection that we didn't have before I…" I choked on the words. *Before I fed on your life's energy.* Lucas lowered his eyes, nodding. "Even the smallest touch, when our fingers meet, our shoulders brush, it affects me more now than it ever has before."

Lucas's eyes welled with emotion. "I feel it, too."

"I'm scared." I kept my eyes fastened to the towel in my hands. "I'm scared that it's just the pull of a Lilitu over her prey."

"It's not." He sounded so sure of himself I couldn't help but meet his gaze.

"How can you know that?"

"Because I don't feel Elyia. Not like this. Not like you." He reached out and caught my hand. I quelled the instinct to pull away. His hand was warm. The touch of his skin was like a balm to my nerves. Our eyes met, and he smiled tentatively. "Braedyn, I slept with her. You and I…"

He let the thought trail off, but I knew what he was thinking. We had fallen short of going all the way. But if he felt a connection to me that he did not feel for Elyia, then maybe… Maybe there was hope for us still. Lucas read my face. His expression softened.

"I'm not afraid of you. I don't want you to be afraid, either. I trust you, Braedyn." Lucas lifted a hand to my cheek. He traced the edge of my jaw, then let his hand slide around to the nape of my neck. Ever so gently, he drew me toward him. The temptation to kiss him drove everything else out of my head. My eyes drifted to his lips, parted in anticipation. He was watching me, a question in his eyes. I leaned forward.

"Oh, sorry."

We broke apart, startled. Matthew stood at the entrance of the kitchen, holding a pair of empty glasses.

"Sorry," he said again. He crossed to the sink, placing the glasses in the dishwater. He flashed us a quick look full of speculation, then returned to the kitchen door. He hesitated in the doorway, then came to a decision. He flashed a quick smile at Lucas and shrugged, sheepishly. "I think your sister wants you in bed at a reasonable hour. You know, school tomorrow."

"Yeah." Lucas reached into the water for one of the glasses. "We're almost done here."

Matthew looked like he wanted to say more, but thought better of it. He turned and walked toward the living room, leaving us alone once more. But the moment had been shattered.

Fifteen minutes later, I closed the door to my room, alone. I rested my head against the door for a long moment. And then a shuddering breath forced its way out. Lucas and I knew, no matter how desperately we wanted to pretend otherwise, that no good would come of us giving into temptation. If we were going to have our night together, it would happen after the war.

When I became human.

If I became human.

Monday morning. I opened my eyes and let out another sigh of frustrated resignation. Another night spent in a fruitless attempt to crack the shield protecting Elyia's mind. And then it hit me; today was the first day of my last year as a high school student.

As I pulled on my school uniform, the scent of pancakes on the griddle wafted into my room. I felt a twinge but smiled. It was good to know some things hadn't changed. First-day-of-school pancakes had become a ritual in our house when I was a little girl. And even though I wasn't hungry, I felt a lightness of spirit that I hadn't felt in months.

As I entered the kitchen, I saw Dad setting out a bowl of blueberries and the canister of whipped cream. They joined a collection of jars and bowls containing all sorts of things. Syrup, chocolate chips, strawberries, peanut butter… he had all the bases covered. He was whistling a light, tuneless song.

"You're happy." I felt myself smile in response to his mood.

"If there's one thing I've learned in this life, it's that you have to take the opportunities to celebrate when they come." He gave me a wistful smile. "My little girl, a high school senior. I'm not exactly sure how that happened."

"It tends to follow junior year." I sat at the kitchen island, pulling a plate toward me.

"Cute." He ruffled my hair, ignoring the dirty look I shot him. "You deserve this."

I looked up at him, surprised at the depth of emotion in his voice. "Dad? Is something wrong? Is something going on?"

"No. No. I'm just… I'm happy you get to go back to school, that's all."

"Okay…" I studied him closely. "You know it's just high school, right?"

"Yes. Exactly. High school. It will be good for you to immerse yourself in normal teenage concerns for a while."

"For a while." I looked up at him, afraid to voice the question that had been plaguing me all summer.

"For as long as possible." Dad turned away, grabbing a spatula and flipping a couple of pancakes onto a plate. He didn't fool me. I might not be able to see his face, but his body language was loud and clear. He was worried.

"How long do you think we have? If Lilith is back... I mean, is this even a good idea?"

"Is what a good idea?" Dad turned to stare at me. There was a hardness in his expression. I dropped my eyes, but not before he saw what I meant. "Braedyn Murphy. You are going to school."

Instead of answering, I just smiled and forked a few pancakes onto my plate. I had to bend my head or risk letting him see the tears lining the corners of my eyes. The pancakes steamed in front of me, their aroma enticing. I reached for the maple syrup. When I looked up, Dad was studying me with a solemn expression.

"You're right. First day of senior year, totally worth celebrating. Sit down. I can't eat all these pancakes by myself."

Dad pulled up a stool and joined me at the island. For a few minutes we doctored our pancakes in companionable silence. But when he picked up his fork, he hesitated.

"You have a future." He looked at me then, and I saw how determined he was. "You're going to graduate from high school. You're going to go to college. We'll take it one day at a time. Just... you have to do me a favor, Braedyn."

A lump formed in my throat. Not trusting myself to speak, I nodded.

"I know the responsibility on you is enormous, and I know we have faced our share of defeats. But I need you to live as though there is a tomorrow. Let yourself be a teenager in those moments you can. Can you do that for me?"

"Even if it means staying out past curfew?" I was surprised by the effort it took to keep my voice level.

Dad gave a soft chuckle. "I trust your judgment. If anything, sometimes I worry that you..." He closed his mouth, leaving the thought unvoiced.

"That I what?"

Dad stared at his plate for a long moment. "I worry you're too hard on yourself for past mistakes. I worry that you don't trust yourself."

I mumbled something in response, then shoveled a bite of pancakes into my mouth. It was hard to focus on the taste. Dad's words bore a hole into my mind. It was alarming to know how easily he could read me. Because he was absolutely right.

I couldn't afford to trust myself. Not after all the mistakes I had made.

Fifteen minutes later, I stepped out of the front door. It was a beautiful morning, clear and cool—one of the benefits of living in the high desert. As hot as it would get today, the sunset would bring relief. I stepped off the porch and felt the sun drape across my back like a warm blanket.

It was a short walk to Lucas's front door. I knocked, then opened the door. Inside, Matthew and Gretchen were sitting at the dining room table. I did not see Thane, but the door to his office was closed. Lucas bounded down the stairs a few seconds later. He must have heard me come in.

"Are you ready for this?" His eyes gleamed with some of his old energy.

"Once more into the breach, right?"

"Let me grab my bag." Lucas slipped into the kitchen, out of sight.

Gretchen weighed me with her eyes. She caught her bottom lip in her teeth, a gesture I'd seen from her before. I dropped my eyes, feeling suddenly exposed. Gretchen had been with us in the mines. She had had to turn her back on Lucas, knowing I would feed on his vitality, knowing I might kill him. She had made it her life's mission, after her young husband's death, to keep his little brother safe. But she'd put that aside when it came down to protecting Lucas or stopping Seth.

Lucas returned, slinging his backpack over his shoulder. He gave Gretchen and Matthew a friendly wave goodbye. "See you guys after school." His eyes settled on my face, and I felt the warmth of his gaze. "After you."

We made it to the front porch before Gretchen stopped us. "Lucas, I need you home right after school. There's some work I need your help with, if you don't mind." Her eyes skipped over to me briefly before returning to Lucas's face.

Lucas looked from Gretchen to me. He bristled a little at her concern, but he nodded. "Sure, fine. I'll see you after school."

Gretchen flashed us a quick smile then retreated back inside. Over her shoulder I saw Matthew watching us. Gretchen closed the door, and Lucas and I were once again alone. Lucas turned to me with a halfhearted smile. He shrugged.

"Sorry. She's been a little weird since…" He ran a hand through his hair and sighed. "It's not you. She… she doesn't trust anyone right now."

"She's probably right to be concerned." We took the front steps down to the walkway, turning our feet toward the street and my waiting Firebird. "I don't know, Lucas. Sometimes it feels like we're too close to going too far."

Lucas shook his head, unwilling to acknowledge the truth. I was afraid the drive to school would be fraught with tension. But Lucas simply changed the subject to our class schedules. He seemed determined to face the day with optimism.

I pulled into the school parking lot and killed the engine. Campus was already full of students returning for the new year. It was a sea of burgundy and gray uniforms. Familiar. Mundane. Kids met across the quad, hugging, laughing, and catching up. Judging from their easy smiles and relaxed faces, they'd had carefree summers filled with vacations and leisure time and maybe even the luxury of a little boredom. My summer—infused as it had been by this crippling grief—left me worn out, not refreshed. Now we were back. It was strangely jarring, looking at this idyllic scene, knowing we could be facing the end of the world sooner rather than later.

Cassie and Royal saw us from the edge of the quad. They were waiting underneath a catalpa tree, talking with their heads together. Cassie saw me first and raised a hand in greeting. Lucas and I walked over to join them.

"Okay, hand them over." Royal pulled a copy of his schedule out of his notebook. He gave it to me, extending his hand expectantly. We traded schedules among the four of us, curious to see which classes we would have together. It felt strange to think that this was the last year we'd be sharing schedules. Stranger still to wonder if we'd all even live in Puerto Escondido next year… assuming we survived to see another fall.

After we had familiarized ourselves with each other's schedules, we headed for the North Hall. We still had 10 minutes before first bell. I noticed Cassie watching me out of the corner of her eyes.

"Okay, Cas, what's on your mind?"

Cassie ran a hand through her silky black hair and shrugged. "I don't even know where to begin to answer that question." She gave me a weak smile. "I guess, I just wanted to know... If there's any news."

"News." She didn't have to specify. Cassie had seen the aftermath of the massacre with her own eyes. In fact, if not for Cassie, we might not know Seth had even performed the ritual to reawaken Lilith. "Afraid you know as much as we do already."

"What about Elyia?" Royal glanced at Lucas. "Has she made any other moves?"

"No." I felt the knots in my shoulders draw even tighter. "I've tried to find her, I've tried to break into her mind. She's still shielded."

"You'll get it," Lucas said. His voice was sure, confident. "You'll break through eventually. I almost feel sorry for her, knowing what's in store for her when you do." A shadow passed over his face. I recognized the expression: he was hungry for vengeance. Just like me.

I bit my lip, trying to decide whether or not to share my misgivings. When I looked up, they were all watching me with bated breath. Royal tipped his head to one side as if to say, *well? Spill it already.*

"Elyia." I cleared my throat, trying to dispel the nervous edge in my voice. "She wasn't strong enough to force me out before. The last time I was in her mind," I couldn't keep the dark, humorless smile from curving my lips, "she was helpless against me." The smile faded. "But now? Someone's helping her. I don't know who."

Lucas eyed me, unsettled. "But you think whoever is helping her is strong?"

"Yeah. Stronger than me." The words hung between us for a pregnant moment. Neither of us wanted to voice the thought we clearly shared. "I think we have to consider the possibility he's still around."

Royal and Cassie traded a look.

"You mean Seth." Royal tried to control his emotions, but a muscle in his jaw jumped, betraying him. "What makes you think it's him?"

I glanced at Lucas, but he deferred to me with a nod of his head. I took a deep breath. "A Lilitu's strength is directly related to how many generations separate her—or him—from Lilith. The closer you are to Lilith, the stronger your power. Seth is Lilith's grandson. He's only once removed from the mother of demons herself. If he's shielding Elyia, I don't know if I'll ever be able to break through."

Lucas shook his head. "You're forgetting, you've already broken one of his shields. The shield around Mr. Hart."

Cassie shot a quick look at me before tamping down her emotions. I gave her an apologetic look. I knew Cassie had nursed a crush on Mr. Hart last year. For all I knew, she might still be a little sweet on him. For a while, I'd had my suspicions about Mr. Hart. But after confronting him, I knew beyond a shadow of a doubt that he was a good man.

"I didn't want to worry you," I said, trying to ease Cassie's fears. "Whatever Seth wanted with Mr. Hart, I think it's over now. And yes, I was able to break through that shield. But that was after months of inattention on Seth's part. We have no idea if Elyia is central to his plan. Breaking through her shield… it's a long shot. Maybe if he's not maintaining it. Maybe if it degrades over time. But if he's monitoring it? It might be easier to break into Fort Knox."

Cassie and Royal looked troubled. Cassie's brow furrowed. "You think he's still in town?"

"Well, that's just awesome." Royal's tone was sour, but he turned away too quickly to sell the indifference he was trying to feign. Seth had hurt Royal more deeply than any of the rest of us. Yes, he'd lied to me. He'd physically attacked Cassie. But Seth had broken Royal's heart. Royal had believed he and Seth were in love.

The timing was terrible, but it would never be good. It was a question we needed to answer. "Have you sensed him?" I tried to read Royal's face, but he wasn't meeting my eyes. "Have you had any more dreams?"

"No. Not since you shielded my mind." Royal shoved his hands into the pockets of his slacks. "But it makes sense. It would be too good to be true to think that he's left town, and when have we ever caught a break?"

"The thing that bothers me is why haven't we heard anything from them?" Cassie played with the hem of her shirt, distracted. "If they're still around, what are they doing?"

"The million dollar question." Lucas looked up as the first bell rang. He sighed. "But it'll have to wait for another time."

Royal straightened, adjusting the satchel on his shoulder. "In that case…" He turned to me, offering his arm as though we were about to make an entrance at some royal event. "Care to join me for AP Bio, Ms. Murphy?" Before I could respond, Cassie spoke.

"Wait. That's it? What about the Guard? What about Idris and the acolytes?" Cassie caught my hand. "What's the plan?"

"Not here," Lucas murmured.

"He's right," I said. "We'll have to pick this up after school. Sophie's?"

"You guys go ahead. I've got to help Gretchen with the make-believe chores she fabricated to keep me and Braedyn away from each other." Lucas grimaced, irritated. I gave him a tired smile, but I knew how he felt.

Cassie seemed satisfied. Royal and I headed toward the science building as Cassie and Lucas made their way to North Hall. I didn't have any classes with Lucas until after lunch. It was going to be a long morning.

The first day of school passed slowly. After AP Bio, I headed off to humanities. As I walked into the classroom, I noticed Amber by her straight blond hair. She turned as I entered and our eyes met. For the briefest moment, she glared at me. Then she turned back to the boy she'd been talking with.

So that's how it was going to be. After training with me for months, after I'd saved her life, Amber was back to her old, hostile self. I found a seat on the other side of class and settled in. By the time the bell rang announcing the end of class, I had managed to push Amber out of my thoughts. I wasn't prepared when she stopped me in the doorway on the way out.

"Just in case it's not clear, I'm out." Amber's fingernails dug into my arm. "So if that means you're pulling my tuition, just let me know now." I stared at her, startled. Amber's father had been arrested last year, something having to do with money and fraud. I didn't know much, but I did know they'd frozen the family's assets. Unlike Cassie, Amber wasn't a scholarship kid—her family had been loaded, and when they lost everything, Amber's life started to crumble. Despite my misgivings, I'd brokered a deal between Amber and the Guard. The Guard would pay her tuition so long as she trained with us as a spotter. Only, she'd made it pretty clear she wanted nothing to do with us after the massacre.

"We've got bigger problems than sorting out your school fees," I said.

Amber's eyes narrowed. "I'm not kidding. Don't think I'll feel obligated to come back to your little band of psychos just because they're covering my education."

"Fine," I snapped. "I didn't like you hanging around anyway."

"I'll bet." Amber's lips tightened in cold fury. "How is Lucas, by the way? Have you guys managed that little tryst yet, or—?"

My fist shot out, launching toward Amber's face of its own volition. But our training had had an effect. Amber moved, knocking my fist aside and slamming me into the doorjamb.

"Whoa! Whoa! Ladies?!" Mr. Baird, our humanities teacher, sprang out of his chair, making a beeline toward us. I felt Amber release her hold on me. I pushed back from the doorjamb and straightened. This was the last thing I needed, getting sent to the headmaster's office on the first day of school for fighting. I forced a smile.

"Sorry, Mr. Baird. We were just practicing a scene for drama class." I shot a warning look back at Amber. "Right?"

Amber forced the tension out of her shoulders. The smile she gave Mr. Baird was perfectly genuine. She even managed a little blush to sell it. "I'm so sorry. We didn't mean to scare you."

Mr. Baird studied us with a shrewd frown. But after a moment, he straightened. "From now on, keep the drama in the theater department, okay?"

Amber and I agreed hastily, then walked off down the hall together. When we rounded the corner, I turned to her.

"Amber, listen…"

Amber didn't wait to hear what I had to say. She turned her back and walked away without another glance. It hurt, which surprised me. Our friendship, if you could even call it that, had only lasted a few weeks. We'd spent hours together sparring before we ever made a real connection. Apparently, that connection had been even more fragile than I had suspected.

I was still mulling this over when the bell rang for lunch. I caught up to Lucas on the way into the dining hall. Cassie and Royal had already staked out a table by one of the picture windows overlooking the mountains. Lucas and I grabbed the food from the kitchen—a few large bowls full of spaghetti and steamed broccoli—and delivered it to our table. Royal and Cassie were already seated.

"No offense," Royal was saying to Cassie, "but are you sure that thing can even make it all the way to the university and back?"

"Are you dissing my ride?" Cassie held her fork up, brandishing it with mock ferocity. "Because that's a forking offense, mister."

"What's at the university?" I asked.

Royal rolled his eyes. "Cassie can't wait for graduation. She's starting college math this year."

"It's just calculus," Cassie said. "Well, second semester calculus. I've taken all the math classes Coronado has to offer, so headmaster Fiedler suggested this."

"And you got a ride out of it?" Lucas gave Cassie an appraising look. "Nice work, Ms. Ang."

Cassie grinned. "She's not going to win any beauty contests, but I like her. I'm thinking about giving her a name."

"Beulah? Old Bessie?" Royal speared another piece of broccoli onto his fork. "No. I know. Mama Sasquatch."

Cassie tagged Royal in the arm, mildly irritated. "At least my car has personality."

"That she does. In spades." Royal handed a slice of bread to Cassie; a peace offering. She took it, mollified.

Lucas and I shared a small smile. It felt good to be around Cassie and Royal again. Actually, it felt good to be at school again. I took a bite of spaghetti, enjoying the savory sauce. I knew why Dad wanted this for me. But it still felt like a luxury. And it was a luxury I didn't know how much longer we could afford.

I parked the Firebird in a half-empty gravel lot just south of the Plaza. Cassie and Royal would be arriving soon; I'd left just five or ten minutes before them. I headed toward the Plaza, squinting against the afternoon sun. Summer's heat was still thick in the air. It would be another month before fall's chill would work its fingers into the breeze. I made my way into the heart of Old Town, planning to head straight for Sophie's and get us a table.

I'm not sure what it was that caught my eye, but I felt the tingle along my spine and turned. She was walking out of another restaurant, holding onto the arm of a tall, kind-looking man. That familiar, dark, curly hair spilled over her shoulders, gleaming in the sun. The man watched her with an engaged smile, laughing at something she said. They looked like a happy couple. But only one of them was human.

I don't remember making the decision to move. One moment I was standing still, the next I was charging toward the couple. The man saw me first, confusion edging into his eyes. I grabbed the Lilitu's arm, digging my fingernails into her skin.

"You should have left when you had the chance."

She sucked in a sharp breath, but didn't try to pull away. Her eyes found my face, searching. The look unsettled me.

The man at her side grabbed my wrist, alarmed. "Hey, what the hell do you—?"

"Why are you following me?" I tightened my grip on her arm. Her eyes narrowed in pain, but again, she made no move to free herself.

"Whoa, easy." The man held up a hand, as if trying to calm a rabid dog. "I think you've got us confused with someone else."

The Lilitu turned to him, giving him a pained smile. "It's okay, Ben. This is Braedyn."

His eyes returned to my face, troubled. "This is Braedyn? And you think she's going to…?" He let the thought trail off, but he didn't take his eyes off of me.

"Could you give us a few minutes?" The Lilitu placed her hand over his, gently pulling his fingers from around my wrist.

Ben eyed her, clearly uncomfortable with this request. But he nodded and—after shooting one last glance at me—scanned the street. "I'll wait for you in the bookshop."

"Thank you." The Lilitu gave him a smile, squeezing his hand warmly. He returned the smile, then left us. She watched him for several moments before turning back to me.

It struck me, suddenly. "You never… You haven't…?"

"Slept with him? No. Ben is a good man." She studied me closely. "He helped me find you."

I released my hold on her arm, uncomfortable. "Who are you?" This whole conversation was making my skin crawl. Just standing in the middle of the Plaza, talking to a demon, as though it were any other afternoon.

"My name is Vyla." She gave me a tentative smile. "As I said, I need your help."

"Why? Why would you… why would *any* Lilitu come to me for help?"

The beautiful creature started to answer me, then stopped. Doubt entered her eyes. "I suppose trust is an issue for us both."

"I haven't had much luck when it comes to trusting strange Lilitu." I heard the rough, low anger in my voice. So did Vyla. It made her flinch, but she held my gaze.

"How many of us have you met?" She sounded genuinely frustrated. "Most Lilitu on earth are struggling to find a way to live among the humans in peace. Most Lilitu on earth want nothing to do with the coming war. This is our home. We do not want to see it destroyed."

"Words are easy," a chill passed through me, negating the warmth of the afternoon sun, "but if you think you'll earn my trust by simply saying the right thing? Sorry. I'm done playing gullible. I've misplaced my trust before, and it brought humanity one step closer to enslavement. I will never make that mistake again."

A deep, piercing pain flickered through Vyla's eyes. She glanced away quickly. "Maybe this was a mistake. I'm sorry."

Curiosity bubbled beneath my suspicion. As she started to walk away, I heard myself ask, "How could I possibly help you, anyway?"

She turned back in an instant. Her eyes latched onto me, like I was some kind of life raft. She drew in a shaky breath. "I've come to you not for myself but for—"

"Braedyn! I thought you were grabbing a table." Royal's voice cut across the plaza. He and Cassie were making their way across the cobblestone street. Cassie gave me a little wave.

I turned back to the Lilitu, but she was already halfway to the bookstore. Royal said something else, but I couldn't quite hear him over the thudding of my heart. It was as if his arrival had broken a spell. This Lilitu knew all the right things to say. And arriving with a human man she'd never attacked... it was smart. Calculated to earn my trust. She'd almost convinced me to listen. I felt a shiver pass over my shoulders. I needed to harden my heart. I needed to be vigilant. The Guard—the world—was counting on me.

I smiled for Cassie and Royal, following them into Sophie's, confident in my new resolve.

A full month passed before I saw another Lilitu.

3

September drew to a close without any indication that mother nature knew fall had arrived. The days were hot and drawn out, the evenings stuffy. Even the few aspens whose leaves had started to turn did little to portray a sense of impending autumn.

It was on one of these hot, wilting afternoons that I returned home and felt something was off. I couldn't pinpoint any one particular thing, but as soon as I crossed the threshold something in the house felt different.

Dad heard me enter from the kitchen. "Hey, kiddo. How was school?" He poked his head out of the kitchen, staring through the dining room into the foyer.

"You're home early." I slid my backpack off, still trying to place the strange feeling.

"One of the benefits of owning your own company." Dad crossed through the dining room into the foyer, drying his hands with a kitchen towel. He gave me a smile, but an unmistakable tension pinched the corners of his eyes.

"Is something going on?" I set my backpack on the bench near our front door, focusing my attention on Dad. He noticed, and turned to set the towel down on the dining room table, hiding his face from me. I felt a rising sense of alarm.

"Dad, what's wrong?"

"Nothing's wrong, just a little hectic." Dad turned back, his face composed in a calm smile that was clearly meant to put my fears at ease. "Terence Clay arrived today."

"The head of the Guard?" I'd heard a little about Terence Clay over the last few years, but I'd never spoken to him or even seen a picture.

"He's a good soldier. Lots of experience, a sharp tactical mind. But... he's old school."

These words sent another bolt of anxiety through my body. Before I could ask what exactly that meant, someone knocked on the front door. Not waiting for a response, the door swung open. Thane stepped into the foyer. His eyes found Dad, slipping past me impersonally.

"He wants to meet her."

"We'll be over soon." Dad took a half step toward me.

Thane's eyebrows ticked up in surprise. "You're going to keep Clay waiting?"

Dad's jaw clenched. His eyes sought my face. After a moment, he came to a decision. "Lead the way."

Thane swept back out the front door.

Dad put a hand on my shoulder. The smile he gave me couldn't disguise the deepening worry behind his eyes. We walked across the lawn separating our house from the Guard's. Thane was disappearing into the house, presumably to let Clay know I was coming. I followed Dad up the Guard's wooden porch steps. His hand closed around the doorknob.

"Wait." I caught his sleeve. "Am I in trouble?"

He turned back and gave me a tight smile. "Don't worry, this is just a formality."

The door opened. Thane stood on the other side, impatient. His eyes flicked from me to my dad. Dad stepped aside, gesturing for me to enter first. He gave me an encouraging smile.

"Just be yourself, and he'll have no choice but to respect you."

I stepped into the old house and stared. The transformation was jarring. Ever since Hale and his unit had moved in, the living room had housed a few comfortable—if beat up—couches, some overstuffed chairs, and some mismatched side tables.

But now, the room was largely empty. An elaborate wooden desk dominated the space, taking up residence in the bay window. It faced the room, flanked by two leather chairs. Beyond the chairs, however, the room was open and unfurnished—unless you counted the pair of area rugs and a few dozen folding chairs resting against the walls. Only the fireplace, with its mission style mantel, felt familiar. And even that had changed; the sword we had placed there after Hale's death was gone. In its place, a heavy glass decanter half full with some amber liquid shared the mantel with a small, silver-framed photograph of a young man.

What drew my attention, though, was the salt-and-pepper-haired man sitting behind the desk. He pored over a few pages of handwritten notes while another man—tall and reserved, with the well-muscled physique of an active-duty soldier—waited at his side.

Thane stood in the entrance to the living room, waiting with a silent deference I'd never seen him pay Hale. I glanced back at Dad. He nodded, gesturing for me to step forward. I took a few hesitant steps into the house and stopped by Thane's side. The silver-haired man looked up. He flashed me a brief smile, then stood, handing the papers to the waiting soldier.

"Thank you, Sutherland." His voice was rich and he spoke with a lilting southern accent that seemed to warm the room. "I'll look the rest over tonight."

"Sir." The soldier—Sutherland—glanced at me with open curiosity. "Would you like me to stay, General?"

"No. Why don't you see if Sandra needs anything?" He may have phrased it like a request, but Sutherland moved instantly, walking toward the back office without hesitation. I felt Dad hovering behind me.

The salt-and-pepper-haired man gestured for me to enter the room. "It's all right, come on in. We don't stand on ceremony here." His eyes slid over my shoulder. "And Murphy, you old son of a bitch. It's good to see you."

Dad walked forward and the two men embraced. "Clay. It's been a long time."

Clay clapped him on the back before releasing him. "Let me look at you." He studied Dad companionably. "Don't tell me civilian life's made you soft?"

"Not too soft, I hope." Dad's tone was light, but his smile was guarded.

"That makes two of us. I'll need my men sharp, you most of all." If Clay saw Dad's unease, he didn't let on. His eyes shifted to me. "So.

This must be Braedyn. I've been looking forward to meeting you for some time. Why don't we sit down, get to know each other a bit."

Clay pulled one of the leather chairs around and gestured for me to take a seat. He rested his weight on the edge of his desk as I lowered myself into the chair. Dad and Thane watched us, but neither made a move to join us at the desk.

"So, Braedyn." He gave me a mild smile, devoid of any hint of malice. "On paper, it looks like you're working for our enemies."

"What?" I was half-convinced I'd heard him wrong. I felt rather than saw Dad take a step closer. Clay only had to glance at him to freeze him in his tracks. He returned his attention to me.

"Tell me if I have this right. You helped an incubus open the Seal. You stood by while the angel Senoy was executed. And you were present for a blood sacrifice facilitating Lilith's return." Clay's smile didn't waver. "Did I leave anything out?"

"I...?" Ice spread through my veins. I turned toward Dad, but he kept his mouth tightly shut. His eyes were locked on Clay's face. Clay saw his uncertainty.

"You didn't think I'd know? It's my duty to keep tabs on what's going on in all my units." Clay's eyes shifted to Thane.

"Thane?" Dad's face was rigid with fury.

Clay put a hand on Dad's shoulder. "Don't get on Thane for keeping me in the loop. He was just following orders."

Thane met Dad's glare, unflinching. "My loyalty is and has always been to the cause." His eyes settled on my face. There was not even a hint of remorse in his gaze.

Dad turned back to Clay. "General, she's made mistakes, yes. But she's brought us victories as well. She killed the ancient Lilitu Ais single-handedly. Helped us infiltrate a cult of Lilith-worshipers. If it weren't for her, we may have lost every remaining Guardsman in the mines—"

"On balance, though..." Clay shrugged. "You have to admit, their side has racked up quite a few wins since your girl joined the fight."

"I can see how it might look..." Dad cleared his throat, struggling for calm. "Once you get to know her, you'll see what a valuable asset she is. It took some time, but Hale grew to rely on her—"

"Hale is dead." All the warmth bled out of Clay's voice. The room went silent. Dad and Clay shared a look, full of tension. I felt the skin crawl on the back of my neck. After a moment, Clay turned back to me, smiling once more. "Even so, I'd be lying if I said I didn't see the benefits of having a Lilitu on our team. Seems to me like you get into most of your trouble when you try to work things out on your own, that about right?"

I nodded quickly. Clay studied me, as if waiting for more. "I… I know I let myself get played. It won't happen again."

"Let's make a deal. You promise not to take matters into your own hands, promise to be a team player, and I promise to trust you until you give me reason not to. Sound good?"

"Yes, sir." I felt my hands unclench at my sides. Relief washed through me, thawing the ice that had settled over me at the first mention of all my past mistakes. But the relief was short lived. Clay was clearly not a man to be trifled with. I forced myself to smile, hoping to hide my uncertainty.

Clay sat back looking pleased. "Then we're done here. I'm glad to have you on the team. You get on home, we'll talk more later." Clay returned to his chair behind the desk, picking up another stack of papers.

I walked back to Dad, feeling like I'd taken some kind of test—but whether I'd passed or failed was yet to be determined.

"Oh, one more thing." Clay glanced up from his work. "When either of you sees Karayan, let me know? We have some unfinished business I'd like to take care of as soon as possible."

"Yes, sir." Dad dropped an arm around my shoulders and guided me out. We passed Thane wordlessly. We made the short walk home in silence, and it wasn't until I'd crossed the threshold that I felt myself truly relax.

That's when it hit me. I walked into Karayan's room, opening the drawers in the dresser. They were empty. Karayan had taken her few possessions and fled.

That strange feeling I'd had? It was Karayan. She was gone.

All that afternoon, I sat in the living room window, watching as the new Guardsmen moved into the house next door. Dad busied himself in the kitchen for close to an hour, and as sunset approached the savory aroma of chicken tortilla soup filled the house.

He joined me in the living room as the last few stragglers arrived next door, duffels slung over their shoulders. I'd counted a few more than 20 new arrivals. Which meant the total number of Guardsmen we'd take into the final battle against Lilith would total around 50, if we were lucky.

"Thane and Clay seem pretty tight." I turned away from the window in time to see Dad sigh. "What's the history there?"

"I guess you could say they share a similar philosophy." Dad popped the cap off a bottle of beer. He looked defeated. "Clay was the one who assigned Karayan's upbringing to Thane."

"That was Clay?"

"He thought Paul was nuts." Dad's voice softened, as it always did when he talked about my biological father. "Told him to his face that raising a Lilitu was inviting disaster. I think he gave Karayan to Thane just to piss Paul off."

"But, if he put Thane in charge of raising Karayan…?" I didn't have to figure out how to ask the question. Dad knew instantly what I was driving at.

"Does he blame Thane for driving her away? No. No way. The second Karayan went off the reservation, she was declared the enemy, Thane was commended for valiantly trying to rehabilitate her despite the odds, and Clay was vindicated for having been right all along. In my opinion, his lack of faith poisoned the whole experiment." Dad chuckled humorously. "Not that anyone's asking."

"So Clay assigned Thane to Hale's unit to spy on us?"

Dad glanced at me. Pain laced his features. He took another swig of beer. "I should have seen it. Maybe Clay's right. Maybe civilian life has made me soft."

"How worried should I be?" I turned back to study the house next door, trying to keep my voice light. Lights filled every window in the Guard's house.

Dad considered this for a long moment before answering. "Clay's a strong leader. His focus has to be getting the Guard ready for the last battle. And if anyone can do it…" Dad took another swig of beer. After a moment's silence, he met my eyes. "Tread carefully around

Clay, Braedyn. It can be hard to spot, buried under all that southern charm, but he's a killer."

It took a few days for the new Guardsmen to move in. Once all the beds had been claimed, all the duffels unpacked, it was time to unite the soldiers who had fought under Hale with the soldiers who'd arrived with Clay.

And so, the next Sunday night, we had a barbecue. I spent the afternoon helping Gretchen and Lucas build a bonfire from salvaged wood in the backyard. Clay's people handled the grocery shopping. Matthew and a few other young soldiers volunteered to man the grill. But for all our preparations, once it was time to sit down and eat the mood was tense rather than festive. Everyone knew why we were here, and a few hot dogs and hamburgers weren't going to make us forget.

Lucas and I stood toward one side of the crowd, feeling out of place among the soldiers. I noticed a few veiled looks from some of the women in the crowd and felt my hand tightening around Lucas's. Spotters. It wouldn't matter that I was fighting on their side; when they looked at me, they'd see the face of their enemy. I'd yet to meet a spotter who warmed to me quickly; each and every one of them only had the ability to see Lilitu because someone they loved had died at a Lilitu's hand.

"We can get out of here as soon as Clay gives his speech if you want." Lucas spoke quietly, his breath warm on my neck.

We heard a rustle in the crowd and turned. Clay strode out onto the back porch. It was only three or four feet off the ground, but it gave everyone a clear view of him. I heard the din of the crowd subside as soldiers noticed his presence. Without ever asking for their attention, Clay found himself facing a sea of rapt faces, eager for a word from their leader.

"Well, we made it. Welcome to the end of the world, my friends." Clay lifted a beer in salute to the assembled.

A dry chuckle spread throughout the crowd. I studied the soldiers. They must have known many of them wouldn't live to see the spring, but they were here of their own volition, committed to a cause greater than their own lives. I felt a swell of emotion.

"I know you must be hungry, so I'll try to keep it brief. Those of you who were lucky enough to serve under Hale, one of our best and brightest... I know what his loss has cost you, cost the whole of the Guard. He was supposed to be here to share this moment with us, and I know I'm a poor substitute. To Hale." Clay lifted his beer again.

A soft echo rippled across the yard as 50 soldiers raised their own drinks. I glanced at Lucas. He kept his gaze fastened on Clay, but a fresh round of pain washed over his face.

"We know what's at stake. We're just the latest in a long line of soldiers stretching back to the Garden, fighting to defend this world from humanity's oldest enemy." Clay's voice rose, ringing with conviction. "But unlike our forefathers, for the first time since a daughter of Lilith murdered a son of Adam, we have the power to bring Lilith's war to an end. Our time is now, and I promise each and every one of you, I will see Lilith dead or I will die to help you stop her from reinstating her reign of terror."

I felt the hair rise on the back of my neck—but for once, it was because I felt like one of the good guys. Clay looked out at us with such fervent confidence, victory seemed possible. No—*probable*.

"Each of us has a part to play." Clay's voice dropped once more, and the assembled leaned in as if afraid of missing even one word. "Yes, our numbers have suffered a major setback. But this is our home. This is our world. And I will not see it fall to the enemy!"

The assembled let out a collective cheer. Lucas's eyes were shining when he turned back to me. I saw it in his face, that same belief that anything was possible. The soldiers turned to the food, helping themselves. Clay stood at the porch rail for several long moments, watching them with a look of wistful pride.

The hand on my elbow startled me out of my reverie. Dad offered me a plate. He followed my gaze and we studied Clay together for a moment in silence. Dad turned back to me with a questioning look.

"He's..." I shook my head, unable to find the right words.

"Yes." Dad looked back at Clay. Clay noticed, and gave Dad a warm smile. Dad nodded in acknowledgement. "He's the one you want to put in front of the crowd, that's for sure."

Dad led me through the line for food. People packed their plates full, then wandered off to find a place to sit in the yard. Lucas and I spotted Gretchen, getting ready to light the bonfire. We joined her, taking a seat on one of the logs we'd decided was too big to burn. It was surprisingly fun. It felt almost like we were camping. After we'd gone back for seconds… okay, thirds… we were starting to get sleepy. Dad offered to grab us some fixings for s'mores.

While he was gone, three strangers approached our fire.

"Mind if we join you?" the first woman asked. She looked like she might be in her forties. She was petite but fit, and her curly, dark auburn hair was cut short.

"Make yourself at home." Gretchen gestured at the logs circling the bonfire. But her eyes flickered over to Lucas and me, and I felt a twinge.

"I'm Marla," the first woman said. "This is Zoe." She gestured to a young woman in her twenties.

Zoe gave Gretchen a reserved smile. She looked out of place among the crowd; an eyebrow stud glittered in the firelight, and her eyes were ringed with dark liner that made them stand out against her extremely pale skin. Her blond hair was partially dyed a vivid indigo blue. She had delicate, almost pixie-like features, but her mouth seemed habitually curved in a cynical smirk. Zoe took a drink from her beer bottle. I saw her eyes slide my way.

"And that is Sandra," Marla finished, gesturing to the striking black woman. Her hair fell past her shoulders in thick ropes. She had prominent cheekbones and a generous smile, and wore chunky glasses that perfectly framed her eyes.

"Archivist," Sandra said in a lilting British accent. She gave Gretchen a sheepish smile. "Guardsmen always assume I'm like you lot because I've got breasts. But those two are the spotters. I'm blind as a civilian when it comes to seeing demons."

Gretchen gave Sandra a warm smile and then turned to the others. "Nice to meet you guys. I'm Gretchen. This is Lucas, and that's Braedyn."

Marla eyed me, and I realized with sudden clarity that I was the reason these three had wandered over to our little corner of the yard. "So, Lucas is your…?" Marla turned back to Gretchen, eyebrows raised.

"My brother-in-law." Gretchen's smile faded. Matthew lowered his eyes. "Eric, my husband, was his brother…" She shrugged, but I could see the emotions welling in her eyes. "He's been gone almost six years now."

"You're okay with this?" Marla nodded toward Lucas and me, then gave Lucas a thin smile. "No offense, kid."

"I know how it looks," Gretchen shot me an apologetic smile, "but Braedyn has saved our lives more than once. She's solid. It took me a long time to come around, but… I trust Braedyn with my life."

"Sure." Marla didn't look convinced. "But… is it… safe to let these two hang out so closely?"

As if on cue, Dad walked up and sat beside me on the log, handing over a bamboo stick. Marla and Sandra exchanged a quick look, then Marla raised her glass to her lips, suddenly thirsty.

"Is that…?" Zoe glanced from Marla to Sandra, but neither would meet her eyes. "Are you Alan Murphy?"

"In the flesh." Dad flashed Zoe a brief smile before turning back to me with a questioning look in his eyes. He must have sensed the tension. I gave him a smile that I meant to be reassuring, but he didn't seem to buy it.

"I see you've met our resident legend." Clay's voice sounded behind us. If I hadn't turned to face him, I might not have seen the muscle jump in Dad's jaw. But then Dad was scooting closer to me, making room for Clay to sit.

Zoe beamed at Clay as he joined us on the log bench. Her eyes were alight with excitement. "Clay tells the best stories about you, Murphy."

Lucas sat up straighter, eyeing Dad eagerly. "Yeah?"

Dad dipped his head. "I'm sure Clay's way too busy to take time out for a story tonight. Maybe another time."

"We do have this roaring campfire… seems like a shame to waste it." Clay grinned at Dad, then turned to Zoe and Lucas with a mischievous glimmer in his eyes. "You know, when we were coming up together, it was pretty much understood that Murphy would be the one to take leadership of the Guard one day."

"Really?" Lucas glanced at Dad, surprised.

"That was a long time ago." Dad kept his voice neutral, but his hands tightened around the plate of s'mores fixings.

"You want a story? Let's see." Clay rubbed his hands together, enjoying the moment. "Murphy and I were assigned to our first unit together a few months after he joined up. I'd been in the Guard already for a few years, but Murphy, hoo. He had a fire in him from day one. I remember this one time, we were hunting a Lilitu who tore up a couple of the loggers in town."

Dad smiled, pained. "Clay…"

Clay didn't even acknowledge the interruption. "Chased her up onto the Blue Ridge Mountains, near this little pass that cut through two peaks. It was rough terrain, but Murphy, he wouldn't back down. Now, we're up there, miles from civilization. Second or third night on the trail our spotter slips and breaks her leg. Usually, that'd end the hunt real quick. This was back before cell phones, you see. But Murphy, he wasn't about to let this demon walk free. So he gets it in his mind to set a trap for her."

Zoe and Lucas leaned in, hanging on Clay's words. Even Marla had forgotten about her beer, intrigued by the story. Dad's eyes flickered over to me. He looked worried. I gave him a small smile, trying to hide my unease. I knew he was a Guardsmen, it wasn't like I didn't know he'd killed Lilitu before.

"I think he's nuts, right? I mean, we'd thrown everything at this one and she was way too wily to let herself get cornered. But Murphy decides to use the spotter as bait, make it look like we'd kept up the hunt without her. That afternoon, we make ourselves a couple of hunter's blinds and wait. Poor Mandy's out there like a sittin' duck, foot swelling worse than a water balloon but damned if she wasn't determined to nab this thing, too."

"It's getting late." Dad turned to me, face drawn.

"What happened?" Lucas leaned past Dad to get a better look at Clay, intrigued.

"Well, it worked, is what. Lilitu circles down that night, slips right past Murphy's blind. Hits a tripwire and bam! Snare's got her ass over teakettle hanging up in a tree. You should've seen her. Petite little thing, but boy was she one pissed off little demon." Clay leaned in closer with a conspiratorial smile. "And that was only the beginning. See, we knew she'd been working with half a dozen other Lilitu up and down the state, only, she was the first one we'd got a bead on. So Murphy, he cuts her down from that tree—"

Dad stood abruptly. "Story time's over."

Clay sat back, eyeing Dad with clear disappointment. "We're just getting to the best part."

"Kids have school in the morning. Lucas, Braedyn, head on inside." Dad caught Gretchen's eye with a steely look. Gretchen sat up a little straighter.

"Probably a good idea. Sorry." Gretchen shrugged at Lucas's frown.

Clay studied me, surprise plain on his face. "You send her to school?"

"She can handle herself, Clay. She was raised human, remember? Keeping her out of school now would just draw more attention."

Clay purses his lips, nodding thoughtfully. "Of course. You're right. Best to keep up appearances."

Dad helped me stand, taking back the unused bamboo skewer. "Sorry. We'll do s'mores some other time."

"Yeah." I dusted the back of my jeans off, then waved goodbye to the group. I felt the spotters' eyes on me all the way home.

It wasn't until I was in bed, pulling up my covers up that I realized I never got to hear the end of Clay's story.

"Braedyn."

She spoke into my ear, her voice low and urgent. It yanked me out of the dream in an adrenaline-fueled instant. I sat up in bed, disoriented, my heart hammering against my ribs with a wild, staccato rhythm.

Karayan sat on the edge of my bed, her eyes fixed on my face. Darkness meant nothing to us; I could see the tension in her face as clearly as if we were sitting in full sun. I rubbed the sleep out of my eyes, trying to get my bearings.

"Where have you been? You left without saying…"

"You need to get your things and get out of here." Karayan whipped the covers off my bed, exposing my bare legs to the night's chill.

"Hey, what the…?"

"You can call Murphy when we reach minimum safe distance. A thousand miles should do the trick."

"A thousand...?" I stared at Karayan. "What are you talking about?"

"I'm talking about *Clay*. He's dangerous, Braedyn. He's a psychotic zealot, and I don't mean that in the warm and fuzzy way."

I looked at Karayan, a feeling of dread seeping into my core. "Clay said you and he had unfinished business."

Karayan dropped her eyes, turning away.

"Karayan, what did you do?"

Karayan stiffened. "I'm trying to help you, Braedyn."

"I can't just run away. What about Dad? Cassie and Royal? The Guard?"

Karayan shook her head, frustrated. "It's not worth your life. And, Braedyn, that is exactly what we're talking about. Stay here, and Clay will find a way to kill you."

"I get it. He's... he's serious business." I caught Karayan's hand. "But we have an understanding. And whether you want to acknowledge it or not, these people are my friends and family. They need me."

Karayan gave a short, mirthless laugh. "Yeah, well, I wouldn't be so sure that your understanding and Clay's understanding are the same thing. He can be slippery." Karayan stood.

I didn't let go of her hand. "Wait. Stay. We need you, too. Clay will see that. Let me talk to him, let Dad talk to him."

"He's not going to come around, Braedyn." Karayan gently pried my hand off her arm. The look she gave me was one of aching sadness. "There's nothing I can say or do to convince Clay I'm anything but a monster."

"Karayan," I swung my feet out of bed, meaning to stop her.

But Karayan froze me with a look. "I tried to warn you." She looked away, biting her lip. "Goodbye, Braedyn."

And with that, she slipped away.

Her words were still ringing in my ears the next morning as I walked down the stairs, doing up the last of the buttons on my school shirt. I found Dad in the kitchen, drinking a cup of coffee. He saw me and pushed a plate of toast my way with a questioning look.

I joined him at the kitchen island. The toast was still warm, glistening with a sheen of melted butter. We ate together in silence for a few minutes. Dad stood.

"Clay wants a word with everyone this morning." Dad downed the last of his coffee and set the mug in the sink. "We're meeting in the Guard's backyard. You want me to wait for you, or…?"

"I'm ready." I slid off the stool and shoved the last bite of toast in my mouth. "What's the meeting for?"

"It's a traditional Guard practice." Dad shrugged. "Like I said, Clay is old school."

We headed next door to discover most of the Guard already assembled. Several guys sat on the back porch, drinking coffee out of paper cups. Others were sparring in friendly competition across the yard. Still others were talking in groups of three or four. More than a few sets of eyes tracked me across the yard. I stepped closer to Dad.

Clay emerged from the house, taking his spot on the back porch. The guys who'd been drinking there moments before moved, clearing the area for him. Clay faced the assembled.

"Before we get down to the business of winning the war against darkness, I want each of you to search your hearts. We go into this fight as the last shield defending humankind from the scourge of the Lilitu. I don't care if you're religious. I don't care what you believe, so long as you believe in this—our mission." Clay looked over the crowd. Each time he made eye contact, a soldier would straighten with new resolve. "It seems fitting that, as we begin preparations for the final battle, we take a cue from our forefathers. Before the Guard was an established force, they were a band of men who refused to sit by while demons plagued the earth. But dedicated as they were, it wasn't until they joined together, committed to a common purpose under a common leader, that they began to turn the tide. And it started with an oath."

Clay turned back to the house. Sutherland emerged, taking his place before Clay on the porch. He drew his Guardsman's daggers with a soft *ssshing* and lowered himself to one knee. He bowed his head and lifted the daggers in his palms, as if offering them to Clay. He spoke in a clear, ringing voice. "I, Dean Sutherland, make this oath: I dedicate my life and my strength to the Guard, to our mission, and to our leader."

Clay closed Sutherland's open hands over the dagger. "I hear and accept your oath. Rise, brother of the Guard."

Sutherland stood. The soldiers around us shifted. I saw a mix of emotions. Some men looked intrigued, some unsettled. I glanced at Dad. His face was hard. But as Clay turned back to the crowd, Dad dropped his eyes, hiding his expression from Clay's searching gaze.

"Old fashioned? Yes. But there is power in an oath. It unites us, defines us, motivates us. I will not demand this of you. But if any among you wish to recommit your loyalty, I will take your oath with the respect and reverence it is due."

An uncomfortable silence descended. Clay waited with the appearance of perfect calm. But when his eyes settled on Dad, I saw a glimmer of something hard and determined in his expression.

Dad must have sensed it, too. He swallowed, then walked through the crowd. Clay moved to meet him, stopping on the top porch stair. Dad had no choice but to kneel on a lower stair. He lifted his daggers and cleared his throat.

"I, Alan Murphy, make this oath: I dedicate my life and my strength to the Guard, to our mission, and to our leader." His voice was hard, it sent a chill prickling down my arms.

Clay's smile was warm, almost benevolent. He closed Dad's hands over the dagger. "I hear and accept your oath. Rise, brother of the Guard."

Dad stood, sheathing his daggers. He backed away from Clay, unable to meet his eyes. Clay, scanning the crowd for the next volunteer, didn't notice. But I saw the hot spots of anger in Dad's cheeks. Dad returned to me as a line of Guardsmen formed before Clay.

"You'll have to pledge," Dad whispered into my ear. I turned to look at him, surprised. His face was stony, and he kept his eyes fastened on Clay as he continued. "He expects it, no matter what he says." Dad's eyes found my face then. "You should get in line. Don't be last."

I nodded, feeling uneasy. I took a step toward the group of soldiers. Marla noticed the movement, tapping the arm of a soldier nearby. I looked away. I couldn't win them over in a heartbeat. But maybe this would start the process. It felt like the line took forever, but when the soldier ahead of me stood after giving his oath, I felt a lump rise in my throat.

Clay's eyes found mine. He hesitated, then gestured for me to come forward. I drew my daggers, contemplating the stairs before me. I'd never kneeled for anyone like this before. It felt incredibly awkward. But the longer I stood there, the worse it would become. I dropped to my knees on the step and raised the daggers toward Clay, keeping my eyes fixed on his gleaming boots.

I'd heard the oath over a dozen times by now, but speaking it felt different. "I, Braedyn Murphy, make this oath: I dedicate my life and my strength to the Guard, to our mission, and to our leader." The words came out in a tumbled rush, and as I finished the oath I felt a wash of relief. Nothing happened. I looked up at Clay, a knife twisting in my middle. If he refused to accept...?

Clay's eyes found mine. After what seemed like a small forever, he nodded. "I hear and accept your oath. Rise, friend of the Guard."

I quickly sheathed my daggers and stood, feeling my cheeks flush with heat. *Friend* of the Guard? I retreated back to Dad, keeping my gaze fixed on the ground. I didn't want anyone to see the shame welling in my eyes—and I didn't want to see the curious speculation on the faces of the watching soldiers.

Dad met me at the edge of the crowd, pulling me close. "You did the right thing," he said, his voice coming out in a gruff whisper. "Don't worry about Clay. He'll come around."

"Can we get out of here?" I asked.

Dad shook his head. "We should wait for Clay to release us. Like I said..."

"Old school." I grimaced. "Right."

It was another ten minutes before the rest of the Guard had given their oaths. Once Clay released the last soldier, he turned back to the crowd.

"Thank you, brothers and sisters. We've got a long road ahead of us, but I'm honored to walk it by your side." He inclined his head to the group. "Now, onto business."

Clay hadn't been kidding when he'd said everyone would have a part to play. He'd been busy drawing up several plans of action over the last few days. The first, and most important plan, being information gathering. Clay gestured to Sandra, who joined him on the porch.

"Sandra will be heading a team at the mission." Clay nodded to Sandra.

"I've secured three badges for the team," Sandra began. "We'll be going in as restoration experts."

"Question?" Gretchen's voice cut across the morning. Sandra glanced up, startled. Clay's brows drew together in a thoughtful frown, but he gestured for her to speak. "The mission's a dead zone. Since the Seal's destruction, we've seen no indication of any activity there."

"Our mission doesn't concern the Seal," Sandra said. "Not directly, at any rate. Let me remind you, the mission was established by a monastic order of Guardsmen several centuries ago. It was customary for these groups to conceal secrets within the structure of their strongholds. Walls may contain vaults, pillars may conceal secret staircases to hidden rooms, and so on and so forth. With the recent loss of the Guard's Archives, we cannot afford to risk anything being overlooked." She smiled a lopsided smile. "This is a research mission, not a tactical one."

Gretchen nodded, thinking this over.

"Sandra will let you know if she needs any further assistance. I'll be handing out more assignments over the next few weeks." Clay closed the small notebook he'd been referring to for assignments. "Thank you all for your attention. Now, let's get to work."

The group started to break up. I let a long breath out, relieved.

"You probably have time for another piece of toast if you'd like," Dad said.

We were halfway to the gate separating our house from the Guard's when Clay caught up to us. "I meant to ask earlier, did Karayan ever come home?" He looked from me to Dad.

Dad shook his head. "I think she's long gone, Clay. Took everything from her room. We haven't seen her since the morning you arrived."

Clay glanced my way again, his eyes taking a quick inventory of my face. "Well. If she returns…?"

"You'll be the first to know." Dad put a hand around my shoulders. "Right, Braedyn?"

"Right." I gave Clay a quick smile, trying to force my body to relax. I could hear the thudding of my heart. I swallowed, hoping Clay couldn't see the panic I was trying to hide. I might not be willing to abandon the Guard, but that didn't mean I was ready to betray Karayan. Whatever was going on between her and Clay, that was their business. I wanted no part of it.

"Things are going to change around here, now that Clay's arrived." Lucas's eyes practically shone with conviction.

Royal paused, a serving spoon of broccoli hovering over his plate. "Change how? You think he'll help you find Seth?"

Cassie glanced at me, curious. She was spooling spaghetti onto her fork, but didn't seem too interested in eating.

"Well, he's not messing around, that much is pretty clear." Lucas bit into a slice of garlic bread. "Tell 'em, Braedyn."

I forced a smile. "Mm. Yeah. He's definitely getting the group fired up." I took a bite of spaghetti, forestalling the conversation. Lucas had jumped onto Clay's bandwagon wholeheartedly. I hadn't been prepared for how quickly Lucas came to view Clay as an inspired leader. But, given the practically worshipful vibe of many of Clay's soldiers, I guess it wasn't such a big surprise. Lucas was living among them now, after all. Some of that enthusiasm was bound to rub off.

I glanced back at Cassie. She moved her forked spaghetti around on her plate listlessly.

"Hey, Cas, you doing okay?"

Cassie shrugged and gave me a self-deprecating smile. "I... yeah. It's been a rough couple of months. You know, finding out the world is on the brink of the apocalypse can really put a dent in your summer vacation."

I set my fork down, taking a closer look at Cassie. She really didn't look good. Her face was drawn, tired. Bags hung beneath her eyes, though she'd done an artful job trying to conceal them with makeup. Even her hair, tied up in a quirky knot-bun, seemed somehow listless.

"Just wait until you meet Clay." Lucas took another bite of his bread. "I'm thinking, five minutes in the same room with that guy and your fears will start to fade. I'm not saying it's going to be easy, but with Clay around… Let's just say, if Lilith thinks she's going to move in and take over, she's going to get one hell of a surprise when she finds us waiting for her."

Despite Lucas's confidence in Clay, not much changed for the Guard in those first few weeks. Yes, Clay assigned more and more Guardsmen to individual and small-group missions, but those missions didn't include me. Or, to his great frustration, Lucas.

After yet another morning meeting ended without Clay enlisting Lucas's help, Lucas turned to me with a despondent frown.

"I guess the Guard still thinks of me as a child."

I bit my lip, unsure how to comfort him. The truth was, I was glad neither of us had been assigned to any formal missions. It meant we had time together after school, to hang out by our lockers for a few lingering moments, outside the watchful judgment of the Guard.

The first day of October dawned crisp and cool. Fall seemed ready to settle in at last. We were well into the school year, things around the house had settled into a new normal, and it seemed the new Guardsmen were growing—if not friendlier toward me—used to me, at least. I was growing almost comfortable in the routine. In fact, I'd been able to spend more time and attention on my schoolwork than I had since learning I was Lilitu. My grades had taken a sharp upturn, and I was even enjoying my coursework.

That's how I found myself sitting out on the soccer field during my free period, pen in hand, ready to start my English homework. Writing a college essay on "one moment that changed my life significantly."

My pen hovered over the blank page. I felt a humorless laugh tickle the back of my throat. The one moment that changed my life more than any other was one I couldn't write about—I couldn't even talk about it with anyone outside of the Guard. It was the moment I'd first understood I was half-demon, and all that that entailed. My normal life had burned to a smoldering ruins in an instant. The future I'd always taken for granted, love, marriage, children… gone.

Unless. Unless I managed to navigate the coming war without giving into temptation. Because only if I somehow managed to help the Guard emerge victorious without straying one step further down the road toward the Lilitu half of me, only then would I be granted my humanity.

Emotions flooded through me. Even if I could write this essay, I wouldn't know where to begin to put my feelings into words.

"Who knows if I'm even going to college," I sighed. The wind carried my words away. A heavy melancholy wrapped around me—

A crack like thunder split the air. Suddenly, a rumpled old man stood on the field beside me.

The angel turned toward me, grizzled face drawn. I scrambled to my feet, breathless. I'd only seen him revealed in his true form twice, but I could feel the power radiating from him, even in this disheveled form.

"Sansenoy?"

"Lilith is vulnerable." His eyes locked onto mine. "She is vulnerable now, as she readies herself to return in force."

"I... okay?" I swallowed, suddenly conscious of being supremely under qualified to be having this conversation. "What does that mean?"

His eyes lost their focus as his thoughts turned inward. He frowned. "The nature of her vulnerability is hidden from me, but it resides here, on the earthly plain." Sansenoy's eyes sharpened once more. "You must act, and quickly. This opportunity will not last."

4

That tenuous sense of peace I'd managed to cultivate over the last few weeks evaporated at Sansenoy's words. I felt knots of tension gathering across my back. The angel looked out across the field, out toward the mountains, as if he could see through them to some distant vista. A breeze stirred the grass at our feet. I wrapped my arms close around my middle, shivering.

Sansenoy's eyes shifted. He turned toward me, raking his eyes over my face. "You've fed on mortal energy."

Fear shot icy fingers through my middle. Even the sun above seemed to dim. If he could see that, just by looking at me... exactly how deeply had that night with Lucas scarred me? And then the inevitable question, the question that had been orbiting the edges of my mind since that night, rose to the surface of my thoughts once again.

"Does that mean…?" I licked my lips, trying to tamp down the panic. "Have I crossed the line? Is it too late?" As the words left my lips, I couldn't help but picture the answer I'd feared. What if he said *yes*? Just like that, the future I'd been clinging to could be ripped out of my fingers. Any hope of ending up with Lucas if we somehow managed to emerge victorious from this last battle would be extinguished.

Sansenoy focused his full attention on me. His eyes narrowed. It felt like he was reading my soul. Every second that passed burned like acid, setting my nerves on fire. After a long moment, he looked away again. "Not too late. Not yet."

I felt my shoulders ease. It was a small thing, considering everything we were up against. Even so, knowing the possibility still existed—that Lucas and I might have our future together after all—kindled a warmth inside of me. It was short lived.

"You stand on the very precipice." The angel's voice was tense. "Each day you spend as a Lilitu is a gamble. Take another risk, and you may slip over the edge, past the point of redemption."

I nodded, feeling suddenly tired. "Tell me something I don't know."

"Your loss would deal a serious blow to the Guard and their hopes of success. Without you, the chances of the Guard prevailing in this fight dwindle to almost nothing."

"What?"

Sansenoy met my surprise with a level expression. "This is something you do not seem to understand." Sansenoy frowned. "Or did I misinterpret your request?"

"But I'm..." I shook my head. "I'm the reason the Seal is open."

For the briefest moment, I thought I saw surprise flash through Sansenoy's eyes. "The incubus Sethyal had his fingers on many strings. He would have found a way to disable the Seal with or without your assistance."

"Seth." I felt a bitter laugh rising in my throat. "I can't even fight one incubus. How am I supposed to help defeat an army of Lilitu? How am I supposed to defeat Lilith?"

Something darkened in Sansenoy's gaze. "Doubt will fetter you if you give it free rein. How can you know what you are capable of until you try?" Sansenoy shook his head. "Every soldier must test their mettle on the field of battle. Become human now, and you will lose the powers you are just beginning to master. Powers that could prove crucial in the coming fight."

A heavy sickness settled in my belly. There was another reason I couldn't become human yet. Lucas. Elyia was still out there, hovering at the periphery of our lives, waiting for another opportunity to sink her claws into him. If I became human, who would protect Lucas from her?

"Right. So I just have to wait a little longer before becoming human. I can deal with that." But then I noticed Sansenoy regarding me with a sad compassion that sent another chill washing through my body. "You don't think I can do it?" I caught his gaze and held it, trying to read anything in the mysterious depths of his eyes. "You don't think I can make it through this conflict with my humanity intact?"

Sansenoy watched me in silence for an uncomfortably long moment. "What I think is of little import."

"Sansenoy...?" My throat caught before I could voice the question.

Sansenoy shifted on his feet. Uncertainty looked strange on his features. "You want me to allay your fears?"

"*Yes*. Allay."

Sansenoy thought for a moment. "You have free will." He looked almost troubled. "Some among my ranks see this as a curse. I, and others, think it a gift. But... it comes at a price."

"Shocker," I muttered. Sansenoy frowned in confusion. "Sorry. What price?"

"If you wish to achieve your humanity, you may have to sacrifice victory against Lilith and her forces." Sansenoy's voice softened. "If you wish to achieve victory against Lilith and her forces? You may have to sacrifice your life."

I swallowed, hard. "That's supposed to allay my fears?" My voice sounded shaky. "You're saying we can beat Lilith, but only if I give up my love or my life. That's my choice? That's what free will gets me?" A knot of anger was beginning to form in my chest.

"The future is unwritten." Sansenoy eyed me with wary unease, as if I were a grenade he'd accidentally pulled the pin on. "One thing I can tell you for certain; if you steal the vitality from another mortal soul, another transgression of that magnitude will tip the scale and you will lose your chance at humanity forever."

"Another transgression...?!" The cold anger in my core erupted into fury. I advanced on Sansenoy. He took a step back, startled. "I wouldn't have had to commit the *first* transgression if you'd been around to help us! Where were you when Seth was preying on my friends? Where were you when he had Royal on that altar, about to slit his throat? If I hadn't taken that energy from Lucas, Royal would be dead right now."

"You made a choice." Sansenoy's voice was low, but it struck me like a slap. "You risked your humanity to save your friend. You were lucky."

"And now?" My fury was transforming into something harder now. "Are you going to stick around, now that we're heading into the final stretch of this war?"

Sansenoy's eyes found mine, tight with an anger all his own. "I am required elsewhere, unless and until the day Lilith returns to this plane."

"So you just pop in, tell me Lilith is vulnerable, and...?"

Another ricocheting crack split the air and Sansenoy was gone. I stared at the space he'd occupied half a second before, gritting my teeth. Whatever this vulnerability of Lilith's was, we were clearly going to have to figure it out ourselves.

I didn't wait for school to end. I figured when an angel shows up to personally deliver a message, that's a ditch-worthy event. Thirty seconds after Sansenoy's abrupt departure, I was rushing toward the school parking lot, shoving my notebook into my backpack.

"Braedyn, what's up?" Lucas caught me at the edge of the parking lot. He glanced back at the school, his hazel eyes tight with worry. "Did Murphy call? Is something going...?"

"Sansenoy." I kept my voice low. "He just popped by for a visit."

Lucas's eyes swiveled to my face. "What, here? At school?"

"I have to go. You should get a ride home with Cassie or Royal."

"Screw that. I'm coming with you." The muscles in his jaw hardened, and I saw it would be pointless to argue.

I filled Lucas in on the drive home. As glad as he was to hear the possibility still existed for me to become human, the news about Lilith overshadowed our relief. By the time we got home, Lucas was as frustrated with Sansenoy's vague message as I was.

"What the hell does that even mean?" He bit the side of his lip, thinking. "Vulnerable, like, this is our best chance to kill her?"

"Your guess is as good as mine." I steered the Firebird onto my driveway and killed the engine. Dad's truck was parked out front, but when Lucas and I checked my house he wasn't home.

"He's probably at our place," Lucas said. I nodded, and we headed over.

We entered the Guard's house to find Dad standing with Clay and Thane by Clay's desk. The men looked up as we walked inside. Thane and Clay shared a veiled look. I got the distinct impression they'd been talking about me. Whatever passed wordlessly between the two, they weren't sharing. A wave of self-consciousness rolled over me and I felt suddenly awkward in my own skin. Thane looked more at ease by

Clay's side than he had since I'd known him. Before I could reflect on this, Dad spoke.

"Why aren't you at school?" Dad's eyes searched my face. "What's happened?"

"I..." I licked my lips, suddenly unsure. "Can I talk to you for a sec?"

Dad took a step toward me, but Thane caught his arm. He studied me with shrewd focus. "Whatever you have to tell Murphy, you can tell us all."

Clay glanced at Thane, then turned back to me with mild interest. Waiting. I glanced at Dad. He shot a small frown at Thane before turning back to me.

"Go ahead, Braedyn," Dad said. "We're all listening."

"Sansenoy found me at school." I forced my shoulders to relax. "He didn't stay long, but he told me that Lilith is vulnerable. He said we had to find the nature of her vulnerability. He also said this is a limited-time opportunity, so we have to work fast. Of course, it would've been nice if he'd given us a clue where to start, but no."

For a moment no one spoke. Clay scratched his temple, smiling slightly. "I'm confused. Why would an angel tasked with rooting out and eliminating Lilith's offspring seek you out to deliver such an important message to the Guard?"

"Sansenoy's sought Braedyn out before," Lucas said, interjecting before I had a chance to say anything. "He gave her Semangelof's sword. He knows she's not like the others. He knows we can trust her." Lucas took my hand, as if to emphasize the point.

Clay's eyes tracked the movement. He glanced at Thane, eyebrows lifting in a silent question.

"It's true." Thane shrugged, as if saying, *there's no accounting for taste*.

Clay thought for a moment, then nodded. "Well. No matter how the message was delivered, the meaning is clear. The fate of the Sons of Adam rests on us now. We must identify this vulnerability and take the fight to Lilith before she gathers her full strength." Clay walked around to sit at his desk, already lost in thought. "Thane, tell Sutherland I need him. Time we convene a full council anyhow. You mind spreading the word?"

"Not at all." Thane turned and strode out of the room, eyes alight with purpose.

"Oh, Murphy, I haven't had a chance to ask you yet, but I'd be honored if you'd join us in the capacity of military advisor. Sutherland's been my go to, but you have a certain expertise I think we'll need in the not too distant future." Clay gave Dad a mild smile then turned back to his work. Again, it may have been phrased like a question, but it was as good as an order.

Dad's jaw tightened. "Of course." He glanced at me, clearly uneasy. "Why don't you head home, I'll be there in a few minutes."

I nodded and turned to go, expecting Lucas to join me. Instead, he released my hand and took a step closer to Clay.

"What about us?" Lucas spoke clearly, but I could hear the tension in his voice.

"Excuse me?" Clay looked up, genuinely surprised. "I'm sorry, did you have something to add?"

"Just…" Lucas glanced back at me, then swallowed. "I know I look like a kid, but I… I'm strong. I can help. I can fight. Sir."

Clay set his pen down and laced his hands together on his desk. He studied Lucas for a moment, then nodded. "I see. Well, thank you for stepping up, son. I have to meet with my advisors tonight, but I'll be handing out some new assignments tomorrow, and I'll keep you in mind."

Lucas nodded. He turned to me and I saw hope burning in his eyes. A deep unease settled in my stomach, but I couldn't put my finger on exactly what caused it. Clay had said all the right things, but he wouldn't actually put Lucas in harm's way… would he?

My question was answered the following morning. I was still getting used to showing up for morning meetings every day at 7:00 AM, but—after that first meeting when Clay had everyone pledge their oath to the Guard—the meetings weren't usually very long, just quick check-ins and a run through of any Guard business for the day.

But today, Clay kept us waiting for a few minutes before he took his now-customary place on the back porch. Word had gotten around about Sansenoy's message. I noticed more than a few sidelong glances aimed in my direction. Some were curious, others were more overtly suspicious.

Dad shifted his weight beside me and I felt a rush of gratitude toward him. Just being close to him made me feel safe. Clay's people might never come to trust or like me, but Dad's reputation was as good as a shield—to cross me was to cross the formidable Murphy. Not something any of these soldiers seemed keen to attempt.

Lucas and Gretchen joined us. Gretchen was rubbing sleep out of her eyes. She must have had another late night on duty at the mission. We kept a presence on guard at the broken Seal, but—as Gretchen had made clear—there'd been no sign of anything supernatural since the Seal's destruction. Lucas, on the other hand, seemed anxious. I didn't need a mind reader to know why; he was waiting to see if Clay had a job for him.

When Clay finally emerged from the house, the troops straightened, giving him their full attention. Clay looked out over the assembled and nodded his acknowledgement.

"I know the rumor mill's been working overtime, so let me just set a few things straight before we begin." Clay smiled, his eyes crinkling with a benevolent friendliness. "We have reason to believe Sansenoy's reached out with some intelligence regarding a possible weakness of Lilith's."

I felt a twisting in my stomach. *Reason to believe…?* I looked at Dad, who glanced at me with a slight frown before turning his attention back to Clay.

"We've got a job ahead of us, both finding out what this weakness may be and exploiting it before this window of opportunity closes. Which brings me to today's assignments." Clay turned to a piece of paper and began reading off names and tasks.

He spent most of the meeting assigning workers to some construction project, making updates to the Guard's basement. It surprised me, I didn't think the basement needed much work, but if Clay was going to ramp up training, it made sense to upgrade the facilities. I let my mind wander as Clay finished up his assignments. He released the group after he read the last name off his list for the construction project, but as we turned to leave, Sutherland blocked our path.

"Clay wants a word." Sutherland gestured, and Dad headed toward the Guard's house. Lucas and I turned to leave, but Sutherland cleared his throat. "You two, too."

"Really?" There was an unmistakable excitement in Lucas's voice. We followed Sutherland onto the back porch. Clay was in consultation with Sandra, but he looked up as we approached. Sandra eyed me with thoughtful speculation, then made her excuses and left.

"Murphy," Clay's eyes settled on Dad first. "I wanted to give you a heads up. I'll be calling on you soon to resume your old duties."

Dad stiffened beside me, but Clay didn't wait for an answer before turning to Lucas.

"I thought about our conversation all night, and I think I have an assignment worthy of your dedication, young man."

"Anything. Just tell me what you want me to do." Lucas straightened under Clay's gaze.

"I need an *Aide De Camp*, and I think you'll fit the bill quite nicely."

"Oh." Lucas's shoulders dropped a fraction. I could tell he was trying to hide his disappointment. So, evidently, could Clay.

"I'm not sure you appreciate the weight of responsibility I'm putting on your shoulders, son." Clay's eyes settled on Lucas's face. "We're going to be spending a lot of time together. As my *Aide De Camp*, you'll be a confidential assistant, a sounding board, an indispensible right hand man. This isn't a nothing position. This is a real job, and I need a good man to fill it. Are you in?"

"Yes, sir. You can count on me." Lucas's voice was full of conviction.

Clay nodded, allowing himself a smile. Then he turned on me. "And Ms. Braedyn. I've got a job for you as well."

"You... you do?" Surprise sent a jolt through my system, chasing away the last fog of sleep from my mind. I glanced at Dad, and saw a shadow of fear pass over his face. It wasn't comforting.

"I need you to draw a Lilitu out. It's important that we trap it alive. We're flying blind at the moment; we need to gain some insight into the enemy's plans."

He was watching me closely, with a look that unsettled me. I swallowed, trying to buy a little time to think. But Clay wasn't interested in waiting for my answer.

"I'll have a group of soldiers on standby. They'll be ready to move the instant you've located a Lilitu, you just give me the word. Understand?"

"I…" I looked at Dad again, torn. "I'm not sure how… I mean, I've never done anything like this before."

Clay frowned. Dad cleared his throat and took a step closer to me. "What about Elyia? Have you broken through her shield yet?"

"Not yet. The shield, it's… it's strong." I shook my head, feeling a heated shame flood into my cheeks.

Clay shifted his weight casually. He inspected a fingernail. "What about Karayan?" The way he asked this, he sounded almost bored. "You two have a connection. Draw her back here, and this could be a way for Karayan to make reparations for some earlier missteps." Clay glanced at me, the intensity of his gaze betraying his interest.

"Oh?" I caught sight of Dad. He shook his head ever so slightly. I dropped my eyes, feigning regret. "I wish I'd known earlier. She's long gone by now."

Clay forced a smile and shrugged lightly. "Well. I don't really care who you bring me, as long as you bring me a Lilitu. And Braedyn, don't keep us waiting too long, okay?" Clay's eyes shifted to Lucas. "Come on, let's get started."

Clay disappeared into the house with Lucas training him like an eager puppy. Dad and I stood rooted to the porch for a long moment after they'd left, each of us lost in our own thoughts, neither of us pleased.

I stepped into the garden of my dreaming mind that night, unsure what path to take. Instead of getting to work seeking Elyia's shielded mind, I turned my attention to the field of black roses shivering in a gentle breeze. I plucked one black stem. Within the stem, the core of the rose was a vibrant green. If these flowers were a metaphor for how far I'd strayed toward becoming Lilitu, that green was vibrant proof that I still held onto one last shred of my humanity. I clutched the stem tight. It wasn't hopeless. Not yet.

I turned away from the roses and knelt on the ground, laying my palm against the warm earth. It was all illusion, of course. As I focused, I became conscious of the edges of my own dream, floating in the vast space shared by all living minds. I honed in on Elyia, and felt the tug as my will drew her mind closer.

A silvery pool rose out of the ground beneath my palm, and within it, a star ascended to hang before me. I reached out a hand, but even before my fingers closed around the gleaming pinprick of light, I knew it was useless. Nothing escaped the shield around her mind; I could sense no hint of Elyia's presence. Just the hard, featureless, impenetrable wall of the shield guarding her thoughts.

Instead of spending the night fighting—again—to break through this wall, I released the star. Elyia's mind fell back into the pool, drifted off into the infinite dream.

"Karayan?" I closed my eyes, willing her to hear me. In half a heartbeat, I felt her attention turn toward me. No matter where she went in the physical world, we'd always be able to find one another in the dream.

"Please tell me this means you're fast asleep on a bus headed to Canada."

I opened my eyes with a grin. Karayan stood at the edge of the garden, scanning the roses as if she could get a read on my physical location from the condition of my dream. "Not yet, but I'm starting to think you may have a point."

"What's he done?" Karayan crossed her arms, instantly tense.

"It's what he wants me to do that's the problem." I got to my feet and dusted the dirt off my knees. Karayan's eyes narrowed as I told her what Clay had asked me to do. When I told her Clay had suggested I try to lure her into a trap, Karayan's lips thinned into a tight line.

"So. What are you going to do?"

"Well, I sure as hell won't give you up. Even if you won't tell me what's going on between you two." I eyed Karayan, but she only tilted her head to one side, clearly uninterested in dishing. "Fine. I'll just have to figure out something else."

"Or..." Karayan bit her lip, looking uncharacteristically concerned. "You could grab your things and leave Puerto Escondido with me."

"You... you're still in town?" Surprise coursed through my garden, manifesting as a blast of cold wind.

"Hoping you'd come to your senses, yeah." Karayan rubbed her arms against the frigid breeze and sighed. "What do you say? Let's put as much distance between us and Clay as money can buy."

"I can't go. I told you." I pulled away from her, frustrated, but Karayan caught my arm. She turned me back to face her, gently.

"Braedyn, right now Clay doesn't know you. But he's learning more about you every day. And when he figures out what's important to you, that's when he'll have all the power. He is dangerous and manipulative and cruel. The smartest thing you can do is get the hell away from Terrance Clay."

I looked down at Karayan's hand on my arm. She released me, frustrated. "I appreciate what you're trying to do," I started.

Karayan nodded, despondent. "Okay. If that's your decision. Guess I'm making my road trip solo."

"You'll take care of yourself?" I felt a lump rising in the back of my throat. It startled me, how much I'd grown to depend on Karayan. Her leaving felt… wrong.

Karayan nodded. "And if you change your mind… you've got my number." Karayan smiled, but it looked strained.

I returned the smile, and Karayan vanished, slipping out of my dream as quietly as she'd entered it. I let out a long breath. Not Karayan. Not Elyia.

But there was one other Lilitu I knew of in Puerto Escondido. I pictured the curly-haired beauty, focused all my energy on her face…

I felt another tug, and when I turned back to the pool of stars, I saw one swirling closer through drifts of gleaming minds. It rose out of the pool to hover before me. I hesitated for a few heartbeats, then closed my hand around her mind.

Vyla looked up as I entered her dream. I glanced around. Vyla's landscape was dotted with cheerful Feverfew flowers, their sunny faces ringed round with fat white petals. Vyla lurched to her feet, taking half a step back. But she stopped herself and—after a moment's recalibration—smiled.

"You've come. I'm so glad." Vyla ran a hand through her thick curls, betraying a nervous energy. "Surprised, but so glad you've sought me out."

"You said you needed my help, but you never got around to explaining what that means." I couldn't keep the suspicion out of my voice. It seemed to work in my favor, though. Vyla winced, so concerned with winning me over she didn't think to question what had changed my mind.

"Yes. Yes. But…" Vyla licked her lips. "The reason I need your help. I need to show you in person." I frowned and Vyla held out her hands, pleading. "Just five minutes. That's all I need. Then you'll understand why I've come to you."

"And if I still don't want to help you, even after I've seen your uber-compelling reasons?"

A strained worry creased the edges of Vyla's eyes. "Well, I guess we'll cross that bridge if we come to it." She smiled again, a painfully vulnerable smile. "But I have to believe once you've seen… I have to believe you'll help."

I nodded slowly, feeling a strange prickle across my shoulders. It couldn't be this easy, could it? A Lilitu begging to meet me in person, right after Clay demanded I snare one for him. I suddenly knew I wouldn't tell Clay about this, not until after I'd met her and heard her story.

"So," I said. "Where do you want to do this?"

The Lilitu detailed a little park near Old Town. I knew it; I'd played there as a little kid. We'd do it tomorrow, during my free period at school. I figured that would be the best way to keep it from Lucas and—by extension—Clay. Once our plans were set, I slipped out of her dream.

But instead of returning to my own dream or waking up, I shifted my attention to Lucas. It had been weeks since we'd shared a night's dream together. Weeks spent in fruitless attempts to crack the shield protecting Elyia's mind. Should I get back to work on it? Yes, probably. But tonight, I needed Lucas.

I felt his dream approaching and turned to meet it. Slipping into his sleeping mind felt warm, familiar, safe. Lucas was mid-dream, something mundane and nonsensical. But when he saw me, the backdrop of his dream began to fade. Lucas was becoming an accomplished lucid dreamer; it only took a few moments for him to approach.

"You're here." He caught my hands and drew me close for a breathless kiss. "It's been too long."

"Agreed." I circled my arms around his neck, pulling him in for another kiss.

We lost ourselves in each other, letting the night slip by as we stretched the limits of our shared dream. As good as things could feel, as nice as it was to spend any time together, nothing in a dream could compare to the sensations of real life. But that was the entire point, wasn't it? Very little of what we shared that night would have been possible between us if it weren't for the dream.

Afterwards, as I became dimly aware of the dawning world outside our dream, Lucas sighed, content.

"I have a feeling we won't be seeing much of each other outside of dreams."

I raised myself onto one arm, studying his face. "What do you mean?"

"Clay wasn't kidding around, making me his secretary."

"You're not a..." I punched Lucas lightly in the arm.

He grinned, rubbing the spot absently. "Well, whatever you want to call me, I'm basically Clay's errand boy now. After so many years wishing I had a job to do, finally having a purpose in the Guard feels... it feels really good. Even if all I do is take notes and sit through meetings."

I lowered myself back down beside Lucas, resting my head on his shoulder. I was glad he felt a sense of belonging. I knew how long he'd sought acceptance from Hale, how much he chafed at Gretchen's trying to keep him out of harm's way. This was probably the best of both worlds, if you thought about it. Lucas was entrenched in the heart of the Guard, but he wasn't expected to fight.

So why did the thought of him spending so much time with Clay fill me with this chilling dread?

Dad was sitting at the kitchen island when I walked in the next morning. I glanced at the clock. It was only 6:15 AM.

"Couldn't sleep?" I knew Dad had been taking some late night shifts every few days, so he'd grown to really appreciate sleeping in on those days when he could. Granted, none of us slept past 7:00 with

Clay's morning meetings, but still… he didn't have to be up for another half an hour, easy.

"Hm?" Dad looked up, startled. I realized he hadn't heard me enter. "Sorry, honey, what was the question?"

"You okay?" I took the stool next to Dad, suddenly worried. His eyes were ringed with deep bags, and shot through with red veins. If I didn't know him any better, I'd say he'd spent the night crying. "You look like crap."

"What every father wants to hear." He raised his mug toward me in mock salute, then downed the contents, wincing. "I'm going to make a fresh pot. You want any?"

"Coffee?" I gave Dad another searching look, surprised. "No thanks."

"Right, sorry." He looked into his empty mug, drifting into unpleasant thoughts.

"Here, why don't I make it?" I took the cup out of his hands and set about refilling the coffee pot. While I worked, I snuck a few furtive glances his way. Dad rubbed a hand through his hair before straightening on the stool. I activated the coffee pot, and we waited in silence for the drip to get going. Once it looked like enough coffee had brewed for a cup, I pulled the pot off its burner and refilled Dad's mug.

"Any luck with Elyia's shield?" Dad took the fresh cup of coffee with a tired smile.

"No. But…" I settled myself on my stool again. Dad gave me a troubled frown. "That Lilitu from the mountain, the one who approached me at Hale's funeral. Vyla."

Dad's expression darkened. "You know her name now?"

I winced, caught. "I… I meant to tell you, but with everything else…"

"Yeah, I understand. Not saying I'm happy about it, but I understand." Dad let out a resigned sigh and nodded his head for me to continue.

"I couldn't break through Elyia's shield, so I thought, maybe I could find Vyla. Last night, I visited her dream."

"Was that wise?"

Before I could answer, someone knocked on the front door. Dad and I exchanged a startled glance. Dad rose to answer it.

Clay and Lucas stood on the doorstep, their breath coming out in puffs of steam against the morning chill. Lucas met my eyes, grinning. He looked pleased with himself.

"Mind if we come in?" Clay entered as Dad stood to one side. He looked around the foyer, impressed. "Nice place you've got here, Murphy."

"To what do we owe the pleasure?" Dad kept his voice level, but I could see his hand on the doorknob. He was gripping it so tight, his knuckles were white.

"Well, I was talking over some things with Lucas this morning and he had an amazing idea." Clay nodded to Lucas with a broad smile. "Why don't you tell them?"

"Well, I know you've had trouble breaking through Elyia's shield," Lucas started, "but then it dawned on me, there's another Lilitu in town." I felt a sick understanding wash through me as he talked.

Of course. Lucas had been there the day I'd met Vyla. He wanted to help me prove myself to Clay.

I forced a smile. "There is?" Dad's head swiveled toward me. I knew I was walking dangerous ground, but I wasn't willing to hand Vyla over to Clay, not yet.

"That Lilitu who attacked you at Hale's funeral. If her mind isn't shielded, you could find her, lure her out into the open."

"Huh." I turned away from Lucas and Clay, hoping they'd buy my silence as thoughtful consideration rather than out and out panic.

"I understand Karayan's fled town," Clay said. "And I know you've had trouble cracking Elyia's shield. So when Lucas proposed this third Lilitu, well, it seemed like an ideal solution to our problem."

I turned back, forcing an enthusiasm into my voice that I didn't feel. "It's a great idea. Thanks, Lucas."

Lucas beamed at me. Clay's eyes shifted from me to Lucas and back. Whatever he saw between us, he kept to himself.

"Excellent. You just tell me when you're ready to spring your trap, and I'll make sure my men are there." Clay clapped his hands together. "Now, I hear you make a mean pancake, Murphy. Would it be too much of an imposition to ask…?"

"Not at all, Clay." Dad gestured for Lucas and Clay to head into the dining room. "I think we've even got some fresh maple syrup in the fridge."

"This wartime planning's hard work. I could eat a horse." Clay and Lucas moved toward the dining room table.

Dad caught my arm. He didn't say anything. He didn't have to. The look he gave me was clear: I was playing a risky game, keeping Clay in the dark about Vyla.

5

I may not have been ready to tell Clay about Vyla, but I wasn't an idiot; I needed backup at this meeting. I considered my options during the first couple of periods at school. I couldn't tell Lucas, not without risking word getting back to Clay. And Royal and Cassie, while they wouldn't hesitate to join me, wouldn't do much good if the Lilitu was springing a trap. Which really left only one person I could turn to.

I hesitated in the hallway outside my AP calculus class. Only three minutes before the bell. I closed my eyes and sought out Karayan's mind. I was in luck; as I contacted her, she was in line to buy a bus ticket out of town.

Change your mind? I could feel her eager surprise through our connection.

No. I'm actually... I was wondering if I could ask one last favor before you leave town. I tried to rein in my anxiety, but some of it must have slipped through along with my thoughts.

What's the trouble this time? Karayan kept her tone light, but I could feel her attention zeroing in on me, trying to glean what she could from our connection.

I'm meeting with that Lilitu, the one I saw at Hale's memorial. Vyla.

Really. Karayan's thoughts came back with an undercurrent of tension. *I wasn't aware she'd made the jump from enemy of the state to lunch-date material.*

I'm just hearing her out, I shot back. *I figured I should see what she has to say for herself before I serve her up to Clay on a silver platter.* That was the wrong thing to say, and I knew it as soon as the thought left my head. Karayan's returning thought was frosty.

I see. And you need me to...?

You're right to be pissed. I let some of the conflict I was feeling bleed into the thought. *I don't know what to hope for, that she's another Lilitu who doesn't subscribe to the whole 'let's destroy the world of men' philosophy, or that she's a bad guy I can hand over to Clay to get him off my back.*

There was a long moment of silence as Karayan considered this. *I'll come with you,* she thought back at last. *But after this is over, you're going to drop me off at the bus station. It's past time I put Puerto Escondido in the rearview mirror.*

It's a deal. I let out a small sigh and opened my eyes. Ally passed me on the way into class. She eyed me up and down. I gave her a neutral smile. Of Amber's posse, Ally was and had always been my least favorite. The feeling appeared to be mutual; we found seats on opposite sides of the classroom.

AP Calc isn't the best class to let your mind wander. I tried hard to keep my thoughts on the lesson, but they kept straying to the meeting. By the time class was over, I was practically buzzing with anxiety. I slipped out of the classroom and dropped my books off at my locker. The plan was to sneak away during my free period and make it back by lunchtime so that Lucas would never know I had left campus. I'd even parked my car on the street instead of in the school parking lot.

I checked the hallway as kids disappeared into classrooms for the start of fourth period. When the coast was clear, I let my Lilitu wings unfold behind me. It always felt strange to stretch them. Most of the time, I pushed them to the back of my mind. They had no place in my human life, and only spotters were capable of seeing them. But, though they were a pointed reminder of my demon heritage, they were also incredibly useful at times like this.

As the intangible wings encircled me, they shrouded me from human view. As far as I knew, the only person on campus who would be able to see me now was Amber, but she should be in class herself right now. I headed for the exit, turning all my attention toward this meeting with Vyla.

Karayan was waiting by my car. She was also cloaked, and under her wings I saw a duffel bag slung over her shoulder. I felt a twinge. She could fit all her worldly possessions in that bag, whereas I had a father, a house, a lifetime's worth of memories in my room. Sometimes I felt like we were very similar, but other times—times like this—I realized how different we actually were, and how lucky I was.

"Well?" Karayan tilted her head to one side, giving me a half-smile. "Are we doing this or not? I was hoping to put a few hundred miles between myself and Clay before nightfall."

I got into the driver's seat and reached across to open the door for Karayan. She tossed her duffel into the back seat and slid in, her movements effortlessly fluid and graceful.

I set the key in the ignition, then hesitated. "Thank you for doing this. I know… I know it's probably the last thing you want to tackle right now." I turned toward Karayan and my breath caught in my throat. I saw the aching sadness in her eyes.

Karayan noticed. She shrugged, but I saw a hint of moisture gathering in her eyes. "What are friends for?"

Fifteen minutes later, we pulled up at the edge of a sprawling grassy lawn. The park was full of kids climbing over a substantial jungle gym, swinging on swings, running as fast as their little legs could carry them.

"Makes me tired just watching them," Karayan said. I grinned at the pained note in her voice. Karayan looked around, curious. "Nice and public. Lots of witnesses. I'm guessing she didn't bring you out here to try and shiv you."

"That's comforting."

We headed toward the fenced-in play area. I scanned the surrounding park for the full head of glossy dark curls. Karayan tapped me on the arm and I turned. She jerked her chin at a figure leaning on the fence, back to us.

"That her?"

I didn't have to see her face to recognize the Lilitu. Her hair was too perfect to be human. The lines of her back inherently sensual. Even the way she curled her hands over the top edge of the post… everything about her was alluring. I met Karayan's gaze and nodded.

"Lead the way," Karayan said. "I got your back."

I swallowed, gathering my courage. Aside from Karayan, my interactions with Lilitu had ranged from uneasy to almost fatal. To say it was hard to trust another one was something of an understatement.

Vyla sensed me coming and turned. Her face broke into a warm smile. Then she caught sight of Karayan and her smile faltered. I glanced back over my shoulder. Karayan was two steps behind, eyes hard and latched onto Vyla with pitiless focus.

"This is my friend, Karayan." I gave Karayan a tight smile and lowered my voice. "Easy. We're here to listen, not instigate world war three."

Karayan nodded slowly, but she didn't take her eyes of Vyla.

"So." I turned back to the dark-haired demon. "What was it you couldn't tell me in the dream?"

"It's what I need to show you." Vyla turned and beckoned to someone in the park. I felt Karayan stiffen behind me, and reached for my own daggers, tucked into the back pocket of my jeans.

But before I could pull them out, Karayan grabbed my wrist. Her face was frozen with a sort of startled amazement. I turned back, searching for the source of this wonder.

I spotted the child instantly. She was cute and lively, and looked completely normal... except for her haunting hazel eyes. I looked from her to Vyla. The girl had the same dark hair, though hers was straight instead of curly. She couldn't have been more than five or six years old. The child danced up to us with an open, guileless smile.

"Mommy, I made a new friend!" Her voice was sweet and clear. "Her name's Elizabeth and she's five, too!"

"She is? That's wonderful! Baby, I want you to meet someone." Vyla turned, placing her arm around the girl protectively. "This is Braedyn. She's the reason we came to this town." Vyla gave me a smile that was half-pride, half-fear. "This is my daughter, Emlyn."

I took a step back involuntarily. There is only one way for a Lilitu to have a child; she becomes pregnant the third night she spends with a man, the night she drains the last of his mortal vitality, the night she leaves him a lifeless husk. In becoming a mother, Vyla had committed murder.

The little girl studied me, curious. I swallowed my shock and forced a smile for her benefit. She gave me a quick wave.

"Hi." But then, like a butterfly alighting on one petal only to flutter away a moment later, Emlyn turned back to her mom. "Can I go play? Elizabeth has to leave soon so her grandma can take a nap."

"Of course, baby. Go have fun." Vyla watched the girl run back to the playground, her eyes deep and troubled. She turned back to me. "I know this looks bad," she began.

"Bad?" Karayan's voice came out ragged, raspy. "You *killed a man*. You're the reason Guardsmen keep hunting us…!"

I put a hand on Karayan's arm. People were turning to stare. Vyla had gone pale in the face of Karayan's wrath. I turned my eyes on Vyla, a cold fury edging into my voice.

"What was all that about living in peace with humankind? About this not being your war?"

"Please." Vyla struggled to keep her voice level. "Try to understand… I'd been on this earth for almost four hundred years before Emlyn's birth. In all that time, I never fed more than once from any mortal man. It was a point of pride among us; we never *hurt* anyone."

"Last I checked, murder wasn't exactly considered benign." Karayan's voice was like iron. Vyla winced.

"Try living for four hundred years without anyone to love." Vyla's face twisted with grief. "I was so lonely, and a romantic relationship was out of the question. I… I was desperate. So yes. I killed. Once. For Emlyn." She met my eyes, and I saw strength there. "She's given my life a whole new meaning."

"Oh, well, in that case, I'm sure the Guard will overlook the premeditated murder." Karayan gave Vyla a cold smile.

"It was wrong, yes." Vyla turned to Karayan, real anger snapping behind her eyes. "And if I have to, I will pay for the transgression. But it was my crime. Emlyn is innocent." Vyla shifted her gaze to me, softening. "She doesn't know what she is, what we are. Up until a few months ago, I only hoped to prolong her innocence for as long as possible. Now? Now I know she could be spared this life. That she might never have to choose between being forever alone or being a killer." The hope in Vyla's eyes was intense. It speared into me like a knife. Here were all my fears, reborn in another little girl. She had no idea what her life held in store for her. What she would become.

Vyla studied my face, as if gathering her courage. "I… I know about your deal with Sansenoy. I want a human life for Emlyn, too."

Karayan let out a soft breath behind me. I met her eyes and saw the same shock in her expression that I felt coursing through my body.

"How...? Who told you about...?"

Vyla gave me a smile that was at once both wistful and knowing. "Lilitu," she said. "Word has gotten around. Most of us have our doubts, but I had to know for sure. That's why I've come to you, Braedyn Murphy. Will you help us? Will you save my little girl?"

My eyes sought Emlyn out on the playground. She looked like any other child at play; laughing, happy digging in the sand. "I... it's not my deal to make." I swallowed, feeling numb. "Sansenoy made the offer. I... I don't know if he'd make the same offer to your daughter."

"Will you ask him?" Vyla wrung her hands. Her voice trembled.

After a moment, I nodded.

"Thank you. Thank you. That's all I need." Relief opened the floodgates within Vyla. She looked away quickly, but not before I saw tears glistening in the corners of her eyes.

"Okay." Karayan stepped forward, drawing Vyla's attention back away from the playground. "Okay, you made your request. Braedyn'll take it to Sansenoy. In the meantime, you need to get your little girl and get the hell out of this town."

"What?" Vyla's eyes clouded. "We're not leaving until..."

"Terrance Clay is here." Karayan dropped her voice. "If he ever got his hands on that little girl...?"

"He won't." A muscle along Vyla's jaw twitched, the only hint of the tension running just beneath her surface. "I'm not leaving, not until we have an answer."

"I don't think you understand." Karayan glanced at me, as if asking for backup. "Clay and the entire Guard are here. Complete with half a dozen spotters and close to fifty trained soldiers."

"I've kept her hidden for the past five years." Vyla glared defiance at Karayan. "You want me to keep Emlyn safe? That's what I'm doing. This is the best way to protect her from the Guard. If she becomes human, she ceases to be a threat. If not? It won't matter where I take her. The Guard will find us eventually, and one of these days I won't be fast enough or strong enough to get us away." Vyla turned back to me, her eyes shining with determination. "I know how my life will end; on the point of some Guardsman's blade. But Emlyn... she could live a human life. Fall in love. Have children. With luck, she will die of old age, surrounded by those who love her." Vyla gave Karayan a thin smile. "We're staying."

Karayan glanced at me, torn. I agreed with Karayan, but if Vyla was bound and determined to hang out until I'd had a chance to talk with Sansenoy…? I sighed, resigned.

Karayan frowned. "Okay, fine. But if they stay, they will need someone to protect and hide them. Someone who knows the town." Vyla watched us with thinly veiled hope.

I nodded slowly. "It can't be me. Clay would notice if I started sneaking away on a regular basis." I met Karayan's eyes. "That bus ticket… I don't suppose it's refundable?"

Karayan shook her head, but I could see she'd already made the decision. "It's not easy being your friend sometimes," she said. Before I could answer, she gave Vyla a smile. "So. You play poker? I have a feeling we're going to need to kill a lot of time."

I felt strangely lighter when I returned to school. It was lunch, and I was five or ten minutes late, so I decided to risk parking in the school parking lot. I figured Lucas would be sitting down to eat with Cassie and Royal right about now. I figured wrong.

Lucas was running late, too. He came out of the North Hall as I emerged from my car. He spotted me and waved, jogging over. I knew by the expression on his face that he suspected something.

"What's going on? Where have you been?"

"Uh…" I swallowed, stalling for time. "Long story. I'll tell you later."

Lucas grinned. "You found her, didn't you?" He must have seen something in my reaction that gave him his answer. "I knew it! I told Clay you'd do it. I told Clay he could depend on you."

Lucas dropped the subject as we headed into the dining hall for lunch, but every time he caught my eye he couldn't help but smile. I knew I needed to defuse his enthusiasm before he reported to Clay. I figured I'd come up with a better story by the end of the day. I spent the last few periods mulling over some options, and finally settled on a decent lie about Vyla being too young and naive to be worth much to Clay. But when Lucas met me for a ride home after school, the story I had prepared fell apart.

"I want to know everything." Lucas's eyes gleamed. I pulled out of the parking lot, steering into traffic while I gathered my thoughts.

"Listen," I started. "I'm not sure she's what Clay's looking for."

"Don't worry about that." Lucas shrugged. "It's not on you to deliver the perfect informant. Anything she knows might be useful. It's more about proving to Clay that you can be trusted, right?"

"Yeah, but she's…"

"How'd you find her?" Lucas eyed me, alive with curiosity.

"Uh… just… got lucky."

Lucas shook his head, grinning. "You're too modest."

I survived the rest of the drive, deflecting Lucas's questions, looking for the right way to talk him out of telling Clay. But by the time I killed the engine in front of my house, Lucas was still gung-ho about the hunt. I eyed the Guard's house.

"Want to come in?" I asked, desperate for more time to figure a way out of this. "Dad made tortilla soup last night and I think there's some left over."

Lucas's eyes lit with interest. "Lead on. Only an idiot would say no to Murphy's cooking."

My front door was unlocked, which wasn't too unusual. Dad went into his office only rarely these days. It was more a front to provide cover for the Guard's soldiers; Dad owned a private security firm and had actually managed to win a contract from the city to guard the old mission after the place was destroyed. The official story was vandals had firebombed the site. The truth was, the mission had suffered substantial damage when the Seal had been destroyed. But try explaining that to the Tourism Commission.

So Dad's security firm was hired to keep an eye on the place while various archeological and restoration experts visited and floated theories about the best way to rebuild the landmark. It made overseeing the restoration, and locating any artifacts that might come up during its renovation, much easier.

But when Dad entered from the kitchen, he wasn't alone. I could tell from his expression that something was wrong as soon as I set eyes on him.

"Honey?" Dad turned as Clay followed him out of the kitchen.

"Well, Braedyn, I must admit I'm impressed. I didn't expect results so soon."

"Results?" I glanced at Dad, confused.

"Modest," Lucas said again, elbowing me affectionately. "I gave Clay the heads up after lunch."

"Oh." I smiled at Clay, but my face felt like stone. "What exactly did he tell you?"

"That you've found our mark, of course." Clay's eyes swept across my face, and seemed to catch on my eyes. He turned to Lucas without missing a beat. "Why don't you gather the team. Send them over here for the mission brief, they'll know what that means. And would you mind grabbing my bag? It should be in the bottom drawer of my desk. You know the one?"

"Yes, sir." Lucas straightened.

"I'll meet you at the car." Clay nodded, dismissing Lucas. Lucas gave me one last smile before heading out. I felt a hole open in my gut.

"Clay." I shifted uncomfortably. "I don't think she's the one you want."

"No?" He crossed his arms, leaning casually against the doorframe. "What makes you say that?"

"She's... she's not like Elyia or Seth." I looked at Dad for help, but he kept his eyes on Clay's face. I cleared my throat, trying to hide my nerves. "I think she could be an ally for us."

"Hm." Clay pushed off the wall, walking a few steps into the foyer. "Well, that's not really your decision to make, is it?"

"I..." I glanced back at Dad. He watched me, intent.

"Don't worry, Braedyn. You've done well. Just let us take it from here."

The door opened behind me. Four soldiers entered. They were all men I'd seen during morning meetings, but I didn't know any of their names. Something crystallized for me in that moment; this was Clay's Guard now. What I wanted was inconsequential.

But then I pictured Emlyn, wrapped in Vyla's protective embrace. I couldn't do this. I couldn't give them up, either of them.

"I... I'm sorry." I took a deep breath and forced my voice to steady. "I just need a little more time. I'll find someone else, someone useful."

Clay nodded thoughtfully. "I understand."

I started to let out a sigh of relief, but I saw Dad's face. It was drawn, tense.

"This is a hard decision. Let me make it a little easier for you." Clay gestured for three of his men. They stepped forward, obeying without hesitation. Straight toward Dad.

His soldiers moved as one. Two of them gripped Dad's arms and wrenched them behind his back. Dad flinched. His eyes latched onto my face. The third soldier stood before Dad. Dad's eyes shifted from my face to the soldier's—

Just as the soldier drove his fist across Dad's cheek. The impact made a meaty cracking sound, snapping Dad's head to one side. Only the soldiers holding him kept Dad on his feet.

"Dad!" I started to move, but the remaining soldier grabbed my arms, holding me back. I tried to pull free but the soldier had an iron grip. "What are you doing? Let me go!" I planted my foot, shifting my weight, preparing to fight back.

"Braedyn, don't!" Dad's voice was gruff. "Don't fight them."

I turned to face him, eyes welling. "Dad?"

Clay approached, looking completely untroubled by the actions of his soldiers. "I need that Lilitu, and I need your help to find her, Braedyn. I'd like it to be voluntary, but if it has to be coerced, well, I can live with that, too." Clay nodded to the soldier standing before Dad.

The man moved, slugging Dad across the face with another meaty crack. Dad let out a harsh breath, then straightened. The look he gave the soldier was one of cold fury. A line of blood trickled from the edge of his mouth.

"Wait." I strained against the soldier holding me. Dad's eyes found my face. Pain and confusion tore through me. I turned on Clay, choking down a sob. "Wait, we can talk about this."

"This isn't a negotiation." Clay tilted his head to one side. His voice sounded almost kind. It sent chills through my veins. "You don't know me, so I'll explain how I work. Once. I give the orders. You obey. So let's try this again. Where can I find that Lilitu?"

"I… I don't know where she is!" It was the truth, but it didn't matter.

Clay lowered his head. "That's too bad." Clay returned to his place at the wall, leaning back as if he had all the time in the world. The soldiers traded grim looks as if understanding an unspoken order. Dad eyed the soldier facing him, bracing himself.

"Wha... what are you...?" My voice broke. Dad turned toward me, so he didn't see the blow coming. The soldier drove his fist into Dad's stomach, doubling him over. "Stop!"

Before Dad could recover, the two men holding him wrenched him back up. Over and over, the soldier drove his fist into Dad's face and torso. I screamed until my voice was raw, but Clay only watched me dispassionately. Dad took the beating silently, until a particularly brutal punch drove him to his knees. He let out a harsh grunt of pain.

"Stop, please. Please!" By this point, I could barely see, blinded by the tears I couldn't wipe away. Every fiber of my being strained toward Dad. The soldier grabbed the front of Dad's shirt, drawing his fist back to strike again. Something broke inside of me. "I'll take you to her!"

The soldiers froze, glancing at Clay for orders. Clay held up a hand. The soldiers holding Dad released him. He dropped forward, catching himself on his hands and knees. Both he and the soldier who'd beaten him were breathing hard.

Clay glanced at the man holding my arms and nodded. A moment later I was free, running toward Dad. I dropped to my knees beside him, grabbing him, holding him tight. Dad grunted with fresh pain and I started to draw back. But he caught me in a tight hug, and pulled me closer.

"I'm sorry. I'm so sorry," I choked into his ear.

"It's not your fault," Dad whispered back. "It's not your fault."

My throat burned. I didn't even try to speak. We held each other, shaking. Tidal waves of emotion rolled over me, rage, fear, anguish, shame.

I was only vaguely aware of Clay giving orders in the background. I looked up when I felt the breeze sweeping across my back from the open door; the soldiers were on their way toward a waiting van.

Dad released me then, pushing himself back to sit against the wall. His face was a mass of red welts and trickles of blood, but his hand strayed to his side and I saw him wince.

"Broken?" Clay asked mildly, as if inquiring about the weather.

"I don't think so." Dad's voice was tight with pain, but there was no hint of anger that I could detect.

"Tape it up, just in case."

Dad nodded, leaning his head back against the wall and closing his eyes. Fury swelled in me, but when I looked up at Clay, it was smothered by an icy wave of fear. Clay glanced at his watch and clicked his tongue thoughtfully. He walked to the open door and looked out. Past him I could see Lucas loading supplies into Clay's car. The soldiers were checking their gear, sharpening blades, testing their swords for balance.

"Looks like the team is ready to move." Clay glanced at me. "Splash some cold water on your face."

"What?" I stared at him, numb.

"This was a private matter, and I'd like to keep it that way." Clay's voice dropped slightly. It wasn't much of a change, but it sent prickles of fear crawling down my spine. "Walk out like that, and your admirer, Lucas, will have all sorts of questions for you. And so there's no confusion, I'll just state it plain; if you tell Lucas about what just happened here, he'll be the focus of your next lesson in obedience."

Clay's words sunk in, worming their way past my anguish. I blinked. Was he really threatening to hurt *Lucas*? I glanced at Dad, suddenly frightened. There'd be no hiding this, no matter what I said. Clay seemed to read my thoughts.

"Training accident." Clay gave me a hard smile. "Accidents happen, even to the great Alan Murphy."

Dad met my gaze. "Go on, Braedyn. Do what he says."

I nodded and got to my feet, stumbling into the downstairs bathroom. I scooped handfuls of cold water over my face, washing away the hot tears. After a few minutes, I patted my face dry and looked into the mirror. The girl staring back at me looked solemn, scared. Something had changed, and there was no changing it back. Like it or not, Clay was calling all the shots, and I had no choice but to obey.

Lucas was surprised to learn Murphy wasn't coming on the hunt. He glanced at me for an explanation. I looked at Clay, too scared to speak. Clay put a hand on Lucas's shoulder and gave him a broad smile.

"Murphy's running the soldiers through a new training exercise."

Lucas nodded, taking Clay's word for it. He turned to me with a lopsided smile. "Imagine that. I didn't think he'd ever let you go on a hunt without him."

I met Lucas's eyes, but I could feel Clay studying me over Lucas's shoulder, watching my face for any crack. I forced a smile. "Guess he thinks I can handle this without him."

Lucas chuckled wryly. "Well there's no question about that. Just never thought he'd acknowledge it. He kind of defines 'over-protective' when it comes to you." But his eyes searched my face, and I got the impression that he could tell I was holding something back.

Clay must have sensed this, too. He drew Lucas closer to his side. "Ride with me, Lucas. Braedyn, you're with the spotters. You can tell them where to go, we'll follow your lead." He gave me a pointed look, then clapped a hand on Lucas's back and led him to the van. I watched them go, feeling a dull chill settling in the pit of my stomach. Lucas had no idea what Clay was capable of.

"Let's get this show on the road." Marla, one of the new spotters I'd met the night of the bonfire, unlocked the front passenger door of a beat up old Ford. She held it open for me with an expectant look.

"Right." I slipped into the car and a sense of panic overtook me. I had to lead them to Vyla. Which meant leading them to Emlyn. If Clay got his hands on that little girl…? I had to warn them. I closed my eyes.

Karayan.

I felt Karayan's attention turn toward me with a sort of amused irritation. *You should just move into my head, you're here so often lately…*

This is an emergency. Clay is on his way!

Karayan's fear radiated through the connection. *Braedyn, I'm not with them… can you warn Vyla?*

I sucked in a breath, feeling my heartbeat kick it up a notch. *I don't know.*

Communicating through the dream is clean, clear. But reaching someone's consciousness—that takes the kind of familiarity that I just didn't have with Vyla yet. Karayan, Cassie, Lucas, I'd managed to connect with all of them while awake, but these were my friends, my loved ones. I turned my attention to the curly-haired Lilitu. I got a sense of her presence… but it was fuzzy. Every time I tried to make a connection strong enough to communicate with her, it slipped out of my fingers like a wet, soapy noodle.

Marla opened the driver's side door. She was laughing over some joke with Zoe.

Zoe peered into the car and saw me. Her smile soured. "Oh. She's coming?"

"She's leading this parade," Marla answered.

I gave Zoe a thin smile then turned away. *Karayan, we're out of time. You have to get there first. Go. Go now!*

I'm on it. But Braedyn, you might want to stall. I'm halfway across town.

Marla turned the key in the ignition. "Okay, navigator." She turned to me with a neutral smile that didn't reach her eyes. "Where to?"

I felt Vyla's presence like a fuzzy dot on a map. Conflict tore through me, leaving a churning anguish in its wake. Images crossed my mind's eye. First Emlyn and Vyla, sharing that smile on the playground. Then Dad, doubling over in pain as Clay's men beat him. I swallowed back a wave of nausea.

"Downtown," I managed. "She's somewhere downtown."

"Okay. It's a start." Marla pulled into traffic.

I balled my fist against the car door. I was running out of time to find a way out of this.

The problem with spotters, with Guardsmen in general, is that they're very short on trust. Marla let me lead her on a meandering route toward Vyla for all of ten minutes before catching on.

"You do know where you're going, right? This isn't some wild goose chase?"

I saw Zoe look up in the rearview mirror. Her eyes shifted from Marla to me. "You want me to call Clay?"

"I don't know." Marla took her eyes off the road to study me shrewdly for a moment. "Do I?"

"No. We're getting close. Make the next right." We *were* getting close. And I hadn't heard back from Karayan.

Marla took the next right. "How close?"

"Up here, at the light, you'll turn left." My throat felt tight. The light ahead turned red. I glanced away, trying to reach Karayan's mind.

Please tell me you found them?

Karayan's reply came a moment later, shot through with a frantic energy. *I'm almost there. One block away.*

We're close, Karayan. Stuck at a light.

Karayan's thoughts came fast, terse. *Small mercies... looks like I'll just beat you.* Then, moments later, I felt Karayan's triumph. *I'm here. Going in now.*

The light turned green. Marla made the turn, and I felt Vyla's presence up ahead. I was concentrating so hard I could almost see the fuzzy outline of her form in the little white house on the corner of the first cross-street.

Marla glanced at me and read my expression. "She's here." Marla found Zoe in the rearview mirror. "Tell Clay, we have confirmation." Marla lowered her voice. "You'd better wait in the car, kid."

I nodded. Behind us, Zoe hit a button on her phone. I could hear the speed dial go through for Clay. Zoe relayed Marla's message as we pulled to a stop in front of the white house. But I was frozen in my seat. I could sense Vyla moving, but then she stopped. Backtracked.

"No," I whispered, before I could stop myself. It was pure luck that Marla and Zoe chose that moment to open their doors and exit the car.

Everything happened so fast. Clay's soldiers stormed the house, moving like the parts of a well-oiled machine. Two took the front, two slipped around to the back. Marla and Zoe split off, one spotter following each team of soldiers into the house.

Clay and Lucas brought up the rear. Clay said something to Lucas, and Lucas fell back, keeping his eyes on the house while Clay slipped around to the back.

A few moments later, Vyla darted out of the house, holding her arm. Blood stained the sleeve of her shirt. If she'd been nicked by a Guardsman's blade she'd be unable to cloak herself. I opened the door and leapt out of the car, forgetting Marla's instructions to stay put.

There was still time... most of the Guardsmen were in the house. If I could convince Lucas to let her go—

"You." Lucas stared at Vyla with a strange expression. His shock drained away, leaving a steely hatred in its place. I'd never seen anything like this from Lucas before. He seemed almost possessed by a murderous rage. Lucas drew his daggers, dropping into a low fighting stance.

Vyla blinked at him, unsteady on her feet. I realized she'd been hurt worse than just a nick on her arm. Lucas didn't seem to notice. He launched himself at her, impacting with enough force to send them both sprawling into the gravel that covered the front yard. Vyla kept her eyes on his daggers, managing to catch his wrists as they fell. The daggers skittered across the gravel on impact.

Vyla rolled to her side, watching Lucas warily. He scrambled to his knees, retrieving one of the daggers.

"Lucas?!" I sprinted toward them, covering the distance between us in a few heartbeats.

Lucas didn't take his eyes off of Vyla. His hand gripped the hilt of his dagger so tightly his fingers were turning white. "It's her, Braedyn." His voice was husky, strained.

"Her…?" I stared at Vyla, not comprehending.

"It's her!" Lucas advanced on the Lilitu. "This is the demon who killed my brother."

Clay emerged from the front door, with Marla by his side just as the soldiers circled back along the side of the house.

"Here! She's here!" Clay's voice sparked something in Vyla. She rolled to her feet like a sprinter taking the blocks, ready to bolt—

But Lucas tackled her once more. This time he managed to pin her arms behind her back, holding her, immobilized, against the gravel. She writhed in his grasp, but Lucas didn't let go. He raised his dagger, setting the edge on Vyla's exposed throat. She grew still, breathing hard.

"Lucas." Clay's voice was soft, calm.

"She murdered my brother." Lucas's hands were shaking.

"And she'll pay for taking his life, I promise." Clay edged toward Lucas, approaching him like you would a wounded bear; slow, ready for anything. "But this? This is too easy a death for her, son."

Lucas blinked, processing this. After a minute, Clay reached out and took the dagger out of Lucas's hand. "Good boy. You did well, Lucas." Clay helped Lucas to his feet.

Seconds later, the four soldiers hauled Vyla off the ground. They wrenched her arms behind her back, locking cuffs around her wrists. Her eyes found mine. For the briefest moment, they darted back to the apartment. She didn't know, I realized. She didn't know if her daughter was safe.

Karayan? I let my thoughts reach out, tentatively.

I've got her. Karayan's thoughts were strained. *Can't talk now.*

I opened my eyes. Vyla was watching me. I nodded faintly. Vyla's shoulders eased. She closed her eyes, and for one moment, she looked at peace. Soldiers dragged her to a waiting van, shoved her inside, and slammed the door.

"Well, well, well," Clay said, stepping into my sightline. I felt a twisting sensation in my gut. Had he seen the nod? Did he know I'd tried to warn Vyla? "Lucas was right about you after all. Why don't you two ride home with Marla and Zoe?"

Lucas nodded, looking numb. Marla led the way to her car opening the back seat for Lucas. Clay put a hand on my shoulder, lowering his voice.

"That wasn't so hard, was it?" He squeezed my shoulder. It made my skin crawl, to be touched by him. I looked at Lucas, sitting shell-shocked in the back of Marla's car. I shook my head. "Good. I hope this is the beginning of a productive partnership between us, Braedyn. I'd hate to have to employ coercive methods a second time." Clay's smile was tight, bloodless. It made me think of a shark. "Now go comfort your friend. He's had a rough afternoon."

Marla and Zoe stood by her car, watching me. I joined Lucas in the back of Marla's car. He looked stunned. I pushed Clay out of my mind for the moment.

"Lucas?" My fingers found his hand on the seat and squeezed. I could feel him, shaking with emotion.

Lucas looked up. "I can't believe you found her. This… this is the moment I've been waiting for since the night Eric… Since he died." Tears stream down his face, unhindered. The raw emotions were naked on his face, grief and anger. Relief and pain.

I leaned close and pulled him into a tight hug. At first he stiffened. But then he melted into me, hugging me back with a fierce need. I looked up and saw Clay watching me, smiling. When he'd caught my eye, he turned and walked to the waiting van. As soon as he'd taken his seat in the front passenger seat, the van peeled away. I swallowed, finally understanding the bigger picture.

Karayan had been right all along. I'd given Clay all the time he needed to get to know me and my weak spots. If I crossed him, he'd know exactly where to apply the pressure to break me. I was trapped. And it was my own fault.

6

The first few minutes of the drive home were silent. I watched Lucas out of the corner of my eye, worry and pain mingling to drown out my other concerns—at least for the moment. Lucas's eyes were unfocused. His hands curled around his knees, knuckles white. He lifted one hand to brush the hair back out of his eyes, and I saw his fingers tremble. A fresh wave of empathy flooded through my body. I knew what Eric had meant to Lucas. They'd come from a broken home, and while Lucas didn't go into a lot of detail, I got the impression he had suffered abuse at the hands of his biological father. Eric had taken custody of Lucas when he turned 18, and Lucas had worshiped the ground Eric walked on. He was more than a brother to Lucas. He was an epic, larger-than-life hero, a knight in shining armor.

I reached across the seat and captured Lucas's free hand. He glanced at me, eyes tight with emotion. And then he seemed to realize something.

"Gretchen." His breath caught, and he took a moment to clear his throat. "Gretchen doesn't know."

I nodded slowly. As stunned as Lucas had been to come face-to-face with the demon that had taken his brother, Gretchen… Gretchen had been there when Vyla had attacked Eric. That was the moment she had become a spotter, able to see through the shadowy cloak hiding Vyla from mortal eyes. Gretchen had watched Vyla take the last of Eric's vital energy. She'd watched Vyla murder her husband just three months after their wedding.

My head was swimming with fear and guilt by the time we returned home. Marla had barely killed the engine before Lucas was out of the car running toward the house. I knew he wanted to find Gretchen, to tell her in person before she saw Vyla arrive. I opened my car door and stood. No part of me was eager to witness their confrontation.

I heard a van approaching and turned. It was Clay and his team. They pulled up to the curb and the van's side door slid open before the driver had fully stopped. Clay emerged from the passenger door and glanced up and down the street. When he felt confident no one was watching, he nodded. Two Guardsmen hauled Vyla out of the back of the van and marched her quickly toward the house. I watched them pass, and when her eyes found my face I forced myself to meet her gaze. I don't know what I had expected to see; anger, hatred, fear. But her expression was blank, as though she was waiting to see exactly how bad the situation was before allowing herself to react.

The moment passed, and then the Guardsmen were leading her up the stairs and into the house. Clay followed, eyeing me with an inscrutable expression. He nodded as he passed, then turned his attention to the house and what lay inside. I stood on the front lawn, full of indecision.

"Braedyn!" Dad emerged from our house next door, gesturing for me.

Clay turned at the sound, his eyes zeroing in on Dad's face. "Murphy. Why don't you join us?"

Dad hesitated for the briefest moment before nodding crisply. But instead of joining Clay on the front porch, he stopped by my side. He dropped his voice, speaking in a low, husky tone. "Braedyn, there's something I need to tell you about my years in the Guard—"

"Time to get to work, Murphy," Clay called from the top of the steps. There was something almost playful—a singsong quality to the way he said this—that made the hairs on the back of my neck stand up. Then his eyes shifted from Dad's face to mine. "You should come inside, too."

"Do you really think that's necessary? She's had a rough day already." Dad put a hand on my shoulder as if warning me to stay put, even though I hadn't moved.

"Nonsense, Murphy. She is as much a part of this victory as any of us." Clay smiled at me, spreading his arms. "After all, we only have the Lilitu because of her."

Clay turned, sweeping his arm with unmistakable meaning; he would wait for us to enter the house first. Dad glanced at me, his jaw tight, but we both knew this was no invitation. Clay had made his wishes known. We had no choice but to obey. My stomach tightened with each step, but my mind felt numb. The day had begun with such promise. How had it come to this, changing so drastically in the span of an hour?

Inside the house, Guardsmen had the Lilitu surrounded. She eyed them like a cornered dog, wary and frightened and looking for an opportunity to attack. I heard something from upstairs, like a strangled sob. A door opened and a moment later, Gretchen appeared at the top of the stairs. She searched our faces, her eyes wild. And then she spotted Vyla.

"You!" Gretchen launched herself down the stairs, driving through the crowd toward Vyla. "You killed him! You killed my husband…!" The Guardsmen watched, no one moving to interfere. Gretchen leapt at Vyla with a fury I had never seen in her before. Gretchen was a skilled fighter—a competitive fighter—with training and skill and discipline under her belt. All of that went out the window as soon as she laid eyes on Vyla. She threw herself at the Lilitu with an almost animalistic rage, clawing at her face, reaching for her neck—

Clay moved, catching Gretchen in a tight grip and pulling her off the shrinking Vyla. He had to struggle to contain Gretchen as she fought to escape him, to renew her attack on her enemy. "Easy, Gretchen. She's not going anywhere. You'll have your revenge. Just not tonight."

Vyla, who'd recoiled against a wall as Gretchen had attacked, barely reacted to this. Her eyes were like steel, fastened on Gretchen with a coldness that seemed completely devoid of humanity. For a moment I reeled, trying to reconcile this Vyla with the loving mother I'd met just a few hours ago.

"Take her below." Clay nodded his head toward Vyla. A handful of Guardsmen moved to obey.

Clay did not release Gretchen until Vyla was out of sight. When he finally opened his arms, Gretchen slumped as though all the fight had gone out of her. She drew in a shaking breath and turned, looking for Lucas. Lucas's eyes welled with tears. Gretchen moved to him, opening her arms. They met in the foyer and gripped one another tightly. For a moment the only sound was the heaving grief of their ragged breath. I had to look away.

After several long moments passed, Lucas and Gretchen straightened. Gretchen wiped at her eyes, but Lucas turned on Clay with a new resolve.

"What are you going to do with her?"

Clay glanced at Dad. "It'll be just like old times." Dad froze. Some of the color seemed to drain out of his cheeks. Clay noticed. "Is there a problem?"

Dad's eyes cut to my face. Clay glanced from Dad to me then back.

"I see. If you're not up for the task…" Clay turned his back on us, facing Lucas. "You ever thought about what you would do to the Lilitu who killed your brother, given the chance?"

Lucas's eyes hardened. "Every day."

Dad stepped forward, catching Clay's shoulder. "I'll do it. Just keep the kids away."

Clay glanced at Dad. After a long moment he nodded. "That's probably a good idea. Lucas, I've been meaning to ask you to look through the files Sandra put on my desk. If you wouldn't mind, I need them sorted by date."

"Now?" Lucas looked at Dad, his eyes wide with frustrated anger. Clay only had to look at Lucas. Lucas's anger faded. He ducked his head and nodded. "Right. Sorry. I'm on it."

I looked at Dad. His eyes found my face, but when he saw that I was watching him, he turned away. He was ashamed. I realized something was very wrong.

"Dad, what's going on?"

Clay clapped a hand on Dad's shoulder, smiling proudly. "You're looking at the finest interrogator in the Guard's history."

"Interrogator?" The word felt strange in my mouth. Images clawed their way into my mind, unbidden and unwelcome. Images from medieval history. From the Inquisition. I glanced at Dad again. He looked like he was going to be sick.

"Oh, yes. Murphy is an artist when it comes to extracting information from the enemy." Clay's eyes glittered as he raked his gaze over Dad.

"You mean…?"

"Go home, Braedyn." Dad turned to Gretchen, who was still standing, shell-shocked, in the foyer. "Gretchen. Take her home. Wait with her until I come back. I don't want her left alone."

Gretchen nodded, glancing at me with an uneasy look. "Come on, I don't think either of us want to be here for this."

"Dad?" I couldn't bring myself to ask the question. But it was a question I already knew the answer to. Dad's history with the Guard, the thing he didn't want me to know, it was pretty clear now. Dad had made a name for himself in the Guard by torturing Lilitu.

Gretchen had to grab my forearm and steer me out of the house to get me to move. My mind turned over slowly, refusing to process this new information. Gretchen was saying something, but none of her words registered. My thoughts remained with Dad in the house. With Vyla in the basement. My dad, who would sacrifice everything to protect me. My dad, who had made sure my childhood was filled with love and affection. How could he be the same Murphy who had done the Guard's dirty work for all those years before I was born?

I stumbled on the front step to my porch and Gretchen steadied me carefully. "Easy. Let's just get you inside."

I looked at Gretchen. She was focused, her lips pursed in a tight line. She did not look surprised. "You knew? You knew about my dad…?"

Gretchen opened the front door and ushered me inside. She turned and closed the door, then locked it for good measure. For a long moment she stood with her hands pressed against the face of the door and her head bowed. Then she straightened and turned to face me.

"I suspected as much." Gretchen's face was drawn with tension. She started to say something else, then her eyes flicked to the top of our stairs. "Someone's in the house."

Gretchen and I edged back from the stairs, suddenly paranoid. I heard someone walking upstairs, drawing closer. When she finally reached the top of the stairs I stared. It was Zoe, one of Clay's spotters. She had a laptop tucked under one arm. And she was wearing my hoodie.

"What are you doing here?" My voice came out harsh, sounding more territorial than I meant it to. "That's mine."

Zoe hesitated on the top step. She glanced down at the hoodie and smiled. "This? No, I think you're mistaken."

"Where did you get it?" I took a step forward. Gretchen caught my wrist, holding me back.

"It was in the closet," Zoe shrugged. "In the room at the end of the hall on the left. The one that looks like an incurable Pollyanna took a stab at decorating."

"Yeah, my room. My hoodie." I felt my hands ball into fists at my side. Zoe's eyes dropped to my hands and her smile deepened.

"Again, I think you're mistaken. You see, this house and all the things inside of it were paid for by the Guard. So really, they belong as much to me as they do to you. Or did you think you'd get special treatment for the rest of your life?"

I opened my mouth to retort, but the words got stuck in my throat. All I could manage was a meek, "get out."

Zoe shrugged again, and made her way down the stairs without any evident concern. When she reached the foyer her eyes flicked over Gretchen. I saw a thinly veiled curiosity in her eyes. But then she was reaching for the front door. She unlocked it glancing back at us with a small smile. "For future reference, Clay doesn't believe in locked doors." With that, she left us standing alone in the foyer.

"What the hell was that?" I turned on Gretchen, feeling a roiling anger in my stomach.

Gretchen met my eyes, but she looked deeply troubled. "Things are changing, Braedyn. Whether we like it or not." She bit her lip, lost in unhappy thoughts for a moment. "Come on. We might as well see if there's anything on TV." Gretchen walked past me and settled herself down on her living room couch. I studied her, full of questions. But Gretchen didn't seem like she was in any mood to talk. I heard the sound of the TV turning on. The thought of sitting down to watch something made my skin crawl.

"I need some fresh air."

"You heard what your father said." Gretchen glanced up from her spot on the couch with a worried frown.

"I'll be in the backyard. Don't worry, I won't leave."

The air was brisk, and it felt clean and fresh as I drew in a deep lungful. I smelled a hint of pine, and something else, something wild and spicy. I spent a moment trying to identify the scent, grateful for the distraction. But my thoughts were pulled inevitably back to the basement next door, to Vyla. Conflicting thoughts warred in my heart.

Vyla was a murderer. Not only that, her crime had indelibly marked someone I loved deeply. She should be my enemy. So why was I so concerned about her fate? I pictured the face of the little girl I'd met this afternoon on the playground. No matter what Vyla was to Lucas, she was that little girl's mommy. Vyla had hesitated in the house, mere moments before Clay and his team had entered. She had backtracked. And I suddenly knew why. She'd stayed behind to give Karayan and Emlyn time to escape. It was an act of self-sacrifice. It was an act of love.

"Sansenoy." I closed my eyes and willed my voice to reach him. Whether or not this would work, I had no idea. He always came when he chose, but maybe if he felt my desperate need he would respond. "Sansenoy, I need you." I waited, letting the wind pull strands of my hair back from my face. Nothing. "I don't know if you can hear me, but if you can, there is a little girl who needs your help."

I told him everything. I told him about the innocent Lilitu child and the mother who'd let herself be captured to buy a few more moments for her daughter's escape. The wind pulled the words away from my lips. Whether they carried them to Sansenoy's ears I couldn't know. All I knew, with a growing certainty, was that Vyla was not exclusively evil… just as I knew that Clay was not exclusively good.

"Please, Sansenoy. You can't leave us alone in this fight. We need you."

I looked up, but all I saw was the high desert prairie sweeping into the foothills, and the rocky mountain terrain, dotted with pines, rising up into the sky.

If he heard a word I said, Sansenoy did not answer.

Dad did not come home for dinner. By the time Gretchen fell asleep on the couch, I realized he wouldn't be returning tonight. I headed upstairs to my room and closed the door. Zoe had clearly rifled through my drawers in addition to ransacking my closet. But that seemed like a small thing after the events of today. I found some pajamas lying on the ground and changed into them.

I felt myself slipping into the dream as my head touched the pillow. Karayan heard my call and came immediately.

"We're safe." Karayan paced, her usually composed features looked worn. "Emlyn is scared. What happened? Where is her mom?"

I filled Karayan in quickly. She grew quiet as I described the events of the afternoon. When I fell silent, she shook her head.

"I tried to warn you." Karayan's voice was tight with anger.

"I know. I'm so…"

"Tell that to Emlyn." Karayan's words struck me like a slap. I dropped my eyes. She was right, of course. "Vyla came to you for help." Karayan took a step closer, her eyes flashing. "And you handed her over to Clay?"

"She's not innocent," I snapped back. "She killed Gretchen's husband. Lucas's brother."

Karayan fell silent. She tipped her head forward, letting the honey blond locks obscure her features for a long moment. When she spoke, her voice was soft, conflicted. "And do you think she should die for that?"

"It's not my choice. I just… She killed him, Karayan. An eye for an eye, right?" but even as I said the words my stomach twisted, rejecting the basic premise of the thought.

"Vyla's not the first to make a mistake, Lilitu or human. You almost led Parker to take his own life, remember? If he'd been found half an hour later, you'd be just as guilty as she is." Karayan looked up at me then, her eyes clouded with remembered pain. "You've been given a chance at redemption. Vyla's not even asking for redemption for herself. She's asking for her daughter. Isn't it hypocritical for you to accept Sansenoy's offer while keeping it away from any other Lilitu?"

I wanted to come back with a snappy argument to defend myself, but the truth of the matter is that these thoughts had been playing through my mind all day. Karayan waited for me to speak, studying me closely. I let out a sigh of resignation. "It's out of my hands. Vyla has to face justice."

Karayan shook her head. "What Clay has in store for Vyla—that's not justice."

I felt something inside of me snap. "What am I supposed to do about it? Look what happened when I second-guessed the Guard before. Dad told me to let the Guard deal with the incubus. I got involved and ended up helping him open the Seal. Everyone warned me away from Lucas. We made a plan to get together and Elyia attacked him. And Hale…" My throat closed with grief, choking off the thought.

Grief washed over Karayan's face. "Hale's death wasn't your fault," Karayan took a shaky breath, "but if Clay tortures Vyla to death? That will be on you."

I turned away, sick. "It won't be Clay. It'll be Dad."

"No, that's…" Karayan shook her head. Her voice firmed. "He wouldn't do that. Not after raising you."

"I think it's me he's worried about." It was my turn to take shaking breath. "Clay knows how much I love Dad… and that Dad would do anything for me. Karayan… Clay ordered his men to…" My throat closed as I tried to muffle a swelling grief. "He had Dad beaten in front of me when I refused to lead him to Vyla."

Karayan crossed the distance between us and spun me to face her. Her eyes locked on to mine, full of cold terror. "Get your Dad and get out."

Until that moment, I hadn't known exactly what kind of toll the day's events had taken on me. I burst into tears facing Karayan. "I don't know how. Clay is two steps ahead of me. Dad didn't come home tonight, and it's not like I can waltz into the basement and get him."

Karayan turned this thought over in her mind for a moment. "He has the upper hand in the waking world, but you have the upper hand here. Let's pay Clay a visit."

I felt an icy trickle of fear at the thought. Messing with Parker's mind had cost some of my precious humanity. But as I weighed my options, it became clear. If manipulating Clay's dreams would protect my father, it was worth the risk.

Karayan made it clear that she was going to help me infiltrate Clay's dream whether or not I wanted it. It was a simple matter to summon his sleeping mind from the infinite dream that all living creatures shared. It rose like a gleaming star, indistinguishable from the billions of others scattered across the darkness. It seemed unfair that his mind should gleam as brightly as Lucas's or Dad's when his soul was so tainted.

"Are you ready for this?" Karayan met my eyes. There was no disguising the determination in her expression. I nodded, trying to project a confidence I didn't feel.

We stepped into Clay's dream as one, doing our best to hover in the background so as not to draw Clay's conscious attention. Guardsmen traditionally tried to practice lucid dreaming, but it was far more art than science. Most failed to gain even a modicum of awareness while dreaming. Still, it was wise to tread carefully, just in case.

"Here goes nothing." I gave Karayan a watery smile before turning to face the heart of the dream.

Seth was waiting for me.

Terror drove all thought out of my head, leaving a wild panic in its wake. Karayan gripped my arm, pulling me back, as though any distance could protect us from the incubus here. Seth wagged a finger at us, smiling.

"Ah, ah, ah... no fair. You wanted to be in the Guard? This is part of the package." Seth's smile deepened in malicious glee. "Let me lay it out for you. You can either stay loyal to the Guard, serving Clay, and trust me you have only barely glimpsed the kind of man he is..." Seth swept his hands wide in a gesture of welcome. "Or you can desert the Guard. At this point, I don't care if you fight for Lilith or if you sit the whole conflict out like your pal Karayan. As long as you're not aiding the enemy, I'm willing to turn a blind eye. This is the best deal you're going to get, and—let's be honest—it's more than you deserve." Seth kept his tone light, but his eyes were snapping with anger.

I was struggling to settle my wildly beating heart, but something plucked at the back of my mind. This didn't make any sense. "You're... helping me? After I killed your sister?"

He dropped all pretense of the smile. Slimmed tongues of purple lightning seemed to crackle in the dream space around Seth. I saw his hands tighten into fists, and knew he was gathering his power to strike— But then he restrained himself, to my utter surprise. He inclined his head, As though ceding a point in some kind of sick game.

"Weigh your options carefully," he said. He turned his head slightly to one side, crooking his finger. Something seemed to tug in the dream fabric around us. I glanced around, and when I turned back to Seth he was gone.

"What did he just do?" Karayan eyed the dream uncomfortably.

"Karayan…?" I turned to face Karayan, suddenly realizing what Seth had done. There was no time to explain. I felt Clay's attention shifting to me as I stood there. I grabbed Karayan's arm and yanked us back to the safety of my dream.

Karayan stumbled into my garden, winded. "What was that for?"

"Clay." I looked at my hands, trying to control their trembling. "I think Clay sensed our presence."

Karayan's eyes narrowed with understanding. "That little scumbag. You think Seth…?"

I nodded, trying to calculate the damage I might have just done to my place in the Guard. Maybe we got lucky, maybe he hadn't identified me. It couldn't have been more than a second between the moment Seth had tugged at Clay's mind and the moment we'd left the dream.

Karayan seemed to be thinking along the same lines. "We got out fast." I nodded, but we both fell silent for several uncomfortable moments. Finally, Karayan shook her head. "Nothing to do for it now."

"Karayan? Was he right? Are you sitting this conflict out?"

Karayan gave me a startled look, then let out a frustrated breath. "Braedyn, I can't be a part of the Guard if Clay is in charge." Before I had a chance to question her further, Karayan's attention seemed to shift. "Emlyn's waking up. I have to go." Karayan turned as though she needed to physically leave my dream. But something stopped her. She glanced back at me, conflicted. "Don't contact me anymore. It's best if you don't know where we're hiding. I'm going to take Emlyn and leave Puerto Escondido."

"Right." It made sense. But that didn't keep it from hurting.

"And Braedyn, tell her mom that she's okay."

I nodded, swallowing. "So this is goodbye?"

Karayan looked down, but she nodded. "Watch your back, Braedyn." And with that, she was gone.

I stayed in my garden for a long moment after Karayan had left. Every part of me dreaded what I knew I had to do next. Finding her dream was simple. The closing my hand around it, willing myself inside? That took all of the courage I could summon.

The landscape of Vyla's dream shuddered and twisted, tossed by a violent storm. Vyla herself huddled at the base of the shaking tree, arms curled around her knees, surrounded by a scruffy patch of Feverfew. I approached slowly, willing the landscape around me to calm. It fought back, churning with intense emotion.

As I approached the tree, Vyla looked up. She eyed me with hostility and suspicion.

"Emlyn's alright. She's safe. We got her out."

Some of the hostility ebbed from Vyla's gaze. But the landscape around us continued to roil. That's when I noticed that Vyla herself seemed weakened, drained. It made sense. If she had been wounded by a Guardsman's dagger, she'd be unable to heal herself, cut off from her ability to draw energy from mortals.

I knelt before her and laid my hand on her shoulder. I meant to comfort her, but as I touched her, I felt energy pass from me into her. I could almost see it bolstering her. Around us, the storm seemed to ease. Vyla took a breath, relaxing.

Her eyes settled on my face. "I don't understand. You betrayed me to the Guard, but saved my daughter. And now you heal me? Why?"

How to answer her? I struggled to find the words. "Clay… he… he hurt…"

Some of the anger seemed to leach out of Vyla's eyes. "Yeah. That seems to be his specialty."

"I… I tried to contact Sansenoy." Her eyes lit with hope. "I haven't received an answer yet, but…"

"Keep asking." Her determination didn't falter.

"Vyla, I'm…" I shook my head. Words wouldn't fix this. I had led them to her, knowing full well they would capture her. I had traded her for my father. That was the simple truth. "I'm so sorry."

She sighed. "How old are you?"

I looked up, startled. "I'm almost eighteen."

Vyla's eyebrows hiked in surprise. "Almost…?" She let out a long breath. "You poor child. I've had centuries to learn the ways of the Guard, but Clay… Clay's the vilest Guardsman I've ever encountered." She studied her hands for a moment. "Don't blame yourself for this. You are out of your league."

Her words twisted the knife in my heart. "Let me talk to Murphy. Maybe if he knew you had a daughter…"

"No." Vyla gripped my forearm, her hand like an iron vice. "Don't tell any of them you've met my daughter. I spent the afternoon convincing Clay that Emlyn is far away from here."

I stared at the desperate Lilitu, shocked. "Clay knows about Emlyn?"

Vyla shook her head bitterly. "The whole reason I sought you out was because Clay discovered she existed."

Guilt settled like a stone in my stomach. "What can I do?"

"Keep Emlyn safe. Keep trying to reach the angel."

"I promise." It was the very least I could do. And I meant it, with every cell in my body. If there was a way to grant Emlyn humanity, I would find it.

Vyla gave me a watery smile. She nodded, and I realized she was too overcome with emotion to speak. She loosened her grip on my arm and I stood. Vyla turned away from me, curling her arms back around her knees. The storm around us may have subsided, but that didn't mean she was out of the woods.

I reached for the edge of her dream. But then something stopped me.

"The man you killed… That was Emlyn's father?"

Vyla nodded, surprised. "His was the one and only life I've ever taken."

I turned away from her before she could see my unease. It seemed strange that I had only put together just now.

Emlyn was Lucas's niece.

7

I was right. Dad did not come home that night.

I awoke to find the dawn sun casting a golden glow into the corner of my room. When I made my way downstairs for breakfast, I found Gretchen and Matthew asleep together on the couch. Matthew must have come over after I'd gone to sleep. They looked so peaceful, nestled on the couch together. For everything Gretchen had suffered after losing Eric, she had managed to find love again in Matthew. They were a good match. Where Gretchen was brash and impulsive, Matthew was quiet and steadfast. It had been Matthew who'd let me kiss him to draw the energy I'd needed to save Lucas from the ancient Lilitu Ais. Not many Guardsmen would have volunteered for that particular task.

I meant to leave them sleeping peacefully, but the bottom stair groaned under my weight. Gretchen stirred and sat up, wiping the sleep out of her eyes.

"Good morning," I said. Gretchen looked as despondent as I felt. But she stood and walked to me, catching me in an uncharacteristic hug. "What's this for?" I found myself smiling. Gretchen had never been the touchy-feely type.

"I know…. Gretchen stopped, gathering her thoughts. "I know this can't be easy for you. But I want you to hear me when I say this: your dad is a good man. Period."

I nodded, but I wasn't ready to let myself dwell on what Dad had been doing all night. "And you? I imagine… you're probably glad that she's…"

Gretchen stared at me for an uncomfortably long moment. When she finally spoke, her voice was tinged with an edge of unease I didn't expect. "I longed for this. For a long time." She fell silent.

"And now?" I watched her closely, but I wasn't sure I wanted to hear her answer.

Gretchen shook her head, curling her arms around herself as if warding off a chill. "I joined the Guard to fight for humanity. The mission was clean and clear. Right versus wrong. Yes, she's the enemy. But this... doesn't feel right."

Matthew stirred on the couch behind us. I glanced at him and was surprised to see him sitting up, watching us. He unfolded himself from the couch and joined us in the foyer. Gretchen looked up at him and melted a little. He reached out and caught her hand, giving it a gentle squeeze.

I studied them, suddenly feeling like an intruder on their moment. I knew they were in love, but until this moment I had never seen it so clearly displayed.

"I was just... Anybody else feel like breakfast?" I hadn't eaten anything for dinner last night. And while I wouldn't exactly say I was hungry, there was an emptiness gnawing at me.

Gretchen had skipped dinner last night, too, so it was no surprise when she nodded. "I'll handle the toast if you'll tackle the eggs."

"I guess that means I'm on coffee duty." Matthew draped an arm around Gretchen's shoulders. The three of us made our way into the kitchen. We cooked and ate in relative silence, each of us sorting through our own private thoughts.

It wasn't until we were heading over for morning meeting that I remembered I had been in Clay's dream last night. The question was whether or not he knew it, too.

The yard was already full of Guardsmen waiting for the meeting to begin by the time Gretchen, Matthew, and I arrived. I scanned the faces, looking for Dad. Instead, I spotted Lucas. His face lit up when he saw me, I could tell he was eager to talk.

He started moving toward me, slipping between soldiers with a single-minded purpose. Someone grabbed his arm, stopping him. Lucas looked up and his face registered surprise. Clay had stopped him. He leaned close to whisper something in Lucas's ear. I felt my eyes narrow as I tried to divine what Clay could possibly be saying. Lucas nodded, then looked down. Clay handed him a notebook and pen then clapped a hand on his back. Clay gestured toward the porch, clearly expecting Lucas to accompany him. Lucas shot a look back at me and shrugged his shoulders apologetically, but turned and did as Clay had directed.

Dad emerged from the house as Clay made his way up the porch steps. Clay nodded at him in passing. Something seemed to pass between them, but I couldn't read my father's expression to guess what. Dad made his way down the porch steps, faltering when his eyes crossed my face. Instead of joining me, he turned back to face Clay. I couldn't be sure, but I think he flinched before looking away.

Clay took his now customary position at the porch railing. The assembled fell silent as every face turned toward him.

"Before we get to the business of the day, I want to praise Braedyn for her excellent work delivering our first Lilitu prisoner." Clay inclined his head toward me and I felt the eyes of the assembled turn in my direction. "It's early yet, but I have great hopes that she will deliver valuable information. I'm leaving Murphy in charge of intelligence gathering while he recovers from his training accident."

I studied the back of Dad's head. He nodded at Clay's words but—as I couldn't see his face—I was unable to gauge his reaction.

Clay flashed an even smile at Dad, then turned his attention back to the gathered troops. "I don't have to tell you that we are facing a time of great importance. Our actions over the coming months may very well seal the fate of humanity. Our victory or defeat will be humanity's victory or defeat. In light of this, I feel a return to some of our older traditions will help to strengthen our resolve. We can't afford mistakes. We can't afford distractions. I've decided it's time to once again embrace one of the earliest tenets of our order. Beginning today, we will keep separate houses for men and women. Men, you will join me in this house. Women, you will take up residence in Murphy's home. I will leave it to you to sort out living arrangements. Any disputes that need to be addressed should be directed to Matthew, who I am appointing head of barracks."

I expelled a sharp breath. Of all the things I expected Clay to do, this hadn't even made the list. I glanced at Gretchen in time to see her and Matthew sharing a stricken look. While they had both maintained their own rooms under Hale's leadership, it wasn't a secret that they shared a bed most nights.

Just one more unwelcome change, courtesy of Terrance Clay, I thought bitterly.

But then my eyes slipped from Gretchen's face. Zoe stood behind her, watching me with the smile of the satisfied cat. Zoe walked over, shoving her hands into the pockets of the hoodie she'd taken from me.

"Hey, guess we're going to be roomies officially now." Her smiled deepened, but there was nothing friendly behind her eyes.

My thoughts wandered for the rest of the meeting. I couldn't wait to get out of there. When Clay finally dismissed us, I pushed my way through the Guardsmen toward Dad. He must have been looking for me as well, because we came face to face in the middle of the yard.

"Dad?" But whatever I'd thought I would ask him, the words slid out of my mind, leaving me grasping to find something to say to him.

"We can't talk here." Dad's eyes cut to the side. I followed his gaze, and noticed one of Clay's soldiers watching us with a mild expression. He looked casual enough, but something in his gaze told me he was on the job.

"Are you being watched?" I heard my voice tick up a notch in surprised outrage.

"Careful." Dad lowered his voice even further, making it almost difficult to decipher his next words. "Given recent events, Clay has decided it would be prudent to monitor my activities. He may well have someone watching you, too."

I stared at Dad, afraid to speak. Who else might be listening? I glanced at the faces of the people surrounding us, but if they were spies for Clay, they weren't being obvious about it.

"I should get back." The muscles along Dad's jaw tensed. "Braedyn, be careful what you confide to Lucas. As far as I can tell, he seems quite taken with Clay. I'm not saying I think he would intentionally…"

"Braedyn, Clay would like a word." Thane stopped by Dad's shoulder, scrutinizing us with a shrewd glance. I felt a spike of adrenaline shoot through my system. I hadn't even seen him approaching. Dad straightened, his features going neutral. He gave me a brief smile and squeezed my shoulder. Only the strength of his grip betrayed any emotion.

"Have a good day at school. I'll see you at dinner." Dad turned and headed back into the Guard's house without another word.

I looked at Thane, trying to keep my voice level. "What does he want?"

"I'm sure he will tell you." Thane's grim countenance gave nothing away. I smiled for his benefit, then turned toward the house. Clay and Lucas were entering through the back door. I followed, forcing myself to take one step after another, comforting myself with the thought that Clay probably would've sent his soldiers to collect me instead of Thane if he thought I was a threat.

I walked into Clay's office trying to cultivate an air of bored indifference, but inside my nerves were screaming. Lucas was taking notes at Clay's side. Neither of them looked up at my entrance. After a few moments, Clay straightened.

"I'd be grateful if you could get that to Sutherland before you leave for school. He'll probably have some questions, but I think you know what I'm looking for so feel free to clarify any points for him."

"No problem." Lucas closed the notebook. His eyes landed on my face, and he gave me a smile that was a painful mixture of pride and eagerness. I didn't need Dad's warning to know that Lucas respected Clay. Somehow, Clay had managed to hide his true colors from Lucas so effectively that Lucas was falling under his spell completely. Lucas left through the front door. Clay waited until the door closed behind him.

"Come in, Braedyn. Have a seat." Clay gestured at an empty chair by his desk. Once I had settled myself, Clay leaned back in his chair and studied me. "So. I know you visited my dreaming mind last night. I'd like to hear your explanation before I decide how to respond."

I felt my mouth go dry. There was no time to generate a convincing lie. I had to tell a part truth. "I was scared. I didn't want my dad to get hurt again."

"I see. And you thought you'd plant a suggestion in my mind, urging me not to hurt Murphy, is that it?"

I nodded. "But it didn't… I didn't go through with it," I stammered.

Clay regarded me in silence for a long moment. "Why do you think I had your father beaten instead of you?"

The question was so unexpected, I couldn't do more than stare at him.

"It's not because I think you're a match for my men, though I understand you are an accomplished fighter. It's because to physically hurt a Lilitu is to hurt a human. You'd simply draw strength from some human to heal yourself, effectively transferring the pain to someone else." Clay stood and turned his back to me, staring out the bay window that overlooked the neighborhood. "But if I hurt someone you love? That leaves a mark you can't easily erase." He turned back to face me, smiling faintly. "You've proven you can be useful to our cause, and you clearly love your father, so I will forgive this insubordination. Once. Your next mistake will cost more than a few bruises. Dismissed."

Clay sat at his desk, picking up a pen, and began to write a letter. The message could not have been clearer: I was no threat to Clay. He held all the power.

I fled Clay's office hounded by feelings of powerlessness and insecurity. But as I reached for the handle of the front door, it opened. Lucas stood on the front step, returning from his errand. He startled when he saw me, but half a heartbeat later his expression had softened into a friendly smile.

"I'm almost done here. Just let me get these figures back to Clay and I can grab my things."

"Actually, would you mind getting a ride with Gretchen today?" I shrugged, giving what I hoped came off like an apologetic smile. "I just remembered... I have to get to school early. There's a quiz." I didn't wait for Lucas's response. I slid past him and rushed across the yard separating our houses. A few Guardsmen stood in conversation by the fence. I felt their eyes tracking me as I fled, and wondered if this was coincidence or if they had been set to watch me.

It dawned on me then, that I had no allies left in the Guard. Recruiting any one of them, Gretchen or Matthew or Dad—and most especially Lucas—would put them at odds with Clay. I didn't want to find out what he might do if he suspected someone of working against him behind his back.

The loss of Karayan crushed into me suddenly. I could have used her advice. Even her admonishment would have been welcomed, as long as it was accompanied by her friendship. I hadn't felt this alone since the day I'd learned I was a Lilitu.

I got to school early enough to see the janitorial staff finishing up their morning circuit. The grass was still wet with morning dew, which made sitting on the quad an uncomfortable prospect. I ended up pacing between the administration building and the dining hall, trying to look like I had a purpose. As other students trickled onto campus, I noticed a few curious stares so I decided to find a seat on one of the cement planters bordering the parking lot.

I was sitting there when Royal and Cassie found me ten minutes later.

"Remind me whose bright idea it was to take three AP classes?" Royal dropped his book bag at my feet before slumping, defeated, onto the planter beside me.

"Yes, but every AP test you pass is a class you don't have to repeat in college," Cassie quipped happily.

"This from the girl who is so excited about college classes that she can't wait until graduation to start taking them, she has to drive to college for one every day." Royal may have sounded exasperated, but the look he gave Cassie was full of affection.

"Braedyn?"

"Huh?" I looked up into Cassie's face.

"What's wrong?" Cassie's eyes narrowed with concern. She exchanged a glance with Royal. "Where's Lucas?"

I meant to give them a smile. I meant to appease their worry. But something inside me broke. "I think… I think I'm really in trouble." Like the first crack in a dam, this trickle of words grew until the whole story flooded out of me.

I told them everything. I told them about Clay, and how he was changing the Guard. I told them about Vyla and her daughter. I told them about Clay having Dad beaten while I watched, helpless to stop it. I told them about how he'd threatened to hurt Lucas if I told him any of this. They listened, and as the minutes passed their shock transformed into horror. I wasn't aware that I was shaking until Royal put an arm around my shoulders and squeezed me tight.

"Okay. I'm driving." Royal stood and offered me his hand.

"Driving where?" I ran the back of my hand across my eyes, brushing away the tears that had gathered while I was telling them my story.

"To the police station." Royal's voice was steady, but something about his tone gave voice to the roiling anger behind his words.

"No!" I lurched to my feet.

Royal studied me with an astonished expression. "What do you mean? That guy is a sociopath…!"

"I can't go to the police. I can't. If I do… You don't know Clay. If I made a move against him, he would find a way to hurt me. He would go after the people I love."

"But if he was in jail…?" Cassie put a hand on my shoulder, trying to calm me down.

"You don't understand! The soldiers who follow him worship him. He would find a way to make his wishes known, he would find a way to get revenge…"

"Okay. First of all, calm down. It's going to be okay." Royal's voice softened; I could tell he was alarmed by my panic.

"That's the thing." I looked at Royal, feeling my strength begin to crumble. "I don't think it is."

"How can we help?" Cassie, all business, took my hands and sat me back down on the planter. "There has to be something we can do."

"I don't know." I felt my mind spinning like the gears of a bicycle after they've slipped the chain. But then, something caught in the back of my mind. I looked up, meeting Cassie's gaze. "Maybe… Maybe there is something."

"Well?" Royal took a seat on my other side. "Don't keep us in suspense."

"Clay won't leave Puerto Escondido until he's gotten what he wants."

"Good. Okay. What does he want?" Cassie gave me an encouraging smile.

"To win the war."

"The war." Royal spoke slowly, as if working through a math problem. "The war… between us and the Lilitu? That war?"

"Yes." I looked at Royal, feeling a sliver of hope breaking through the fog of the morning's panic. "Yes, exactly."

"Oh." Cassie's voice sounded faint, and her smile looked a little fixed. "Is that all?"

"Lilith is vulnerable," I said in a rush. "We just have to figure out how." I saw the look Royal and Cassie exchanged and shook my head. "It's not crazy. Sansenoy told me Lilith was vulnerable. Something is keeping her from accessing her full strength. If I want Clay out of my life, I just have to figure out her weakness so the Guard can defeat her."

Royal made a strangled snort of disbelief, but Cassie looked thoughtful. "Okay. So we have our goal, now we just have to figure out how to achieve it."

I let out a long breath. It wasn't exactly a plan, but it was a direction to head in. And more importantly, I realized I wasn't alone in this. Cassie and Royal had my back. They'd proven themselves capable of more than I would have imagined back when we were all freshmen together. Maybe it was selfish, getting them involved. But I didn't have time to second-guess my motives right now. We had work to do.

Cassie bit her lower lip. "Do you think… Do you think that's why Seth is hanging around? Could he know what this vulnerability is, too? Maybe he's trying to protect Lilith until she's gathered her full strength."

I stared at Cassie, stricken. "I hadn't even thought about that," I whispered. "It would explain why he's still hanging around after opening the Seal and completing the ritual." I filled them in on Seth interfering with my attempt to infiltrate Clay's dream.

"Awesome," Royal breathed. "Just what we need. More Seth."

Cassie frowned. "On the plus side, the fact that he's still around could mean that the secret to Lilith's vulnerability is close. Maybe that's why he's keeping such a close eye on you, Braedyn."

I nodded, mulling this over.

"Lucas! Over here!" Royal waved toward the parking lot. I looked up quickly. Lucas spotted us and smiled, heading in our direction. I lowered my voice, pulling Cassie and Royal in close.

"Just promise me you won't tell Lucas about any of this," I hissed. That got their attention.

"Braedyn, what the hell…? It's Lucas." Royal frowned, showing more unease than I'd seen from him yet.

"He's loyal to Clay." They stared at me, stunned. "Please," I said, urgently. "Just trust me. Until I can be sure he won't run to Clay, we can't let him know what we're doing."

Neither of them looked happy about this, but they nodded.

"Fine," Royal muttered, just before Lucas reached us, "but for the record, I think keeping him in the dark is a terrible idea."

8

By the time I got home, I was exhausted. I headed upstairs, hoping to grab a few minutes of solitude. But as I approached the door to my room, I realized it was occupied. Zoe was lounging on my bed, flipping through a magazine. She glanced up as I entered but made no effort to move.

I saw a duffel bag tossed in the corner. Zoe's laptop computer was resting on top of it. Next to that, a folded cot leaned against the wall beside my window. I recognized the cot. It was one of several dozen from the Guard's house. Apparently, Zoe had literally meant "roomies."

"Isn't there somewhere else for you to crash?" I tried to keep my voice level. Something told me that letting Zoe see how much this invasion of my personal space bothered me would only encourage her.

Zoe shrugged and flipped a page. "Sandra and Marla are sharing Murphy's bed."

"What about Gretchen? Wouldn't you be more comfortable sharing a room with her, seeing as how you're both spotters?"

Zoe looked up, hearing the edge in my voice. "Gretchen claimed the downstairs bedroom, and it doesn't exactly take a genius to guess why. I'd really rather not walk in on her and Matthew, if you catch my drift." Zoe gave me a cold smile. "Besides, it's not like you and Lucas are going to be doing any canoodling, right?"

I clenched my jaw shut, refusing to rise to her bait. It was clear I had no say in this. Fighting her would only make things worse. Besides, I was too tired to get into it right now. I shrugged out of my sweater and turned to hang it up in my closet. Zoe had squashed all of my clothes onto one rack to make room for hers on the other rack. I gritted my teeth and hung my sweater on the packed rack.

Zoe didn't look up as I left the room, but under the fringe of blue hair I could've sworn I saw her smirk.

Days passed, but if there was a silver lining to the cloud that was becoming my life it had yet to reveal itself. The days were growing steadily shorter and colder. Autumn had the land firmly in its grip now. All the things I used to love about this season were fast becoming painful reminders of a life I no longer led. I caught myself staring at the pumpkins lining hay bales set up outside of grocery stores as I drove past on my way to school. Dad and I used to make an event of carving up our annual jack o' lanterns. As I passed the bright orange globes, memories swelled in my head; giggling with Dad as we lugged our heavy treasures home, pulling out handfuls of slimy pumpkin guts, watching our breath steam in the cold air, sitting down with a cup of hot cocoa to warm up after…

This Halloween there would be no pumpkins. No hot chocolate. No giggling with Dad. In separating me from my father, Clay had taken away the one constant I had always relied on. My house no longer felt like my home. My room was no longer a sanctuary. I felt exposed all the time. There was no safe place for me to hide.

When she wasn't training, Zoe was almost always in my room. She was there when I got home from school, sprawled out with her computer or a magazine or a notebook or just listening to music through my headphones. At first, I wondered about this. Why didn't Clay have her training with the others, or researching, or doing anything other than hanging out? But then it became clear. Clay had assigned Zoe a mission. Her mission was me, and her presence was a message: Clay wanted me to understand that I was always being watched.

The only place I could go to escape her was school. But even there I had to keep my eyes open for Lucas. I was racked with internal conflict, torn between keeping Lucas safe by keeping him ignorant, or telling him everything and risking Clay's wrath. My inaction itself became a choice; the longer I debated with myself whether or not to tell Lucas the truth, the further he fell under Clay's influence. Part of me hoped that spending time with Clay would open Lucas's eyes so I wouldn't have to say anything. I became obsessed with the hope that Clay would do something to expose his true nature to Lucas. But Lucas seemed to fall more and more under his spell by the day. The few times I floated doubts about Clay, or questioned his motives, Lucas was quick to defend him.

"I know he's a little rough around the edges," Lucas would say, "but he is struggling with enormous problems. You of all people know the threat we're facing. And Clay has to figure in logistics, troop development, and maintaining the morale of everyone under his command. Trust me, it's not as easy as it sounds."

I would invariably back down, telling myself Clay would eventually show Lucas his true colors. But Clay outmaneuvered me every passing week. By the time Halloween arrived, Clay wasn't even bothering to come up with excuses to separate Lucas and me. It was as though he knew he held Lucas's loyalty firmly in hand and there was nothing I could do to pry it from his grip.

It would have been easy to sink into a deeper and deeper depression. Without Royal and Cassie, that's probably what I would have done. But with their help, I had a goal to work toward. I had something to pour my energy into. I had a purpose. And if we had to work in secret, guarding our conversations against the fear that Lucas would overhear something, that was just the way it had to be. At least, that's what I told myself each and every time Lucas stumbled onto one of our conversations.

At first, our stolen moments were spent turning the problem over and over in our minds. But we were not going to be able to guess Lilith's vulnerable points, not without knowing more. If I were being completely honest, those last few weeks in October bore very little fruit.

The problem was Lucas. Now that Clay was keeping Lucas busy at home, the only time we really had to speak freely was at school. And so Lucas would seek me out whenever we had a moment. Which made plotting with Cassie and Royal extremely challenging. There just aren't as many private places on a high school campus as you would think. Each time Cassie and Royal and I would start digging into the problem, Lucas would invariably find us and bring our work to a screeching halt. After a few awkward interruptions, Lucas started to catch on; he knew there was something going on. I saw him swallow his hurt feelings, respecting our desire to keep this secret from him, and it made me ache. I wanted to tell him, but at the same time, I was afraid of what telling him might do. If he didn't believe me, he could expose our plans to Clay. And if he did believe me...? If Clay began to suspect I had disobeyed him by telling Lucas what he'd done to my father, Clay might retaliate by hurting Lucas. It had me worried enough that—despite my growing urge to tell Lucas everything—I held my tongue.

One thing was certain; no matter how I sliced it, it was getting harder and harder to keep Lucas out of the loop.

Halloween brought with it a surprise gift. Mr. Hart had asked Cassie to manage the theater department's Halloween Parade. Missy would be reprising her role as Guinevere, wearing the stunning gown Cassie had crafted for her the previous year. Beyond that, a couple dozen theater kids had signed up to join the parade, and Cassie was given oversight of doling out the rest of the costumes. The parade itself would only last about 15 minutes, but it would take a few afternoons to handle all the fittings and make any necessary changes to the costumes before the big day.

And so three days before Halloween found Cassie, Royal, and me with our heads together in the costume closet, doing our best to discuss strategy in this private stolen hour.

"That's the whole problem." I closed my eyes, feeling the now familiar pangs of helplessness. "If Idris or Ian knew anything, they took it with them to their graves. Unless Cassie remembers overhearing something useful...?" I glanced at Cassie, leaving the question unvoiced.

"I'm sorry." Cassie lowered her eyes, miserable. "There has to be some other way for us to research what this weakness of Lilith's is." Cassie refused to be daunted by reality. "Maybe Seth...?"

"*No.*" Royal and I spoke the word in the same breath.

Pink spots of embarrassment colored Cassie's cheeks. "I don't mean corner him in a dark alley or anything." Cassie let out an irritated breath. "What I'm trying to say is, maybe if we look at what we know about Seth it might shed some light on Lilith."

I set up a little straighter. "Actually, that's not a terrible idea."

"I disagree. Anything having to do with Seth automatically qualifies as 'terrible idea' as far as I'm concerned." Royal crossed his arms. He looked like he was ready to fight.

"When Seth was working with the Guard," I stopped, shrugging unhappily. "Or… against the Guard, I guess. Anyway, he seemed pretty interested in everything having to do with the mission."

"Yeah?" Royal gave me a bland look. "At the time, the mission contained the Seal that was locking Lilith out of this world. Now the Seal is broken and the mission is pretty much a pile of rubble."

"It wasn't all about the Seal, though." I closed my eyes again, this time trying to recall something. "He was after information. Those rubbings he took of the stations of the cross, there were stories in the borders. One of them was about Seth and his sister, but there were a lot of other things carved into those borders. Maybe something important."

"I hate to repeat myself, but the mission is pretty much a pile of rubble." Royal had not uncrossed his arms.

"Yes. Because of Seth. He also torched everything that the archivist Angela brought with her. I think…" I looked up into Cassie's eyes. "I think the answer might actually be out there. I think Seth was trying to destroy the information we would need to stop him—to stop Lilith."

"Um…" Cassie raised her hand. "At the risk of sounding like a total downer, it kind of looks like he succeeded, doesn't it?"

"Clay's archivist doesn't think so." I quickly painted them a picture of Sandra, and told them what she had said about the mission, and how monks of the time built in secret compartments and vaults and passageways. "The Seal is gone. And the roof is gone. But a lot of the columns, and whatever secrets those walls might contain, those are still there." I started to say something when someone knocked on the costume closet door.

Half a second later Lucas entered. "Still working on the parade?"

Royal sat back, giving Lucas a winning smile. "We're still looking for a Lancelot. Are you interested?"

"Uh…" Lucas's smile grew a little strained. "Is that a trick question?"

"Don't worry, I'm not going to stick you in purple taffeta or anything." Cassie's eyes twinkled with a mischievous gleam. "How do you feel about tights?"

"This isn't going to do any favors for my reputation, is it?" Lucas walked into the room and closed the door. "What the hell. I'm always willing to take a bullet for the team." He flashed me a heart-melting smile. Something inside me tightened. "You guys look kind of serious. Did I interrupt something important?"

I turned toward Royal and he saw the emotion in my eyes. "Braedyn's birthday," he lied smoothly. "We have less than two weeks to plan something. It's going to be tight, but I've faced challenges like this before and I have emerged victorious."

Lucas looked stricken. "I can't believe I completely forgot. With everything that's been going on…" He turned to me, pained. "No excuses. I'm a terrible boyfriend."

"Yeah. You're awful." I gave Lucas a playful smile, doing my best to keep things light when all I wanted to do was break into a million pieces.

Royal rolled his eyes. "Okay, okay. You two can flirt on your own time. We have serious business to discuss. Is this going to be an exclusive affair or are we inviting the whole school like we did for your sixteenth?"

"Please, don't." I grabbed Royal's arm and forced him to face me, willing him to hear my plea. "Seriously, Royal. I don't feel like celebrating this year."

"That's not an option." Royal covered my hand with his and gently pried my fingers off of his arm. He gave me a smile that looked almost wistful. "Aside from the fact that this is your eighteenth birthday, welcome to adulthood, it might also be the last time we're all able to celebrate your birthday together."

The words shot a bolt of shock through me. Lucas must have felt the same rush of anxiety and fear. We looked at each other, exchanging a loaded glance.

"Go straight to the worst possible outcome, why don't you?" Royal let out an irritated sigh. "I meant, we might all be in different colleges next year. You know, after we save the world and life goes on. Am I the only one who's keeping a positive attitude about this?"

"Royal's right." Lucas's voice softened. "We should take advantage of any excuse to celebrate. This year especially. It reminds us what we're living for. What we're fighting for."

I met Lucas's eyes and felt my heart skip a beat. His gaze held me, and I felt another swell of emotion rising in my chest. Lucas had this way of making me feel seen. As though in this moment, no matter what was going on in the world, 100% of his focus was devoted to me. I relented.

"Fine. But let's keep it between us. I really don't want to have to perform, or pretend. If it's just the four of us…" I looked around at my friends.

Cassie took hold of my hand and gave it a warm squeeze. They understood.

"Fine, if you want to waste this last opportunity to have me plan something spectacularly extravagant for you, I suppose I have no choice but to respect your decision." Royal sniffed in mock irritation.

Cassie punched him lightly on the shoulder. "Don't worry, Braedyn. I'll make sure he doesn't go off the deep end."

With that settled, we turned back to the work at hand, rooting through the racks of clothes for the best costumes. After a few minutes of working in silence, Cassie gave a delighted squeal and emerged with a pair of matching costumes for a boy and a girl.

"Romeo and Juliet! Braedyn, you and Lucas should join the parade as star-crossed lovers…" Cassie's voice abruptly cut out as she realized what she had said. "I… I'm sorry. I don't know why I said that."

A new tension seeped into the room. It was something we didn't talk about much, but both Cassie and Royal new that Lucas and I had to tread very carefully. Romeo and Juliet might have been separated by society, but at least Juliet didn't have to worry about draining Romeo of his life's energy if they gave into their attraction for one another. It didn't help that everything that Lucas and I had been through together had only strengthened our bond, deepening our love for one another. You want star-crossed lovers? It didn't get too much more star-crossed than Lucas and me.

I reached out and took one of the costumes from Cassie's hands, running my fingers over the velvet doublet. "I do think you would look dashing as a brooding young lover." I looked up at Lucas through my lashes, giving him a warm smile. Some of the tension seemed to ease out of Cassie's shoulders. If only all of the conflicts in my life were so easy to resolve.

The conversation resumed, touching lightly on topics ranging from homework to school drama, staying several ZIP codes away from all things supernatural or apocalyptic. It felt good to just be hanging out with my friends. I glanced from Cassie to Royal. Maybe they were right. Maybe it was a good idea to take some time out and celebrate turning another year older. If nothing else, it was one small glimmering light to look forward to.

I woke up on November ninth, shivering. Zoe had taken the bed last night before I came upstairs. I'd been left with the choice of sharing the bed with her or sleeping on the cot. I chose the cot, but Zoe had snaked all the best blankets as well. My shoulders felt stiff and sore. With a heavy sigh I rolled out of the cot and stood, picking my way to the closet to get dressed for the day. After pulling on my uniform, I ran a brush through my hair just a few times before heading out the door. I wasn't eager to spend any more time in Zoe's presence than absolutely necessary.

I was halfway down the staircase before I remembered that today was my birthday. The thought stopped me cold. The house was quiet; any spotters who were not on duty were still asleep. They would most likely drag themselves out of bed in time for morning meeting, but not a minute sooner. And Dad didn't live here now. I hadn't anticipated how lonely this would feel. Dad usually made pancakes on my birthday. It was our tradition, one I hadn't expected to miss this badly.

I heard a door open downstairs and finished descending. Gretchen emerged from her room, rubbing sleep out of her eyes. She saw me and nodded in greeting.

"Has anybody made coffee yet?"

"I was just going to ask the same thing." Zoe emerged from the hallway at the top of the stairs above. She walked down the stairs and passed me wordlessly.

Gretchen groaned. "I'll take that as a no." The spotters stumbled toward the kitchen and their morning caffeine fix, leaving me alone in the hall. I felt invisible.

I tried to tamp down my disappointment. After all, Gretchen couldn't be expected to know today was my birthday. It's not like we had talked about it, and in all fairness I didn't know the exact date of her birthday, either. But still, I felt a sinking sensation. I was 18 years old, and no one seemed to care. This thought was followed immediately by a rush of shame and guilt. We were facing the end of humanity. Our concerns were so much bigger than one girl's forgotten birthday.

I headed into the kitchen, made myself some toast, and took it out to the front porch. I ate it slowly, hoping Dad might emerge from the house next door. I finished the toast, staring at the door. When it finally opened, it was Lucas who emerged. He had his backpack slung over one shoulder and he looked surprised to see me waiting on the porch. He jogged over, and brushed my lips with a kiss.

"Happy Birthday, Braedyn Murphy."

I smiled, lacing my fingers through his. Not forgotten completely. Lucas studied me, concern deepening in his eyes.

"Everything okay?"

"Yeah, just… Did you see my dad?" I tried to keep my voice neutral, but a plaintive note slipped in.

Lucas winced, giving me an apologetic smile. "Clay sent him on a mission this morning. I don't think he knew today was your birthday."

I wouldn't bet on that myself. I released one of Lucas's hands and turned toward the Firebird, parked in front of the house. "We should probably get to school." If Lucas sensed any of my hostility, he didn't let on. It was going to be a long day.

When the final bell rang, I let out a sigh of relief. Lucas found me by my locker. He waited while I collected the things I would need for homework.

"You think you can finish all of that before sunset?" A small smile played across his lips.

"Why?" I studied him, as though by scrutinizing him I would be able to divine his plans.

"Don't worry, this is all within the guidelines you established. Much to Royal's frustration," he added with a grin.

And so, as a heavy sun dropped low in the west, Lucas drove me out to Lookout Point. The point had a spectacular view of our little valley. From here we could see the whole of Puerto Escondido nestled within the spreading arms of the mountain ranges.

Royal and Cassie were waiting when we arrived. I emerged from the car, my breath catching. They had spread a variety of blankets across the ground, making a luxurious quilt for us to rest on. In the center of the blankets they had placed a low table. It was loaded with candles. Set against the backdrop of a glorious sunset, the effect was magical.

"You guys…" I beamed at my friends, moved. "This is perfect."

Cassie took the lid off a pot in the middle of the table. "And your dad sent this." I didn't have to hear her say the words to know it was Dad's homemade green chili stew. Steam wafted out from the pot, filling the air with an enticing aroma. I don't know when he'd had time to cook it, but I knew it was Dad's way of saying happy birthday. He hadn't forgotten me, either. I nodded, wishing he could be here to celebrate with us.

We settled around the small table and dug into the delicious meal. It was cold on the mountaintop, but the stew and the candles were enough to keep us warm. And even if they weren't, the view more than made up for the chill. The aspens were changing color, scattering pockets of russet and gold across the valley. We could see the whole of the western horizon as the sun set. It was a perfect evening.

As we sopped the last of the stew out of the bottom of the pot with bits of tortilla, Lucas stood.

"I'll be right back."

Royal and Cassie traded a quick look as Lucas headed back to the car. When Lucas was out of earshot, Cassie spoke. "I found an online archive of ancient texts. It includes a lot of Mesopotamian lore." She shot a quick look over her shoulder, making sure Lucas was still out of earshot. "I figure it's worth looking through."

"It's definitely an idea." I knew they could hear the hesitation in my voice when they frowned. "It's just, Zoe—she's one of Clay's spotters—she's sort of his techie go to. I think she would have found anything useful if it existed online."

Cassie's face fell.

"That doesn't mean you shouldn't look." I meant to encourage her, but she just shook her head.

"There's got to be something we can do…" Cassie fell silent as we heard the crunching sound of Lucas's steps on the gravel behind us.

Lucas joined us, glancing around at the group. "Something we can do about what?"

When no one spoke, I cleared my throat. "I was just telling them I'm still freaking out about Vyla."

Lucas turned to face me, surprised. "Braedyn? Should we really be talking about that with civilians?"

"*Civilians?*" Royal's voice sounded sharp.

"No offense." Lucas tried to appease Royal with a smile. "It's just… That's private Guard business."

"Guard business." Royal nodded slowly, but I could see the anger heating his cheeks. "And you don't think we've earned the right to be kept in the loop? After everything we've seen and done? Cassie put her life on the line for you guys going undercover with that Lilith cult. I was almost sacrificed over an altar to bring Lilith back. Or have you forgotten all of that already?"

Lucas stared at Royal, taken aback. "I haven't forgotten. But Clay… He wants to run a tight ship. Can you blame him? If the wrong person overheard you talking about the demon we're keeping trapped in our basement…"

"You mean the Lilitu you're keeping trapped and *torturing* in your basement?" Royal kept his eyes fixed on Lucas's face.

Lucas's eyes narrowed. "Yeah, so?"

"Doesn't it bother you, knowing what they're doing to her?"

"Bother me?" Now it was Lucas's turn to get angry. "She's a murderer. She deserves whatever's happening to her. No. It doesn't bother me."

I felt a chill, and it wasn't from the mountain air. "What if it were me in the basement?"

"You've never killed a human being." Lucas turned his frown on me.

"You think Clay cares about that? He told me to bring him a Lilitu. Any Lilitu. He didn't care if whoever I brought him had murdered anyone or not."

"Then it's a good thing you found that particular Lilitu, isn't it?" Lucas glanced around the circle. "She murdered my brother. She ruined my life. And Gretchen... You weren't there. You don't know what it was like in those first few weeks after Eric was killed. What Gretchen sounded like... how she cried so hard she threw up almost every day." His eyes landed on mine once more. "And you want me to feel sympathy for the cause of all our suffering? No. No."

Royal and Cassie turned to me, eyes full of pain. I just shook my head, unable to respond. It was Cassie who broke the silence.

"I get it. Your anger is totally justified. None of us understand what that must have been like for you. None of us have had to live through what you've had to. But can you honestly tell me you don't care how this must be affecting Braedyn's dad?" Cassie spoke quietly. "Your Clay has ordered Murphy to torture this Lilitu—*Murphy*, who's spent the last eighteen years raising a Lilitu as his own daughter. You think he doesn't see Braedyn in this Lilitu you captured?" Of all of us, she wasn't speaking from anger. Lucas hesitated, caught off guard by the question.

"Clay is a great man," Lucas started.

"Who exactly are you trying to convince?" Royal picked an imaginary piece of lint off his pants.

"Maybe he has to do unpleasant things, but it's for a good cause." Lucas's voice firmed.

"Do you really believe that?" I spoke slowly, trying to keep my voice gentle. "Do you really believe what they're doing to Vyla is justified?"

Lucas cut his eyes toward me. "You know what she did. What she took from me. I... I can't talk about this anymore. Here." Lucas dropped the little box into my lap. "Happy birthday." Lucas drew in a shaky breath. "You guys should stay. I'm going to walk home. I just... I need to clear my head." He turned on his heel and walked away without waiting for a response.

Royal let out a long breath. "You weren't kidding." Royal eyed me in the gathering darkness, concerned. "He really is on Clay's side, isn't he?"

I opened the present Lucas had left behind. Underneath the wrapping paper I found a small velvet box. When I opened it I discovered a simple silver ring. Realization struck me in that moment, drew my mind back to our conversation at Hale's funeral.

Our symbol. This was supposed to be the reminder of what we were striving for; the end of the war, the moment when I could become human, the beginning of our future. I stared at the ring, feeling numb.

"Cassie. Let me know if you find anything online worth investigating. We need to figure this out ASAP." I didn't have to say it, we were all thinking the same thing.

The sooner we got Clay out of town, the better.

9

Cassie's search had turned up nothing one week after my birthday. And, as much as I wanted to devote everything to finding Lilith's weakness—thereby moving closer to getting Clay out of my life—I was still a high school student, with high school obligations. It was easier to just do the homework than it would have been to start failing classes, get called into the headmaster's office, be referred to our school counselor, or—worst of all—have to face the disappointment in Dad's eyes.

Which is how I ended up sitting at the dining room table one evening, trying to finish up some math homework. It was hard to focus with the spotters watching TV in the living room, but it would've been harder to focus in my room with Zoe there. As had become my habit over the last week, I brushed my fingers across the ring hanging from a necklace hidden in my shirt. It didn't feel safe to wear the ring openly just yet. It would raise too many questions. But having it close was a comfort. I grew used to feeling the weight of the ring against my skin. A reminder of Lucas's feelings for me, and mine for him. Something Clay couldn't take away from us.

I was puzzling through a difficult calculus problem when something caught my attention. Marla and Sandra were talking about Vyla in the living room. My pencil froze over the paper. I strained to hear more.

"Do you think she's telling us everything she knows?" Sandra's lilting British accent rose above the din of the television. They'd been watching some prime time drama about cops working on a murder case.

"If she hasn't yet, she will." Marla's voice sounded grim. "You've seen her, haven't you?"

"Yes." Sandra's voice grew tense as well. "They've certainly done a job, haven't they?"

"Murphy's thorough," Marla agreed.

An icy chill flooded through my veins. I looked over at them, unable to stop myself. Marla saw me watching her and had the grace to look embarrassed. They fell silent, turning their attention back to their show. I sat frozen for another moment, trying to decide which would be worse, finishing my homework in my room with Zoe distracting me or turning in an incomplete assignment. I felt my cell phone vibrate in my pocket and fished it out.

The caller ID only gave a number, no name. I was about to hit ignore, when something stopped me. I answered the call, raising the phone to my ear.

"Hello?"

"Braedyn, turn on the news." It was Karayan.

I shot a glance at the spotters in the living room, then turned away, lowering my voice. "I thought you wanted radio silence."

"This is an emergency." Karayan's voice came through the line, strained with a sharp urgency. "Channel seven."

I left my math book open on the dining room table and walked quickly to the living room. The remote was sitting on the coffee table. I picked it up and flipped to channel seven.

"Hey." Sandra looked up, irritated. "We were watching that."

"Look. Sandra, look." Marla tugged on Sandra's sleeve, eyes glued to the screen. Sandra and I turned back to the TV. The news was covering the restoration of the mission. Somebody had taken cell phone footage of the discovery of a secret chamber. How it had gotten to the local news station was anyone's guess. On the screen, Sandra and her team of undercover Guardsmen worked side-by-side with archaeologists from the local university.

"Bloody hell." Sandra was on her feet in an instant, attention fixed on the screen.

"It's been called an ancient time capsule of incredible value," the newscaster was saying. She smiled into the camera, unaware that her news report may very well be jeopardizing the fate of humanity. "Within the hidden chamber, restoration experts have already recovered over 100 volumes. Local authorities are now working with the university to create a special collections vault dedicated to studying and preserving these valuable tomes."

"Oh, shite," Sandra moaned. "Clay's going to go full mental when he hears about this."

A second clip of footage from the secret chamber played as the reporter droned on. One of the university archaeologists was opening a book with white-gloved hands. The camera traveled to the book, panning down to show elaborate illustrations.

The pictures stopped my breath. They depicted a ritual I had witnessed through Cassie's eyes. Three young women, dressed in white robes, standing in the moonlight. The chalice, the knife, the thurible—it was drawn here exactly as it had occurred when Idris recruited the three acolytes for Lilith. The acolytes… something tugged at the edge of my memory, back when Royal and I had been trapped with Idris in the cave beneath the mission. Just before the Seal had crumbled to dust…

"Come on, let's get out of here!"

I let Royal help me across the Temple. He stopped along the way to pick up one of the lanterns harboring a flickering candle inside. But as we reached the tunnel, I froze. "Wait." I spun back to face Idris. "The acolytes."

Idris's eyes flicked to my face, suddenly alert.

"Three girls, with 'courage, conviction, and a lightness of spirit akin to that of a child.'" I saw once more the selection in my head. Idris had been looking for specific qualities among the eager volunteers. She chose the girls she chose for a reason. "What did you need the acolytes for?"

It was as if a veil came down behind Idris's eyes, obscuring her emotions. "I'm sorry, child, but until you are willing to open your mind to the truth, you are an enemy of Lilith." She shrugged her shoulders sadly. "Unless that changes, I cannot—I will not answer your questions."

"You initiated them—"

The ground lurched under our feet. Royal and I braced ourselves against the walls of the cave. I clung to the rough wall, once again rocked from within by the spiritual upheaval in the dream world.

"It's not over." Royal reached for my hand, his voice strained with urgency. "We need to move."

"The ritual," I hissed, glaring back at Idris. "Their blood—what was it for?"

Idris met my gaze evenly. "You ask all the right questions, Daughter of Lilith. But again, I will not provide answers to an enemy."

"One of those acolytes is my friend. You'd better believe you're going to answer my questions." I took a step toward her, meaning to cross the distance between us and grip her forehead; if she was unwilling to give me the truth, I would take it directly from her thoughts.

The ground heaved once more, and a few chunks of rock broke off from the walls surrounding us. While I stood there, still dazed from the tremors shooting through the dream world, Royal grabbed me around the middle with one arm.

"That's it." Royal hauled me into the tunnel. "We are leaving now." In his free hand, he held the candle aloft, lighting our way.

I was too weak to offer much of a fight. "Wait. She knows something. We have to find out what she's done to Cassie—"

I let out a sharp breath, unable to stop myself. I'd never gotten an answer from her. I felt a dull terror seeping up through my core. Cassie.

Marla and Sandra studied me with sudden interest. I ignored them, thinking fast. The camera panned up, passing a strange man. He was looking directly into the camera, and his face was anything but friendly. Something about his expression alerted me.

"Who is that man?" I asked the question to Karayan, still on the phone with me. But the spotters turned back to the TV. Sandra saw the man I pointed out immediately. She frowned.

"I don't recall him. He's not one of our team. I don't think he's from the university, either." Sandra exchanged a grim look with Marla. "I'll notify Clay."

Marla said something in response, but I didn't hear her. My eyes had caught on something else. As the camera panned away from the strange man, I caught the barest glimpse of another figure hovering in the background.

I heard Karayan's hiss of surprise. "Did you see that? Did you see him?"

"No," I whispered. Not because I hadn't seen him, but because I didn't want to believe it. I left Marla on the couch and ran upstairs to my room. Zoe must have stepped out, but she'd left her computer open and on. I did a quick search for the news report. A moment later I was watching the video again. I scanned forward to the segment I was looking for, then stepped through the video one frame at a time. As the camera panned up and away from the book, across the face of the strange man, I waited. A few frames more, and I saw him again.

"Karayan." Despair filled my voice. "It is him. It's Seth."

"What's he doing there?" Karayan sounded astonished. "I would've thought he'd be long gone by now."

I didn't answer her. I played the video again, stopping on the clearest frame of his face. He looked… angry. What if the archeologists had already found whatever it was that held the secret to Lilith's vulnerability? Could the answer be within our grasp?

I was running across the yard that separated our house from the Guard's just a few moments later. I didn't know what to do, I needed to talk to my dad. I ran into the house, and stopped the first Guardsman that I saw.

"My dad… Murphy. Where is he?"

"I think he's below," the Guardsman started.

Without thinking, I darted for the basement door. Behind me, the Guardsman shouted for me to stop. I wrenched open the door and raced down the stairs. What I found at the bottom silenced me. The basement was almost unrecognizable. Clay's construction project had not been about improving our training facilities. He had turned the basement into a prison. Barred cells lined one wall, while another wall was set with chains and manacles. It looked like something from a medieval dungeon. I let out a startled breath.

Dad turned at the sound. He held a rag in one hand. It dripped with red. Behind him, I saw Vyla, crouched against the stone basement wall. She was wheezing, and her face was crisscrossed with cuts and bruises.

Dad let out a strangled curse and moved toward me. I recoiled from him, stricken.

"Braedyn, it's not what it looks like." He raised a hand toward me as though trying to soothe a startled animal.

"What it looks like?" My head felt light, too light, like it was filled with helium and trying to escape from my shoulders. "It looks like…" But I couldn't bring myself to say the words. Part of me knew what he must be doing down here, but seeing it…

At that moment, Guardsmen flooded into the basement.

"I'm sorry sir," one of them said, looking at Murphy with obvious fear. "She got past us before we could stop her." Two of the men grabbed hold of my arms.

Dad moved. "Release her!" The men holding me recoiled. "Get out of here." His gaze followed the men as they tripped over themselves in their haste to flee back up the stairs. Then his eyes settled on my face. All the rage drained out of them, leaving a deep sadness in its wake. He took a step toward me. I jerked back against the banister reflexively. He saw the movement and stopped.

"Dad…?"

Behind us, Vyla lifted her head. Her eyes found my face, and I saw surprise gleaming there.

"He's your… father?" Vyla eyed Murphy, curious. "It begins to make sense."

Dad saw me staring at Vyla. He stood aside, clearing my path. I went to the Lilitu, knelt beside her. She was holding her side, and when she pulled her hand away, I saw fresh stitches closing a gash along her ribs.

"Makes sense…?" I looked up into her eyes. "What makes sense?"

She gave me a bitter smile and shrugged. "Your father is not the worst Guardsman I've ever met, though he could use a little more practice with a needle and thread."

"Then he didn't…?"

"Stab me?" Vyla's eyes darkened. "No. That was Clay."

I choked down a swell of revulsion and turned back to Dad. "You have to let her go."

Dad's face fell. He looked haggard, exhausted. "I can't. Clay is watching me like a hawk. This is a test. Any mercy I show her…" Dad ran a hand through his hair. "Clay has… suggested… that he thinks my mind has been tampered with."

"Tampered with? You mean, by me?"

Dad only shrugged in answer.

"He really thinks I would do that to you?"

"The more important question is: what can he get the others to believe?" Dad glanced at the stairs, and I suddenly saw how anxious he was. "I'm doing what I can to buy Vyla some time. Clay is focused on the mission's library for the moment."

"What happens when he loses interest in the mission?" I saw Dad wince, but I couldn't stop myself from pushing. "What are you going to do if he asks you to hurt her?"

Dad dropped his gaze. "Not if. When." His voice was soft, but it carried through the basement like a shot. Beside me, Vyla stiffened. I felt her hand tighten on my wrist, and fury boiled up inside of me.

"I don't even recognize you." I hurled the words at Dad, fueling them with all the helpless rage I could find no other outlet for.

Dad nodded slowly. He made no move toward me. "Braedyn, if I disobey Clay, he will use it as evidence that you have poisoned my mind. There will be no way to disprove that kind of accusation from the head of the Guard. Who do you think they will take it out on?"

His words burrowed into my mind, dragging unwelcome images with them. He didn't need to elaborate for me to understand his meaning. Dad was valuable to the Guard. I was the enemy. All they needed was an excuse, and I would join Vyla as a prisoner in this basement.

Dad was watching my face closely. When I looked up into his gaze, he risked a step closer. "I figured out how you and I can escape the Guard. But it means leaving our life behind forever. I'll have to gather money and supplies without drawing attention, it will take some time. And when we are ready to flee, we will have to fight—or kill—the Guardsman Clay has ordered to watch me. The timing has to be perfect. If we miscalculate, Clay will have the Guard down on both of us in a matter of minutes. As good as I am at fighting, and as strong as you are, even working together we would be no match for the forces of the Guard under Clay's command."

I stared at Dad. The skin along my shoulders prickled uneasily. It was clear he had given this a lot of thought, run through every conceivable scenario. All this time, while we had been separated, he'd been planning our escape. Hot tears blinded me. I brushed them out of my eyes, ashamed.

"I'm so sorry, kiddo." Dad's voice was husky with emotion. It made my nose sting in response, and I choked down a sob. "My only regret is not taking you and running the day Clay arrived."

The floor creaked above us, as footsteps flooded the hall. Dad glanced up, worry etched into every line of his face.

"Braedyn, this isn't a safe place for you. Why are you here?"

It dawned on me that we might not have much time to talk. I crossed the remaining distance between us, dropping my voice to a near whisper. I told him about the newscast, Seth, and about the pictures of the acolyte rituals that I had seen on the television. His eyes sharpened on my face.

"Cassie." He understood instantly. "I'm sure Thane has told Clay all about the acolyte rituals Cassie took part in. If Clay gets his hands on that book and it indicates the acolytes might be a problem, he will send a team to eliminate them."

"You don't mean... Are you saying you think he would *kill* Cassie?"

"That doesn't actually surprise you, does it?"

I stared at Dad, wracked with new fears that threatened to overwhelm me. Dad glanced up as we heard another creak from upstairs.

"You shouldn't be here. Go home." Dad gave me a thin smile, trying to soften his tone. "Try to get some sleep. We'll be able to think more clearly in the morning."

I did as he told me, but I couldn't wash the image of Dad and Vyla out of my mind. After tossing in my bed for an hour, running through everything I had learned that evening, I was no closer to coming up with a plan than I had been standing in the basement with Dad.

I was tired of feeling helpless. I needed an enemy I could fight. A steely determination took root in my belly. She wouldn't get away this time. I slipped into the dream.

Elyia's spark flew straight toward me like a gleaming arrow. I gripped my hand around it, once again encountering the featureless shield that kept her mind safe. I focused all my directionless rage and anxiety on the shield. I ran my mind over every inch of it, pushing against the barrier, seeking any weakness.

I almost missed the one tiny chink in Elyia's armor. Almost.

Triumph flared in my mind, brighter than a thousand suns. I drove all my energy at the weakness, spearing through the shield. It shredded under the force of my attack, stripping Elyia's mind bare. She turned, looking up from the field of daisies that dotted her dreamscape. Elyia's flower. Bright white and gold.

"No. You can't be here." Elyia fought to expel me from her mind. I felt the pressure building as she turned all her willpower to pushing me out. But her champion was absent. Whoever had crafted her shield might have been able to withstand me in that moment. Elyia could not. I pushed back and felt her strength pop like a soap bubble.

Elyia staggered back, breathing hard. I saw the panic across her face a millisecond before she made the decision to flee. I clenched my fist, and the dream caught Elyia, holding her fast. She faced me, eyes wide and shining with fear.

I held the spark of her existence in the palm of my hand. If I pushed just a little harder... I could extinguish her. It was what she deserved. I wanted to end her for what she had done to Lucas. I wanted to make her suffer the way she had made us suffer. But she had something that we needed. Information. With great effort, I stayed my hand.

"What is Lilith's vulnerability?" I took a step toward her. Elyia gave a low moan and shook her head. "Lilith's weakness. What is it?" I took another step toward her.

"Please, don't." Elyia struggled, but her efforts were futile and we both knew it.

"You can give me the information I want, or I can take it."

The threat made Elyia go pale, but she kept her mouth tightly shut. My stomach twisted as I heard the words echoing in my mind. What I was doing, was that any better than what I condemned Clay for? I pushed the uncomfortable thoughts to the back of my mind and tilted my head to one side. "If that's the way you want to play it."

I lay my hand on the ground at her feet, sending my consciousness searching for the secret she was keeping. It threaded through her mind, but once I had grasped the edge of it, all I had to do was pull —

"Wait!" Elyia threw out a hand, forestalling me. "You can save your friend. The acolyte. Cassie. That's what you want, right?"

I was so stunned by these words that I released Elyia's secret. "Tell me everything."

"I don't know much." Elyia licked her lips, but she spoke quickly, as though eager to prove her value. "Only that Seth freaked out when your Guard learned of the secret chamber and its contents."

"Why?" I moved closer, desperate for the information.

Elyia cringed back, but her words didn't slow. "There's a book. A book that talks about how to sever the tie between Lilith and an acolyte."

"What tie?"

Elyia met my gaze and I saw surprise flicker through her eyes. "Isn't that why you're here?"

The dream rocked around us. Elyia turned, her face transforming into a mask of abject terror.

"I didn't tell her, I swear it!" Whatever fear I inspired in Elyia, she feared something else a great deal more. Something with enough power to keep itself hidden from me. I shivered, sensing the malevolent force but unable to see it.

Then the dream wrenched shut, and I was shoved out into the vast blackness containing all sleeping minds. As I watched, the shield around Elyia's spark healed itself, grew tighter and harder. I felt a wash of unease. I'd been lucky to crack her mind once. It wouldn't happen again.

At morning meeting the next day, Clay asked for a status update from Sandra. She joined him on the porch and told the assembled that the university archivists had removed everything from the mission to their campus vault. The news report had shed unfortunate publicity on the find, and it was the university's opinion that the only way to protect the collection from further vandalism was to put it under lock and key. Sandra had managed to secure credentials that would grant her access to the vault, but she wouldn't be able to walk out with more than a few volumes without the theft being detected. Which meant Sandra and her team would need to spend time searching through the library for the most important volumes.

"And there's another problem." She turned to Clay, her expression grim. "It seems like there may be another interested player involved."

For a moment I was afraid she meant Seth. But then Sandra described the other strange man we had seen on the broadcast the previous night. Clay took all this in, nodding slowly.

"Do you need reinforcements?" He kept his voice level. I couldn't tell exactly how he felt about the news, but it was clear he wasn't pleased.

Sandra shook her head. "Not yet. I will keep you updated."

"What is your current plan?" Thane glanced from Clay to Sandra. He didn't say it out loud, but the tone of his voice implied he questioned whether she was up for this.

Sandra gave Thane a cool smile, failing to hide her irritation. "Not to worry. We've already put a plan into motion."

I felt my breath catch. Of course she had a plan. She'd had all night to think through the ramifications of all this unwelcome publicity. It dawned on me then that we didn't have much time. If we didn't move fast, someone—either an archaeologist from the university or one of Sandra's crew—would stumble upon the acolyte ritual. Once it was on Clay's radar, there would be no hiding it. I didn't know if it incriminated Cassie and the others, but I wasn't about to risk finding out.

Which left me with only one course of action: I needed to get the acolyte book before Sandra did.

10

The next morning, I drove Lucas to school at our usual time. But when we parked in the parking lot, I told him to go ahead into the building without me.

"I need to catch Cassie before first period," I explained when he gave me an odd look.

"Okay. I'll catch you later. Say hi to Cassie for me." Lucas shrugged his backpack on and made his way into campus.

It still felt wrong, keeping him in the dark. But until we could have a conversation about Clay that didn't end with us fighting, I wasn't going to risk tipping my hand by telling Lucas what I was up to.

While I sat there, waiting for Cassie, Missy and Ally walked past.

"I feel like we've done all that ice and snow stuff before," Missy sighed.

"Yeah, because it's Winter Ball." Ally sounded exasperated. "It's kind of built into the name."

"Maybe we could try something different this year." Missy bit the corner of her lip, thinking.

"Like…?" Ally surveyed Missy from the corner of her eye.

"I don't know. Maybe something like 'A Midwinter's Dream,' or something. Do a twist on something a little bit more whimsical."

Ally's eyebrows hiked up. "Hm. That's not the worst idea I've ever heard. But I don't know if the guys are going to go for a fairy-themed school dance."

"Call it Shakespearean and avoid the 'f' word all together." Missy beamed at Ally, clearly growing more excited by the second. "Did we just do it? Did we just pick the theme for this year's ball?"

They drifted out of range before I heard Ally's reply, but if I knew Missy she'd find a way to sweet talk Ally into agreeing with whatever she'd set her heart on. I shook my head with a small smile. It was the strangest sense of misalignment. Other high school students were thinking about dances and dates. My friends and I, we were thinking about surviving the battle that would decide the fate of humankind.

I spotted Cassie's car pulling into the parking lot and stood. She saw me as she emerged. She must've read something in my face, because she grabbed her things and rushed to meet me.

"What is it?"

"We have to move fast," I said. "I had an idea, but I need your help. Yours and Royal's." I filled Cassie in as she walked me to my first period—AP Bio. By the time we reached the door of the classroom, Cassie's eyes were gleaming with anticipation.

"I'm in," she said. "I have to get to class. You'll fill Royal in?"

I nodded, and Cassie hurried off to make her first period. Royal was already in class, flipping through his AP Bio textbook. He looked up when I joined him.

"Are you up for running interference for me with Lucas today?"

Royal sat back in his seat and gave me a piercing look. "You have my full attention."

I filled Royal in on the plan over the course of the class. It had come to me at the end of morning meeting. Cassie had to drive to the university for her calculus class. I would stow away in her car. No one should miss me; it was my free period. And if we were late, we'd only be missing lunch. Which was why I needed Royal. He'd keep Lucas company if Cassie and I were late coming back from the university.

"And you don't think Lucas will have any questions about why you're not eating?" Royal frowned.

"Hopefully, we'll be back before lunch even begins. If not, just tell him I have a research paper I forgot about."

"Uh-huh." Royal didn't look too pleased, but he nodded. "One of these days you're going to return all these favors, right?"

"How about I save the world from the ravages of a demon horde?" I gave him a mild smile.

"Yeah, all right." Royal sniffed. "That sounds fair."

The plan was set. I'd stow away in Cassie's car while Royal kept Lucas distracted. Once we got to the university, Cassie would go to her class like normal, but I would cloak myself and slip into the university's vault. Once inside, I'd find the book, snatch it, and sneak back out. With any luck, Lucas would never know I'd left campus.

As if he knew I'd been thinking about him all morning, Lucas chased me down in the hall after third period.

"Okay. Tell me I'm just being paranoid, but are you avoiding me?" Lucas tried to read my face. He looked miserable. "Is this because… I've been thinking about what you said about Vyla."

"Yes, you're being paranoid." I caught his hand, pulling him closer. He smiled, and some of the worry eased from his expression.

"Just because I'm paranoid…"

"I'm not avoiding you," I said. The half-truth tasted bitter in my mouth. I told myself it was just for a little while longer. "And just in case I'm late to lunch, I have to research this paper I totally spaced."

"Ah. So you're saying if you end up ditching lunch…?"

"It's not you, it's me." I gave him a mischievous smile. He threw an arm around my shoulders. It felt good to be tucked against his side.

"Right." Lucas glanced at his watch and sighed. "In that case, research like the wind. Lunch isn't the same without you." He released me and melted into the flow of students heading to class.

Five minutes later I was standing at the edge of the parking lot, cloaked in my Lilitu wings. Cassie approached, scanning the area. Her eyes slid past me two or three times before she was close enough for me to call her name.

"Cassie, over here."

"Oh!" Cassie startled, then gave a halfhearted smile of embarrassment. "Sorry. Sorry." She kept her voice low, and her eyes focused on the car. We had discussed this. It had to look like she was leaving alone, we didn't want anyone seeing her talking to thin air. They might think she was crazy, but if Lucas heard the story, odds were good he'd guess she'd been talking to me, which would open up a can of worms we couldn't afford to open.

Cassie unlocked her driver side door, then opened the back passenger door. She took her time arranging her book bag on the back seat. I climbed into the front seat through the driver side door and scooted into the passenger seat.

"Are you in? You're in, right?" Cassie kept her face angled toward the back seat.

"I'm in."

"This is so James Bond of us." Cassie closed the back door and slid into the driver's seat. After buckling her seatbelt, she hesitated. "Are you... I mean, it's kind of a long drive."

"Right. All we need is for someone to look into the car and see a seatbelt restraining an invisible body."

Cassie frowned, conflicted. I saw her unease and sighed.

"Fine. I'll put the seatbelt on once we hit the road."

"I can live with that." Cassie turned her key in the ignition. The engine turned over with a grumbling protest. It shuddered to life slowly, but after she gave it a little gas, it was humming cheerfully enough.

The drive to the university was uneventful. Cassie was used to the commute by this point, she had the route down pat. So we spent the drive talking—mostly about the book and what it might contain. But then she glanced in my direction before remembering she couldn't see me.

"That is so weird," she murmured. "What's it like, being invisible?"

I smiled, then realized she couldn't see my face. "Well... you kind of nailed it. It's so weird. Useful, occasionally. But weird. And... every time I cloak myself it reminds me how different I am. That I'm not... you know. Human."

Cassie drove for a moment in silence, mulling this over. "I used to fantasize about being invisible. I guess, in middle school for sure, I just wanted to be left alone. The thought of being able to move through school without attracting any attention at all... It just seemed like heaven." She shrugged, unhappily. "But I guess everybody feels like that sometimes, right?"

"Yeah. I guess... I guess I used to think the same thing. Not exactly being invisible, but there were definitely times when it would've been better to be invisible than to be a target." My mind scrolled through memories of middle school. Amber and Ally had made an art form of excluding girls they deemed weird. Cassie and I had both been in their crosshairs at one point or another. What a difference a few years can make. Now Amber knew my greatest secret. We'd trained side-by-side. There had even been a time when I thought we were becoming friends.

"We're here." Cassie turned off the street into a large parking lot ringed around with aspen trees. Here, in the heart of the older part of our little town, the trees had had close to a century to flourish. In the summer they provided lush canopies of shade. In the winter, their skeletal arms created intricate patterns against the sky. And in the autumn, like now, they painted the landscape in vibrant oranges and golds.

Cassie parked her car in the first empty spot we came to. We got out of the car the same way we climbed in; Cassie left her driver's-side door open while she got her back out of the back, giving me enough time to crawl out. When it was time for us to separate, Cassie glanced at her watch.

"I still think I should skip class," Cassie said. "In case something goes wrong and we need to get out of here fast."

"No. We need to stick to the plan. If anyone checks, you attended class like always." I stood close to her, keeping my voice low. I didn't see anyone nearby, but the campus was full of students and I didn't want to risk being overheard.

Cassie nodded. She didn't do much to disguise her unease, though. "Okay. You have fifty minutes. Then we'll meet back at my car."

"Fifty," I agreed. "Have a good class."

Cassie snorted. "Right, because I'm going to be paying so much attention." She headed off towards the south end of campus.

I made my way to the west edge of the university. I had done my homework last night, poring over an online map of the campus. The vault where the collection from the mission had been transferred was in the archaeology building. I made my way through campus, following a winding flagstone path. The university campus was beautifully kept with xeriscaped borders lining the walkways. Native plants bobbed and danced in the gentle breeze, and a beautiful dappled light filled the campus with a peaceful glow.

I came around a bend in the path and saw the archaeology department. It was an old building, one of the oldest on campus. But they had recently completed an addition that included a high-tech vault. The archaeology department was one of the strongest schools at the university, which wasn't surprising considering the wealth of archaeological sites in the area. Humans had been living in this area for tens of thousands of years. Some of the cultures were so ancient that all we knew about them was what we could glean from a few shards of pottery or the remnants of an old adobe village.

I followed a student through the main doors. Inside, I found a directory that included the room number of the new vault. I set out down the hall in the direction of the vault. I'd been picturing something out of a bank heist movie, a large round door with the wheel built into its face. What I found was much less dramatic.

The vault was less "bank security vault" and more "secured library room." There was a small access room you had to pass through before you could enter the vault. I stood by the door for several minutes before someone approached. He was either a graduate student or a young professor. *Graduate student,* I decided. He had a disheveled look about him that suggested long nights spent in study. He fumbled to pull out a picture ID badge and flashed it at the security guard posted in front of the main vault door. The security guard nodded and hit a button. I heard a deep buzz and the graduate student reached for the door.

I moved quickly, slipping through the door close on his heels. He hesitated for a moment, glancing back over his shoulder. I held my breath, but his gaze passed through me and he gave a small shake of his head. We moved into the vault as one, and the door swung shut behind us. I heard a mechanical lock reengage. I'd be trapped here until someone left. I pushed the thought to the back of my mind; there was plenty to worry about aside from how I'd get out of here. First things first. Time to find what I'd come for.

The vault seemed to contain a few different sections. One was a room full of metal shelves lined with boxes. Each box was labeled with a series of numbers, but no description of what the box contained. The numbers must correspond to some kind of catalog. For the first time, I felt uncertain about this plan. I hadn't expected the vault to be so large. I couldn't exactly look through every box. Somebody was bound to notice if the boxes started sliding themselves off of shelves. Even if I was the only person in the room, there were security cameras everywhere. I passed the room of metal shelves and continued into the heart of the vault. It opened up into a massive room with a soaring ceiling. It was lined with bookcases, but the center of the room contained several large white tables.

Groups of people stood around the tables, hunched over the objects assembled there. From my place at the edge of the room, I saw a few familiar faces. Sandra stood shoulder to shoulder with a Guardsman whose name I did not know. They looked completely at home in the academic setting. One table over, I spotted the strange man we'd seen on the newscast. He lifted a volume from a metal box gingerly. Like the others, he wore white gloves. But unlike the students around him, this man seemed more alarmed than excited. I wondered who exactly he was, and what he knew about this collection of books.

My eyes slid past him and I froze. Marla, one of Clay's spotters, stood across the table from the stranger. If she'd bothered to look up, she would have seen straight through my cloak. With my heart hammering in my chest, I slipped into the room and ducked beneath the closest table. Marla was facing away from this table. I kept my eyes locked onto her back while I tried to decide what to do next.

While I sat there, I heard snippets of conversation from the various teams working in the vault. Two students behind me were focused on an old clay vase.

"No, that's why I contacted the antiquities department. We don't have the right equipment to keep this kind of clay stabilized. Now that it's been exposed to the atmosphere, we need to get it under glass."

"What a pain in the ass. We are going to have to slog all the way across campus every day for the next two months?"

"Hey, that's the glamorous life of an archaeology grad, right?" The students shared a chuckle.

That's when I noticed the book. It was resting on top of the pile of large tomes on the table where Sandra was working. I recognized the distinctive leatherwork instantly. It was the book containing the acolyte ritual. I crawled forward, as far as I could go. Sandra had not seemed to notice the book yet. She was flipping through a different volume with rapt concentration. I glanced back at Marla. She was watching the strange man out of the corner of her eye while pretending to examine a shallow metal bowl.

This might be the best opportunity I would get. One of the students in front of me left the table. I slipped out from under my hiding place, keeping low. I made my way quickly to the table where Sandra was working, hiding behind another pair of grad students before Marla could spot me. This wasn't a great place to hide, I was in the middle of the floor. Anyone walking by could trip right over me. I had to move fast.

"Sandra, take a look at this." Marla's voice cut through the quiet conversations of the vault. Sandra looked up, turning away from me. I held my breath. The students right in front of me turned, too, curious. I moved, surging toward the table and snaking the book off the pile. I drew it close, letting my wings render it invisible along with the rest of me. Well, invisible to all but Marla. But she was leaning over her table, shoulder to shoulder with Sandra. It was time to go.

I turned toward the hallway leading back to the vault's entrance. I'd only made it a few feet before one of the students noticed the book was missing.

"Hey, did you take a little book off this pile?" He glanced around, ducking to check under the table. I shrank back, even though there was no chance he'd be able to see me.

"What?" His companion looked at him with a blank expression.

"It was right here. Leather binding, elaborate tooling… you didn't see it?" The grad student's voice was growing more strained by the moment. "Prof. Jenkins asked me to catalog it for her."

"I didn't move it, if that's what you're asking." The other student straightened, his tone defensive.

"Just, help me look for it." The panicking grad student walked over to the next table. "Hey, did any of you guys move a book from that table?"

I looked back at Sandra and Marla. The commotion was drawing attention from the other grad students. The strange man took the opportunity to slip out of the room, adjusting his jacket carefully. Another thief? What was he taking? I bit back a hiss of frustration. There was nothing I could do about it now. I had my own book to steal.

Marla and Sandra traded a quick look, then I saw Sandra slip a pair of books under her voluminous sweater. Sandra and Marla made their excuses and left. No one suspected them, as they'd been at another table when the book went missing. As Marla vanished from sight, I straightened, relieved. With the spotter gone, I could stand up again.

My legs were cramped and it felt good to stretch them. I found a place to stand between two bookcases, out of the way.

The grad students were soon all caught up in the search for the missing book, combing through piles of artifacts.

I checked my watch. I had 10 minutes to make it back to Cassie's car in time for us to get back to school before the end of lunch. I counted to 100 to give Marla enough of head start to minimize the chance that she might see me emerging from the vault. While I was waiting, I overheard the grad student describing the book.

"It was full of apocryphal mythology. Old Mesopotamian stuff. Stories about the Lilith figure. It was some kind of latter-day documentation of ancient Lilith worshiping rituals or something." He shook his head, miserable. "I've never seen a book like this. And Prof. Jenkins, it's exactly the kind of thing she's made her career studying. She's going to kill me."

"Lilith? As in Adam's first wife Lilith?" One of the other grad students joined the conversation, curious. Her eyes shone with a newly ignited interest. "One of my friends had a roommate who was really into Lilith last year. She got crazy obsessed with some old lady who was telling women to reclaim their power."

"Yeah, this book seems to indicate that the monks who wrote it believed Lilith would return to claim the world unless they could stop her."

Adrenaline shot through my system. I took a step closer, forgetting Cassie for the moment. People were gathering closer, curiosity piqued.

"The best part?" The grad student smiled, shaking his head. "It had hand-written notes all over it from some fifteenth or sixteenth century monk. I mean, he was probably certifiable, writing down incantations and counter-rituals. It was incredibly detailed stuff. Delusional, but super interesting."

I felt my hands tighten on the book. Every molecule in my body was urging me to run. I had the key in my hands. But it would do us no good unless I got it home.

Cassie was waiting by the car when I returned. She looked up, hearing my steps.

"Braedyn?"

"Let's get out of here." I looked down. I'd been holding the book so tightly my fingers were starting to ache.

Cassie let out the breath she'd been holding. I must have been later than I'd anticipated. She'd been freaking out. I felt a twinge of guilt. Cassie opened the car door and I dove inside. She didn't speak again until we were three blocks away from the university.

"So? Did you get it?"

"I got it. I got it, Cassie." I couldn't keep the excitement from my voice. I told Cassie the whole story. She listened, her eyes getting wider with each passing minute. By the time we pulled into the school parking lot, Cassie was shaking her head.

"Let's hope it was worth it," she murmured. She glanced at her watch and sighed. "No time for lunch. Fifth period is going to start any minute."

"Right."

Cassie and I had fifth period English with Lucas. Missing lunch was one thing, but missing class would be much harder to explain. Cassie stood lookout while I found a secluded spot against the back of the auditorium to uncloak myself where no one would see.

We made it to English with two minutes to spare. Lucas looked up as we entered. He gave me a smile full of empathy.

"Did you get anything to eat?"

"Not exactly." I shrugged. "I mean, I had a bottle of water in my bag, so that's something, right?"

"Wrong." Lucas shot a furtive glance at the head of the class where Ms. Barnhouse was putting her notes in order. "Here. I thought you might need something." Lucas slipped me a bag of trail mix.

"My hero." I looked up into his eyes, feeling a swell of gratitude. I ripped the package open, spilling a handful of the mix into my palm. "What would I do without you?"

Lucas shrugged happily. "Waste away to nothing, I'm guessing."

More guilt wove its way into my chest. I gave Lucas a faint smile before eating the handful of trail mix. I savored the salty sweet mixture. I hadn't realized how hungry I was until this moment.

The bell rang, signaling the start of class, and I lowered the trail mix to my lap. Ms. Barnhouse turned to face the class.

"Okay. *A Picture of Dorian Gray*. Everyone finished the reading, yes?" She glanced around the classroom before turning to the board. "First thoughts?"

"Oh…"

I turned, hearing the startled fear in Cassie's voice. Blood streamed from her nose onto her desk.

"Cassie?" Ms. Barnhouse reacted, grabbing a box of tissues and rushing to Cassie's side. "Tilt your head forward. Here. Hold this to your nose." She spent a few moments huddled next to Cassie, getting the bleeding under control. The class exchanged glances of curiosity, revulsion, empathy. When Ms. Barnhouse was satisfied she'd done all she could to help Cassie she looked up. Her eyes caught on me. "Braedyn, would you mind walking Cassie to the nurse's office?"

"Of course not. Come on, Cas." I gathered Cassie's things and held out my hand. Cassie took it, looking mortified.

"It's just a bloody nose," she said. "I've been getting them lately. My mom thinks it's the dry air, or maybe allergies."

"My sister's getting them, too," Missy said from the front of the class. "It must be going around." She gave Cassie a friendly smile, but her words struck ice into my heart. Missy's sister and Cassie shared more than bloody noses. They'd both been acolytes initiated by Idris.

I steered Cassie out of the classroom, doing my best to hide my alarm from her. I needn't have worried, though. Cassie was completely enmeshed in her own embarrassment.

"Why does this keep happening to me? I'm bleeding like a stuck pig," she moaned. "It's bad enough when it happens at home. But now…" Cassie pulled the tissues away from her nose. The blood seemed to have slowed to a trickle, but her mouth and chin were covered. "How bad is it?" Her eyes studied my face, looking for any reaction.

"Cassie, how long have you been getting bloody noses?"

Cassie ducked her head, caught. "Since the beginning of the summer," she admitted.

"Since the ritual, you mean?" My voice came out sharper than I intended it to. "You and Carrie."

"Maybe it's a coincidence?" But even she didn't sound like she thought that was a remote possibility.

I didn't argue with her. We walked across campus to the administration building, and I saw Cassie safely to the nurse's office. She gave me an unhappy wave when I left her to return to English class. Walking back, I let myself feel the rage that had been building since Missy mentioned her sister's bloody noses.

I knew it beyond a doubt; Idris had done something to Cassie and the others. I was going to find out what.

Cassie had managed to talk the nurse out of sending her home or calling her mom. She returned to English just a few minutes before the end of class. Ms. Barnhouse looked surprised to see her, but didn't make a big deal out of it.

Royal found us during passing period. He'd heard about Cassie's bloody nose. When Royal learned that Cassie had been keeping her bloody noses from us for months he grew uncharacteristically quiet. When he finally spoke, his voice sounded clipped with tension.

"Library. After last period." It wasn't a question. Cassie and I exchanged a look, but nodded.

A few minutes after last bell, we met up in one of the study rooms on the ground floor of the library. Royal reported that he'd managed to keep Lucas oblivious to the fact that I had left campus. I filled him on what I'd learned, and then I pulled the book out of my backpack and set it on the table.

"That's it?" Royal eyed the book, as if afraid it might bite.

"That's it."

We stared at it for a long moment in silence. Then Royal reached out and flipped it open. The pages were filled with beautiful calligraphy—which was entirely in Latin. I could pick out a few words here and there, but I wasn't the Latin scholar.

"Well?" Cassie watched Royal, eager for his opinion. "Can you read it?"

"I think so." Royal met her eyes with a weak smile. "Looks like the Latin classes will be good for something other than making my father happy after all."

He flipped through the book until Cassie gave a startled gasp. He'd opened the book to the illustrations I'd seen on the news; the depictions of the ritual Cassie had participated in.

"Wait… is this about the acolytes?" Cassie turned on me. Her expression looked caught between surprise and anxiety.

I took a breath and let it out. "Cassie, there's something I have to tell you." Reluctantly, I filled both Cassie and Royal in on what I'd learned from Elyia. Cassie didn't take the news very well.

"What do you mean, tied to Lilith? What does that mean?" Cassie reached for the book, flipping through the pages. "I can't… Royal?"

Royal met my eyes. "Don't worry, Cas. I'll have this thing translated in no time." He put a hand on the book, sliding it gently out of Cassie's grip and into his backpack.

"The important thing," I said, trying to calm Cassie's frayed nerves, "is that there's a way to break whatever connection exists between you. I'll figure it out. No matter what it takes."

Cassie nodded, but she licked her lips nervously. "How much danger am I in?"

I wanted to comfort her, to allay her fears, but anything I might have said would have been a lie. "That's what we have to figure out."

Cassie blanched, and I felt my stomach twist in response.

"So what do we know?" Royal glanced from Cassie to me. The question wasn't an accusation. I knew Royal well enough to know he wanted all the facts. The problem was, I had no facts to give him.

"All I know is we have to keep this book out of the Guard's hands." I met Royal's eyes. He studied my face, then nodded in grim understanding.

We had to protect this book. Cassie's life might depend on it.

11

As hard as it was to let the book out of my sight, I knew it was safer with Royal. If I took it home with me, it would only be a matter of time before Zoe or one of the others discovered it. Add to that the fact that Royal was the only one among us who stood much of a chance of being able to read and understand it, and there wasn't really any other logical option. Still, I felt a twinge leaving the book behind, knowing it was our best hope of figuring out what was happening to Cassie—and what we'd have to do to help her.

I slipped out of the library and made my way toward the school parking lot. It was late enough that Lucas was probably hanging out by my car, worried that he'd missed me in the halls. After all, I was his ride home. I was getting tired of inventing white lies to explain my absences and late arrivals. But when the school parking lot came into view, the excuses I'd been turning over in my mind evaporated.

I saw the police car first, lights still flashing though the siren was silent. Two uniformed officers were speaking with headmaster Fiedler, while a third was handcuffing Lucas's wrists behind his back. A crowd was gathering, drawn by the spectacle. Lucas's jaw was clamped tightly shut. His face had a strange, closed look about it. But when he saw me, his eyebrows lifted and for a moment he looked vulnerable and scared. I pushed through the crowd and made a beeline for Lucas.

"I refuse to believe there wasn't a better way for you to handle this." Headmaster Fiedler kept his voice low, but his eyes were practically sparking with fury. "This school is private property, these students are my charges."

The police officer addressing headmaster Fiedler was a fit, middle-aged man. "As I explained, sir, we obtained a warrant for this young man's arrest." He rested one hand on the butt of his service pistol casually. "But in future, if you like, I'll make sure to stop by your office before performing my duty." While his tone was civil enough, there was something underlying his words that made it clear no part of him actually cared what Fiedler thought.

"In future? In future?" Fiedler's eyes narrowed. "Given that this is the first time a student has ever been arrested on my campus, you'll understand if I hope I never see you again, Officer Wess." Officer Wess nodded his head slightly. Headmaster Fiedler noticed me standing nearby. "Braedyn, go wait with the others."

"I don't understand. What's happening? What do they think he did?" My eyes sought out Lucas once more. He wasn't talking, but his expression was grim.

"I'm sorry, I'm not at liberty to say," Officer Wess said.

"They think I vandalized the old mission." Lucas's voice was strained, but it carried. Kids traded shocked looks behind us.

Officer Wess frowned. He nodded his head toward my car. "We also have a partial plate match for this car. Can I assume, based on your interest in the suspect, that you and he are dating?"

Before I could open my mouth to respond, Headmaster Fiedler stepped forward.

"If you want to question my students, I suggest contacting their legal guardians." Headmaster Fiedler put a hand on my shoulder. "Unless you have a warrant for Ms. Murphy's arrest as well?"

Officer Wess frowned, his eyes sliding from Fiedler to me.

"No? Then I'll thank you not to interrogate her on school grounds. You don't have to talk to them without a parent present, Braedyn." His eyes shifted to Lucas. "That goes for you as well, son. As far as I know, we still operate under the expectation of due process in this country."

Officer Wess gave us a faint smile, devoid of any amusement. "Let's get him down to the station."

The officer who'd cuffed Lucas led him by the elbow into the back of the waiting squad car. Lucas climbed awkwardly into the back seat. When he was settled, the police officer closed the door on him and got into the driver's seat. Lucas found me with his eyes, staring out of the back of the police car. Now I understood the worry I'd seen in his face. We'd been out to the old mission on more than one occasion. It was possible some stranger had seen him, had remembered part of my license plate. Or maybe it was Seth, messing with us in an attempt to show his power, or derail our investigation into the acolytes.

Whoever it was, they'd have to show up to the police station to identify Lucas, right? As the police cars pulled out of the parking lot, Fiedler turned toward me.

"Do you know anything about this?" His eyes searched my face. He looked genuinely concerned for Lucas.

"No, sir." I shook my head quickly. "I have to call his sister."

He didn't try to stop me as I fished my keys out of my pocket. I glanced back at the crowd and saw Cassie and Royal's faces among the onlookers. I couldn't spare the time to fill them in. I slid into the driver seat and engaged the engine. Before pulling out of the parking lot, I hit my speed dial for Gretchen's phone. It rang and rang before going to voice mail. I wondered if Lucas had already contacted her. Maybe they were talking right now and she just wasn't picking up my call. I ended the call, then tried Dad. Again, the phone rang before going to voice mail. Frustrated, I tossed the cell phone into the passenger seat and slipped the car into reverse. The drive to the police station took only 10 minutes, but it felt like hours had passed since Lucas's arrest.

The police station had recently undergone a renovation—it had made the news a while back for the design. The walls were clean brown stucco, and a neat flagstone path led the way to the front doors. It looked nice enough that you might mistake it for an office building instead of the police station. I left my car in the parking lot and raced up the flagstone path. The lobby of the police office was mostly quiet, with a few people waiting on benches across from a set of glass security doors. There was an officer on duty at the front desk. I approached her, trying to keep my voice from shaking.

"My friend, Lucas Mitchell. I think he was just brought in?"

The police officer kept her face neutral. "I'm afraid I can't divulge that information to a nonfamily member."

"Well, can you tell me if his sister, Gretchen Mitchell has been notified?"

The police officer shook her head, lips pursed. "Why don't you have a seat. Try to contact your friend's sister." She nodded her head toward the benches behind me. I stumbled towards one of them, sinking onto the seat while my hands fumbled to dial my phone again.

I made over a dozen attempts to reach Gretchen or Dad, but after leaving several messages saying basically the same thing, I gave up and pocketed my phone. I let out a startled gasp when someone sat next to me, despite the empty benches surrounding us. Then I saw who it was, and my surprise morphed into a cold fear.

"I understand you took a little field trip today." Clay's warm drawl jolted me out of my stupor.

"What?" I stared at him, uncomprehending.

"The vault at the university. Marla saw you grab a book off one of the research tables." Clay picked at one of his cuticles before meeting my gaze. The smile he gave me sent a fresh chill coursing down my spine. "Was any part of my warning unclear?"

"I... I don't..." But then the realization bloomed inside my mind. "This was you? You arranged for Lucas to be arrested?"

"If you want Lucas released, you'll tell me what you took." Not even a flicker of shame crossed his face. For a long moment I could do nothing but stare at him in horror. Clay shifted position in his seat, looking like he had all the time in the world. "Did they tell you the charges? He's facing felony vandalism. Lucas could be looking at 10 years in prison."

"A... a felony? This is Lucas we're talking about. *Lucas*. I thought he was your protégé."

"And yet, here we are." Clay's eyes hardened. "You're forcing my hand, Braedyn. I like Lucas, I do. But if it comes down to a choice between protecting Lucas and doing everything in my power to defeat Lilith, I'm sorry. The boy is gonna lose that fight."

"Terence Clay." The officer manning the front desk stood up, glancing into the waiting room. "Is a Mr. Terence Clay here yet?"

Clay glanced at me. He looked completely relaxed. "In case you're wondering, I don't bluff. Just like I don't make idle threats. I told you what would happen if you gave me any reason to doubt your loyalty. Well, sweetheart, welcome to the consequences." Clay stood and raised his hand, drawing the attention of the police officer at the front desk.

I caught his hand before he got two steps away. He glanced back at me, unhurried. "I took a book." The words came out of me in a rush, low and urgent. My mind spun, spilling out the story before I had time to think it through. "I knew Sandra and her team wouldn't be able to take very many books out of the vault. I figured, going in cloaked would give me an advantage."

"Why not announce yourself to Marla, then?" Clay scrutinized me. I could tell he didn't believe me. "Why hide yourself from her?"

"I panicked. I didn't know she'd be there. If I had, I would have consulted with her before hand. Once I was there, I figured it would look suspicious no matter what I said." This last part, at least, had the benefit of being true.

"Something we can agree on," Clay said. He still did not look convinced.

"I swear. I wanted to prove myself to you, and I thought this was a way to do that."

"You expect me to believe you meant to hand over that book you took?"

"Yes!" I poured out all of my urgency and fear and shame into this one word, hoping the intensity of my emotion would do enough to disguise the lie. Clay hesitated, eyeing me with uncertainty.

"Where is it?" Clay's eyes flicked over to my backpack, resting on the seat beside us.

"I… I was on my way to get it from my locker when I saw the police arresting Lucas." I swallowed, hoping Clay mistook my shaking voice for the conviction of truth.

"Mr. Clay? They're waiting for you." The police officer frowned at us, impatient.

Clay considered me for another heartbeat. "Wait here. Lucas will need a ride home. But Braedyn, once we're done here, I'll expect the book within the hour." With that, he straightened his jacket and strode across the waiting room to the security doors. The police officer buzzed him through, then led him into the bowels of the station and out of sight.

I picked up my cell phone, fingers fumbling on the lock screen. When I had the phone unlocked, I hit the speed dial for Royal.

"I need the book." I lowered my voice, turning away from the front desk just in case.

"What? I haven't even had time to open it yet."

"Clay knows I have it, Royal. He wants it. Now."

Royal answered me slowly. He sounded shocked. "I thought the whole idea was to keep the book out of Clay's hands."

My voice caught, but I forced myself to speak against the rising swell of emotion. "It was Clay. Clay had Lucas arrested. If I don't give him the book..." My throat closed against a sob.

"What about Cassie?"

"We have time to help Cassie, but Lucas... Please help me, Royal. They could convict him of a felony! He'll have that on his record forever. Forget college, or finding a decent place to live or a decent job or..."

Royal heard the rising panic in my voice. "Okay, just take a deep breath. I'll bring the book to you. Where are you?"

"No, you can't bring it to me. Just... Could you park around the corner from my house? I'll come find you. Just stay in your car. I don't want anyone to see you." Royal didn't sound happy about it, but he agreed.

About 10 minutes later, Lucas emerged from behind the security doors looking shell-shocked. Clay followed a few steps behind. When Clay saw me, he gave me a broad, friendly smile.

"I imagine you'd like a few moments alone with your girlfriend after the events of this afternoon." Clay clapped a hand on Lucas's shoulder and gave it a friendly squeeze. "I'll see you at home." And then Clay was gone, striding past us and out the front doors of the police station.

I turned back to Lucas. He swallowed, trying to get his bearings. I caught his hands, and felt the touch like an electric spark. His eyes focused on my face, and he opened his mouth to say something. A tear slipped out the corner of my eye. Lucas saw it. Instead of speaking, he reached up with a thumb and gingerly brushed the tear away. I leaned into his palm.

Lucas let out a soft breath. I heard the longing in his sigh; I felt it too. My lips parted, and for one frozen moment, we hesitated. Then we came together, seeking one another wordlessly. His lips found mine, warm and firm. I ran my hands up his chest and encircled my arms around his neck, clinging to him. As though by holding him close, I could protect him from all the threats that awaited us the moment we walked out of this station. When we finally drew apart, breathless, I felt the weight of anxiety crushing back into me.

"Lucas..." But what could I say? Would he even believe me if I told him Clay had had him arrested because of me? Lucas misunderstood my fear. He smiled.

"Don't worry. I knew it was going to be all right." He reached up and brushed a lock of hair back from my forehead. "I had complete faith that Clay would get me out."

I stared at Lucas, fighting the urge to tell him everything. Anger simmered through my core, threatening to boil over. But I was on the clock. I had an hour to get the book into Clay's hands. This would have to wait. "I parked outside. We should probably get home."

Lucas caught my hand, stopping my flight. "Hold on. What's wrong? Is it Fiedler? I'm not getting expelled, am I?"

I turned back to face him, struggling. Could I keep the truth from him now? Now that he'd been placed in Clay's crosshairs on my account? "Stop working for Clay."

Lucas released my hand, stepping back in confused surprise. "Why the hell would I do that?" His cheeks flushed.

I bit my lip, choosing my words carefully. "What if Clay isn't the man you think he is?"

A sudden exhaustion seemed to descend on Lucas. He let out a long breath. "I know he's got his own way of doing things, but there's a lot more to him than you'd think. The guy you see at morning meetings, that's only one part of Clay."

"Lucas, I've seen more sides to Clay than you think." I drew a breath, suddenly determined to tell him what Clay had done to Dad. But before I could voice the words, Lucas took my hand again.

"Wait. Don't judge him yet." Lucas dropped his eyes. "I'm not going to say he hasn't made any mistakes," Lucas shook his head, "but he's struggling to restore order and honor to the Guard."

"Honor?" I shook my head, battling the urge to laugh at the irony.

"I know you disagree with some of his methods." Lucas met my gaze. "I'm just asking you to try and understand."

I shook my head again. "Lucas, whatever you see in that man…"

"That's the thing, Braedyn. It's not just about Clay. I finally have a place in the Guard. Hale… I loved Hale, but he treated me like a kid. I never belonged, not really, not until Clay gave me a propose."

"As his assistant?" I couldn't keep the derision of my voice. It was a mistake. Lucas winced, stung. I instantly felt regret for the harsh words. "Wait, that came out wrong. I don't mean you're not valuable…"

"*Aide de Camp* might sound like a stupid nothing title, but it's not." Lucas shoved his hands into his pockets. For a long moment he didn't meet my eyes. "Clay talks to me. He confides in me. He asks me for my opinions. And he listens."

"I… I didn't know that." I tried to disguise my astonishment, but Lucas read it in my face. He shook his head and looked away, offended.

"What did you think 'confidential assistant' meant?" When he turned back to me, his gaze was cold. "I keep Clay's secrets."

Whatever hopes I'd had of turning Lucas against Clay died on the vine. Clay had given him something I couldn't, something not even Hale had been able to provide: a father figure.

Lucas wasn't likely to forgive the person who damaged that relationship. Royal, Cassie, and I would have to figure out how to sever the bond connecting Lilith to her acolytes on our own.

12

I found Royal's car parked against the curb around the corner from my house. Towering aspens shaded the street with the last of their autumn leaves. I walked through drifts of fallen leaves, my steps making a dry brushing, crunching sound. As I watched, a sudden breeze teased out a few more leaves from the canopy overhead. They swirled and drifted, riding eddies of wind to the ground. Royal couldn't have been parked here for long; there were no leaves resting on his car, though the leaves were scattered over everything around us.

I glanced back down the street, checking for any unwelcome eyes. But if Clay was having me followed right now, my watchers were good at hiding. I crossed into the street and opened the passenger side door of Royal's car. I slipped inside and quickly pulled the door shut.

Royal eyed me, deeply troubled. "Are you sure about this?"

"No." I looked down at my hands resting on my lap. They were still trembling. I clasped them tightly together. "But I don't see any alternative. Clay is… ruthless. I don't know what else to do."

Royal's frown deepened. "Fine. But I'm not quitting." He pulled something out of his backpack and tossed it into my lap—a stack of copy paper fastened with a binder clip.

"What is this? Where's the…?" But then I turned the first page of the stack and realized what I held my hands. Page after page was covered with black and white calligraphy, illustrations, margin notes. "You copied the whole thing?" I looked up, charged with new hope. "Why didn't I think of that?"

"Well, your boyfriend was facing hard time." Royal smiled and shrugged. "You weren't thinking clearly. It happens to the best of us."

I reached across the car and caught Royal in a tight hug. "Thank you. Thank you, Royal."

Royal chuckled, then tapped my arm lightly. "Can't breathe."

I released him, turning my attention back to the copy in my hands. I flipped through it. The copies were slightly muddy, legible, but just barely. Royal saw my concern and sighed.

"I know. I messed with the settings, trying to get the cleanest possible copy, but this was the best I could do on short notice. That book is old, some of the ink has bled through, and the pages themselves are kind of dark. I tried to up the contrast, but then the notes in the margins started to fade, so…"

"You did great, Royal." I caught his hand and gave it a warm squeeze, hoping this was enough to convey the rush of love and gratitude I felt for him.

Royal met my eyes, looking suddenly uncomfortable. "Okay. You probably want this." He pulled the book out of his backpack and handed it to me. I took it gingerly. "How is he, by the way? Lucas?"

I hesitated, playing over our last discussion. "He thinks Clay saved him."

"Hold on. You didn't tell him it was Clay that had him arrested in the first place?" Royal shifted in his seat, facing me directly. "Braedyn…"

"He practically worships the man." The words tasted like ashes in my mouth. "You should have seen his face when I asked him to stop working for Clay. It's… Royal, I'm afraid if I ask him to choose between me and Clay, he will side with Clay."

"That's insane. Lucas loves you. He just met this guy…"

"It's the final battle, Royal. This is something Lucas has been training for since his brother's death. Clay has promised him revenge. It's because of Clay that the Lilitu who murdered Lucas's brother was caught." I felt my cheeks growing hot. Royal sat back. I took a deep breath. "I'm just saying, I think the situation is more complicated than either of us want to acknowledge."

"Apparently." Royal stared unhappily out the window, his gaze unfocused.

I leaned back in my seat. "I hate this. But I think we need to assume that Lucas is Clay's eyes and ears at school. If he catches sight of you with that copy of the book…"

Royal nodded grimly. "Yeah, I worked that out myself. Don't worry. I'll make sure Lucas never sets eyes on this thing. What about you?"

I looked at Royal, unsure how to answer. Royal studied me, growing concerned.

"I mean, Clay knows you stole the book. Are you in trouble?"

"I don't know. I think… I think I managed to convince him I did it for the Guard." I looked down at my hands, still cradling the ancient volume. The truth was, I couldn't read Clay. I couldn't tell if he believed me or if he was biding his time until I was no longer useful. I couldn't tell if he valued Lucas at all, or if Lucas was just one more pressure point Clay could push to keep me in line. I didn't share any of this with Royal. Why give him one more thing to worry about? I needed him focused on the book. Cassie needed him focused on the book.

"Just be careful." Royal looked like he wanted to say more, but instead of talking, he bit his lip.

I nodded, though I couldn't make any promises. It was hard to know how to be careful when I didn't fully understand the nature—or number—of the threats I faced.

A few minutes later, I ascended the front steps of the Guard's house clutching the book to my chest. Everything about this felt wrong. I hesitated on the threshold, but the hour was up. With a deep breath of resignation, I opened the door.

Clay was seated behind his desk. Lucas stood to his left, scribbling some notes onto a pad. They both looked up as I entered.

"Ah, Braedyn. Come in." Clay stood and gestured for me to come forward.

I walked into the room, forcing myself to cross the distance between us. Like a wooden puppet, I jerked my hands out, offering the book. Clay took it and set it on his desk. His eyes never left my face.

"I'm very glad to see I can trust you to live up to your word."

"What is this?" Lucas glanced at the book on the desk. His eyes returned to my face, full of questions.

"Braedyn managed to retrieve this for us from the university vault today." Something flashed through Clay's expression—something malicious and triumphant—before he turned toward Lucas. "She didn't tell you?"

"No." Lucas forced a smile for Clay's benefit, but I could see the tension in his shoulders. "It was kind of a crazy afternoon. It probably slipped her mind." Lucas glanced back at me, studying my face.

"I'm sure you're right." Clay's tone was warm enough that it sounded sincere, but I heard the mocking undertone that Lucas appeared to miss. "Come on, Braedyn. There's someone I'd like you to meet." Clay walked around the side of the desk and led me toward Thane's office door, set into the wall at the far end of the living room. With an afterthought, Clay turned back to Lucas. "Bring that book, would you?"

Clay rapped his knuckles against the closed door. A moment later the latch turned and Thane opened it. Beyond Thane, I could see Sandra speaking with the strange man we'd first spotted in the news broadcast. He was tall and broad shouldered, with a full head of dark brown hair only lightly dappled with silver. I gauged his age to be around 40, but he had the kind of face that suggested experience beyond his years.

"Sandra, Braedyn's brought the book we've been waiting for." Clay stretched his hand out without looking and Lucas placed the volume in it. Clay tossed the book to Sandra. She snatched it out of the air, startled. The stranger frowned at Clay, then swiveled his gaze to me.

"Why was a child in possession of this volume?"

Sandra looked up from examining the book in her hands. "That is a very good question."

"Braedyn, this is Father Jerome. Jerome, this young lady is Alan Murphy's daughter." Clay put a hand on my shoulder casually. I had to fight the urge to shrink away from him. "Father Jerome is something of a colleague of ours."

I studied Father Jerome, surprised. "You're a Guardsman?"

"No." Father Jerome straightened. If anything, his expression grew even grimmer.

"Father Jerome is a priest. He's a member of a very old religious order, the Order of Saint Marcel." Clay watched Father Jerome with a faint smile.

"Saint Marcel?" I wasn't sure if that name was supposed to mean anything to me.

Father Jerome's eyes flicked from Clay back to me. "It was my order that established the mission in this town five centuries ago. Once we learned of its destruction, I was sent to recover whatever I could from the wreckage." His tone sharpened. "Of course, that was before our library was exposed to public scrutiny."

"You... You know what kind of books this library contained?" I shot a quick glance at Sandra. She inclined her head toward Father Jerome, deferring to him.

"I do. And I take it from your question that you do as well." Father Jerome turned back to Clay. "There are a handful of rare volumes I need to reclaim for my order for which no other copies remain in existence. Most of the books contained in that library were redundant volumes, volumes we are resigned to losing to the university. I understand there may be a few volumes of interest to you as well. I am willing to offer them to you in payment for your assistance in helping me reclaim the *lamia* volumes."

I glanced at Lucas, standing just behind me. "*Lamia*?" I whispered. Recognition brought with it a prickle of goose bumps cascading down my arms. "That's Latin for Lilitu, right?"

Sandra turned her attention to me. "Technically, it's Latin for vampire, though the term was used interchangeably for both Lilitu and vampires until the early seventeenth century."

Father Jerome nodded once in acknowledgment. "You Guardsmen have your monster, and we have ours."

"Wait." Lucas took a step forward, crowding against me in the doorway. He sounded stunned. "Hang on. You're saying... You're saying *vampires* are real?"

I couldn't help it; a mirthless chuckle escaped my lips. Lucas glanced at me, surprised. "I bet that's how I looked the first time you told me about Lilitu." Sandra ducked her head, hiding a small smile.

Lucas swallowed. I watched him as he struggled to adjust his worldview to accommodate this news. "Right. Vampires. Anything else we should know about?"

"Most mythology has some basis in reality," Sandra said, turning her attention to Lucas.

"That lesson will have to wait. We have a limited amount of time to secure the missing volumes before they are fully integrated into the university system." Father Jerome eyed Lucas and me with undisguised irritation. "I'd really rather not leave the state with the FBI on my tail for antiquity theft."

Sandra pursed her lips. "*Lamia*, you say?" She turned to a small stack of books on the table behind her. "I actually think I may have grabbed one of those on my last visit. Ah." Sandra turned back around, holding a small book with a wine-red leather cover. "Is this one of the volumes on your list?"

Father Jerome took the slender book and turned it over in his hands almost reverently. He opened the book and scanned the first few pages. "Yes. Yes, this book is on my list."

"We're happy to help you," Clay said. "And we'd be most obliged if you could identify, or possibly list, any of the books from the mission that might contain information on Lilitu."

"Of course." Father Jerome slipped the wine red book into his satchel. "I have a catalog of the mission's volumes. It was last updated in the late seventeen hundreds, but with any luck, the collection has remained relatively undisturbed since that time. Considering the amount of books discovered in the vault, I have high hopes that many if not all the books we seek can be recovered." Father Jerome's eyes slid back to me. "And, of course, Ms. Murphy has already brought you one of them."

Genuine surprise flashed across Clay's face for a moment. But then his mask was back in place, and he turned to me with a friendly smile. "Is that so? You'll have to tell me how you knew which book to retrieve."

I smiled weakly and ducked my head. When no one spoke, I looked up. Clay was studying me, waiting. "Oh, you mean now?"

"That would be one hell of a coincidence, if you just happened to pick up a book concerning the Lilitu out of over a hundred of inconsequential volumes." Clay's smile did not alter, but his eyes glittered with an unfriendly focus.

"Not a coincidence." I cleared my throat and turned to face Father Jerome. "I saw the book on the news." Alarm shot through my system. I knew it was dangerous, coming this close to the truth, but it was also the only way to get Clay off my back. "There were some illustrations, it looked interesting."

Father Jerome's jaw tensed. "Yes, I saw the broadcast. It would have been better for all of us if that footage had never found its way into the hands of a reporter."

Clay gave him a tight smile. "No use mending the barn door now that the horses have fled."

Jerome nodded, then turned to Sandra and inclined his head. "If you'll excuse me, I need to report back to my superior. I look forward to working with you." He offered a hand to Clay, who shook it firmly. "I will get the catalog to you as quickly as I can. I assume you are fluent in Latin?"

"Not me, father." Clay chuckled richly. "But we have two excellent archivists who probably spend more time reading Latin than they do English."

Father Jerome hesitated in the doorway, unsettled. "Forgive me for asking, but you do realize the Seal has been destroyed?"

Clay's eyes hardened. "Yes, we are aware of that."

"Then you are aware that Lilith is preparing her endgame as we speak." Father Jerome glanced from Sandra back to Clay. When Clay nodded, Father Jerome shook his head. "Given your time constraints, it may be difficult to work through all the volumes regarding the Lilitu with just two translators. Let me put a call into the head of my order. We could have half a dozen translators out to you in a matter of days."

Clay clapped a hand on Father Jerome's shoulder and gave him a tight smile. "Why don't you let me worry about that. You and Sandra just focus on getting the important books back." Clay turned, gesturing toward the living room. It was a clear dismissal. Father Jerome's eyes tightened, but he offered no resistance. He simply ducked his head in farewell, and strode through the living room toward the front door.

"How long do you think he'll remain in town?" Clay asked Sandra quietly, moments after Jerome had left.

"Until he's satisfied that he's recovered the books he's seeking for his order." Sandra was staring after Father Jerome with a thoughtful look.

Clay frowned. "Let's see what we can do to help him on his way, then."

Sandra seemed to come back to the moment. "Right. Braedyn, what was it about the illustrations that you found so interesting?" They turned to me, waiting.

"I thought I saw… Wings." It was an outright lie, but Sandra nodded thoughtfully.

She opened the book and flipped through the first few pages. I saw her eyes scanning the calligraphy.

"Can you read it?" It was an effort to keep the terror out of my voice. If Sandra could unlock this book's secrets before Royal had had a chance to work through it… I swallowed. We just didn't know what it would say about the acolytes, or their bond with Lilith.

"Hm?" Sandra looked up, distracted. "Oh. Yes. You have good instincts. There've been two mentions of Lilitu on this page alone. I'll be interested to see what other books show up on Jerome's catalog list." Sandra flipped through a few more pages, then set the book aside. She turned to Clay with a slight shrug. "I'll look through it."

Clay nodded, then glanced at me. "Good work today, Braedyn. You're free to go." There was something almost predatory in the smile he gave me. He didn't have to finish the sentence for me to know what he meant. I was free to go, *for now*. "Lucas, would you mind joining me for a meeting with Sutherland."

"No problem." Lucas turned his attention to Clay, and I took the opportunity to leave.

I wanted to run, but I kept my steps measured. For three years now I had served the Guard. I had tried to be a good soldier. I had fought for this cause, on the side of humanity. But the more I saw of Clay's methods, the less I trusted him. I couldn't push Karayan's words out of my mind; *I can't be a part of the Guard if Clay's in charge.*

But me? I couldn't leave the Guard, not now. Not until I knew what kind of danger Cassie was in—from Lilith… and from Clay.

"If you put this much effort into all your classes, you would be valedictorian by graduation." Cassie dropped into the seat beside Royal. We had taken up residence in one of the study rooms of the library, meeting here every day for the last few weeks. November had settled in and the sky outside was dark with building clouds. There was no snow promised in the forecast, but Mother Nature had taken us by surprise before.

Royal looked up from the smudged photocopy. He blinked, bleary-eyed. "What?"

"Nothing." Cassie smiled at him, and shot me a concerned look. "So, how's it going?"

"Slow. It's going slow." Royal sat back, setting his pen down. He ran both hands through his hair, scratching his scalp. He looked exhausted. "There's a lot of stuff in here about the ritual. But it's stuff we already know, because you lived through it. Only I'm afraid to skip over anything, just in case there's something important I might miss." Royal gestured at the spiral notebook already half-filled with his notes. "Also, I'm only sure about 80% of my translation. It's… It's not exactly conversational Latin."

"Um… Is there any such thing as conversational Latin, it being a dead language and all?" Cassie tried to win a smile from Royal, but he was not amused. "Sorry."

Royal sighed. "No, I'm sorry. I'm not the greatest company right now. I just can't help but feel like there's something in this book that we have to know, that we have to find out before the Guard does, and I'm the only one who reads Latin. So basically, if you're in danger, I am the one who is responsible for keeping you safe…"

"Royal, that's not…" Cassie put a hand on his shoulder. Royal closed his eyes, dropping his head forward in resignation. Cassie looked at me again, helpless. "I mean, you're not the only one working on this book. The Guard has it too, right? Braedyn, have they learned anything?"

"I don't know." Tension spiraled through my back, as though my muscles had been coiled for weeks, waiting for an enemy to attack. "Clay assigned Sandra to this book, but she's not exactly reporting her findings to me."

"Is there a deadline?" Royal looked up at me, his face solemn. "I mean, it's almost December…"

I bit my lip. No one had to say it out loud. The longest night of the year was also the night of greatest power for the Lilitu. If Lilith had a vulnerability, we would have to find it and exploit it before winter solstice. Cassie and Royal studied me in silence for a long moment. Then Cassie forced a chipper smile and shrugged.

"Well, let's just assume no news is good news for the time being." Cassie squeezed Royal shoulder a little harder. "And you better take it easy. You can't translate twenty-four hours a day. If there's one thing I've learned from all my AP classes, it's that you can't force your brain to work on no sleep and no food."

Royal shot Cassie a lopsided grin. "That's all you've learned? From five AP classes?"

Cassie smacked Royal on the back of the head, but she was smiling. "All right. Braedyn, you should get going. Lucas is going to be looking for you. I'll stay here with Mr. Hilarious. I might not be able to read Latin, but I can look for important words. Maybe I can help narrow our search."

"Right." I turned back to Royal, searching his face one last time. "She's right, you know. Take care of yourself."

Royal nodded, making an exasperated gesture for me to leave. I walked out of the room as Cassie settled down for a long afternoon by Royal's side. It felt wrong to be abandoning them with this, but Cassie was right; we didn't want Lucas asking any questions.

You want to know the definition of incongruous? Try eating Thanksgiving with 50 Guardsmen under the shadow of the last battle. No amount of roast turkey, stuffing, mashed potatoes and gravy, yams, or cranberries could dispel the pervading feeling of impending doom. And yet, the soldiers of the Guard pulled out all the stops for the feast.

We lined up folding tables in the great room of the Guard's house, draping them with linen tablecloths. The food was store-bought, but it still filled the house with an enticing aroma. Someone had dug up a mismatched collection of candlesticks, and merry little flames danced on each of the tables.

But when I walked into the room, the only thing I could think about was Vyla, still trapped in the basement below. Her daughter, Emlyn, would be spending this Thanksgiving in the company of strangers. Who knew if the mother and daughter would ever share another Thanksgiving feast together?

Dad drew me into the room, guiding me to one of the end tables. I glanced at him and saw the concern mirrored in his eyes. He gestured at a chair by the wall.

"Sit." Dad glanced around the room then took the chair beside me, effectively separating me from the room full of Guard soldiers. "Eat."

I glanced at him, detecting the note of tension in his voice. "How? How am I supposed to...?"

"You need to participate." Dad lowered his voice, not looking directly at me. "We need the Guard to see you as one of them, not the enemy."

One of them...? It was the first time I'd ever heard Dad talk about the Guard like he wanted no part of it. A pit opened in the bottom of my stomach at his words. "Do you know something I don't?"

Dad's mouth tightened into a thin line. "I know Clay." He shot a quick glance at me. "And I know we can't make any mistakes."

"Braedyn!"

I looked up as Lucas entered the room, descending down the stairs. He had changed his clothes for the occasion. He still wore jeans, but he'd swapped his standard long-sleeve T-shirt for a button down. It hugged the muscles of his chest and arms in a way his school clothes didn't. I stared at him, breathless. Some part of me knew that Lucas had kept up his training since Clay's arrival, but I hadn't realized the effect it would have on his build.

Dad cleared his throat beside me. I dropped my eyes, blushing, but then Dad was sliding over, making room for Lucas to sit beside me.

"Hey." Lucas met my gaze, smiling. He smelled wonderful, fresh from a shower. "I've missed you."

"Me too." The room full of Guardsmen, the spotters, even Clay... everything seemed to fade to background noise as I looked into Lucas's hazel eyes. Right now they flickered a beautiful green-gold, warm and inviting. Suddenly I didn't feel so out of place.

"I was thinking the other day. About us. About this... whole situation. You know, one day, the war will be over." Lucas studied his hands, resting on the edge of the table. "I hope we win. But if we lose," he looked up at me again, his expression solemn. "I guess what I'm trying to say is, once the war is over, one way or the other, human or Lilitu, I want to be with you."

"Lucas?" I stared at him, stricken. "No. Not if it means..."

"Braedyn." Lucas caught my hand, silencing me with a look. "Sansenoy can't deny you, not if we win. And if we lose...? Then it won't matter."

I pulled my hand free, tears welling in my eyes. "Suicide by Lilitu? I won't do it. I won't kill you…"

Lucas reached up and brushed an errant lock of hair back from my forehead. "How long do you think Lilith would let any remaining Guardsmen live if she ends up winning?"

I recoiled from him. "Where is this coming from? Do you know something…? Did Clay learn something about Lilith, or the final battle, or…?"

"No." Lucas let out a long breath. "That's the whole problem. None of the books Sandra's been able to pilfer from the university's vault have done anything to shed light on Lilith's vulnerability."

"So…" I chocked down my terror. "So she's finished translating them already?"

Lucas looked startled. "What? No. Not even close. Clay ordered her to skim through them looking for any mention of Lilith's potential weaknesses." Lucas shook his head. "There's just so much. And it takes so long to translate even one passage. Thane's working on it all day long, too, but…" Lucas shot a veiled look at Clay, sitting several tables away. "I don't think Sandra understands why Clay turned down Father Jerome's help."

"Turkey?" Dad held a platter full of sliced turkey in front of Lucas. There was an edge to his voice. Lucas and I looked up and saw the warning in Dad's face.

"It's Thanksgiving, kids. Why don't you eat something." Dad inclined his head slightly. I looked over his shoulder, and saw Clay watching us.

"Lucas, would you serve me, too?" I lifted my plate up, forcing a smile. Out of the corner of my eye I saw Clay turn away.

"Sure." Lucas glanced from me to Dad, but whatever questions he wanted to ask he kept to himself.

We did our best to enjoy the meal. Or, rather, we did our best to look like we were enjoying ourselves. I managed to choke down a respectable amount of food on the off chance anyone was watching. But I barely tasted anything that passed my lips. As the evening wore on, people sat back in their chairs, passing bottles of wine around the table.

Marla carried a fresh bottle to our table. She poured a glass for Dad, then reached for the empty glass in front of me. Dad clamped his hand over the glass and gave Marla an irritated smile.

"Oh come on, Murphy. She's eighteen years old. A small glass of wine won't kill her." Marla gave me a friendly smile. "It's Thanksgiving, after all."

Dad hesitated. After moment's consideration, he withdrew his hand. "A small glass."

Marla poured the liquid into my glass. "Cheers."

"Thanks." I picked up the glass, feeling conspicuous. I touched the wine to my lips and took a small sip. Marla grinned and turned to Lucas.

"How about you sweetheart?"

"I better not." Lucas glanced at Clay, but the old man was engaged in conversation with Thane and Sandra. "Just in case."

"Suit yourself." Marla shrugged and headed back to her table. As soon as her back was turned, Dad plucked the wine out of my hand and downed it in a few gulps. Lucas glanced at me, surprised.

"Dad?"

"The last thing we need is for you to get tipsy." Dad set the empty glass back in front of my plate. "Sorry, kiddo." He flashed me a wistful smile. "I promise, once Clay and his men have moved on I'll buy a really nice bottle of wine and we can share it. Deal?"

Lucas gave Dad a thoughtful look at this, but said nothing.

"Does that mean you think we're going to be dealing with Clay until I turn twenty-one, or…?"

"No. I fully plan on contributing to the delinquency of a minor." Dad smiled. "Hopefully we'll be sharing that bottle before you turn nineteen."

The meal was winding down 20 minutes later when the doorbell rang. Clay glanced up from his spot in the center of the room. His eyes found Lucas, and he nodded his head toward the door.

Lucas understood. He rose from his chair and walked quickly to the front door. I couldn't see the door from where I sat, but I heard Lucas's surprised voice.

"Cassie?"

Whatever Cassie said in response was lost against the noise of the Guardsmen finishing their meal. But a few moments later, Lucas and

Cassie walked into the great room. Clay looked up, clearly displeased. The room, spotting the stranger, grew quiet.

Cassie froze, uncomfortable with all the attention. She cleared her throat. "Sorry to disturb your dinner." She glanced around until her eyes landed on Sandra. "Are you Sandra?"

Sandra shot a veiled look at Clay before rising to her feet. "Guilty. And you are?"

"I'm Cassie Ang. A friend of Braedyn and Lucas's from school." Cassie smiled nervously. "I was hoping I could talk to you."

Sandra turned back to Clay. He gave her permission with a small nod. Sandra crossed to Cassie and Lucas. I pushed back from the table to join them. Dad caught my hand.

"What is she doing?" His eyes creased with concern. I shook my head, mystified. Dad released me, but he didn't look any less worried. "Be careful."

I headed into the foyer and found Sandra and Lucas listening to Cassie with astonished looks on their faces.

Lucas glanced at me when I entered. "Did you know anything about this?"

"About what?" I glanced at Cassie, and a wave of butterflies exploded in my stomach.

"I didn't tell her I was planning to come," Cassie said. "I didn't want her to tell me not to." Cassie gave me an apologetic shrug and smiled. "Sorry."

"I still don't know what we're talking about." I glanced at Lucas. "What's going on?"

"Your friend has offered to help us out." Sandra studied Cassie with undisguised suspicion, then turned to me. "Do you make a habit of telling your schoolmates about the Guard and what we do?"

I opened my mouth to respond, but Cassie spoke first.

"You think she had to tell me?" Cassie's voice was suddenly hard, filled with a strength that seemed to surprise Sandra. "My best friend, Royal, was attacked by an incubus. That same incubus tried to brainwash me."

Lucas nodded slowly. "She's right, Sandra. And… she was there when they opened the Seal."

"Really?" Sandra turned back to Cassie, suddenly interested. Alarm bells raged in my mind, but Cassie pressed on.

"I might not be a spotter, but I have just as much right to join the cause against Lilitu as anyone else. I want to help."

"While I can respect your desire to join the fight..."

Clay strode into the foyer, placing a hand on Sandra's shoulder. The archivist turned toward Clay, startled.

"This must be Cassie." Clay's rich southern accent filled the room with a friendly warmth. Cassie looked up at him, startled. "Thane has told me all about you and your devotion to our cause."

Cassie smoothed a wisp of hair back from her forehead, then her hands dropped to brush the front of her skirt nervously. "He has?"

"Volunteering to infiltrate a cult of Lilith-worshiping zealots?" Clay inclined his head in admiration. "You're a brave young woman."

Cassie blushed, pleased at the compliment. I stared at Clay amazed. Cassie knew everything about this man, but he still managed to flatter her. Cassie dropped her eyes to her hands. "I wanted to do something to help."

"And I'm sure we can find a job for you." Clay turned to Sandra expectantly.

Sandra looked at Clay with wide eyes, but when he nodded for Sandra to continue, she swallowed her surprise. "Right. Well. You're not a spotter... Am I correct in assuming you're not a fighter, either?"

Cassie glanced at Lucas, unsure. "I'm more of a research-oriented girl."

Sandra frowned, thinking. Then she brightened as an idea came to her. "Hang on. Do they make you lot study dead languages in your schools? Do you read Latin?" When Cassie shook her head, Sandra sighed, her sudden hope fading.

"But..." Cassie straightened, desperate to find a way to help. "Do I have to understand Latin to help? I mean, couldn't you give me a list of words to look for or...?"

"That's not a bad idea," Sandra murmured.

Clay's gaze returned to Cassie. "Excellent. You can start tomorrow."

"Awesome!" Cassie's squeal cut through the Guardsmen's chatter. She saw some of the soldiers staring at her through the foyer entrance and waved nervously, then cleared her throat. "Awesome," she said again. "See you tomorrow."

Cassie caught me in a quick hug, planted a kiss on Lucas's cheek, then turned and practically skipped out the front door. I felt my stomach churn.

Cassie had been right, if she'd floated this plan past me I would have shut it down. I would never have willingly given Clay one more person to hold over my head. And now that Cassie was on Clay's radar, I might not be able to protect her from him.

Cassie thought she was helping.

She didn't understand that she was walking into the lion's den.

13

"You can start on these. I've written out a list of twenty words to look out for. See any of those words, you should mark the page and copy the sentence out. We can look through your notes once you've finished the first book." Sandra handed a stack of books to Cassie. A small slip of paper rested on top with a list of Latin words written on it in black ink.

The second volume in the pile was a slender book bound in red leather. It was the book I had taken from the university vault. Finally, we'd caught a break. I glanced at Cassie, barely able to contain my glee. She saw the look in my eyes and understood. We'd had a long conversation the previous night about how we were going to get our hands on this book. This, at least, was a problem we no longer needed to solve.

We stood in the former living room of the Guard's house, just outside Thane's office. Clay's desk sat empty at the opposite end of the room. He and Lucas were off on some errand or another, which suited me fine. It was increasingly draining to have to hide things from Lucas.

"Any questions?" Sandra glanced from Cassie to me, sensing something.

"No questions. I think I've got it." Cassie pulled the books close to her chest with an impish grin.

Sandra hesitated. "You know this isn't a game, right? One of those books might contain the secret to defeating the Lilitu. You could literally be holding the key to mankind's salvation."

"No, I know. I'm just... I'm just glad I can offer something in this fight." Cassie blushed.

"Right. Well, chop chop. There are plenty more where those came from." Sandra inclined her head at the books in Cassie's hands. "I'll be in the study if anything comes up."

"Sandra, would you mind if we went back to my place, I mean…" It was now my turn to blush. The house I'd grown up in wasn't exactly my house anymore. "I mean next door." When Sandra gave me a searching look I shrugged. "Fewer distractions." I tilted my head toward Cassie.

Cassie turned as a young Guardsman walked past. She watched him disappear down the hall with a dreamy look on her face. I bit the inside of my lip to control the urge to laugh. But Sandra frowned.

"Right. Probably not the worst idea," She turned back to me with a warning look, "but I'm holding you responsible for the books."

I nodded, and then Cassie and I were heading out the Guard's front door and down the steps. I felt myself breathe a little easier, away from Clay's headquarters. It wasn't like we would have much more privacy at my house, but at least it felt more comfortable.

We settled down to work at the dining room table. I didn't see any spotters downstairs, but that didn't mean Zoe wasn't hanging out in my room. We kept our voices low, just in case. Cassie flipped open the book detailing the acolyte initiation ritual. I saw her brow furrow as she turned the pages, recognizing—as I had—each step of the ceremony.

After a long moment, Cassie looked up. "What do you think we should do?"

"I think you should work through the other books. Save this one for last. Give Royal as much time as possible to make headway with the translation." I thought I heard something at the top of the stairs. I closed my mouth, straining to concentrate. It might have been the settling of an old house, but neither Cassie nor I wanted to take any chances. Cassie saw the look on my face and slipped the volume to the bottom of the stack of books in front of her.

"Well, here we go." Cassie picked up two books and handed one to me. She set the list of Latin words between us on the table, then opened her book and began poring over the dense calligraphy within.

We'd only been working for about 15 minutes when the front door opened and Clay walked in. Something about the way his feet shuffled into the foyer set my nerves on edge. I stiffened, my finger marking a passage in the book before me. Cassie started to push back from the table as Clay entered.

"Hello, Ms. Ang." Clay pulled a chair out and sat, indicating Cassie should stay seated. "I hope you don't mind if I join you for a moment. I like to get to know the people working with the Guard."

Cassie flashed him a nervous smile, curling a lock of black hair behind her ear. "Sure. No problem." After a moment's awkward silence, Cassie gestured at the book in front of her. "Do you want me to keep working or do you have questions for me or...?"

"You seem a little nervous." Clay studied her with a neutral expression. "Is everything all right?"

Cassie glanced at me, uncertain. Clay followed her gaze, watching every move between us.

"If you're worried about Cassie, you shouldn't be." I gave Cassie an encouraging smile. "She's been a loyal friend to the Guard, just ask Matthew or Gretchen or Lucas."

"And you do seem surrounded by loyal friends," Clay said. His voice was mild, but there was something underneath the words that set off alarms in the back of my mind. Before I could suss out exactly what he meant by this, Clay was on his feet again. "Well, I should let you get back to work." He inclined his head toward Cassie and offered her a smile. "Glad to have you aboard, Miss Ang."

Cassie and I watched as Clay made his way back to the front door. He left without a backward glance, but his presence seemed to linger in the room.

Cassie let out a shaky breath. "Yikes. You weren't kidding. That guy... he's intense."

"Yeah." I studied the closed front door. Something about Clay's visit left me feeling cold. I might not know what he was planning, but I knew with certainty that whatever it was—it wasn't good.

December arrived with very little fanfare the following week. We were back in school, gearing up for midterm exams in all our classes. Royal was devoted to translating the acolyte book, but if anything his progress had grown even slower as the book delved into arcane and technical language.

I headed into English after lunch with Lucas and Cassie. It was the one class the three of us had together. The bell rang but before we could delve into the reading, Missy walked through the door. Her eyes were red and puffy. It looked like she'd spent the morning crying.

Ms. Barnhouse took one look at Missy's face and rushed to her side. "Missy? What's wrong, sweetheart?"

"It's my sister." Missy clenched her jaw. She looked on the verge of more tears, as if the slightest thing might tip her into a whirlpool of grief.

"Carrie?" Ms. Barnhouse's voice tightened. Of course she would know Carrie. Carrie had only graduated from Coronado Prep a few years ago. She was as sweet and pretty as Missy, and—if possible—even more charismatic. "Has something…?"

"She's in the hospital," Missy breathed.

Ms. Barnhouse's eyes filled with concern. "Sweetheart, if you need to go, just tell me."

"No. It's… they're watching her right now. My mom will call if things get worse." Missy offered Ms. Barnhouse a watery smile. She headed to an open desk beside Amber and sat. I saw them put their heads together. Amber's expression grew from concerned to outright alarmed.

I tried to focus on class, but all I could think about was Carrie. She'd had bloody noses, just like Cassie. She'd undergone the acolyte initiation, just like Cassie. Did this mean Cassie might end up in the hospital too? I glanced at my friend. Cassie appeared unaware of my concerns, engrossed in the lesson. But Lucas was looking at me with undisguised worry.

After class, I gathered up my things and followed Missy and Amber out onto the quad. Ally ran up to them, her face drawn with concern. She threw her arms around Missy and gave her a tight hug. The three girls turned and headed across campus. I hurried to catch up to them. As I approached, I overheard part of their conversation.

"The doctors don't know what is wrong with her. She just… keeps getting weaker." Missy took a shuddering breath. Amber caught her around the shoulders and gave her a gentle hug.

I cleared my throat, uncomfortable. "Missy, I'm so sorry to bother you but..." I had trouble forming the question. Missy and Ally turned to look at me, startled. Amber's eyes narrowed, but before she could tell me off, Missy wiped her eyes and gave me a weak smile.

"What's up?" Missy had a genuine kindness to her. It continued to amaze me that she was such good friends with the likes of Amber and Ally.

"Your sister… I'm sorry, but can you tell me what happened?" I heard Cassie and Lucas approaching but I didn't take my eyes off of Missy's face. Missy blanched.

"What the hell is your problem?" Ally stepped between Missy and me, instantly defensive.

"I know she was having nosebleeds." I tried to keep my voice calm, despite my instinct to snap back. That's when I heard Cassie's sharp intake of breath. Amber heard it too. Her gaze sharpened on Cassie.

"I just want to know if the doctors think this is connected to the nosebleeds, or…?"

"I…" Missy shook her head, trying to clear her thoughts. "Yeah, I mean, they're taking everything into consideration. She did have a nosebleed last night. Kind of a bad one."

"Oh God." Cassie's eyes were two pools of liquid fear. She clutched her hands over her mouth.

"What? What is it?" Amber glared from me to Cassie and back. "Do you know something about what's going on with her sister?"

Missy stared at Amber, stunned. "What? Why would they…?" But then she turned toward me. Her eyes were full of unvoiced questions.

I hesitated. My eyes slid to Ally. Amber followed my gaze. She seemed to understand, her expression clouding. She cleared her throat.

"Ally, would you mind grabbing my Bio textbook from my locker and meeting up with me outside class?" Amber gave Ally a smile, but this was clearly a dismissal.

"Excuse me?" Ally's eyes widened in astonishment, but Amber gave her a pointed look. "Fine. I have to grab my book anyway." Ally left, affronted.

Amber glared at me, pissed. "Spit it out. What's going on?"

I turned to Missy, trying to keep my voice gentle. "I think… Your sister might be in trouble."

"What kind of trouble?" Missy glanced at Cassie, struggling to manage her rising panic. "What makes you say that?"

"You remember that group Carrie and I were a part of last year?" Cassie took a hesitant step forward.

Missy nodded, her eyes full of questions. "Yeah, the Lilith thing."

"I don't know how much Carrie told you, but she and I were selected to become acolytes. There was an initiation ceremony." Cassie broke off. Amber closed her eyes.

"And?" Missy's voice betrayed her anxiety.

"And... I felt... Something during the ceremony. A presence."

Missy shook her head again. "I don't understand. Presence...? Like...?"

"Like something supernatural." Amber spoke through gritted teeth. "What they're trying to tell you is Lilith is real. Only she's not some kind of beneficial lady mascot. She's a demon. And now her acolytes are getting sick."

Missy stared at Amber blankly for a moment. Then her face darkened. "What are you...? Why would you say that to me? My sister could be dying and you're...?" Amber reached a hand outward Missy, but Missy jerked away. "Don't touch me. This is beyond cruel." Missy turned to face me, her eyes welling. "I thought we were friends."

"We are friends, Missy." I took a step closer to the petite strawberry blond. "That's why I'm trying to help. We don't have time to do this the gentle way. Just watch me." I scanned the surrounding area, waiting for my opportunity. We were nearing the end of passing period, and most students were already inside heading to their classrooms.

Missy's eyes narrowed in confusion. "Watch you? What is that supposed to...?"

I willed my Lilitu wings to unfurl behind me. Amber took a sharp breath as they stretched wide. Of all of them, Amber was the only one who could see my Lilitu aspect. It took only the smallest effort of will and then my wings were enfolding me in a shield of invisibility.

Missy let out a strangled scream, turning to run. Lucas caught her arm, stopping her. Her books spilled onto the grass at our feet. I uncloaked myself quickly, and then dropped to help pick up Missy's things. She stared at me, frozen with fear.

From across the quad, the school counselor heard her scream and came running.

"Don't say anything," Lucas hissed into Missy's ear. Missy stared at him, uncomprehending.

"Missy! What is it? Did something happen to Carrie?"

Missy turned haunted eyes on me. I held my breath. For one agonizing moment, I thought she might tell him what she'd seen. But then she swallowed, took a deep breath, and faced the councilor. "I'm sorry. I… I guess I'm feeling a little high strung today."

"If you'd rather be at the hospital, I can excuse you from afternoon classes." He put a hand on Missy's shoulder.

"Yeah. Actually, I think that's a good idea." Missy's eyes flicked back to me.

"Okay. But I'm not sure you should be driving. Is there someone you could call, or some other way for you to get to the hospital?" the counselor asked.

"Actually, I have free period now," Lucas said. He glanced at Missy. "I can drive you, if you want." Missy nodded.

"Good. It's settled. Why don't you both come to my office. I'll write your permission slips." The counselor glanced at Lucas. "Just make sure you're back before your next class."

"I just have to put some things back in my locker," Missy said. "Can I meet you there in five minutes?"

"Of course. Take your time." The counselor flashed Missy and understanding smile. "Lucas?" He led Lucas back to the administration building. When they were safely out of earshot, Missy turned back to the group.

"This… ?" Missy swallowed again, eyeing me with frightened fascination. "What are you?"

"Don't worry, Braedyn's a *nice* demon." Amber's voice was heavy with sarcasm.

Missy's eyes grew even wider. "Demon…?"

"We shouldn't do this here." Royal spoke quietly, eyeing the campus around us uneasily. "Why don't you go to the hospital. Be with your sister. And then we can meet up this afternoon and answer all your questions."

Missy nodded slowly. "Fair warning, I'm going to have a lot of them."

Cassie and I headed to Sophie's that afternoon. We claimed one of the large booths in the back dining room, promising the skeptical waitress that there would be more people joining us soon. A fire burned low in the hearth. It filled the room with the soft crackle of charred logs and helped to keep the December chill at bay. Amber spotted us a few minutes later and joined us, sliding into the booth with a grim expression.

"Listen, I'm only here for Missy. Don't expect my help with any Guard stuff. I was serious when I said I wanted out." Amber flipped her hair back over one shoulder.

"Fine." We stared at each other in silence, waiting. Twenty minutes later, Royal and Missy slipped into the booth as well.

Missy didn't waste any time. But her first question was to Amber. "How long have you known about this?"

Amber looked surprised at the heat in Missy's voice. "About two years."

"Two years?" Missy nodded to herself. Then she looked up at Cassie. "Is my sister going to die?"

"Not if we can help it." My voice was hoarser than I intended. Cassie heard the emotion behind my words. She flashed me a small smile.

"What exactly can you do?" Missy fixed her eyes on me. She was taking this revelation a lot better than I had when I had first learned about the Lilitu.

"There's a book. As far as we can tell it's all about the acolytes. We have reason to believe there might be a way to break the connection between Lilith and her acolytes."

"What?" Amber's voice cut through the comfortable din of the restaurant. A few patrons glanced our way. Amber lowered her voice, leaning over the table to face me directly. "I'm sorry, there's a connection between Lilith and her acolytes? And you learned this when?"

I turned to Missy. Her face was still, emotionless. "Missy, I… I didn't want to say anything until we had a plan."

Missy's eyes swiveled to my face slowly. "This book, you think the answer is in there? You think it can tell you how to break the connection between my sister and... and Lilith?"

"That's what we're hoping." I looked at Amber. She glared at me, lips tight with anger.

"Hoping?" Amber scanned the faces at our table. "Hoping doesn't sound like a plan."

"The book is in Latin. It's taking a long time to translate." I met Amber's glare directly. "We're doing the best we can."

"Wait, Latin?" Missy turned to Amber. "Ally. Ally could do it."

"That's a bad idea." I glanced at Royal, looking for backup. "The fewer people that know about this, the better."

"She's got a point, Braedyn." Royal stared at his hands on the table. "When it comes to Latin, Ally is the best student at Coronado. I'm taking too long to figure this out. Maybe we need more help."

I stared at Royal. "So, what? We just tell Ally hey, by the way, demons are real. Would you mind helping us translate something that may or may not turn the tide against them but will definitely get their attention, preferably before midterms?"

"I don't know what you want me to say." Royal met my eyes, seething. "If we had unlimited time? If Cassie's life wasn't on the line? Sure, I'd be totally willing to go it alone. But we don't, and it is, and I'm not going to let my friend die because I don't want to scare some high school girl."

Before I could argue the point, Missy straightened. "If you're worried about her learning demons exist, just don't tell her what she's translating."

Royal eyed Missy. "Won't she figure it out? I mean, she'll be *translating* a *book about demons*."

"So tell her it's some weird mythology book, or something for a D&D game or... I don't know, get creative!" Missy slammed her hand down on the table. I saw Cassie jump beside me. Missy ran her hands through her strawberry blond hair. "Sorry. Sorry. This is turning out to be a really weird day."

"You don't have to apologize." Royal's voice softened. "I know this is a lot. And I know you're worried about your sister. But Missy, if anyone can help her it's Braedyn. I've seen her do amazing things. I've seen her fight harder than I've ever seen anyone else do anything. And

I mean that both metaphorically and literally. We don't know what's wrong with Carrie yet. But I can pretty much guarantee if it has something to do with Lilith, Braedyn's the one you want fighting by your side."

Missy and Amber glanced at me. I sighed. "Okay. Call her."

Amber rose from the table to place the call.

While we waited, Missy looked at Cassie, worried. "What about the other one?"

Cassie looked up, startled. "The other... you mean the third acolyte? Emma?" Cassie turned to me, stricken. We hadn't thought of contacting her. There was no point, not until we knew what we could do—if anything—to help her.

Missy studied us, frowning. "You have to tell her. What if she's got the bloody noses, too? She won't know what's happening to her. She's all alone in this."

I nodded, feeling more than a little chastened. "You're right. We need to find Emma and loop her into the conversation."

"Promise me," Missy said.

I swallowed. "I promise. I'll find her as soon as possible."

Missy nodded, satisfied, then lapsed into a worried silence. Twenty minutes later, Ally wandered into the room. She spotted us in the corner and headed over. I don't think she was expecting to see me or Cassie or Royal. She eyed us with suspicion, but slid into the booth next to Amber.

"So what's the big emergency?" She turned her attention to Missy, dismissing us for the time being.

"Actually, you should probably explain it." Missy looked directly at me when she said this. Ally followed her gaze, eyes narrowing.

"We need your help." I glanced at Royal. He nodded slightly, urging me to continue. "Missy says you are good with Latin. Do you think you could take a look at a manuscript and help translate it?"

"What about him." Ally jerked her chin at Royal. "He's decent at Latin. Ish."

"You're too kind." Royal shot Ally an irritated smile. "No, please, stop. You're going to make me blush."

"Would you take a look?" Missy touched Ally on the arm. Ally considered this and then sighed, frowning.

Royal pulled the manuscript out of his backpack and slid it across the table to Ally. She picked it up and began to study it. After a moment, her frown deepened. When she looked up, her eyes found my face.

"Okay. I don't know what's going on with you, or whatever weird occult thing you're into, but I don't want any part of it." Ally set the manuscript back down on the table. "Seriously. Why are you guys listening to her?" But Ally didn't look at Missy. This question was for Amber. I suddenly remembered that Amber had tricked me into confessing I was a demon during our sophomore year. We'd been standing in the locker room when Amber had confronted me. I let her bait me into admitting what I was, and then Ally had stepped out from her hiding place behind the locker bay. I realized I had no idea what Ally had made of that conversation in the intervening years. But if Royal was right, we needed her help.

"Occult? Really?" I forced a smile. "Don't you think that's a little Salem witch trials?"

"I just know, whatever messed up thing you're into… or whatever messed up thing you think you are…" Ally glanced at Amber again. Amber seemed to understand Ally's hesitation. She shot a quick look at me then laughed humorlessly.

"You don't seriously still believe she's a demon, do you?" Amber stared at me, hostility edging her words. Missy glanced at Amber and Ally, but she kept her mouth shut. "That was just some weird affectation or something."

Ally sniffed. "No, of course not. Do I look like the kind of New Age-y, crystal-hugging freak who would fall for that crap?" She might have affected a dismissive tone, but her shoulders were still tense. Her eyes shifted to my face. "But I know you did something to Parker. You got into his head somehow and… Changed him."

"He hurt my friend." It was an effort to keep my voice quiet. Cassie looked down. I knew she felt responsible for what I had done to Parker.

"Thanks for the newsflash. Why do you think I dumped his sorry ass?" Ally's lips peeled back from her teeth in a sneer. Everything about her set my nerves on edge. I took a breath, ready to chew her out, but Missy intervened before we could really get into it.

"Ally, please. This could help Carrie."

Ally eyed Missy suspiciously, but there was nothing about Missy that was calculating or manipulative. Still, Ally wasn't convinced. She turned to Royal. "Seriously, though. You're in Latin, why can't you do it?"

"I've been working on it," Royal said stiffly, "but it's kind of straining the limits of my abilities."

Ally turned back to the pages once more, a glimmer of interest flickering to life behind her eyes. "Really?" She pulled the pages closer, letting her eyes run over the calligraphy one more time. Finally, she seemed to come to some decision. "Fine. I'll help. For Carrie."

I left Royal and Ally to sort out the details of who would translate what on their own. They weren't exactly study-buddy material. Each of them took some pages home every night and returned with the translations the next morning. We all met up at the end of the day to go over what, if anything, had been gleaned from the book. With Ally's help, we started to make some real progress.

We learned, for example, what each element of the ritual was for. The bloodletting, the chalice, the thurible with its distinctive incense… each piece of the puzzle had a specific purpose. What we had thought of as the initiation of the acolytes, the book described as *the anointing*. There was no mention of bloody noses or weakness or any side effects of the ritual on the acolytes. The book was more concerned with what the ritual provided for Lilith herself. The whole purpose of the ritual, it seemed, was to establish a bond between the acolytes and Lilith through which Lilith could draw power. Which made no sense to me. Lilith had at her disposal the sleeping minds of all humankind. If she needed energy, why not take it from them? What was special about the acolytes? What could they provide her that the rest of humanity could not?

More than once, I found myself about to ask Lucas for his thoughts. And then it would crash back in on me: Lucas didn't know what we were doing. He had no idea that Royal was working off a copy of one of the books taken from the mission vault. Lucas had no idea that Ally was involved, either.

I found myself on the verge of deciding to tell Lucas everything at least once a day. But then there would be a moment, maybe a call from Clay, or Lucas would recount something that Clay had said to him, and I would see again how devoted he still was to the man. Maybe he would keep our secret, but I couldn't risk finding out. Until I could get Lucas to see Clay for what he truly was, I couldn't trust him with this.

Cassie continued to come over every day after school and chip away at the books Sandra had entrusted her with. As far as we could tell, neither Sandra nor Thane had any particular interest in the acolyte book. They had identified a few volumes that they thought might be instrumental in preparing a defense against Lilith. Those were the books they were focusing their time and attention on. It gave us a window of opportunity. As long as we made progress on the books Sandra had assigned to us, they didn't look too closely at what we *weren't* working on. Sandra would check in on us at least once a day. She'd read through the phrases we copied from the books. Every once in a while, she would ask to see the passage noted, and either Cassie or I would flip through a book until we had located it for her. For the most part, we uncovered nothing earth shattering. But we kept Sandra happy—and we kept the acolyte book off her radar, which was the main goal.

The one big difference was Father Jerome. He and Sandra began spending more and more time together, poring over volumes and offering each other insights as to the nuances of various potential translations. Father Jerome realized Clay was not interested in bringing any outsiders in to help, so he filled in as a third Latin expert. Sandra seemed to understand this without ever having to discuss it. While Clay was eager to see Father Jerome on his way, Sandra began to utilize Jerome's expertise more and more. He became a regular fixture at the Guard's house. The only way we would've seen more of Father Jerome would be if he had moved in. But that would've been pushing Clay a little too far. And so Father Jerome kept his hotel room, and Sandra got her Latin expert, and Clay said nothing.

As impatient as I was for answers, I got used to hearing Royal and Ally say they hadn't found anything useful yet. So when I sat down for lunch the second week in December, I was surprised when Ally joined us at our table.

"I found something interesting in my pages last night." Ally pulled a chair out and sat, not waiting for an invitation.

"What pages?" Lucas looked up from serving himself a second portion of broccoli. We typically didn't leave much in the way of leftovers, thanks in large part to Lucas's amazing metabolism.

Ally started to answer him, but Royal cleared his throat quickly. "It's a Latin assignment. We're supposed to work on it together. For class." Royal took a swig of milk, shooting Ally a warning look.

Ally glanced at me. For a moment, I worried she'd expose everything we'd been working on to Lucas, and—by extension—Clay. I held my breath. Ally reached across the table and plucked a piece of broccoli out of the serving bowl.

"Yeah. So, about our assignment. There's a passage I think you should look at." Ally slipped one of the photocopied sheets to Royal. I didn't see much, but it looked like Ally had written her own notes all over the margins. Royal took the paper and skimmed Ally's notes. He looked up.

"Yeah. Interesting. Good catch." Royal kept his tone light, but his gaze flicked to me and I noticed instantly the urgency behind his eyes.

Lucas looked from Royal to me. After a moment's awkward silence, he popped the last piece of broccoli in his mouth, then stood. "You know, I should probably cut out early. I have a quiz to study for." He flashed us a smile, but his eyes caught on my face. He knew we were hiding something from him. I felt my stomach twist, but it was a problem we would have to deal with later.

Once Lucas had left the dining hall, Royal, Cassie, and I gathered close around Ally.

"What did you find?" Cassie craned her neck, trying to read the margin notes.

"Well, based on what Royal has told me, I think I might have found what you're looking for. It's this part here, somebody wrote a note alongside the text." Ally pointed out some Latin scrawled alongside a dense passage of calligraphy. "It's a discussion about the connection between acolytes and the night demon."

I looked up, meeting Cassie's gaze. The *night demon* could only mean Lilith. "What does it say? What does it say *exactly*?"

Ally gave me a shrewd look. "I haven't finished translating the whole thing yet, a lot of this is very odd phrasing, but it seems to be some kind of counter-ritual or something. He keeps using the word 'ameliorate,' which is weird because as far as I can tell he's talking about curing somebody from a dream."

"Curing? It actually says curing?" I couldn't keep the urgency out of my voice.

Ally looked up at me again. "Yeah."

I let out a breath of stunned relief. And then I was embracing Ally, hugging her tightly in the middle of the dining hall. "Thank you." I managed, releasing her.

"Okay, easy." Ally pulled back, surprised and clearly uncomfortable with the display. "You do realize," she said after a moment's hesitation, "you're going to have to tell me what this is all about. Soon."

Ally's news sent my spirits soaring. It wasn't much to go on, but I'd take it. Now, it was just a matter of waiting for Ally and Royal to finish translating the margin notes. I let myself relax that night, turning to schoolwork as a welcome distraction. I finished a book for English class. I even studied for a quiz. It felt great to be normal for one night. To not have to sit by and worry about my best friend, feeling clueless about how to help her. We had a glimmer of hope.

But when I returned to school the next day, Missy was out. Word was, her sister had taken a turn, and the doctors feared she might actually die. That was bad enough. But things were about to get worse.

I spotted Cassie on my way to first period. She looked awful. Worn, her face drawn. Her eye sockets looked sunken. It was almost as though I could see the skull beneath her skin. When she spotted me, Cassie made a valiant effort to smile.

"Cassie, are you feeling all right?" I was almost afraid to touch her, she looked so fragile.

"Yeah. Did you hear about Carrie?" Cassie's eyes swept the hallway, but no one was standing close enough to overhear us.

"I heard." I bit my lip. "You have any more bloody noses?"

"I have bloody noses every night." Cassie smiled mirthlessly. "I'm thinking about buying red sheets."

"Why didn't you say anything to me about this before?" I couldn't keep the tension out of my voice. Cassie winced.

"Um, because it's gross?" But then Cassie sighed. "And because you couldn't do anything about it anyway."

"Okay, this is not a coincidence. Something is definitely affecting the acolytes."

Cassie's eyes shifted focus. "I wonder if Emma's getting bloody noses, too."

I studied Cassie, pained. I'd had no luck locating the third acolyte so far. Emma didn't go to our school. She was older, maybe 20 or 21. I had no idea where she lived, if she went to college, if she worked. I hadn't known where to begin looking for her, and I'd gotten distracted by everything that was going on with the translation and the Guard. But I'd promised Missy we'd find her, and it needed to be sooner rather than later. If Cassie and Carrie were sick, there was a good chance Emma was, too.

Cassie glanced at her watch. "We should get to class. Are you coming?"

"Yeah. Just have one thing I need to take care of. I'll meet up with you later." I gave Cassie a smile and watched as she walked away. When she was out of sight, I fished my cell phone out of my pocket and dialed. Missy picked up on the third ring. "I heard about Carrie. Are you okay?"

Missy's voice came through the line, shaking with emotion. "I don't know. She's in and out of consciousness. It's so weird. One minute she seems fine, and then she just passes out and they can't wake her up. She got all these tubes in her face now and…" Missy took a shuddering breath. "Do you need something? I should probably get back soon, so…?"

"If…" I swallowed and cleared my throat. "Sorry. *When* she wakes up again, if you remember, could you ask her what she knows about the third acolyte, Emma? I haven't been able to find her yet, and anything Carrie might know could help."

"Sure." Missy sniffed on the other end of the line. "Hold on, I think… I think she might be coming out of it again."

"Go. We'll talk soon." We hung up. The bell rang, announcing the start of first period.

I didn't expect to hear from Missy for the rest of the day, but she called at lunchtime. "Emma works at a pizza place, that's all Carrie knows. She thinks it's downtown, but she's not 100% sure. I'm sorry I couldn't get anything more specific, but…"

"No, Missy, that's great. We'll take it from here. Just be with your sister, and call us if you need anything or if anything changes."

"Braedyn, I meant to say this before, but thank you. For telling me… everything. For trusting me. And for doing everything you're doing to help Carrie."

I felt a lump in my throat. "Of course." It felt wrong that Missy was thanking me. We had known that Lilith was real, and we'd figured out that Idris knew it, too. But we let Carrie and Cassie—and Emma, for that matter—go through the entire initiation without interference. It was hard not to feel responsible for what they were suffering now.

That afternoon I filled Cassie and Royal in. There was no good way to figure out which pizzeria Emma worked at, so we decided to hit as many restaurants as we could every day after school. Even though Missy hadn't been sure about the location, we decided to start with the pizzerias near downtown. That gave us a list of 12 restaurants to start with. 12 restaurants, and only 11 days until winter solstice.

Despite our good intentions, over the next week we only managed to hit one or two pizzerias a day. We'd order a slice, and as the others ate I would slip away to ask the workers about Emma. Nothing, nothing, and more nothing. It wasn't until the 18th that we hit pay dirt.

The place was called Salieri's. It was a cute little walk-in pizzeria near the university. We had to eat our slices at the standing counter. I finished mine and spotted a manager. By this point I had gotten pretty good at fishing for information.

"Hey, is Emma in today? I missed her in class." I gave the manager my best smile. He hesitated, then shook his head.

"Actually, she's out sick. Some kind of headaches or something. Bloody noses." He shrugged. "If you see her, pass on my good wishes? We'd love to have her back. She's a great kid."

"Oh." I struggled to keep the urgency out of my voice. "I'd totally love to take her some chicken noodle soup or something. But I think she's moved since the last time I visited her place. I don't suppose you could tell me her current address?"

"No, I'm sorry. I'd love to help, but it's against company policy to hand out employees' personal information." He gave me a pained smile and started to turn away.

"Well, maybe you could make an exception just this once." I put my hand on his shoulder. He turned back to face me, and I could see the irritation in his eyes. I locked eyes with him. A soft breeze seemed to kick up, even though we were standing inside. The breeze teased the hair back from my face. The manager stared at me, his words dying on his lips. I'd never been on the receiving end of a Lilitu's enthralling, but I'd seen it in action before… and I'd done it myself a few times. It's not something I'm proud of, but it gets results. "I mean, if it wouldn't be too much trouble?"

The manager licked his lips. After a moment he nodded. "Sure. Sure. For a friend of Emma's, anything."

On the way to Emma's, we stopped to pick up a carton of chicken noodle soup from a 24-hour diner. Fifteen minutes later, we were knocking on Emma's door.

Emma's roommate opened the door. "Hello?"

"Hi." Cassie smiled and hefted the carton of chicken noodle soup. "I'm a friend of Emma's. I heard she wasn't feeling too good. Do you think she'd like some soup?"

The roommate's face relaxed. She held open the door for us. "Come in. She's been feeling awful for about two weeks. It started with the nosebleeds, but now," she shrugged, concerned. "I keep telling her to go to the urgent care center on campus, but she doesn't want to leave the apartment."

We headed back to Emma's room. Cassie knocked on the door quietly. Emma's voice sounded weak when she asked us to come in. When we opened the door, Emma's face lit up at the sight of Cassie. "Hey, you. It's been too long."

I hung back at the doorway as Cassie went into the room. She set the soup on Emma's nightstand and took a seat on the edge of her bed. They talked quietly together for a long time. They hadn't seen each other since the night Idris had died. I tried not to look at them. It felt awkward, like I was spying on a private moment. But then Emma said something that caught my attention.

"It wouldn't be so bad, if I wasn't having all these weird dreams."

I happened to glance up at that moment. If I hadn't, I might not have seen Cassie flinch.

"What dreams?" I asked. The question was more for Cassie than Emma, but Emma answered.

"Just… really vivid, strange dreams," Emma said. "Nightmares, I guess. There's always this feeling, like something… evil… is just waiting to jump me." Emma laughed weakly. "I'm sure my therapist would have a field day with that."

"You look tired," Cassie said. She stood. "Try the soup, it's supposed to work miracles. And then hopefully you can sleep without dreaming tonight."

"Thanks, Cassie. You're sweet." Emma gave Cassie a warm hug.

When we were back outside the apartment, I turned to Cassie. "You've been having dreams, too." It wasn't a question, and Cassie knew it. She bit her lip, caught.

"I… I didn't tell you about them because I didn't want you to freak out. They're… Well, just like Emma said. Nightmares with this weird… presence in them." Cassie didn't look at me.

I held my tongue for a moment, fighting down the urge to yell. "It didn't strike you that this might be connected to Lilith?"

"I don't think… I don't think…" Cassie couldn't finish the sentence. She raised a hand to her head with a sharp intake of breath, eyes squeezing shut in pain. A trickle of blood escaped her nose. "No, not again…" Cassie held her nose with one hand while trying to pry her bag open with the other.

"Let me." I opened her purse and fished out a pack of tissues, peeling one off for her.

"Thanks." She held the tissue to her nose and gave a frustrated sigh. "I'm so tired of these."

I stood silent. Cassie's bag was stuffed full of packs of tissues. I looked up, studying Cassie clearly for the first time in a long time. Something was clearly wrong—and it was more than just the nosebleeds. Cassie wasn't usually this obtuse. If she was hiding something, there was a reason. I felt a strange prickling sensation spread across the back of my neck. What if there was an actual reason Cassie hadn't told me about these nightmares? What if something in the dreams was preventing Cassie from discussing them?

"Let's get out of here," I said. I gave Cassie a fresh tissue and led the way back to my car. When I opened the door for her, she flashed me a sheepish smile.

"Thanks, Braedyn. I should have told you, I'm sorry."

"It's okay," I said. And I meant it. Because I'd already decided what was going to happen next. If Cassie couldn't tell me what was going on in her dreams, I'd find out on my own. Even if it meant going in uninvited.

14

Even though I'd made the decision—even though I knew this was the best way to help her—it was hard to force myself to breach the edge of Cassie's dream. I knelt in my dream garden, staring at the flickering gleam of her sleeping mind. It hovered like any other dream, a twinkling pinprick that somehow managed to exude an inherent Cassie-ness. It was an odd sensation, feeling comforted by the familiar presence of one of my best friends while planning to disregard her privacy in the most invasive way imaginable.

"Just do it," I murmured under my breath, as though hearing myself voice the order would make it easier to accomplish. But this was still Cassie. In the end, the thing that pushed me to act was the thought that Cassie's dream may have already been invaded. If something was lurking in her subconscious mind, we both needed to know.

I closed my hand around the spark of her sleeping mind and found myself standing in the middle of Cassie's nightmare. Cassie herself sat in a nondescript chair, hands folded demurely in her lap, staring blindly ahead. I'd been in other nightmares, I'd watched as friends clawed their way through terrifying landscapes. Yet, somehow, watching Cassie simply sit was more chilling than the most frantic of nightmares I'd navigated before. I wanted to go to her, to comfort her, but she wasn't supposed to know I'd been here. I had a job to do.

Aside from Cassie, the first indication I had that something was amiss was a vague, gray miasma that shrouded the landscape with a uniform shadow. It was as though something had tainted the entirety of Cassie's unconscious mind. The more I focused on the miasma, the more anxious I became. And there was something else, something lurking in the haze. Once I caught wind of it I tried to sharpen all my attention on identifying it.

For a moment, the haze seemed to resist me, slipping like oily residue through my fingers. But then something changed. I had only a moment's clarity to think. The presence Cassie and Emma had spoken of seemed to become *aware of me*. Around me, the nightmare took form. The miasma congealed into a lithe body, but its edges were blurred as though someone had captured it through a broken camera lens. Where a face should have been there was only a shifting smudge of darkness.

It reached one insubstantial hand toward me and laid a finger against my forehead. A searing pain shot through my body. It felt like being shoved into an icy bath. The wind was driven out of my lungs but I knew better than to take a breath. In front of me a world opened up, gray and lifeless. An overwhelming rage burned at its heart. I simultaneously tried to see and *not see*; some deeply buried part of me, instinct or animal fear, urged me to locate the threat so I knew in which direction to run. But another part of me simply wanted to close my eyes and forget—

The next thing I knew, I was gasping for breath, clutching my sheets tightly to my chest. Zoe stirred on the cot beside my bed. Instead of waking, she slipped back into whatever dream was playing inside her mind. I forced myself to breathe deeply, trying to gain control of my racing heart. One moment later, I had a thought that nearly stopped my heart cold.

The miasma. That insubstantial form both graceful and terrifying. That was no figment of Cassie's imagination. It had had real power, power it shouldn't have been able to wield in Cassie's dreaming mind... unless it was a Lilitu. A Lilitu with the power to infect every corner of a mind. A Lilitu whose touch could plunge my consciousness into another reality.

Lilith.

I wanted to run to Lucas. I wanted to feel his arms around me, warm and strong, even though I knew he lacked the power to protect me. But I couldn't. Telling him was not an option. If I went to him, he wouldn't stop digging until he knew what had terrified me so deeply. And that would lead him to Cassie. And if I told Lucas the connection

I had just discovered between Cassie and Lilith, he would feel duty bound to report her to Clay. Telling Lucas would be as good as handing Cassie directly to the enemy.

As my fear began to subside, frustration took its place. It felt like I had slowly been isolated, my most powerful allies stripped from my side one by one. Lucas. Dad. Karayan. But I needed help. And even though I'd promised not to, I focused my thoughts on Karayan. After a moment's pause, I felt her attention turn to me.

What do you need? Karayan's thoughts felt guarded even as they spilled into my head.

For a moment, no words came to mind. There was so much, I didn't know where to begin. I took a breath and opened my mind, letting the memory of my encounter flood out to Karayan. It was like reliving the dream-encounter. But this time, I had company. When the memory had played itself out, I felt a profound terror from Karayan.

It's really happening. Karayan sounded deeply shaken. *I've heard about the final battle my whole life, but now… It's actually here.*

So what do we do?

A dark, mirthless laugh was Karayan's only response.

Come on, Karayan, please! I don't have anyone else who… Lilith has some kind of hold on Cassie and until we figure out how—or if—we can break it… I let my thoughts fall silent.

After another long silence, I felt Karayan's resigned sigh. *Lilith isn't like you and me. She's not like anything you've encountered before.*

What do you mean?

I overheard Ais and the others talking, back before I joined up with Team Braedyn. I sensed Karayan considering her next words. When she continued, her voice sounded tired. *She's as ancient as the garden. A being who has lived that long… She doesn't think like a human any longer. She's closer to a force of nature than a woman. Braedyn, if she's become aware of you…*

I shivered. *But we have to face her eventually, right? Isn't that the whole point of this war?*

The swell of pity threading through Karayan's next thoughts chilled me. *If Lilith does return? I don't know who could stand up to her. Mankind's best hope is to keep her out of this world for as long as possible.*

Everything I'd been clinging to, my hopes of becoming human, my hopes of being with Lucas, my hope of seeing the end of this war…

they blackened and curled like paper tossed into a roaring fire. Despair overcame me.

Come back, Karayan. Please. I can't do this alone. I didn't care that I was begging her for help.

Clay will never let me back in. Not even if it would save humankind from Lilith. There was something so certain in Karayan's tone that I had no choice but to believe her.

Why?

I don't want to… I didn't have to be sitting in the same room with her to sense the sudden tension that gripped her.

Damn it, Karayan! What did you do? She didn't answer me. I don't know if it was the helplessness, the fear, or coming face-to-face with the indescribable power that meant to destroy us, but something inside me snapped. *Tell me! You owe me that much, if nothing else! Why won't you come back? Why won't Clay let you return? Is it because of whatever happened between you and Thane?*

It's none of your business. Shock and anger shot through Karayan's thoughts. I ignored it.

Did you enthrall someone? Did you kill…? I felt her reaction like a shockwave. *Karayan? You killed someone?*

All the resistance bled out of Karayan. I sat for several moments in silence while she gathered her thoughts. I could feel her summoning the courage to speak, long before she began the story.

Clay had a son. John.

It wasn't what I had expected her to say. But I kept my thoughts to myself, just listening.

He was… well, let's just say that asshole didn't fall far from the tree. He was three years older that me. Confident and cool and he knew I had a crush on him. He'd tease me about it whenever Clay wasn't around. When I turned sixteen, my Lilitu powers started to emerge and he… he was suddenly around everywhere I went. I thought he was falling for me. It was exhilarating and terrifying and forbidden, of course, but that only made it seem so much more…

Karayan fell silent for a moment. I sensed something through our connection. A shudder.

One day he followed me into my room. Karayan's voice quivered. *He'd started to get a little handsy before that day, but suddenly he was all over me. He laughed when I told him to stop before I accidentally hurt him. He said he'd thought it all through and he was okay with it, that one time wouldn't damage him, not permanently anyway. He might have been okay with it but I wasn't. I should have kicked him in the nuts. But I still thought he might... I guess it doesn't matter what I thought. When it was over, he told me not to say anything, that he'd keep our secret if I would. Like he'd given me a gift. He said I wouldn't have to wonder about what sex was like after this. He told me he'd made a sacrifice, by sleeping with me.* Karayan's voice broke.

I felt these words like a knife in my gut. Karayan's anguish was potent, but it was overpowered by a stinging shame. I grasped for anything to say, but my mind drew a blank.

I had to tell someone. I thought I could trust Thane. It was hard... but I told him everything. He looked horrified. I thought he'd do something, protect me or... I don't know. Do whatever fathers do in this situation. Karayan's voice drifted off.

What happened? I asked, feeling sick.

Somehow, John found out I'd told Thane. Thane confronted Clay that night, but it was already too late. John had spent the afternoon convincing his father that I'd enthralled him, manipulated him into sleeping with me. When I tried to defend myself, Clay ordered his men to lock me up while he deliberated, just to be safe. Bitterness tinged Karayan's thoughts with a sour pain. *Thane stood by me at first. Even though he practically worshiped the ground Clay walked on.*

I let out a breath, processing this.

John came to my cell that night. He was pissed, hurt. He told me I should have kept my mouth shut. I begged him to tell Clay the truth, but he looked at me like I was losing my mind. I could see he was scared, but when I tried to reason with him he pulled back. He said it was my fault. That if I hadn't flirted with him, he'd never have come to my room in the first place.

What?! I couldn't keep the outrage from my thoughts. I felt the swell of emotion in Karayan's thoughts in return.

Yeah, he was a real prince. He unlocked the door and told me to run and never come back. I was too angry to speak. I mean, this was the only home I'd ever known. And as screwed up as he was... Thane was my only family. I left the cell and walked up the stairs. He followed me, tried to put some money into my hand but I told him where he could shove it. I was going straight to Thane to tell him everything. Johnny lost it. He grabbed onto me, tried to pull me back down the stairs. Karayan's words were somehow subdued, as though she was afraid to voice them, even in her own mind. *I kicked him off of me and he fell. I heard a snap and then... nothing. So I went down. He must have broken his neck. I didn't have to touch him to see he was dead; I tried to reach his mind. There was this dissipating feeling, like an afterimage... I don't know. I just knew he was gone. I panicked and he ended up getting what he wanted; I ran. By the time I'd worked up the courage to call Thane, they'd found the body. It was seen as proof that Johnny'd been telling the truth. Thane told me if I ever came back he'd kill me... unless Clay got to me first. And that was the last conversation I had with Thane until we both ended up in Puerto Escondido.*

Suddenly I had a window into Thane and Karayan's past that allowed me to see the roots of all that tension and pain and anger I had sensed between them over the years. I shook my head, overwhelmed. *But... It was an accident.*

I didn't mean to kill him. But that doesn't change the fact that he's dead. Karayan's voice was grim but firm. *You see? Even if I wanted to come back, I can't. If Clay catches me, he'll kill me.*

I let out a long sigh. She was right. I'd seen Clay go ballistic when I'd hesitated to hunt down a Lilitu for him. What would he do to someone he blamed for his son's death? Karayan could not come back. Not while Clay was in charge.

I understand.

Braedyn, it's not too late to leave.

I can't go. The thought filled my mind with a bitter pang. *I've made my choice. I'm going to help Cassie, and I'm going to do whatever I can to see the Guard through this last battle.*

I wonder... Karayan's thoughts grew wistful. *I wonder if you can have it both ways. It might not be possible to help your friend and remain loyal to the Guard.*

I released our connection, but Karayan's words stayed with me. It was getting harder to separate the Guard from Clay in my mind.

My phone buzzed on the nightstand, waking me. I picked it up and my eyes caught on the date. It was December 19. Two days until winter solstice. I blinked, and saw the text from Royal.

Found something important. Come early?

My drowsiness evaporated. I flew through my morning routine, asking Gretchen to take Lucas to school. I made up some excuse about meeting up with Royal for a project, but Gretchen didn't seem to care too much about the details. She was still rubbing sleep out of her eyes when I rushed out the front door.

I found Royal in our study room in the library. He looked up as I entered, his eyes tight with concern.

"So I found this passage last night. It talks about preparing a vase, maybe some other step in the ritual that still has to be performed? I'm having trouble with the last bit, but I think… I think it says without her acolytes, Lilith cannot return."

"What?" I dropped my things and leaned over Royal, scanning his notes. There were several holes in his translation, words that he either guessed at or flat-out couldn't decipher, but the gist was there. The acolytes were crucial to Lilith's return. Without them, she might not be able to rejoin the physical world. I sat down heavily. Ice flooded my veins. If Sandra translated this passage and showed it to Clay, Clay wouldn't stop until Cassie and the other acolytes were dead. I knew it as surely as I knew the sun rises in the east. Clay wouldn't hesitate to take drastic measures to stop Lilith's return.

But when I tried to explain that to Royal and Cassie, they looked at me like I was insane.

"Hang on." Royal eyed me with frank disbelief. "Some random book mentions Lilith needing her acolytes. We don't know why or what she needs them for. Do you really think Clay would kill Cassie over that?"

"That is exactly what I think. Which is why that is exactly what I said." I walked to the library door and peered out the little window into the library's main hall. "We need to get Cassie out of town."

"Sorry. Sorry. Are you saying you want me to leave school right before midterms?" Cassie stared at me aghast.

"You're not going to be able to take your midterms if you're dead." There wasn't time to sugarcoat it, but I did feel a twist of regret when I saw the panic growing in Cassie's eyes.

"There is no way my parents will sanction a trip out of town in the middle of the school year." Before I had time to argue with her, Cassie plowed on, "besides, if I leave now, how are you going to cure me once you figure out how to break the connection between Lilith and her acolytes?"

I opened my mouth to answer her, but nothing came out. There was so much more at stake now, the fact that we were even talking about midterms made me feel like screaming.

"She makes a damn fine point." Royal glanced from Cassie to me. "Correct me if I'm wrong, but breaking this link between Cassie and the mother of all evil just jumped to the top of our list of priorities. Right?"

I nodded, but I didn't let them see my eyes. "I don't know how far Sandra and Jerome have gotten translating their books. But when they're done, they're going to come for any of the books we haven't finished. And right now, that means the acolyte book."

"Yes, but they haven't picked it up *yet*. So there's still a little time." Cassie turned to Royal and put her hand on his arm. "You should show this passage to Ally. Get her thoughts. Maybe she can fill in some of the blanks."

Royal nodded. "Hopefully, we'll have some news by lunch."

If you'd asked me to pick one student at Coronado prep who was least likely to sacrifice anything to help us out, I would have said it would be Ally. But when Royal took the passage to her, she ditched all of her morning classes to focus on it exclusively.

When lunchtime rolled around, Ally and Missy joined our table wordlessly. Lucas glanced from me to Royal and back, surprised when neither of us offered any objections to the girls joining us for lunch. Technically, it was Royal's turn to bring the food to our table from the kitchen. But when he turned to Lucas, summoning all his charm to ask for a favor, Lucas held up a hand.

"Let me guess. Latin homework?" Lucas glanced at me, his eyes flat.

"That's right." Royal shrugged apologetically. At this point, we all knew that Lucas knew we were keeping something from him. But we kept up the fiction, for the sake of our friendship.

Once Lucas had left in the direction of the kitchen, Missy turned to Ally, anxious. "What did you find?"

Ally pulled out her notes. She spread three pages on the table. Her handwritten notes intertwined with Royal's, making a mess of the margins. But as he looked through them, Royal's eyebrows hiked higher up his forehead.

"Oh, no. No, no, no." Royal looked up, meeting Ally's eyes. Ally's only response was a grim nod.

"What? What did you find?" Cassie could barely contain her anxiety.

"I mistranslated something," Royal muttered. "It's, um, kind of a big deal." Royal met my eyes, then turned the page he was looking at toward me and slid it across the table. "Third passage down."

I found the passage he was referring to, then read the translation he and Ally had jotted down beside it. "The night demon will have her choice of vessels, prepared for her on the night of the anointing." I looked up, confused.

"I thought it was 'vase,'" Royal said.

"Okay?" They must have read the confusion on my face because Ally and Royal traded an exasperated glance.

"It's not a 'vase' it's a 'vessel,'" Ally said. When that did nothing to clear up the confusion, Ally let out a frustrated breath. "They're not describing a jar. They're describing a body. Like, a human body."

The realization sunk leaden claws into my heart. "A body? You mean…"

"Lilith. She's going to possess one of the acolytes." Royal's voice was so faint, I could barely detect it above the noise of the dining hall. "She needs a body to occupy until she's strong enough to remake her own."

Cassie covered her mouth with her hands, growing several shades paler than usual.

Missy looked from Royal to Ally, panic swelling behind her eyes. "There's… there's got to be some way to stop it. What does it say about stopping it?!"

Ally eyed her friend uneasily. She glanced around the table, reading all our faces. She swallowed. "This isn't just some weird ancient mythology stuff, is it?"

"No." Amber joined us, startling Missy out of her building panic. "It's real. So answer the question."

Ally glanced back at the stack of pages in her hands. "I did find…" She shuffled through some sheets of paper, looking for something. "Yes, actually, I just saw something that mentioned the anointed…

something about warding them... I haven't gotten very far with it yet, but if I had a couple of hours to work..."

"Great. I'll help you after lunch, seeing as how this is 90% of our grade." Royal's voice suddenly became a little too chipper to sound completely normal.

Amber looked up, irritated. "Your grade?"

Lucas set the tray of food down in the middle of the table. We startled visibly. Lucas gave Amber a thin smile.

"It's their cover story." Lucas turned to me, and suddenly I saw the depth of hurt he could no longer hide. "If you want me to go, just ask. But do me a favor. Stop pretending like you have nothing to hide from me." With that, Lucas turned and walked out of the dining hall.

I surged to my feet, feeling awful. Every part of me wanted to race after Lucas. I wanted to catch him. Tell him everything. Win him back. But what I wanted? That was about 100 items down on my current list of priorities. I forced myself to turn back to our table. Everyone was staring at me with varying expressions on their faces.

I forced myself to swallow my frustration and turned to Royal. "So, what's the plan?"

"Well... Aren't you supposed to tell us?" Ally studied me. There was no hint of sarcasm behind the question. She waited for my answer.

I frowned, unsettled. "Winter solstice is in two days," I started.

Ally glanced at Royal, confused.

"Don't ask," he murmured under his breath. "I'll fill you in later."

"Which means we're out of time," I explained. "I know you ditched morning classes, but..."

"Got it." Ally stood, gathering the pages in her arms. She glanced at Royal, impatient. "You coming?"

Royal got to his feet, helping gather the rest of the manuscript copy. "We'll call you as soon as we learn anything," he said. And then he and Ally were walking out of the dining room.

Amber watched me with a small frown. But whatever she was thinking, she kept it to herself, returning to her own lunch table, where her friends sat, presumably waiting for an explanation as to why she and Ally were suddenly hanging out with my friends and me.

"I should see what I can do to help." Cassie started to stand. I caught her hand, stopping her.

"Cassie." I lowered my voice. "I hope Royal and Ally figure this thing out, but... we have to assume that Lilith is going to possess one of the acolytes. I'm not going to let it be you." I had made this decision the morning after I'd visited Cassie's dream. I felt guilty about the others, and responsible, but if it came down to only being able to protect one of them, I was going to save Cassie.

Cassie licked her lips, and I suddenly saw clearly how hard she was struggling to contain her fear. "What can you do?"

"I can shield your mind. It worked to protect Royal from Seth."

"Yeah, just barely." Cassie frowned. "Isn't Lilith stronger than Seth?"

"I've been thinking about that." I leaned in closer, lowering my voice even farther. "I'm going to ask Karayan to work with me. Together, I think we can weave a stronger, thicker shield. It might not stop Lilith, but it's possible it might slow her down."

Surprise flashed across Cassie's face. "I thought Karayan was gone."

I gave Cassie a small smile. This, at least, was something I knew how to accomplish. "It doesn't matter where she is in the waking world. What we have to do won't happen here."

I expected Karayan to be holding some residual anger at me for forcing her to share her story. So when I asked, almost timidly, if she could help me with one more favor, she snapped.

Of course I'll help you, Braedyn. You're my best friend. She sounded exasperated, but there was nothing sarcastic in her tone.

I felt a burst of shock ricocheted through my body. I counted Karayan as a friend, but I hadn't ever really thought about what I was to her. *Right, sorry. I just... I know you wanted some distance.*

It's the Guard who can go screw themselves.

Some part of me still resisted painting the entire Guard with one brush. *Clay is just one man...*

No. This is what you don't understand, Braedyn. While he's in charge, Clay is the Guard. A grim note pervaded Karayan's thoughts.

I didn't want to fight about this again, not now, not while Cassie was still walking around, unprotected. So I dropped it with a sigh.

Karayan must have felt my frustration, because she gave a dry chuckle. *You are the single most stubborn person I've ever met.* But the thought sounded almost affectionate. *Okay. Let's do this.*

I cast my memory back to the night I had woven the shield around Royal's mind. This one needed to be stronger, even more convoluted. I opened my mind and sent the images through to Karayan. After a few moments, I *felt* her begin to understand. Comprehension swelled between us until a unified thought cemented itself in our minds, taking shape into something between an image and a map of what we were after.

Accessing the universal dream while awake takes a little practice, but both Karayan and I were able to do it without much trouble. I sent my conscious mind into the vast space of the dream and sought out Cassie's mind. It wouldn't matter that she was awake. We weren't trying to enter her subconscious. All we had to do was build a wall that separated Cassie from the prying eyes of Lilitu.

I felt Karayan drawing close. When we were both in position, I began to weave my shield. She watched for a few moments, then joined in. We each encircled Cassie's mind, laying down layer after layer of the convoluted maze that would become our shield. As the shield began to take shape, I noticed something intriguing. I couldn't sense Karayan's shield, and I would bet money she couldn't sense mine, but together they seemed to make two parts of a whole.

We worked for close to an hour, pouring all of our energy into the shield, until it seemed to take on a life of its own. When I noticed the shield beginning to swirl I pulled back, willing Karayan to join me at a safe distance. The shield spun around Cassie's mind, picking up speed by the second. It seemed to flash brilliantly and then in the next moment, it was gone. She was gone. I stared at the place where Cassie's mind had been just moments before.

What the...? Astonishment radiated from Karayan's mind beside me. *Where did she go?*

Look. I stared. Against the unrelieved black of the universal dream, there was the palest shadow of something...

Cassie's mind was still directly in front of us. But the shield had worked so well, it not only hid her thoughts from us, it hid almost every trace of her mind's *existence*. If we weren't hovering right next to it, I'm not sure I would've been able to find her against the darkness.

For a long moment, Karayan remained silent. When she finally reached out, her thoughts were tinged with amazement. *It might not keep Lilith out forever, but I'd like to meet any other Lilitu who could break through this shield. Nice work.*

When I returned home that evening, Cassie met me at the door to my house. I could tell immediately that something was wrong.

"Cassie?" My first thought was that something we had done with the shield had harmed Cassie in some way.

"Inside." Cassie drew me into the house. Marla was working on something in the kitchen, but the living room was empty. Cassie took me to the farthest corner and lowered her voice. "It's gone. The acolyte book. It wasn't here when I arrived. I think Sandra or Thane might be translating it right now."

"That little red book?" Zoe walked down the stairs nonchalantly. We looked up, startled. Cassie stared at her. "Oh, she's been translating that book for at least a week. She just puts it back before you get home." Zoe gave me a predatory smile. "Clay figured it might be important, seeing as how it's the one our resident Lilitu personally pilfered with her own little demon hands."

I stared at Zoe, numb. But of course—*of course*—Clay would pay special attention to that book. I felt like an idiot for not suspecting earlier.

While I was still trying to gather my wits, Cassie took a step closer to Zoe. "Do you know how far they've gotten in the translation?" I stared at Cassie, surprised by her brazenness.

Zoe shrugged. "Not my job."

"Then I'll ask her myself." Cassie strode for the front door. I had to run to catch up with her.

"Cassie, wait." But I couldn't say what I wanted to say. Not with Zoe listening in. Cassie didn't stop.

I followed her next door and into the Guard's house. Sandra was sitting at the dining room table with the acolyte book open in front of her. She glanced up as we entered. Thane stood over her shoulder, reading her notes with a look of interested speculation on his face.

"Hello girls." Sandra flashed us a neutral smile. "Fascinating book you brought us, Braedyn. And Thane tells me Cassie was actually anointed as one of Lilith's acolytes this past year?"

The spark of fear that had jumped to life in my heart with Zoe's words roared into a full-fledged blaze. I swallowed, stalling for time to think of something—anything—to say to this.

Clay walked into the room. He didn't look surprised to see either Cassie or me. "Sandra, did you tell the girls what you discovered?"

"I was just about to, actually." Sandra turned back to the slender volume, translating on the fly. "I found this fascinating passage regarding a vessel that's the key to Lilith's return."

"Have you identified what kind of vessel it's describing?" I asked, my voice faint.

Sandra shook her head. "Not yet. This book in particular has some very odd passages. It's almost like it was written by someone who was thinking in a language with more Germanic than romantic roots."

"That's why we have a backup," Clay said. "Murphy, you're up!" Clay bellowed up the stairs.

A few moments later, Dad emerged from the upstairs hallway, bleary eyed. I stared. He looked awful. Deep bags encircled his eyes, and judging by the amount of five o'clock shadow, his face hadn't seen a razor in several days. But it was the way he walked that disturbed me most of all. He shuffled down the stairs, shoulders hunched.

He didn't see me until he reached the bottom step. Then his eyes landed on my face and he hesitated for half a second. His eyes swiveled to Clay.

"What is it?" His voice sounded hollow, strained.

"I need you to find out what our… guest… knows about a vessel. Apparently it's pertinent to Lilith's return. Sandra, brief him before he goes down."

I straightened, eyes latching onto Sandra's face. If Sandra told Dad what she'd learned, we'd know just how much they'd managed to translate.

Sandra stood, tucking the book under her arm. "I've got my notes in the study. Come on, then, I'll fill you in."

I could have screamed with frustration. Dad passed me without meeting my eyes. I made a move toward him but someone caught my arm.

"Don't." Gretchen's whisper moved the hair beside my ear, she was so close. "Clay is watching."

15

I glanced back at the older man. Clay's eyes, fixed on my face, glittered with an unreadable expression. I forced the tension out of my shoulders. Gretchen released her hold on my arm and shifted her weight, masking the fact that she'd had to stop me from going after Dad. The conversation continued around me for several more moments. Even if I'd been closer to the little office, even if Sandra hadn't closed the door behind herself and Dad, I wouldn't have been able to hear much over Clay's droning voice.

Ten minutes later, the door to the office reopened, and Dad and Sandra emerged. Again, he refused to meet my gaze. I watched him make his way to the basement stairs before disappearing below.

I stood, frozen. This was the moment he'd warned me about—the moment he'd been so sure would come. The moment when Clay would order him to hurt Vyla and he'd have to do it or risk his own life and mine. That was the choice he was making on my behalf—to trade my wellbeing for hers. Vyla, who'd only come to Puerto Escondido seeking salvation for her daughter. Who was only trapped here, now, because of me. Guilt and revulsion chased themselves through my thoughts until I felt like crawling out of my own skin. Nothing about this was right, but I felt powerless to stop it.

Sandra returned to the group, turning to Thane with an uneasy frown. "Just in case, we should organize everyone present to search the volumes for any other mentions of this vessel. Cover all our bases."

Thane nodded slowly, his eyes shifting toward Cassie and me.

"Good idea. We can help. Right, Braedyn?" Cassie turned toward me, her eyes gleaming with thinly veiled terror. Something in her tone alerted me and I cleared my throat.

"Yes, absolutely." I forced a smile for Sandra's benefit. "Just tell us what to do."

"I'll grab everything we've recovered from the university. Hang on." Sandra hurried back to the office. A few moments later she returned with a decent stack of old volumes. She set them on the dining room table, and a cloud of dust wafted up from the impact. Sandra dusted her hands off and gestured to the pile. "Right. Pick a book. Look for anything referencing *alveus* or *vas*."

"We'll work together, here." Thane's voice was cold. I glanced up and saw the suspicion plain on his face. "Sit."

He pulled out two chairs from the dining room table. Cassie took one and I followed, lowering myself into it with a leaden feeling growing in the pit of my stomach. I was too focused on the basement below us to concentrate on the book Thane slid into my hands, but Cassie took the book he offered her and began flipping through it with intense focus.

"I think I'll join you, too." Clay took a seat at the table one chair away from me.

"Excellent. You can start on this one." Sandra handed a book to Clay, then picked up another volume for herself.

Sandra and Thane took seats on the far side of the table. I felt Clay's gaze on me but didn't look up. Like a robot, I flipped the book in front of me open and began scanning the first page. My eyes slid over words without registering anything. My mind was fractured, zipping from Vyla in the basement to Cassie and what the Guard might have learned about the connection between Lilith and her acolytes… The longer I sat there, the more my insides twisted up until I felt ready to snap like an over-stressed spring.

Out of the corner of my eye, I saw Cassie freeze. I turned toward her and was jolted out of my spiraling thoughts by the expression on her face. She looked up at me, eyes hard with determination. Clay shifted in his seat, glancing up at that moment. Cassie bent her head back over the book. Her hair swept forward, just obscuring the image drawn onto the page before I could get more than a glimpse of it. But a glimpse was enough; it was an impressive vase, not unlike the vase Seth had manipulated me into stealing for the ritual that had opened the Seal last year. And… something about it seemed vaguely familiar.

Suddenly, Cassie's determination became clear. She was forming a plan. I risked a quick glance at Thane and Sandra, but they were both engrossed in their own books. My eyes shifted to Clay. He met my gaze with a tight smile. I gave him a smile in return, hoping it looked more bored than terrified, and bent over my own book, flipping the page and pretending to scan the dense calligraphy.

Cassie slid something into my hand under the table. A scrap of paper. I took it from her, flipping another page in the book. After a few minutes, I shot a quick glance at Clay. He was studying the book in front of him. Thane and Sandra were similarly engaged. I carefully unfolded the scrap of paper in my lap, then glanced down at it. It was a short note scrawled in Cassie's neat handwriting that read—*Can you reach Vyla?*

I balled the note in my hand, understanding. We might not be able to stop Sandra from translating the acolyte book, but according to Royal and Ally, the text was vague enough that we might be able to throw Sandra and Thane off-track. Give them something else to chase and hopefully buy us enough time to figure out how to break the connection between Lilith and her acolytes *without* killing them. I nodded once without looking up. Cassie straightened beside me, clearing her throat.

"Could this be the vessel you're looking for?" Cassie's voice sounded almost timid. Sandra and Thane glanced up from their books. Cassie held up the image of the vase. While Sandra and Thane studied the image, Clay glanced from Cassie to me. Whatever he was thinking, he hid it behind a flawless poker face.

"Let's see it." Sandra stood and took the book out of Cassie's hand. Thane and Clay rose to join her a moment later. Thane and Sandra traded a look.

"What do you make of it?" Clay glanced at the book over Sandra's shoulder.

"There's not much to go on here." Sandra flipped a page, looking for any clues to the vase's purpose.

"Oh. Okay. I just thought… it's a vase, so…" Cassie shrugged, then shot me a pointed look.

Right. I had a job to do. I let out a breath, and allowed my consciousness to drift below. It took all my nerve to seek Vyla out, fearing what I would find when I did so. But… Vyla's mind was closed to me. Of course. She was a virtual stranger, and she was awake. This wasn't slipping into her dream. The conscious mind guarded itself in a way the sleeping mind did not. For a moment, I panicked. This would only work if Vyla could substantiate Cassie's theory. But then I realized: I was very familiar with the other person in the basement.

I adjusted my target and felt Dad's mind like a beacon of light in the darkness. I slipped into the back of his mind. As it had been with Lucas and Cassie, I found myself experiencing the world through his eyes. When he looked at Vyla, he couldn't see her Lilitu aspect. He only saw the slight woman glaring at him from behind the bars of a cell.

Relief flooded through me—he hadn't laid a hand on her, not yet at any rate. Vyla spoke, her words sounding strangely muffled. I focused on her and the words grew clearer.

"And I'm telling you, I don't know anything about any vessel." Her voice was strained.

Dad turned away from her. I watched through his eyes as he walked toward a metal cabinet against the far wall. He opened the cabinet, revealing a gleaming array of wicked looking tools.

"Murphy, I swear I'm telling you the truth." Vyla's voice sounded scared, vulnerable. "Please believe me, if I knew of a threat against this world I would offer it up freely."

"I'm sorry," Dad breathed. "I have orders." Dad reached for a slender knife—

Dad, stop! The force of my horror bled through the thought, stronger than I had intended.

Dad doubled over, dropping to one knee and clutching his temples. For a moment, I was too scared to speak, worried I had hurt him. Then he rose to his feet. "Braedyn?" His voice came out hoarse with emotion.

I'm here, I sent.

"Don't… please, baby, don't watch this." Dad's voice cracked. "I can't do this if I know you're…" he choked back a ragged sob.

We don't have a lot of time. I tried to fill the thought with urgency. It got Dad's attention. I felt him focusing inward, waiting. *The vessel they're looking for, it's an acolyte—Lilith has to possess one to physically return to this world.*

"Cassie…?" Dad's concern warmed my heart.

I've done what I can to protect her, I sent. *But Royal and Ally are working on a way to break the connection between Lilith and her acolytes.*

"Why are you telling me this?"

We need time, time for Royal and Ally to figure it out. If Clay realizes what the vessel is…

Dad nodded. I didn't have to spell it out for him; he knew exactly what Clay was capable of. "What do you need from me?"

There's a vase pictured in one of the books up here. I focused on the image in my mind, willing it into Dad's head. I heard him breathe in sharply.

"Tall. Inscriptions along the base?"

That's it. I felt a swell of triumph, but had to push it down. *Can you describe it to Vyla? If we can convince Clay that it's worth investigating…*

Dad turned to Vyla before I'd had time to finish the thought. "I've got it. And kiddo, be careful."

Vyla eyed him through the bars of the cage, uneasy. "What? What's going on?"

"I think there's a way out of this for both of us that doesn't involve violence. How good are you at acting?"

Vyla gave him a hollow smile. "Today? I'm Oscar worthy."

"Listen up, we don't have much time. You're going to have to describe a vase in intricate detail, when Clay comes asking."

"What about your orders?"

Dad grew quiet. I felt the turmoil in him. He didn't seem to know I was still eavesdropping, but I couldn't pull myself away. "Let's just say, I'm more concerned about my soul right now. Braedyn was right. I don't even recognize myself anymore."

"What about you, Braedyn?"

"Huh?" I looked up, my consciousness jerked back to the dining room table. Cassie watched me, eyes tight with anxiety.

"Have you seen anything like this before?" Sandra frowned at me, holding the book out. Clay studied me over Sandra's shoulder, suspicious.

I took it from her, focusing on the image of the vase. "It does look familiar," I said. Then, like a lightning strike, the memory of the vase returned. "In the university vault." I looked up at Sandra, excited. "You were there. Those two grad students were handling the vase. Remember? They said they had to store it in a different department, antiquities or something?"

"Holy shite." Sandra took the book back and stared at the image. "I think she's right."

Clay took the book from Sandra, his surprise almost palpable. "We should call Jerome. See if he recognizes it, or knows its significance." He looked up at Sandra. "He's at the university now, isn't he? Maybe he can get a look at this thing up close."

"Yes, but he'll be in the wrong vault." Sandra frowned again.

"It's something to work off of, at the very least," Thane murmured.

Clay handed the book back to Sandra. "I'll check with Murphy. See if he's managed to glean anything from the Lilitu." He strode toward the basement door. I knew Dad would hear him coming; I just hoped he and Vyla had had enough time to sort out the specifics of the vase to sell it.

"Sandra, do you still need me? We've got midterms coming up." Cassie wrung her hands, looking for all the world like an anxious high school kid worried about her exams.

"Go ahead, love." Sandra gave Cassie a warm smile. "I think we can spare you for an afternoon or two."

"Thanks."

I walked Cassie to the front door before Clay had time to return. "Keep your cell on," I whispered.

Cassie nodded. "Royal and Ally, they're going to figure it out, I know it." She gave me a smile full of faith. "We just have to give them a little more time."

I heard the door to the basement open and pushed Cassie out the front door. "Go. Tell them to hurry."

Cassie nodded and darted toward her car, parked on the opposite side of the street. I watched her go for a beat longer, then closed the door.

"Braedyn, would you join us for a minute?" Clay's warm drawl reached me in the foyer, sending a chill over me.

"Coming." I took a breath, trying to settle my racing heart. A million scenarios played through my head in the short walk back to the dining room. What if Clay had unearthed our subterfuge? What if he'd hurt Vyla and she'd let something slip? What if Sandra had already completed the translation and Clay had simply let us think Cassie was safe?

I entered the dining room, feeling a cold sweat beading along my scalp.

Clay looked up as I joined them at the old wooden table. "Tell me, how do you contact Sansenoy?"

"I... I'm sorry?" I stared at him, caught off guard.

"The angel. How do you contact him?" Clay straightened, his eyes narrowing.

I swallowed, glancing at Thane nervously. The archivist studied me with an unreadable expression. "I don't. He comes to me."

"You can't call to him in any way?" Clay's frown deepened.

"No." I shrugged, letting some of my frustration rise to the surface. "I've tried everything I can think of to get his attention, but he comes and goes when he wants to."

Clay scrutinized me for a moment in silence. Then he scratched at his temple. "I've been thinking. Why would a powerful angel choose to confer with a demon girl when he could bend the ear of the leader of the Guard? The Guard has worked closely with those three angels since Adam was expelled from the Garden. But this angel comes to you, at school no less, where there are no witnesses to corroborate your story."

I stared at Clay, anger filling my stomach like a stone. "Are you suggesting... you think I made it up?"

"I don't know. Maybe you felt an urgency to prove your worth to the Guard. It's understandable. You show up with 'a message from Sansenoy' just when we need direction, I can see the logic in wanting to feel indispensible."

Heat flooded my cheeks. "I wouldn't lie about that."

Clay shrugged. "Odd that such a powerful potential ally for our cause prefers to keep his distance."

"Yeah." I crossed my arms. I suddenly felt like I was on trial. "But like I said, he comes and goes when he wants."

"Well." Clay flashed an easy smile and waved this away as if it wasn't important. "Just let us know if he makes contact again."

"Of course." I stood rooted to the floor, rigid with fury.

Clay turned back to Sandra and Thane. After a moment, he glanced over his shoulder at me. "You can go now. I'll call for you if I need you."

I fled onto the front porch of the Guard's house, closing the door behind me. For a moment, I was too stricken to make the walk home. I leaned against the side of the house, trying to get my breathing under control. Clay had picked a scab I'd thought was healed over. But now, fresh pain and frustration welled within my heart.

It had been months since I'd last seen Sansenoy. Why was he ignoring me? Why now, when I needed him—the cause needed him— more than ever before?

The door opened beside me and I bolted for the stairs, caught.

"Wait." It was Dad. I turned back to him, swallowing the urge to cry out and throw myself into his arms. He stood in the doorway, solemn. He looked tense, strained. He shot a quick look over his shoulder, then froze. One of Clay's men—his name was Simon, I think—joined us on the porch. He moved casually enough, but I would have bet good money he was there to monitor us.

"Sorry, Murphy. Clay's got some more questions for you." Simon gave Dad a mild smile.

"Right." Dad held the door open. "After you."

Simon's eyes flicked over to me before he shrugged and headed back inside. As soon as his back was turned, Dad caught my gaze and mouthed; *My dream.*

Before I could respond, he was pulling the door shut and I was standing on the porch alone.

"Something's shifted in the Guard." Dad's dream had faded almost as soon as I'd found him that night. He was a decent lucid dreamer, which surprised me.

"Shifted, how?" I perched on a nondescript ledge that hadn't completely dissolved as Dad's attention had turned from his dream to me.

"I can't quite put my finger on it." Dad frowned. His frustration pulsed in the space around us, made almost palpable as his dreaming mind tried to interpret the intensity of the emotion into something physical. "But I know I'm being deliberately excluded from Clay's confidence. Which scares me." Dad's eyes settled on my face. "I think it's time to move."

I stared at him, my breath catching. "You mean… run?"

"I have the money we'll need to put some real distance between us and the Guard. I've been gathering it steadily for weeks now. And I can see to it that Vyla is released before we go."

"What about Cassie? There's a way to protect the acolytes. We can't leave until I know she's going to be okay."

"Braedyn, we might not get another opportunity…"

"It's Cassie."

Dad studied me for a long moment. He looked torn. "You're putting a lot of faith in a couple of high school kids," he started.

"Then… what if we approach Sandra?" I swallowed, thinking fast. "We could tell her what we've figured out… I mean, if we can break the link between Lilith and the acolytes, won't that hurt Lilith, too? Maybe even keep her from returning to earth. Sandra might help us finish the translation and…"

"*No.*" Dad's voice ricocheted across the dreamscape. "If you tell Sandra about this, she'll take it directly to Clay. Clay won't care if there's a way to release the acolytes from this bond, he'll want to eliminate the threat they pose by any means necessary."

"But if she doesn't go to Clay," I started. "If *you* ask her to trust you… I mean, you're The Alan Murphy. You're their hero or something, aren't you?"

Dad's lips tightened as he gathered his thoughts. "When I said something was shifting in the Guard… I feel it in all these little interactions. The way the rank and file soldiers watch me out of the corner of their eyes. The way Sandra, and now Thane, pick and choose their words when I'm around." Dad shook his head. "I may have been their hero once. But I'm not anymore."

I felt something tighten inside my chest. Some part of me had clung to the belief that Dad's presence would be enough to shield me from the Guard. But if they no longer trusted him, then he no longer had the influence to protect me simply by vouching for me. Maybe Dad was right. Maybe we were living on borrowed time. But that didn't change the fact that if I left now, I would be abandoning my best friends.

Dad seemed to read the conflict in my face. He let out a slow breath. "Whatever you're going to do, kiddo, you better move fast. Vyla and I can string Clay along a few more days at most."

"Thank you." I looked up at Dad. "For freeing her."

"Don't thank me yet." Dad gave me a solemn look. "I'll do my best, but if it's a choice between freeing her or escaping with you…"

"Don't say it." Another wave of guilt and pain coursed through me.

Dad studied my face, concerned. "Honey, it was her choice to come to Puerto Escondido. If not her, Clay would have forced you to hunt down some other Lilitu…"

"She didn't come to Puerto Escondido." My voice came out harsher than I'd intended. Dad jerked back, surprised by the vehemence. "She came to *me*. She came to find me because she wants her daughter to become human."

Dad's expression shifted from surprise to astonishment. "She…?"

The shrill buzz of an alarm rocked the dream. Dad's dream aspect flickered as his body began to stir in the waking world. We were out of time. Dad turned back to me, his expression urgent—but before he could finish the thought, his dream dissipated.

I bit back a frustrated curse and focused on his mind. But when I slipped into the back of his consciousness, I saw Simon—Dad's minder—entering his room. We wouldn't be free to talk, not with Simon present.

I drew back, returning to my own dream to contemplate my next move in the last few moments before waking.

An alien wind rustled through the field of roses. I turned.

Seth faced me, eyes snapping. I recoiled from him, grasping for the escape of the waking world. Seth gestured, and I was suddenly flattened, pinned like an insect onto the ground, unable to stir or wake from my dream. A new brand of terror seeped into my bones. The pressure of Seth's will increased. It was like being squeezed in an invisible giant's fist.

"Do you really think you can undo what has been set in motion?" Seth advanced on me, studying me with an almost apathetic frown.

My heart fluttered wildly in my chest, but a surge of something else rose inside me, overwhelming the panic. "I sure as hell can try."

Seth tilted his head to one side and the pressure around me increased. I gasped against the crushing sensation. "You'll fail. Lilith will return." Then he smiled, a chilling, malicious smile. "I hope she chooses Cassie."

I couldn't help but react. Seth saw my fear. His grin broadened.

"You know what happens when something as powerful as Lilith takes possession of a human body?" Seth lifted a hand and gestured lazily in the air. A transparent plume of smoke appeared, solidifying into a girl's body as I watched. It didn't take much imagination to see Cassie in the slight figure. "Her power will burn through the vessel… slowly at first, devouring the spirit, then the mind." A flame flickered to life within the shadow-figure. As Seth spoke, it grew, filling the form with searing light. "Eventually, not unlike a butterfly emerging from a chrysalis, Lilith will emerge, shedding the host body like an empty shell."

The flame spiraled out of the shadow-figure, which broke apart into motes like the settling ashes of a fire.

My eyes shifted from the shadow to Seth's face. He was smiling, feeding off my helpless agony—when something changed.

A building rage had taken root in my chest, and like a boiler with no way to release the pressure, it fought the walls struggling to contain it. Something gave, just slightly, but I felt the pressure around me lessen. Seth's smile faltered. I pushed myself to my hands and knees, then looked up into Seth's eyes. His face was taut with concentration. I rose to my feet, facing him as I strained with every ounce of strength against the crush of his will.

Seth's jaw clenched with effort. He lifted a hand, trying to regain control. I took a step toward him, and the power holding me snapped. Seth's body rocked back, as though it had absorbed the full force of a blow from a sledgehammer. He staggered back, just managing to keep his feet.

"Get out." I kept my voice level. Around us, the garden shivered with a building power.

Seth shot a quick glance at the shuddering roses. When he turned back, he was smiling again. "It's almost endearing, how hard you fight for lost causes. Your little puppy-love romance with Lucas. Your devotion to an all-but-decimated Guard. Your futile efforts to save Cassie from her destiny…"

I lifted a hand, stopping Seth's mouth with the effort of my will. Seth's eyes narrowed. I could feel him pushing back, struggling to exert his will over the dream.

"Enough." I closed my fist.

For a split second, Seth's face registered astonishment. Then he was gone.

It hadn't been a restful night. I stood, shivering in my winter coat, at the start of morning meeting. Around me, Guardsmen and spotters huddled in groups, talking quietly and drinking mugs of steaming coffee to fight off the chill.

Dad wasn't around, but I saw Sandra and Thane emerge from the house with Clay. They had their heads bent close together in conversation. My heart skipped a beat when I saw what Sandra was clutching tightly in her hands—the acolyte book. I tried to read their faces, but I was too far away to make out much. Uncertainty surged through my mind.

If they didn't know about the link between Lilith and her acolytes yet, I didn't want to tip them off and risk them acting rashly. But if they did know… I needed to make them understand there was a way to protect the acolytes. I bit my lip, finally resolving to see what came out at the meeting before taking any action.

During the meeting, Clay gave the standard updates and assignments. Lucas scribbled down the meeting minutes at Clay's side. Sandra presented an update, touching on the vase without giving any details. No one mentioned the acolytes at all. Clay called the end of the meeting and relief washed through me. One more day. We had one more day to figure out how to break the link.

One more day until winter solstice.

The group broke up, hurrying for the warmth of the houses. I made my way home, meaning to pack and leave for school early. With any luck, Royal and Ally could be waiting with news of a breakthrough.

I walked through the front door of my house. Someone gripped my arm and pulled me inside, shutting the door behind me. I recoiled, then froze—

"Dad...?"

Dad pressed his eye to the peephole, scanning the front yard. "They're moving on Cassie *now*."

"What?!" I felt the bottom drop out of my stomach. The walls seemed to waver around me, but all I could focus on was Dad's face.

"Matthew overheard some of Clay's soldiers preparing." He pulled his gaze away from the door. "It's time to move. We'll have to take Cassie with us."

Dad pulled the front door open and set one foot outside. I moved to follow him, but he caught me with one hand and pushed me against the wall just inside the door.

"Murphy. We missed you at morning meeting." Clay stepped out from behind the gate leading to the Guard's backyard.

Dad's voice sounded easy enough, but his hand didn't loosen its grip on my jacket. "Lost track of the time. It won't happen again."

"Mind if I ask what you're doing in the women's barracks?" Clay's voice was equally neutral. I held my breath, feeling each second pass.

"Ran out of razor blades," Dad said. I felt him pull something out of his pocket. This must have been his contingency plan. "Plus, they've got all the good coffee."

"Next time put it on the list. We're due for a supply run anyhow." Clay cleared his throat. "I wanted to get your opinion on something. Mind joining me in my office for a chat?"

"No problem. Let me just turn the kettle off. Don't want to burn the house down."

"Fine." Clay's voice was starting to sound strained.

Dad turned away from the door, leaving it ajar. He pulled a wad of cash out of his pocket. "You'll have to go without me," he whispered.

"Dad, no—"

"Get Cassie and get out of town." Dad shoved the money into my hand and closed my fingers over it. "I'll keep Clay busy for as long as I can."

"But when they realize I'm gone...? What are they going to do to you?"

"I can take care of myself," Dad hissed, "but if you don't go *now*, Cassie will be dead within the hour."

16

Dad left me in the foyer, huddled against the wall. I gave myself to the count of 30, then opened the front door and slipped outside. Morning sunlight slit across the yard, cut into ribbons by the bare arms of the oaks and aspens lining our street. I saw Dad follow Clay into the Guard's house. He risked one glance back, and when he saw me, he gave me a slight nod. My nose stung in response. It felt entirely too much like a goodbye.

I pulled my phone out of my pocket to check the time. Only 7:14. Cassie was probably still at home. I fished my keys out of my pocket and darted down to the street, unlocking the Firebird and slipping behind the wheel. I checked the rearview mirror once before turning the key in the ignition. There was no one in sight. I shifted into drive and pulled away from the curb, battling nausea.

Was this the last time I'd ever see my childhood home? I pushed the thought to the back of my mind. The route to Cassie's was one I'd travelled hundreds of times before, but today, each street felt strange and hostile. I kept my eyes on the mirrors, watching for anyone who might be following.

By the time I pulled up at Cassie's house, tension had knit the muscles of my back into stones.

Cassie was opening the driver's side door of her car. She didn't look up as I pulled to a stop at her curb. Why would she? She wasn't expecting anyone at this hour.

"Cassie, I need you to come with me."

Cassie turned, blinking against the harsh morning light. "Braedyn? What are you doing here?"

"Cassie, get in my car *right now!*"

Cassie heard the urgency in my voice and snatched her backpack out of her car. It was open; a few books tumbled onto the driver's seat. Cassie reached for them reflexively.

"Leave them!" My voice sounded shrill in my ears, but it got the point across. Cassie abandoned her textbooks and raced for my car. I reached across the seat and shoved open the passenger door, then shifted into reverse. Cassie dropped into her seat and I peeled away from her curb.

"Whoa!" Cassie pulled the door closed and yanked her seatbelt down across her chest. I heard the buckle click into place.

I floored it and the Firebird leapt forward, slamming Cassie and me back against our seats. We reached the corner and I blew past the stop sign, squealing into the turn. I heard the Firebird kicking up a scatter of gravel as we skidded onto the cross street.

Behind us, a familiar truck turned onto Cassie's street from the opposite end. I spotted them a split second before a house obscured my view. With any luck, they hadn't marked my sky-blue Firebird. It wasn't exactly designed to blend in, but the sun was working in our favor, slanting into the truck's windshield. With any luck, whoever was driving would have shielded his eyes against the glare as we were making our escape.

Cassie watched me from her seat, gripping her seatbelt so hard her knuckles had gone white. "How scared should I be?" Her voice, thin with fear and tension, struck a nerve.

"Call Missy. Tell her the Guard knows about the acolytes. They'll be coming for Carrie, too."

Cassie drew her phone out of her pocket wordlessly. Only her hands, shaking as she dialed Missy's number, gave voice to her terror. She cleared her throat when Missy picked up. "They know. Get Carrie and hide." Cassie thumbed her phone off and leaned back in her seat.

I spun the steering wheel, taking an unexpected turn. This street was lined with skeletal trees. Only a few leaves clung to the branches here and there; most had already dropped as the winter approached. I saw an alley ahead and turned into it. The alley cut through to the next residential street. I pulled onto the street and waited, keeping my eyes on the alley behind us. Cassie glanced at me, then back at the alley.

After a few minutes, I let out a breath. "I think we're clear."

Cassie turned back to me, her eyes haunted. "Now what? I can't go to school, can I?"

I shook my head no.

Cassie swallowed. "I can't go back home, either?" She sounded faint. I shook my head again. Cassie nodded, but it looked like she might break at any moment. "What about... what about my parents? Are they in danger?"

"No. No. Clay only wants you." I gripped the steering wheel, fighting the helpless rage that threatened to blind me. "We're going to figure this out," I managed.

Cassie hissed. I looked at her, startled. A bright trickle of red snaked down the front of her face. She held a hand to her nose, wincing. "Oh crap." She fished in her purse for some tissues, then blotted up the blood. "I'm sorry."

A rush of grief rolled over me. I reached out and squeezed Cassie's shoulder, unable to put my feelings into words for a few breathless seconds. "It's getting worse, isn't it?"

Cassie glanced at me, but the blood was already seeping through the tissue she'd wadded against her nose. She turned away, grabbing another handful of tissues.

Karayan, I need you. I closed my eyes, willing the thought to find her. I felt her attention honing in on my plea. *I know we agreed on distance, but I need to know where you are hiding.*

Why? But it wasn't suspicion bleeding through Karayan's thought. It was alarm. *What's happened? Something's happened.*

It's Cassie. I need to put her on a bus. She's coming to meet you. So just tell me what city I'm buying a ticket for.

You don't need a ticket. Karayan's thoughts echoed through my mind, charged with tension.

I can't drive her myself. My mind had been turning the problem over and over. If we fled together, we have to leave the car behind. It was too noticeable, and we didn't know who was on Clay's payroll, or how far his reach extended.

Braedyn. You don't need to put her on a bus. I'm still here. I'm in Puerto Escondido. Karayan must have sensed my shock. I felt her grim admission like a slap. *I couldn't take Emlyn away. I couldn't take her away without her mom.*

You're hiding in Puerto Escondido? I repeated the question in my mind, numb. *But the Guard…*

I know! Don't you think I know? I felt Karayan gathering her thoughts. *But we've been careful. And… We have someone helping us.*

What? Who?! I felt suddenly disoriented. Karayan was relying on some secret stranger to protect her from the wrath of Clay and his soldiers. It had to be someone who knew about the Lilitu, and it had to be someone *human*. The Guard would have sussed out any Lilitu skulking around town, no matter how carefully she hid. Who would willing help a Lilitu, knowing what we are? Who could we trust? Unless… *Karayan, what did you do?*

Nothing. The hurt threaded through Karayan's thoughts.

Then why…? But before I could finish my question, Cassie cleared her throat.

"Braedyn?" Cassie stared at me from her seat. She'd managed to stem the flow of blood from her nose. But dried red streaks stained the front of her face from her nose down to her chin. Cassie's eyes shifted to my hands, still gripping the steering wheel.

"It's Karayan." I glanced at Cassie, distracted by the internal dialogue. "I just need a minute…"

Cassie nodded, her eyes widening in understanding.

He wanted to help. Karayan's thoughts changed, permeated with an awed gratitude. *His name is Ben. He came here with Emlyn and her mom. He doesn't know much, but he knows enough. He knows we're not exactly human, and he knows Clay will kill us if he gets the chance.*

The image of a kind looking man in his 30s appeared in my mind's eye. I'd seen him in the Plaza, that day when I had confronted Vyla. They had looked happy together. I remember noticing she hadn't fed from him. Ben. I bit my lip, thinking.

Do you have room for one more? I wasn't thrilled about the prospect of keeping Cassie in town. But they'd managed to hide for months without raising any suspicions, so whatever they were doing seemed to be working. So far.

The more the merrier, Karayan sent back. I could feel the worry behind her words. *In fact, we have room for several more than one in case you and Murphy were looking to upgrade your life expectancy.*

I let out a long breath. *One step at a time. How do I get to you?*

It took me 20 minutes to drive to the old duplex in the heart of downtown.

Ben met us at the front door and led us inside. The duplex was built in a modified Hacienda style. The two separate units surrounded an inner courtyard. The courtyard itself was completely enclosed by the duplex, perfectly hidden from the surrounding streets. Karayan and Ben had managed to secure both units, giving everyone their own room, with one more room to spare. But the best part of the setup was the courtyard. There was space for Emlyn to play, complete with a little patch of grass and a modest swing set. Knowing that two of the three occupants hadn't stepped foot beyond the walls in months, the house felt vaguely like a prison, but until the Guard learned how to fly, it would keep Emlyn and Karayan hidden from prying eyes.

As Cassie and I followed Ben into the first unit, Karayan looked up from her seat at a small kitchen table. She rose, unfolding herself from the chair like a ballerina. I'd forgotten how graceful she was. She crossed the distance between us and caught me in a fierce hug.

There were so many things she could have said, with "I told you so" topping the list. But when she released me from the hug, she simply held my gaze and asked, "what now?"

My resolve broke a little, and hot tears gathered in the corners of my eyes. I quickly ducked my head, fixing my gaze on the floor between us. "I know. I should have listened to you. Clay… He's everything you said he was and more. Dad tried to get me out, but…" I clamped my mouth shut, refusing to give into the wracking sobs trying to work their way out of my chest. I cleared my throat. "He wants us to go. He told me to leave without him."

"Agreed." Karayan's voice firmed. "It's past time. We can be ready in fifteen minutes. I just have to pack a few things for Emlyn." Karayan turned toward the back of the house. I caught her hand, stopping her.

"Wait." My eyes slid back to Cassie. She watched me, waiting. The skin around her eyes had taken on sunken look, and the nosebleeds… they were symptoms of a disease we had yet to diagnose. "Wait." My mind felt sluggish, but I knew if we left now it would mean Cassie's death, one way or another. "We can't leave."

"If this is about Lucas, or saying goodbye to your friends…" Karayan studied me with a frown.

"She's getting sicker by the day." I dropped my voice, but I didn't have to glance at Cassie for Karayan to take my meaning. Her eyes flicked over to the slender figure of my friend. "If we don't find a way to break the connection between her and Lilith…" I saw the shadow figure consumed by fire once again in my mind's eye. I shivered, trying to push the image out of my head. "We're so close to figuring it out. Royal and Ally… they could literally finish the translation *any minute* now. If we leave before they do…"

"Mommy?" A little girl ran into the room, eyes bright with a wild hope. She stopped short when she saw my face. The glimmer of excitement in her eyes guttered and went out. "Oh." She turned to Karayan, suddenly shy. "How much longer?"

"I told you." Karayan turned and knelt to face Emlyn, smiling kindly. "Your mom has an important job to do, but as soon as she's done, she'll come find us."

Emlyn's gaze slid over Karayan's shoulder. She eyed me with a suspicious fear that had no place on a little girl's face. Emlyn had had to grow up fast these last few months, and whatever pretty lies Karayan had had to tell her, it was clear Emlyn wasn't buying them anymore. "That's what you keep saying. But I want to know *when*."

"I wish I could tell you, sweetie." Karayan turned to me then, her face full of pain. "Emlyn, Braedyn and I need to talk for a minute. Why don't you go back outside with Ben. We can make our cookies this afternoon, okay?"

Emlyn frowned unhappily, but she took the hand Ben offered her and let him lead her outside.

Karayan watched them go, then let her head dip forward in resignation. "Fine. Stay. Figure it out. I'll keep Cassie safe until you do." She turned back to look at me then, her eyes solemn. "You'd better get to school or Clay will know you're involved in Cassie's disappearance."

"He'll suspect me no matter what," I said dully.

"Yes, but he might not act immediately if he *only* suspects. And isn't this whole thing about buying your friends time to finish their translation?"

I didn't need to be told twice. I left Cassie standing beside Karayan and slipped back to my car. With any luck, I'd make it to school in time for first bell. Some part of me knew I was playing with fire by going back to Coronado Prep, but I told myself I'd be safe, that Clay wouldn't send someone for me while I was at school.

Because no part of me expected to be going back home.

I pulled into the parking lot at school 15 minutes later. There was a crowd gathering on the quad, and I saw the flashing lights of the police car glinting off the windows of North Hall. What now?

I parked my car and emerged, feeling as though I were trapped in a dream. I made my way toward the quad. Lucas saw me and broke from the crowd of students. His face was drawn with an anxious tension.

"Have you heard from Cassie?"

"What?" I had to swallow to keep the fear out of my voice. "No… no. I haven't." The lie tasted sour in my mouth, but Lucas's face fell.

"She's missing. Braedyn, Cassie is missing. The police are asking if anyone's seen her. They found her car abandoned on the street in front of her house, the door was open and some of her schoolbooks were still inside. They think… they think someone took her." Lucas's brow furrowed. He peered into my eyes, his concern wrenching a knife in my chest.

"What does…?" I swallowed again, hating this. Hating the need to lie to Lucas. Hating the fact that I couldn't trust him not to run to Clay if I told him our friend was safe.

Lucas took my hand in his. His fingers curled through mine, warm and strong. I felt the tears I'd fought down earlier return, but this time I let them spill. Grief and shame and guilt, they poured out of me. Lucas pulled me to him, wrapping his arms around my shoulders.

"It's going to be okay." He whispered the words into the hollow of my neck, his breath warming the hair beside my cheek. I heard the agony in his voice, knew he was suffering on Cassie's behalf. She was one of his best friends, too. He didn't know she was safe. I did. And yet, he was comforting *me*.

Revulsion forced me to push out of his arms. Lucas stared at me, stricken. I shook my head, dragging the back of my hand across my eyes. I couldn't do this. I couldn't face him.

"Braedyn." The school counselor approached, his face solemn and composed. "I'm so sorry, but Headmaster Fiedler would like to speak with you in his office. Would you please come with me?"

I glanced back at Lucas. Behind him, I saw Royal emerging from his little sports car. There wasn't time to get to him and explain. He would hear the story from our peers, and he would be left wondering if Clay had taken Cassie. If Clay had *murdered* Cassie.

"Braedyn." The school counselor took hold of my arm and pulled me gently forward. I glanced back at him, reeling. Lucas gave my hand one last squeeze before releasing me. And then I was following the counselor across the quad toward the administration building.

I don't remember the walk to the headmaster's office. I only remember looking through the door as headmaster Fiedler stood behind his desk. He was speaking to a police officer. When he saw me, he nodded his head toward me.

"This is one of Cassie's closest friends, Braedyn Murphy." Headmaster Fiedler gestured toward the officer. "Braedyn, this is officer Wess."

The police officer turned toward me and I recognized him in an instant. Adrenaline hit my system like a zinging bolt of electricity. "I remember. You're the one who arrested Lucas."

The officer nodded his head, keeping his expression neutral.

"You can leave us," Fiedler was saying to the counselor. "I'll stay with Braedyn and the officer. I'm sure you'd be more use to the students right now."

I turned back in time to see the counselor pull the office door closed behind him.

"Braedyn Murphy. Whenever a student at Coronado Prep gets into trouble, I seem to run into you." Officer Wess's voice resonated off the office's wood-paneled walls. I forced myself to take a deep breath, then I turned to face him. His eyes glittered in the dimly lit room. "I have a few questions."

By the time they were finished with me, it was well into second period. As soon as I got clear of the administration building, I fished my phone out of my pocket and dialed Royal. He picked up on the first ring.

"Did they take her?" Royal's voice sounded like it had been scraped raw.

"No. She's safe. She's hiding." I heard Royal's breath release on the other end of the line.

"Why didn't you tell me?!" Royal's fear morphed into fury.

"There wasn't time." I glanced over my shoulder. A few other officers were taking statements from teachers and students on the quad. "We shouldn't do this now. Where are you?"

"Ally and I are finishing the translation. You'll just be in the way. If we learn anything I'll call you. But right now…"

"Right. Right. You should be working. So stop wasting time talking to me."

"Braedyn?" Royal's voice sounded hoarse. "Thank you. For getting her out." He didn't wait for my response. The line went dead. I thumbed my phone off and slid it back into my pocket. There was nothing to do now but wait.

I drifted through morning classes with my head in a haze. The school was buzzing about Cassie. It seemed like her name was on everyone's lips. I felt eyes on me every time I walked into a room, down a hall, through a door. But when I saw Cassie's mom and dad being led toward the administration building, the floor seemed to drop out of my stomach. Cassie's mom clung to her dad, too blinded by her tears to navigate the pathway without stumbling. Headmaster Fiedler met them at the front door of the administration building. Officer Wess stood by his side, arms crossed over his chest, the picture of official responsibility.

"You recognize that guy?" Lucas's voice startled me out of my reverie. His eyes were locked onto Officer Wess. "He's the same cop who arrested me." There was something in Lucas's tone, something dark and dangerous. "Do you think it's a coincidence?"

At that moment, Wess turned his eyes toward me. The smallest smile flashed across his face. A malicious smile. A *knowing* smile.

"No." The word slipped out, half breath, half growl. But Lucas heard it. He turned toward me, suddenly alert.

"What do you know?"

I opened my mouth, fumbling for the next story. But I couldn't force myself to lie to him again. Lucas's brows furrowed. He stepped in front of me, blocking my view of Cassie's parents. He brushed a hand beneath my jaw and gently tilted my face up until I met his eyes.

"Braedyn? What aren't you telling me?"

"Don't ask." I closed my eyes, struggling for strength. "Don't make me lie to you."

"I've been waiting." Lucas's voice wavered. "I've been waiting for you to trust me enough to tell me what's going on. Why can't you trust me?"

"It's not safe." I forced my eyes open. Lucas's gaze was fixed on my face.

"Safe for who?"

I shook my head. It was the only answer I could give. Lucas licked his lips. I could see the effort it took for him to keep from screaming.

"I don't need you to protect me, Braedyn." By some miracle, he managed to keep his voice steady. "I want to help. Let me *help*."

My phone buzzed and my heart leapt into my throat in response. I fished the phone out of my back pocket. Royal had sent a text. One word.

Library.

"I'm sorry. I have to go." I pulled away from Lucas, shoving the phone back into my pocket before he had a chance to see the screen. Lucas moved to follow me.

"I'll come with you."

"*No.* No. If you want to help… Just please, let this go." I turned my back on Lucas, but not before I saw his face crumble. My lungs burned in my chest, but I forced myself to move.

When I made it to the library, I glanced back to make sure Lucas wasn't following. He wasn't. I expected to feel relief. Instead, all I felt was empty.

Royal was pacing in the study room when I arrived. Ally was jotting notes down in a spiral. She didn't look up when I entered, but Royal ran to my side.

"We found a note scrawled in the margin this morning. Ally thinks she might have…"

I pushed past Royal toward the table where Ally was still working. "What note? What does it say?"

"Royal has good instincts. This is one of B's notes."

"Bees?" I glanced at Royal, uncomprehending.

"B." Royal gestured at the manuscript. "Sorry, it's… there's the original text, right? But there are also all these margin notes throughout. We've been able to identify at least four different people's handwriting. A, B, C, D…" Royal shrugged. "Not the most creative nicknames but when you're operating on triple-shot espressos and quesadillas…"

"B, right." I turned back to Ally. "What did you find?"

"Well, B is the one who's always testing out theories, recipes…" Ally finished writing and pushed the manuscript copy away. She ran a hand through her hair, "but this… this is something different. Ally looked up at Royal, a slow smile spreading across her face. "I think they're complete. All we have to do is identify the last few elements…"

"What…?" I shook my head, afraid to voice the question.

Ally saw my confusion. "They're instructions."

"For?" I glanced back at Royal.

His eyes gleamed with a fierce satisfaction. "As far as we can tell? A separation incantation."

I felt my heart skip a beat. For a moment, the air seemed to press in on my ears. "An incantation…?"

Ally planted her hand over the manuscript copy. "This is how you're going to break the link between Lilith and the acolytes."

I turned to Royal. Suddenly the room seemed to be swimming, like there was too much oxygen. It felt like a vise had been released from around my heart. "You did it?"

"Well, it's not 100% finished yet but…" Ally frowned down at her notes.

"We did it." Royal's grin widened. I let out a ragged sigh, and then Royal and I caught one another in a tight hug.

Ally eyed us with a little half-smile. Royal noticed her and pulled back.

"Get in here, you." He pulled her out of her chair and drew her into the group hug. "You earned it."

"Oh, yay." Ally feigned distaste, but the smile on her face was anything but irritated. She noticed me watching and blushed.

"Thank you," I said. "This is… this is the best news we've had in months."

"It's going to take a little more time to work through the details," Ally said, "but... I think... by the end of the day, we'll know everything we need to know to help Cassie and Carrie."

I left the library, feeling like I was floating. If I'd thought it was hard to sit through morning classes, that was nothing compared to the agony of afternoon classes. I must've checked my phone 1000 times, afraid I'd missed a text from Royal. Waiting for the signal that we could leave to find Cassie and cure her.

Lucas found me in the hall after last period. I turned the corner toward my locker and came face-to-face with him unexpectedly. I flinched before I could guard my emotions. Lucas saw. He dropped his eyes, hurt.

"You're worried about Cassie. I get it." He took a deep breath and met my eyes. "Look, if I did or said anything..."

"Lucas." The emotion loaded into that one simple word silenced us both for a few moments. I looked down, taking his hand in mine.

"Yeah." Lucas nodded, smiling wistfully. "Trust is a bitch."

I looked up and met his gaze, but whatever he was thinking he kept to himself. The bell rang, calling us to our last class of the day. Lucas released my hand and bit his lip.

"You know I can make up my own mind, right?" Lucas studied me with a look that pierced right through me. It felt like he was trying to tell me something without *telling me*. Like we were talking in a code but only Lucas held the key. I opened my mouth to say something, but at that moment Royal put a hand on my shoulder.

"Sorry, Lucas. Braedyn. I need you." Whatever it was must've been urgent because—of all of us—Royal had seemed the most comfortable living the fiction that we weren't keeping Lucas out of anything. I turned back to Lucas. He saw the decision in my eyes and nodded once.

"Okay." It sounded like defeat. Lucas flashed me a small smile, turned on his heel, and walked away.

"What is it?" I turned my full attention to Royal.

"It's done." Royal glanced at the end of the hallway. Ally stood, framed in the glass exit doors, clutching her spiral notebook tightly to her chest. We made our way to Ally, and she led us to a secluded spot on the quad.

"We're going to need to get some things." Ally wasn't smiling. Royal turned to study me, his expression equally grim. It gave me an uncomfortable feeling my stomach.

"Okay. What kind of things?"

"Some sacred oils and tinctures, wherever the hell you shop for that stuff…" Ally glanced down at her notes.

"No problem." I knew exactly where to go for both the oils and the tinctures. Ironically, it was because of Seth. The ritual that we had preformed to open the Seal had required similar ingredients. "What else?"

"Well, we need a priest to oversee the ritual." Ally looked up at me, frowning. "I don't suppose you have one of those on-call, do you?"

Father Jerome. If there was a priest who would understand the importance of what we were attempting, it would be Father Jerome. We'd have to convince him to join us, and we'd have to do it without Clay finding out. Difficult, but not impossible. I nodded sharply. "Priest. Consider it done. What else?"

Ally's eyes widened with slight surprise, but she shrugged this off. "Location location location."

I glanced at Royal, trying to tamp down my impatience. "Translation?"

"We need to find a place with a clear view of the western horizon." Royal kept his eyes on Ally, as though waiting for her to drop a bomb.

"Okay. We'll figure something out. What else?"

Ally bit the side of her lip, looking uncertain for the first time. "There's just one more thing. We have to complete the entire ritual before," and here she paused to read from her notes, "'the sunset begins the long night.' Any idea what that means?"

"Yeah." A seeping dread spread throughout my stomach. It was like coming face-to-face with an old enemy. "Winter solstice."

"Winter solstice?" Ally glanced from me to Royal. "Winter solstice… Isn't that…?"

Royal's eyes slid to my face, tight with anxiety. "Tomorrow night."

Tomorrow night. Which gave us 27 hours to save Cassie or risk losing her forever.

We moved as fast as we could. We recruited Amber and Missy. But even with the five of us splitting up duties, it took the rest of the day to locate most of the necessary ingredients. More than once I found myself wishing Cassie could join us. But having her help wasn't worth the risk that some patrolling Guardsman might spot her. So we did it without her. We pored over maps of the town and surrounding area, finally settling on Lookout Point as our location. It was far enough away from the city that we shouldn't have to deal with any traffic, and it was a school night, so with any luck, it would be free from teenage couples on the lookout for some privacy.

"That just leaves the tinctures," Ally said, looking up from the map we'd settled on. School had let out 20 minutes earlier, so the library was filling up with kids meeting for midterm study groups or diving into last minute research for term papers. Ally glanced at Royal and dropped her voice. "You have your ID on you?"

"Yeah." Royal held up his wallet. "I never leave home without it."

"I'll drive." I picked up my backpack and led the way out of the library. We'd placed the order at lunch, and the lady had said it'd be ready for pickup at 4:00. Royal had been elected to make the purchase—he was the only one with a passable fake ID. I already knew the shopkeeper wouldn't sell tinctures to a minor because they contained alcohol. But with the extra spotters in town, it felt like a foolish risk for me to cloak myself in order to swipe a few vials off a shelf when we could just buy them with the right card.

We piled into my car for the drive to Old Town. Ally sat in the backseat, her legs crossed under her. I caught a glimpse of her in the rearview mirror. She was flipping through the manuscript copy, frowning. Something about the look on her face sent a cold rush through my chest.

"Ally? Is something wrong?"

Ally looked up, caught. "I... was just trying to make sense of something. I'm sure it's nothing."

"How sure?" My voice sounded strained. I traded a worried glance with Royal.

Ally looked up, conflicted. "I never thought I'd wish for a PhD in archaic Latin, but... Something about this passage... the long night..." Ally shook her head. "Just give me a minute."

"We'll get into it after the supply run," Royal murmured. "Just in case there's something we missed."

"We can't afford to make any mistakes." I kept my eyes on the road. The car fell silent. We reached the edge of Old Town and I pulled into an empty space alongside a curb. Royal left to head to the tincture shop. I turned to face Ally. "Any luck?"

Ally caught the edge of her lip in her teeth. "You know how I said the ritual had to be completed before the sun sets on the long night?" She looked up, her eyes strained. "I think I made a mistake. I think it means the ritual has to be completed *as* the sun sets on the long night."

I felt an icy fist take hold of my heart. "What?"

"We can't do it tonight." Ally ran her finger over the Latin margin note, rereading the passage to herself once more. "We have to wait for tomorrow's sunset." She looked up and saw the undisguised terror on my face. "Braedyn?"

"I... was hoping to finish this tonight." My mouth felt suddenly dry. I'd resigned myself to leaving. I'd come to terms with the understanding that it might be a long time before I walked through the front door of my house again. But now... now I found myself facing an excruciating choice.

If I went back home for one more night, I'd have a better chance of contacting Father Jerome without drawing too much attention. I'd also delay the manhunt Clay would order if I disappeared. It just meant I'd have to rely on the hope that Clay wouldn't act on any suspicions he might have tonight.

If I went into hiding, I'd rest easier being out of Clay's reach. But I might not be able to contact Father Jerome, and we needed a priest to perform the ritual. I'd also confirm whatever suspicions Clay may have been harboring, which meant I'd have to rely on the hope that Clay's soldiers didn't catch us before we'd had a chance to finish the ritual, save Cassie and the others, and flee Puerto Escondido for good.

In the end, it was Lucas who tipped the scales. He called as I spotted Royal walking back onto our street, tinctures in hand. I answered it, my hands shaking.

"Gretchen's getting pizza. I thought maybe we could..." Lucas let out a sigh. "Actually, I just thought it be nice to sit with you. Forget talking. Talking's for chumps."

I gave a soft chuckle. "And everything's...?" I didn't know how to phrase the question. But I had a feeling that if Lucas sensed I might be in any trouble, even if he didn't believe Clay would actually harm me, he would warn me. I tried a different tack. "Have you seen my dad?"

"Yeah, he's been in and out all day. Clay has all the guys out on patrol. Actually, I think he just got back. Does he know about Cassie?"

I hesitated. Then cleared my throat. "I haven't called him yet. I should probably do that."

"So. Pizza?"

"Yeah. Sure. I'll be home in an hour."

Dad was not thrilled when I called with my plan. But, like Lucas, he hadn't picked up any unusually suspicious vibes from Clay. "Going to school might have been the best thing you could have done," he said grudgingly, "but after this..."

"Who knows?" I tried to keep my voice bright. "Maybe this ritual will thwart Lilith's plans to return, and we'll have averted the final battle for a few more centuries." When Dad didn't respond, I felt my confidence waver, but the decision had been made. I was going home.

Dad was waiting in the kitchen when I joined Lucas for pizza at the Guard's table, but he didn't approach us. I had a feeling he was there as backup, in case something happened. Sandra and Thane passed us a handful of times, and neither gave me a second glance. I forced myself to relax as much as possible.

What I hadn't counted on was how hard it would be to sit with Lucas, pretending everything was normal. Knowing I'd be leaving, it made me more attuned to Lucas than I'd been in months. I found myself dwelling on the line of his jaw, the striking contrast between his dark hair and his skin, the almost magical way his hazel eyes caught and reflected the colors around us. I longed to lean into him, to breathe in his warm, musky scent, to feel the strength in his arms as he held me close.

The pizza lost its flavor, but I forced myself to eat. I caught Lucas watching me with a speculative look. I swallowed the bite, waiting. I expected... I don't know. Questions. Anger. Hurt. But true to his word, Lucas didn't try to pry anything out of me. We just sat together, not needing words. Finally, Lucas pushed his plate back. He hadn't even finished one slice. He saw my concern.

"Guess I'm not as hungry as I thought I'd be. I can't stop thinking about Cassie."

I looked down at my plate, fighting another surge of guilt. "Yeah. You're a good friend."

A few Guardsmen walked through, stopping as they caught sight of me. One of them whispered something to the other, who chuckled dryly. Lucas must have seen the expression of fear on my face. He glanced back at the soldiers as they headed up the staircase.

"Just ignore those guys."

His words came back to me as he closed the box on the nearly whole pizza... *I can make up my own mind, you know*. What had he meant? Was someone—Clay?—trying to turn him against me?

"Do the Guardsmen... do they talk about me?" I glanced at the staircase.

Lucas sat back in his chair, uncomfortable. "Nothing important. Just guys, talking." He met my eyes. "But I'm here to set the record straight. So... you know... you don't have to worry."

I nodded, but I wasn't comforted. One teenage boy's testimony against the long and sordid history of the Guard's war against the Lilitu...?

"I should head home," I said, rising. "It's been a long day." And tomorrow would be even longer. I left Lucas at the table and headed back home, feeling strangely unsettled. I let myself slip into the dreamless void that night, but awoke hours before the sun crested the eastern horizon. The last piece of the puzzle was still missing. We needed our priest.

I slipped into the Guard's house, making my way across the dark great room toward Thane's office. I eased the door closed, but didn't turn on the light. My Lilitu sight rendered the dark as comfortable to me as daylight was for most people, and it meant I didn't have to risk someone walking through the house and spotting light shining from under the office door. But I still had to worry about sound. So I moved slowly, searching the office as quietly as I could.

I searched for close to two hours in vain. If Sandra or Thane had contact information for Jerome, they weren't keeping it in the office. I eased the office door open, planning to head upstairs and search Thane's room—

Someone crossed into the room and flicked a desk lamp on. Clay.

I felt my Lilitu wings snap around me reflexively. Even cloaked, I felt exposed, standing in the open office door. Clay sat at his desk, pulling a stack of pages out of a drawer. He flipped through them, looking for something. I was too afraid to move, afraid the wooden floor of this old house would give me away if I tried to walk past him. And so I stood there, frozen, until the house began to stir.

The only mercy to Clay's decree separating men and women's sleeping quarters was that I didn't have to worry about a spotter coming down the stairs.

But when Lucas emerged, buttoning up his school shirt, I felt my heart lurch against my ribs.

"Morning," he called to Clay. He looked exhausted.

"Good morning, son." Clay looked up, giving Lucas a concerned smile. "How did you sleep? Any… dreams?"

"I told you." Lucas dropped his eyes, suddenly uneasy. "She hasn't visited my dreams for a while now." My body went rigid with shock. Lucas was reporting on our dreams to Clay?

"Well, not that you remember." Clay's smile grew neutral, as though he wanted to disagree but was too polite to directly contradict Lucas.

"She's not the enemy." Lucas met Clay's gaze directly. "I keep telling you, she's more human than demon. You should have seen her yesterday, when Cassie went missing. She was… she was twisted up inside."

Clay sat back, his fingers steepled. "She was surprised?"

"Devastated." Lucas shook his head. "They're best friends. You've seen them together, you know how much they mean to each other."

"You think Braedyn would do anything in her power to protect Cassie?"

"Anything," Lucas agreed.

Clay studied Lucas for a long moment before nodding. "All right. I believe you." He glanced at his watch and stood. "It's getting late. You should hurry, school will be starting soon."

"Right." Lucas's face eased. He flashed Clay a grateful smile. "I left my bag upstairs." Lucas darted for the stairs.

Clay's eyes shifted to me. My heart stopped beating as terror edged out the rational part of my brain that knew Clay couldn't see me. Clay walked out from behind his desk and headed straight for me. I forced myself to move, stepping away from the office door, timing my steps to coincide with Clay's to disguise any potential creaks. Clay's eyes remained fastened on the doorway. He passed within a few inches of my leg, disappearing into the office behind me.

My heart thundered in my ears and I had to blink to clear my vision. I heard Lucas pounding down the stairs and forced myself to move, moving as quickly and quietly as I could toward the front door. Lucas opened the door, pausing to call back to Clay.

"See you this afternoon."

I didn't wait—I darted through the open door past Lucas, taking care not to brush him as I passed. But his head turned, as though he could sense me. I crouched against the wall of the house, afraid to move. Clay said something from inside, and Lucas waved in response, then closed the door.

Lucas didn't move for a long moment. He seemed to be struggling with something. He shook his head, coming to a decision, and headed down the porch steps, walking toward my house.

I waited for him to reach the front porch, then raced into the Guard's backyard, vaulting over the fence into my yard. The back door was open—Zoe hadn't been lying about Clay's aversion to locks. I slipped into the kitchen, dropping my cloak as I passed through the doorway.

I was pouring myself a glass of milk when Lucas poked his head into the kitchen.

"Hey." He studied me, trying to conceal his suspicion. "Ready for school?"

"Yeah, just a sec." I forced a smile, then drank the milk, trying to keep my hands from shaking around the glass.

I went through the motions, driving Lucas to school, sitting through our first class together to keep up the fiction. But my mind was spinning. As soon as Lucas and I parted ways, I headed to the library computer lab. I performed every kind of computer search I could think of to locate Father Jerome, but there were only a few sparse mentions of the Order of Saint Marcel on some medieval history blogs.

"How do you even know Jerome's his real name?" Royal had joined me during fifth period, but neither of us made any headway. "Maybe they take different names, like nuns. Don't nuns change their names? And Popes. Popes definitely change their names." Royal looked up at me with sudden inspiration. "Hey. Do you think it'd work if I got ordained online?"

"Not helping, Royal." I glanced at the clock on the wall. School would be ending in less than five minutes and we had everything we needed for the ritual.

Everything except the priest.

17

"What now?" Royal followed me to the parking lot after school. He was all out of sarcasm. "God, I miss Cassie. We could use a little of her logic right now."

"Go to the university. He might be in the vault. Just tell the guard at the window you need to speak with him."

"And where are you going?"

"Jerome's been hanging out with Sandra and Thane a lot these past few months. With any luck he'll be there when I get home." I finished my keys out of my backpack. Royal caught my arm, concerned.

"Hang on. If you're suggesting approaching Jerome at the Guard's house…"

"We're out of time, Royal. If you have any better ideas, I'm all ears."

"What if he's not there? Look, you're right. We are out of time and we have no idea where to find Jerome. We need a backup plan. I don't know, maybe we can convince a local priest that we're not completely insane and get him to read the spell or whatever."

"It's not a *spell*." I turned on Royal, frustration building with every passing moment. "None of this is *magic*. Don't you get it? This is *spiritual*. We *can't fake* it." I saw the agony in Royal's eyes and stopped. "I'm sorry. I know you're trying to help." I closed my eyes, struggling for calm. "Okay. If he's not there, I'm going to Sandra."

"No, Braedyn. Bad idea. Isn't she one of the ones that came with Clay? How do you know she isn't blindly loyal to him like some of those others? How do you know she won't take this information and…"

"What choice do we have? Cassie is out of time. If I have to, I'll tell her everything we've learned."

"Why don't you just tell me?" Lucas stepped out from behind an SUV parked beside the Firebird. His face was rigid with suppressed anger. Royal turned away, muttering a curse under his breath. Lucas caught him by the shoulder and spun him back around. "Did I hear that right? You guys know where Cassie is?"

"We don't have time for this." Royal glared at him. "Let me go, Lucas."

"I know what today is. It's winter solstice" Lucas turned back to me, and I saw suspicion behind his eyes. "And I know you were at my house this morning. Cloaked. I'm trying to trust you, Braedyn. But you're making it really hard."

"*You're* trying to trust *her*? Is that supposed to be a joke?" Royal's incredulity stopped Lucas cold.

"Why? Does it strike you as funny?" Lucas's voice dropped dangerously low.

"None of this is funny." Royal stepped closer to Lucas, his face radiating fury. "Take your hand off of me."

"And if I don't?" Lucas's voice grew even softer.

"Guys!" I reached between the boys, planting a hand on each of their chests and pushing them apart. "We can't do this now." I turned to Royal. "Just go." But when Royal tried to walk away, Lucas grabbed him in an arm lock.

"We're not done here," Lucas started.

I moved without stopping to think. The muscle memory took over, and I wrenched Lucas off of Royal with a power fueled by rage. I spun Lucas around, catching his wrist and wrenching it behind his back with one hand and slamming his chest into my car with the other. He impacted the Firebird with a startled growl of pain. I released him, jerking my hands away as though burned. Lucas slowly pushed himself off the side of my car, touching his shoulder gingerly.

"He's been warning me about you. But I'm guessing you already know that." Lucas turned, meeting my gaze with an anguished expression on his face. "I didn't want to believe anything he had to say."

A white-hot anger shot through my core. "And now?" I kept my voice measured, but Lucas read the anger behind my eyes.

"You think I want to believe it?" Lucas's face twisted in pain. "You think this is easy? I've been defending you to him for months. And you've been keeping me in the dark. For *months*. It makes me sick to my stomach, asking myself whether or not I can really trust you."

"It's Braedyn." Royal looked into Lucas's face, seething. "She saved your life, did you forget that?"

"No." Lucas shifted his gaze to Royal. "I haven't forgotten. Just like I haven't forgotten that she broke into my mind and stole a secret she had no right to take. Or that she tried to get Parker to kill himself. Or that she helped Seth open the Seal. Or that she stood by while Senoy was assassinated…"

The world seemed to tilt around me. I felt the pull of the dream, trying to rescue me from the agony of this moment. But I pushed it back. I stumbled against the Firebird, struggling to keep from buckling. Nausea welled in the back of my throat. I may have wondered about the poison Clay might be pouring into Lucas's ears. But hearing it spilling out of Lucas's mouth was almost more than I could bear.

"Whose words are you speaking?" Royal stared at Lucas, aghast. "That's Clay talking, isn't it?"

"You don't know anything about him." Lucas's voice tightened with renewed anger. "He's been trying to support her. He's given her so many chances…"

"Oh hell, no." Royal advanced on Lucas, stabbing a finger into his chest. "This ends now. You're the one who doesn't know anything about that psychopath. He sent soldiers to kill Cassie yesterday!"

Lucas scoffed, biting off a humorless laugh. "That's crazy."

"Is it? He's the one who had you arrested. He had Murphy beaten in front of Braedyn when she hesitated to lead him to that Lilitu."

Lucas's gaze cut to me. I saw a glimmer of surprise fighting through his rage. "No. If any of that had happened… I would know. Braedyn would have told me."

"She didn't tell you because Clay threatened to hurt you next, you idiot!" Royal shoved Lucas again, and Lucas stumbled back, catching himself against the Firebird beside me. "The only reason they released you from jail is because Braedyn promised to hand over the one thing we needed to save Cassie."

Lucas processed this for a moment. "The acolyte book?"

I nodded. "Clay was the witness who gave the cops your description and my partial plate. He showed up at the police station for the lineup."

"No, that doesn't make…"

"He told me it was my decision. I could either deliver the book I had taken from the university or you would go to prison for felony vandalism."

Lucas shook his head. "Okay, there must be some misunderstanding."

"Yes, exactly." Frustration made Royal's voice sound clipped. "Yours."

Lucas opened his mouth to argue, but I spoke first. "People see what they want to see." I caught Lucas's gaze. The words silenced him. They were the words he'd told me two years ago, when he'd first introduced me to the notion that demons walked among us. Lucas wanted to see Clay as a good man. That didn't make it so.

Lucas took a deep breath. "The training accident? You're saying that was Clay…?"

I nodded. My breath caught. Was it possible that Lucas could set aside his hero worship?

Lucas straightened, but he kept his eyes on the ground, thinking. "This… This doesn't gel with the man I know." He turned to face me, choosing his words carefully. "I've spent time with him, Braedyn. Maybe… maybe he felt he had to do some awful things. Maybe we don't understand his full purpose. But you haven't seen the other sides of him…"

Exhaustion draped over me like a blanket heavy with water. This was the conversation I'd longed to have with Lucas for so long. But we couldn't afford the time it would take to convince him of Clay's true nature. I looked up into Lucas's eyes and hardened my heart.

"I don't care." I spat the words out, imbuing them with all the helpless frustration and anger I'd been bottling up since Clay's arrival. "I don't care about Clay. I care about Cassie. She's in danger. We only have three hours before sunset. You can either help us or you can get out of our way."

Lucas swallowed, looking sick. After an agonized struggle, he shook his head. "I can't betray Clay. If you're wrong…"

Royal let out a hiss of fury. "Then get out of our way. If you have any decency left, you keep your mouth shut for three more hours." Royal turned his back on Lucas, dismissing him completely. He looked at me, face tight with anxiety. "Go. I'll call you if I find Jerome at the university. Before you ask Sandra, see if Murphy has any ideas of how to contact Jerome."

I nodded and reached for the door of my car.

"I can find Jerome." Lucas hadn't moved.

"What?" Royal turned back to Lucas, stunned.

"Father Jerome knows I'm Clay's aide. He's kind of a… He won't meet with a bunch of teenagers, but if Clay sends for him, he'll come."

"So now… you're offering to help us?" Royal glanced at me, uncertainty plain on his face. "Why would you do that?"

"I might not be willing to go against Clay, but if there's another way to stop Lilith…" Lucas shrugged. "I say we try everything."

I gripped Lucas's hand. "Do it. Set the meeting now."

Lucas pulled the phone out of his back pocket, giving me one last speculative look before thumbing it on. He scrolled through a list of contacts and selected a name. He lifted the phone to his ear and waited. A few moments later, he spoke. "Father Jerome, it's Lucas. Clay was hoping to meet with you. I know it's short notice, but this is urgent." Lucas listened, then nodded slightly. "As soon as you can. I don't know the details, I just know we're on a very tight deadline." Lucas's eyes widened in alarm. "No, not at the house, he wants to keep this meeting under wraps. There's a restaurant in Old Town, Sophie's. Do you know it?" Lucas nodded quickly. "Great. 4:30 at Sophie's. He'll be there." Lucas thumbed the phone off, ending the call. He turned back to face us. He looked uneasy.

"Thank you." I bit my lip, wanting to say so much more. But there wasn't time. I turned to Royal. "Go get Cassie. Meet us at Sophie's. We might need her help to convince Jerome."

Royal nodded and darted into the parking lot toward his car. I fumbled with the keys, trying to get them into the car's door lock. Lucas took them out of my hand and opened the door for me.

"Clay really had your dad beaten?" Lucas's voice was soft. He still sounded conflicted, but the edge of defensiveness I'd heard earlier was gone.

I nodded, fighting the building pressure behind my eyes. "I'll tell you everything," I whispered. "Just let me save Cassie. We've got to get her to…"

"Don't." Lucas took a step back. "Don't tell me any details. Clay… he's good at reading people. It's probably better if I don't know anything concrete."

I nodded, swallowing hard. Lucas gave me back the keys. He lifted a hand to my cheek and his lips parted, as though he wanted to say something else. But then he closed his mouth, turned away, and left.

I was pacing outside the restaurant 20 minutes later when Missy and Ally arrived. I stared at them.

"Royal called," Ally said, reading my confusion. "He said something about a priest."

"I figured we could use the backup," Royal said, approaching behind us. I turned and spotted Cassie clinging to his arm. She had the hood of her jacket on, and she kept her face angled toward the ground. It was doing a decent job at hiding her face, but it also looked like she was trying hard to go unnoticed. Royal saw my gaze and frowned. "Yeah, we should probably get inside. I don't think Cassie's going to be making the top 10 list of 'people who hide well in broad daylight' anytime soon."

I led the way into the restaurant. The first two dining areas were sparsely populated, but I didn't recognize any of the people seated at the tables. We moved into the far dining area, where a small fire was crackling merrily in the hearth. Jerome was seated at a small table meant for two. He looked up as we entered and was about to dismiss us when his eyes caught on me.

"Take the booth in the back," I told the others. "We'll join you in a minute."

Royal gave me a concerned look, but he didn't argue. They started to head back towards the circular booth. Jerome tracked them with his eyes, then flicked his gaze back to me. I crossed the dining room to his table.

"I thought I was meeting Clay." Jerome sat back in his chair, clearly pissed. "In case you hadn't noticed, we're facing some fairly serious challenges. I don't have time to play with children." He pushed back from the table and stood.

"You think you're the only one trying to save the world?" I spat the words out, my raw nerves getting the better of me. Jerome's mouth tightened with distaste. I forced myself to calm down and started again. "You're already here. Just give us five minutes. If you still want to leave after that, we won't stop you."

I saw a muscle along Jerome's jaw twitch. He glanced at the booth where the others sat, waiting. His frown deepened. "Five minutes. And then you can explain yourself to Clay." Without waiting for a response, Jerome made his way to the round booth. My friends were crowded around the back of the booth, giving Jerome a wide berth. Everyone eyed him with deep distrust as he took a seat at one edge of the curving bench. I slid onto the other edge so I could look across the table at him.

"Talk quickly." Father Jerome glanced at his watch, marking the time.

"Lilith is about to return."

Jerome's eyes swiveled to my face. For a long moment, no one at the table took a breath. Jerome licked his lips, struggling to regain is poker face. "I'm listening."

"He didn't tell you, did he?" I phrased it like a question, but I had already seen the answer in his surprise. Clay didn't want any information making it out of the Guard, not even to someone like Jerome, who could help us.

"Historically, the factions are not typically forthcoming with members outside their own organizations." Father Jerome folded his hands on the table in front of him. "Out of curiosity, what makes you believe her return is imminent?"

"That's going to take more than five minutes to explain." I held his gaze, unflinching.

"Then answer me this, first. Why am I meeting a collection of teenagers instead of the head of the Guard?" Jerome's eyes flicked over the faces of my friends before returning to settle on me.

"If Clay knew what I'm about to tell you, he wouldn't be sitting down to talk. He'd be burying the bodies of three teenage girls."

Jerome's eyebrows hiked up his forehead a fraction. But instead of asking any further questions he glanced at his watch. The message could not have been clearer: he was still waiting for us to convince him to stay.

I took a deep breath. This was the moment of truth. We needed Jerome, and he needed the truth. "Six months ago, a priestess named Idris recruited three girls to become acolytes for Lilith. At the time, they thought it was harmless. A female-power thing. But now we understand that these acolytes are instrumental for Lilith's return."

Father Jerome's expression altered only slightly, but I saw the tension edging into his fingers, still poised on the edge of his watch. I pressed on.

"There's a way to break the connection between the acolytes and Lilith. We can save their lives, but we need a priest to perform the incantation." I swallowed. "We need you."

Father Jerome sat back against the booth. "You're telling me you've identified a way to keep the mother of demons out of our world? How can you justify keeping this from Clay? He's the head of your Guard."

"Because Clay is a kill now, ask questions later kind of guy," Royal spat. "And one of the acolytes is my best friend."

"Another one is my sister." The emotion in Missy's voice silenced the table for several painful seconds.

When Jerome looked up, I saw the pity in his eyes. "You have my deepest sympathies," he started, "but…"

"Wait." I reached toward Ally, gesturing toward her bag. "Before you make any decisions. Just look at what we've found."

Ally pulled the manuscript copy out of her bag. She offered it to Jerome. He frowned, glancing at me, but then he took it. He set the pages down, pulling a set of reading glasses out of his pocket.

"The margin notes, the ones highlighted in green…" Royal pointed at the page.

"Yes, I see." Jerome sniffed, impressed. "Who did your translation?"

"Um, that was us." Royal glanced at Ally across the table. "Ally and me. Ally, mostly, though, she's the better…"

"I'm trying to read." Jerome looked up over the rims of his glasses, silencing Royal with a frown. Our five minutes had long expired by the time Jerome set the manuscript down. "You're cutting it awfully close, aren't you?"

I felt my heart leap in my chest. "Does that mean you're going to help us?"

"I'll need the original volume. This copy is too difficult to read with the notes scribbled over everything." Jerome's words were like the antidote to a paralytic. Royal slumped over in relief. Cassie balled her fists to her mouth, choking down a sob. Missy and Ally traded a watery glance.

But I stared at Jerome. The original volume was back at the Guard's house. He read my consternation.

"Will that be a problem?"

I shook my head. "I'll get it." I didn't know how, yet, but it had to be done.

Jerome glanced back at the notes. "I'm assuming you've gathered the ingredients listed here?"

"Yes."

"And the location? Clear view of the western horizon?"

Royal pulled the folded map out of his pocket and slid it across the table to Jerome. "Lookout Point."

"Maybe he should catch a ride with one of us." Missy eyed the map nervously.

"That's probably a very prudent idea." Jerome glanced at his watch again. "We've got a few hours. I'd like to run through the ritual at least once before performing it for real."

Missy glanced at Ally. "We'll pick up Carrie." Ally nodded confirmation. "But that still leaves the third acolyte."

I stared at them, stricken. "Right. Emma." Only Cassie and I knew where Emma was staying, but Cassie was in no condition to make the drive. "I'll pick up Emma after I get the book."

"Okay, sounds like we have a plan." Royal gave me a tense smile. He didn't have to say it—we were both thinking the same thing.

This had better work.

I made the drive home in record time. The whole way there I was running scenarios through my mind, trying to figure out how I would get the book out with the least amount of drama. But the best laid plans…

I pulled to a stop at the curb in front of my house and killed the engine. Before I even opened the door of my car I heard the commotion. Men were shouting. The door to the Guard's house flew open and pairs of soldiers raced around the back of the house. I almost got back in the car and fled. But without the book, we were hamstrung.

I made my way toward the Guard's house, my senses on heightened alert. Matthew spotted me on the porch steps.

"Braedyn. This may not be the best time." Matthew moved to stand in the open front door, effectively blocking my view.

"What's going on?" I felt the pressure building in the back of my head. We had overcome so many obstacles to get this far, we couldn't fail now.

"It's the Lilitu. She's escaped." Matthew's voice was a grim. He knew Vyla only as the demon who had murdered Gretchen's husband and Lucas's big brother. I stared at him, stricken. "I have to tell Gretchen."

"Of course." My voice sounded faint in my ears. Matthew slipped past me, and I saw into the heart of the chaos. Thane stood in the center of the great room, berating a pair of Guardsmen.

"How is that even possible? There were two of you! You cannot tell me you both just happened to fall asleep at the same moment!" Thane pressed toward the men. They faced him down, clearly terrified.

I saw Dad then. He faced the men, but kept his back to the wall. His face was stern, but something about the way he watched the scene unfold… I felt my breath catch. Vyla had had help. It suddenly dawned on me that I couldn't have asked for a more perfect distraction. I glanced back at the house behind me, looking for any of the Guard's spotters. With any luck, they'd all been dispatched to hunt down the escaped Lilitu. It was time to act. I shrunk against the wall just outside the Guard's front door. With one final scan of the surrounding area, I took a deep breath and cloaked myself.

I slipped into the house. Thane alone was making enough noise to cover the sound of my footsteps, but even if he'd fallen silent that instant, no one would have heard me over the sounds of the Guardsmen rallying upstairs. They must have just discovered her disappearance.

I darted into the back office, trying to focus my thoughts enough to concentrate on the task at hand. I scanned the shelves and the desktop for the small red volume. It only took a few moments to spot it, peeking out from under a pile of notes. I grabbed the book and clutched it tight to my chest.

"She's not in the backyard and she's not on the street." Marla's voice cut through the din. I shrunk against the wall inside the office, my heart leaping into my throat. A spotter was standing directly between me and my freedom. If I came out of the office cloaked, no excuse would be enough to talk my way past her. I waited, breathless, hoping that she would leave to continue the search. But it seemed my luck had run out.

"Clay will be back momentarily." Thane's voice grated in the sudden quiet. "Wait here."

I had to think fast. I slipped the book into the back of my pants, covering it with my shirt. I uncloaked, and peered around the side of the door. Marla was facing Clay's desk so she didn't see me emerge. But Dad did. His eyes tightened with sudden fear.

"Braedyn, there you are." Dad gestured for me to join him. Thane looked up as I emerged from the office. Marla glanced over at me, too, but she looked distracted by other worries. "How about you, Braedyn? Did you see her outside?" Dad gave me a pointed look. I knew he was trying to give me an alibi. I swallowed.

"No. Nothing."

"Maybe you should check back at the house?" Dad took my shoulder and guided me toward the front door. I felt his hand tug on the back of my shirt, covering the book perhaps? As we passed into the foyer, I heard Dad whisper at my shoulder, "whatever you're up to, please, please be careful."

I turned to face him at the door. "Did you do this?" I couldn't resist asking the question. Instead of answering, Dad simply kissed my forehead and pushed me towards the door. I felt a swell of love for him. Dad saw the emotion filling my eyes and nodded, once. He gave me a faint smile then turned back to the waiting Guardsmen.

I let out a soft sigh. Last obstacle overcome. We had done it. I took a step onto the porch. What I saw there made no sense. Lucas was struggling in the grip of two of Clay's soldiers. One of them had a hand around Lucas his mouth. I recognized Clay's military advisor with a shock of fear. Sutherland. Lucas's eyes were wild with panic as he struggled against his captors.

I took a step toward him, but something stopped me in my tracks. "*Braedyn...?!*"

It took a split second to recognize Dad's voice, warped with terror. I looked down, startled to see the edge of a blade protruding from my chest. It was covered with fresh blood, but through the red stain I could make out the oily sheen of a Guardsman's dagger.

I've been stabbed. The thought struck me simply, divorced from any emotion.

And then a searing pain burned every other thought from my mind.

18

Like a blossom of fire, pain bloomed through my chest. Lapping tongues of agony radiated out from the blade. It was so intense it drove all thought from my head, muted every other sense. Only the pain seemed real. After the first crush of agony, I returned to myself, senses roiling, fighting for each breath before another tsunami of pain slammed through me.

I blinked to clear my vision before realizing something else had changed. The afternoon sun was slanting away from the porch, leaving deep pools of shadow across the face of the house. The details within those shadows were fading before my eyes. I'd grown so accustomed to my Lilitu sight that losing it felt like going blind. It was another heartbeat before I fully understood what was happening.

Clay's dagger, it was a Guardsman's blade. A unique weapon forged to wound both the physical and spiritual aspects of the Lilitu it was used on, severing her from her supernatural abilities until body and spirit had had time to heal.

I felt someone grab me from behind. I glanced down and saw Clay's fingers curling over my shoulder, above where the blade protruded. And then I felt a wrenching sensation. The tip of the blade retracted back through my chest, unleashing a new flood of searing pain.

I was dimly aware of dropping to my knees on the porch. My body felt leaden, sluggish. I'd been stabbed once before by the ancient Lilitu Ais. She'd driven a dagger through my shoulder, pinning me to a door. I remembered the sensation vaguely. This pain was different. It was unlike anything I'd ever experienced. I looked down, surprised to see blood only now beginning to seep through my shirt. It felt like I'd been stabbed minutes ago, but it must have only been a second or two.

Sounds returned in a rush—Dad's howl of rage, Lucas's panic, the commotion of the soldiers trying to contain the situation.

"Get away from her, you son of a bitch!" Dad's voice tore through the din. I glanced up and saw him fighting to free himself from the soldiers holding him back.

Clay still gripped the shoulder of my shirt. It must have pulled up as I'd dropped. I heard Clay's sharp intake of breath. He reached down and wrenched the acolyte book free from the waistband of my jeans.

"What other proof do you need?" Clay's voice was hard, pitiless. But he wasn't talking to Dad. I looked up and met Lucas's gaze.

Lucas stared at me, face twisting with conflicting emotions.

"If she was fighting with us, why would she need to steal?" Clay held the book up as though it explained everything. Doubt entered Lucas's eyes and a stabbing bolt of anguish shot through the physical pain. Clay seemed to see it, too. I heard the satisfaction in his voice. "Let him go." The soldiers holding Lucas released him. He rubbed at his arms where they'd gripped him, but made no other move.

Clay released his hold on my shirt. I pitched forward, just managing to catch myself on my hands and knees. The necklace with Lucas's ring on it swung free from my shirt. I heard a soft breath and looked up. Lucas stared at the ring. He lifted his gaze to meet my eyes, then his face transformed with alarm—

I turned half a second too late. Clay had walked around to face me. He planted a boot on my wounded shoulder and kicked, sending me crashing back against the wall of the house. Pain exploded behind my eyes, blinding me with red-gold bursts. When the bursts faded, I saw Clay standing over me, looking down, face radiating triumph.

"We knew you'd slip up, girl." He held the book out, and someone approached to take it from his hand.

Thane turned the book over as if examining it for damage, then his eyes settled on me. "It was only a matter of time." He sounded tired. Resigned. Thane had never disguised his distrust of me. So why did this feel like such a stinging betrayal? My vision went blurry, but this time I knew why. A tear snaked its way down my cheek. Thane studied my face, his expression unreadable. I shifted my gaze back to Clay, pushing Thane out of my thoughts. The air burned with each breath, but more excruciating than that was the thought that struck me next.

I'm going to die and they'll be left waiting for me… Images played through my mind. Cassie, Royal, Jerome, waiting for the book that would never come. The shadow-figure consumed by fire taking on Cassie's features. Lilith's forces covering the earth, unopposed, no longer needing to hide as they attacked… I felt the strength ebbing out of my body and let my head rock back against the side of the house.

"Ah ah ah." Clay kneeled beside me, catching my jaw in his hand and wrenching my head around to face him. "No checking out just yet. I have some questions for you."

"Don't touch her!" Dad broke free from the soldiers holding him. He launched himself at Clay. Clay jerked back, alarm flashing across his face.

I saw Sutherland move. Before I could draw the breath to scream a warning, Sutherland brought the hilt of his dagger down across the back of Dad's head. Dad pitched forward, hitting the porch just feet away from me. He lay there, still. I reached for him reflexively then crumpled, waylaid by another bolt of shooting pain.

"Dad?" I stretched out my good arm and touched his face. He didn't respond. Clay grabbed the back of my shirt and pulled, slamming me back against the side of the house.

"Take him below." Clay jerked his head at Dad and a couple of soldiers moved to comply. They hauled Dad off the porch. He hung between them, limp. For a moment, I feared Sutherland had killed him, but then he let out a semi-conscious groan. Relief pulsed through me, but then the soldiers were dragging Dad inside. Clay turned back to me. "As I was saying. I have some questions for you."

I didn't have the strength to resist him, but a new anger ignited in my core. I gritted my teeth against the pain, refusing to utter a cry. Clay seemed to read the anger in my face. He flashed me a chilling smile.

"Your father isn't the only one who knows how to make demons talk," he said quietly. "Do yourself a favor and answer the question. Where are the acolytes?"

I swallowed against the bile rising in the back of my throat.

Clay studied me for a long moment before nodding. "Lucas wouldn't tell us either."

"Lucas?" I glanced up, startled. "You think Lucas…?"

"I think you've had too much time alone with the boy." Clay stood, brushing imaginary dust off his knees. "Too much time to work your Lilitu wiles on him. Once you've been executed, his head will clear."

"Wait, *what*...?!" Lucas took a step toward us. The soldiers behind him moved but Clay stopped them with a gesture. He turned to face Lucas head on.

"This is what they do, son." Clay flicked a glance at me. "They worm their way into your mind. Make you believe and do things you would never do in your right mind. Whatever you feel for this creature, you can't trust her."

Lucas shook his head, thinking fast. "Clay, I... I hear what you're saying. But I knew Braedyn before her powers manifested. She's a good person, believe me. If she took this book, she has a reason."

Clay stared Lucas down. "I'm sorry, Lucas. I thought we'd made some real progress over these last few months. But it seems she's got her talons in you deep. Trust me, you'll come to your senses once her power over you is broken."

Lucas seemed to shrink under Clay's glare. Maybe that's why Clay made the mistake of turning his back on Lucas. Lucas hurtled toward Clay without warning. The soldiers moved too late to stop him. Lucas impacted into Clay and they hit the porch together. Clay let out a sharp grunt of surprise. Lucas straddled Clay, pinning him down.

Lucas turned to me, eyes alight with panic. "Braedyn, run!"

I forced my body to move, rolling to my feet and darting toward the stairs—but the wound I'd sustained was too severe. I gasped and stumbled, hobbled by the pain. Three Guardsmen circled around me, but even they could see I wasn't going anywhere.

"I'm sorry," I managed, clutching the wound in my chest.

Sutherland hauled Lucas to his feet with a grimace. Lucas stared at me. His eyes had a hollow look about them, and I realized he knew it, too. I was going to die.

Clay stood. He calmly walked to Lucas and drove his fist into Lucas's stomach with almost no expression. Lucas jackknifed in Sutherland's hands. Sutherland let him drop. Lucas curled on his side. His breath came in sick, wet gasps. Clay reached down and hauled him up by the scruff of his shirt. When he had Lucas on his feet, he shoved him toward another Guardsman.

"Clearly we're facing a crisis." Clay turned to address the gathering crowd of Guardsmen. "Respect for authority is not a courtesy, it is the thing that will keep us whole. Insubordination will be dealt with harshly. Lucas has just volunteered to provide us with an example. I want the entire Guard assembled in one hour."

Thane glanced at Lucas with unmistakable pity.

Lucas saw this. He turned to Clay, his features tense. "Why? What are you going to do?"

"I'm reinstituting corporal punishment." Clay glanced at Lucas, as if it were the obvious conclusion.

Lucas swallowed, struggling to keep his voice under control. "You're going to have me beaten?"

"No, son." Clay shook his head almost sadly. "I'm going to have you flogged."

My head swam with chaotic thoughts. Flogged. I could hear Lucas's shouts at the edge of my consciousness. Clay's men were dragging us down the basement stairs. I saw the thick-barred cells awaiting us—soldiers already held two of the doors open. Through one I saw Dad, who lay unmoving on the basement floor.

Lucas was shoved into the cell with Dad.

I was pushed into the empty cell next to it. When the Guardsmen released me, I staggered forward, catching myself on the far wall. It took all my concentration not to fall. I heard the metal door clang shut behind me.

"We'll do it on the back porch." Clay pocketed the keys to my cell. He was talking to Sutherland.

"Don't." I forced the word out, tasting blood. "Clay, don't hurt him. Whatever you think I've done, Lucas wasn't a part of it. We couldn't trust him *because* of his loyalty to *you*."

Clay shot me an impersonal frown, then turned back to Sutherland. "Do you have the cat?"

Sutherland's eyes shifted to Lucas, troubled. "He's just a boy."

"Do you have it?" Clay's tone hardened.

Sutherland hesitated, then nodded. "It's in the armory."

Someone burst through the door at the top of the basement stairs. "Get out of my way!" Gretchen pounded down the stairs. She skidded to a stop in the basement, staring at the scene before her. "Clay? Did I hear this right? Are you planning to *flog* Lucas?"

"I have no choice." Clay eyed Gretchen, his voice rich with empathy. "Lucas's will has been usurped by the Lilitu in our midst."

Gretchen's eyes latched onto me. "Braedyn? That's impossible. I'd trust Braedyn with my life."

I felt my heart warm at her words, but the comfort didn't last long.

"Then perhaps Lucas isn't the only one who's fallen prey to the demon." Clay studied Gretchen. The threat was plain as day, but Gretchen pressed on.

"This is paranoia. You can't honestly believe…" Gretchen stared at Clay, seeing the grim determination in his face. She crossed the distance between them, bearing down on him with growing anger. "Clay… You can't *flog* Lucas. This isn't the seventeen hundreds! You don't have absolute power to do—!"

Clay whipped the back of his hand across Gretchen's face. She wasn't prepared for the blow, but she kept her feet, staggering back out of his reach to recover. I saw her blink hard to clear her eyes. When she looked up at Clay, her face was a mask of icy rage.

"That's how you want to keep discipline, is it?" Gretchen thumbed at her lips, wiping a thin streak of blood away. "You're going to beat us all into submission?"

"If I have to." Clay's voice was stony.

"I'm not going to let you hurt him." Gretchen turned toward the stairs.

"Mind telling me where you're off to?" Clay followed Gretchen with his eyes.

"To the cops. News flash: child abuse is a serious crime." Gretchen spat the words over her shoulder. Clay's eyes shifted slightly to the Guardsmen stationed in the basement. They moved as one, blocking Gretchen's path to the stairs. She turned back to Clay, incredulous.

"I applaud your moral outrage," Clay said. "In any other situation, I'd agree. But we're too close to the end. I need absolute obedience from my soldiers if we're going to have any hope of beating Lilith. Need I remind you, both you and Lucas swore an oath of loyalty to the Guard and to me."

"Clay..." Gretchen licked her lips, looking scared for the first time since she'd entered the basement. "Be reasonable. He's a kid. What you're talking about... you'll scar him for life."

Clay dropped his gaze to the floor. "It has to be done."

Gretchen hesitated, thinking hard. Then, without any warning, she turned and sprinted toward the stairs. She dodged the first soldier, but the second caught her arm. She clasped a hand over his, shifted her weight, and twisted. The motion sent the soldier flipping over her back. He impacted with the floor, hard. Gretchen's path now clear, she bolted toward the stairs.

She didn't see the third soldier reaching for something in his pocket. He took aim and fired—

The taser hit Gretchen in the back. She dropped at the foot of the stairs, back arching, biting back a howl of pain and rage.

"Gretchen!" Lucas gripped the bars of his cell, watching in horror as the slender woman spasmed on the floor.

"That's enough," Clay said. The soldier who Gretchen had flipped straightened, rubbing at a sore shoulder. The other two each took Gretchen under an arm and dragged her to the last empty cell. They dropped her on the floor, then one of them knelt to rip the taser's barbs out of her back.

Gretchen hissed in pain, but otherwise made no sound. The cell door clanged shut behind her. I expected Clay to leave us in the basement. But instead, he walked back toward the door of my cell. I pushed myself off the wall, still pressing a hand to the wound in my chest. I felt faint, and a slick sheen of sweat now covered my face and back.

Clay studied me for a moment, a slight smile playing around the corner of his mouth. Without taking his eyes off of me, he called to his waiting soldiers.

"One of you, go get Zoe. Have her bring her laptop." Clay leaned his forearm against the bars of the cell as one of the soldiers left, sprinting up the stairs. "I had Zoe put a tracking app on your phone."

The skin along the backs of my arms prickled.

"So I guess now's your last chance to prove yourself, Braedyn." Clay smiled. He was confident. "Anything you want to tell me before Zoe digs it up?" I stared at Clay, wordlessly. He shrugged, unconcerned. "Suit yourself."

A few minutes later, Zoe came down the basement stairs, trailed by Sandra, Marla, and Thane. Sandra and Marla glanced at the cells, curious. Sandra's eyes hesitated on me, but she didn't say anything.

Thane moved to stand by Clay's side. He held his hands clasped behind his back; it couldn't have been more clear where his allegiance lie. Clay glanced at him before turning to Zoe.

"You wanted to see me?" Zoe turned to Clay, curious. She carried her laptop under her arm.

"The tracker you put on Braedyn's phone." Clay moved a small table into the center of the basement. "Can you access the data from your computer?"

"Sure." Zoe set the computer on the table and opened it. I heard the machine humming to life. Zoe's fingers moved over the keyboard, filling the basement with the soft click of the keys. "Are we looking for anything specific?"

"The morning Cassie went missing. Did Braedyn make any unusual trips?"

At Clay's words, my heart leapt into my throat. Clay was watching me like a hawk. He saw my reaction and a slow smile spread across his face.

"Yep. Looks like she left from here, drove to Cassie's house, then drove to a third location... here." Zoe turned the computer to face Clay. I saw a map of Puerto Escondido. Zoe pointed to a red dot in the heart of downtown.

"What's there?" Clay moved toward the computer screen, captivated.

Zoe typed a few things into the computer, then glanced up. "Looks like... it's a duplex. It was rented out two months ago."

Clay turned back to me. "What will I find if I send a team back to that duplex?"

I closed my eyes, turning away from Clay, leaning heavily on the bars separating my cell from Lucas and Dad's. There was no hiding my horror. Karayan and Emlyn were still hiding there. They wouldn't leave unless I could warn them. I took a breath, trying to steady my nerves to reach out and make contact with Karayan's mind. Only... I couldn't. A ragged breath tore itself out of my throat. None of my Lilitu powers were available to me. I couldn't see in the dark. I couldn't send a telepathic warning to my friends. Until my wound healed, I was as helpless as a human girl.

My eyes snapped open. I saw Lucas watching me with concern.

"I know about your friend," Clay murmured. He'd moved closer when my eyes had been closed, and his proximity startled me. "I know about the connection between Lilith and her acolytes. I know she's going to possess one of them to make her return to this plane." Clay held my gaze. "Is that why you took the book? To keep us from finding out?"

"No. No." My voice wavered. "There's a way to break the connection between the acolytes and Lilith."

Over Clay's shoulder, I saw Sandra's head lift. She edged around Zoe's table, moving closer, interested. But Clay's expression darkened. "Even if I believed you, which—for the record—I don't, it wouldn't matter. The only sure way to keep Lilith from returning is to eliminate the bodies she has the potential of possessing."

"No!" I forced myself to walk toward Clay, gripping the bars to keep from falling. "I'm telling you the truth. Call Father Jerome. We can save them. There's no reason to kill the girls. They're *innocent*."

Sandra stopped a few feet away from us. She exchanged a startled look with Thane behind Clay's back. Thane kept his expression neutral. Whatever he was thinking, he wasn't sharing it with anyone.

"Innocent?" Clay shook his head, deadly serious. "They chose this fate when they decided to devote themselves to the mother of demons."

"Not Cassie!" I reached the door of the cell and gripped the bars with both hands. Blood covered my right hand, making the bar slick. "Cassie only went through with the initiation to help us figure out what Idris had planned."

"Thane." Dad was awake. He pushed himself into a sitting position. "You know she's right." Thane's eyes slid to Dad. I saw his lips tighten, but he gave no other response.

"Cassie took a huge risk to help us," Gretchen added. "One you encouraged, Thane! She put everything on the line for us. Are you really going to turn your back on her now?"

Thane's eyes shifted back to me for half a heartbeat before he turned to face Clay. "It's already been decided."

I'd never been so aware of how completely and utterly helpless being human could feel. I stared through the bars at Thane and Sandra and Marla. *I* was helpless. But *they weren't*. A sudden fury boiled up within me. I glared at Thane.

"Decided by Clay, you mean. And you'll follow his orders as mindlessly as you always have." My words seemed to prick something within Thane. His eyes narrowed. I pressed closer to the bars. "You let him make the decisions, and you fall in line. Even when it was your own daughter's life on the line. She told me. Karayan came to you for help after being assaulted and you took Clay's side over hers."

Thane's face drained of color. I had never seen him look so stricken. Clay spun on me, eyes flashing.

"Your demon friend seduced and then killed my son." Clay gripped the hilt of his dagger—the one he'd just stabbed me with. Some part of my mind noticed drops of my blood still visible on the dull metal.

I took a step back from the bars, trying to put distance between myself and the weapon. Thane had a strange, far-away look on his face.

"He attacked her, Thane." I kept my eyes focused on Thane's face, willing him to listen. "He assaulted Karayan and he lied about it. Then, when everyone else turned their backs on her—including the one man she trusted most in all the world—he attacked her *again*."

"Lies!" Clay drew the dagger. It made a soft *shhhing* sound as it slid free from the sheath. "She tried to poison me against my own son, and when she failed, she killed him!" Clay fumbled for the keys in his pocket. I backed into the far wall, trapped.

"Braedyn!" Dad clutched my hand through the bars, his eyes locked on Clay. Clay fumbled to get the key in the lock with one hand and clutched the dagger in his other hand.

"It was an accident," I said. But I wasn't talking to Clay. I caught Thane's eyes, desperate to be heard. "She didn't mean to kill him, but that doesn't mean he was innocent. Those girls Clay's ready to murder? They are. Cassie is innocent."

Behind Thane, I saw Marla and Sandra trade an uncertain glance.

"We know how to stop it," I gushed. "Father Jerome's looked over the ritual, he believes it will work. We gathered all the ingredients, the only thing they need is the book—"

The lock clicked open.

"Clay, don't. Don't." Dad's voice was hoarse through the bars. I felt his hand tighten around me. "Thane, don't let him do this."

"She's blinded you all." Clay took a step into the cell. I pressed myself farther into the back corner, but there was nowhere to run. Thane reached out and caught Clay by the shoulder. Clay spun on him, furious. "Don't tell me she's gotten to you as well?"

"No." Thane flicked his eyes over me, coldly dispassionate. "But you lose a valuable opportunity by slitting her throat down here. You want a demonstration of strength? Gather the Guard. Hold an execution."

A strangled sob broke from Dad's lips. Lucas took a few steps away from Clay then collapsed, sitting on the floor with a hollow look. Gretchen gripped the bars of her cell and screamed, something about Clay being a power-hungry psychopath.

But I was staring at Clay. I could see the wheels turning in his head. After what felt like forever, he sheathed his dagger, turned on his heel, and left, pushing the cell door keys into the hand of a Guardsman. The Guardsman returned to lock the door, but I wasn't paying any attention to him.

I watched Clay walk back to the stairs, trailed up and out of the basement by Thane and Marla. The last thing I heard before they closed the basement door was Clay's voice.

"Search the duplex. Kill whoever you find there. Then locate and eliminate the acolytes. All three of them."

It's easy to become paralyzed when you feel overwhelmed by helplessness. I stared through the bars of my cell, feeling myself on the knife's edge.

In mere moments, Clay's men would leave with nothing more than an address to a little duplex downtown. They'd break into the house and storm the rooms. They'd find Karayan and Emlyn, maybe even Ben. Karayan would die first; no way would Clay send the men without a spotter, and as soon as whoever they sent got a good look at Karayan's Lilitu aspect, it would be over. Ben, he seemed like the kind of guy who'd fight back, trying to protect Emlyn. They'd cut him down without a second thought. But Emlyn… would they hesitate before assassinating a little girl?

Fury and fear had burned through me, left me feeling charred, hollowed out. But as I pictured Emlyn's face, something moved in to occupy the hole they'd left behind. I looked up, directly into the eyes of the two Guardsmen Clay had left behind—Simon and a soldier I recognized, but whose name I'd never learned.

"Is this what you signed up for?" My voice cut across the space between us. "Standing by while Clay murders a couple of helpless girls?" The Guards shared a veiled look.

Simon glanced from Dad to me. "Clay is willing to make the hard calls. He's willing to sacrifice innocents if it means defeating Lilith."

"But he's not willing to find out if there's a way to defeat her *without* spilling innocent blood." I could see my words had an effect on them. They'd been listening to our fight. They'd heard my plea. I'd thought it had fallen on deaf ears. Maybe it hadn't, at least not entirely. I straightened, summoning a strength that surprised me. "Clay is wrong. And you know it."

Simon and the other Guardsman traded a look. They did know it, I could see it in their eyes. But neither of the men spoke. I felt my frustration building. I gripped the bars separating us a little harder.

"Someone has to stand up for what's right." I fought to keep the frustration out of my voice. "You joined the Guard to fight. You joined because you believe in right over wrong. Good over evil. Clay's lost the mission, can't you see it?" Some of the anger I was fighting to conceal bled back into my voice. "Clay isn't fit to lead the Guard! Why are you following him?"

"It's no use." Dad's voice sounded hollow. I turned. Dad eyed me from the back of his cell. "He's trained them not to think for themselves."

I glanced at the soldiers. They stared at the ground, jaws clamped tightly shut. I looked at Dad, angry. I'd been getting through to them, I could feel it. But he raised a finger to his lips, urging silence. He nodded his head back at the soldiers standing guard. When I turned back, I saw Simon glancing up the stairs with a thoughtful frown. It wasn't much, but it was a start.

I slumped with my head against the bars. The searing pain in my chest had faded to a throbbing ache. Either my body was getting used to the sensation, or I was going into shock, or… I was healing.

19

With shaking fingers, I pulled the neck of my shirt open. I had to force myself to look down to examine the wound in my chest. Part of me knew that if I wasn't a Lilitu, I'd already be dead. I pulled a corner of my shirt up and mopped the blood away from the wound. It was still seeping red, but the flow had stemmed to a trickle. I let out a long breath and looked up.

Lucas was there, just a foot away, looking devastated. "I didn't know. I couldn't... see his..." He swallowed, then dropped his head forward. "Braedyn, I'm sorry."

I was too tired, too angry to acknowledge the apology. As edifying as it was to know that Lucas believed us now—that he had finally seen Clay's true nature—it was too little too late.

I turned my back on Lucas and slid down the bars, sitting on the cold basement floor. It took several long moments to tamp the slow-burning rage. I closed my eyes and tried to open my heart.

Sansenoy, please. If you can hear me, please answer. We need you now, more than we've ever needed you. I waited. Silence. I tried again to release my hold on the anger threatening to boil over within me.

"What can I do?" Lucas knelt behind me. Only the bars separated us. I could hear his remorse in every syllable. It reignited the anger. Lucas reached through the bars and brushed his fingers against the side of my arm.

"Don't," I breathed.

"Braedyn, I..."

"I can't help you!" I pushed away from the bars, lurching to the other side of the cell. I heard Lucas stand behind me.

"I'm not... I'm not asking you to help me." He spoke quietly, but I could hear the pain in his voice.

"You're not?" I spun on him, letting loose my anger on the only available target. Even though I knew he didn't deserve it, even though I knew he'd been played by Clay, I couldn't help but attack. "You're not secretly hoping I'll tell you it's okay, that you were only doing what you thought was best?"

Lucas stared at me, frozen. Behind him, I saw Dad lower his head into his hands. Lucas shook his head, blinking back the tears welling in his eyes. "I didn't know."

"You didn't *want* to know. There's a difference." I clung to the bars, feeling dizzy. Blood raged in my ears, but once I'd started, I couldn't seem to stop the words. Like a dam bursting, my rage and frustration poured out of me and there was no holding it back. "I tried to get you to see. But every time I criticized Clay, you shut me down." I had to choke back a sob of fury. "You want to help? What could you possibly do? We're stuck in here. Cassie…" My breath caught as a fresh wave of pain cascaded through me. "Cassie is going to die tonight because I can't get the book to her and you… you were supposed to be on my side." Tears flowed down my cheeks. "You chose him."

Lucas nodded, accepting the blame. His chin trembled, I could see the tears he fought to hold back. And then he turned away from me, pacing the cell like a caged beast. After a few moments of this, he launched himself at the cell door, again and again, each time impacting with a heavy clang.

"Lucas!" Gretchen tried to reach him through the bars separating her cell from his, but she couldn't. "Murphy…?" She turned to my dad, but he was already on his feet, moving toward Lucas.

Dad caught Lucas in a tight bear hug. Lucas shuddered, but he didn't fight.

"It's okay, Lucas," Dad murmured. "I loved him too, once. He has this way of making you feel… irreplaceable."

Lucas let out a shaky breath. He swallowed.

Dad turned toward me. His face was drawn. I closed my eyes, wishing I could slip into unconsciousness, lose myself in the velvety blackness of the universal dream. But even that avenue of escape was closed to me now.

"What time do you think it is?" I asked, to no one in particular.

Simon was the one who answered me. He'd been watching, listening to every word we'd said. "4:30."

I sank back to the floor, curling onto my side. The sun would be setting in an hour. And just like the fading light of day, Cassie's chance to be free of Lilith's taint would dim and then, finally, gutter into darkness.

This cell wasn't my prison. My prison was my mind, and Clay had locked me in when he'd stabbed me with the Guardsman's blade. I felt the seconds scraping my nerves raw as they passed. My thoughts flew to Cassie at Lookout Point, waiting for release. To Father Jerome, who'd set aside his better judgment to listen and then offered his help. To Royal and Ally, who'd sacrificed their time and risked academic sanctions to translate the book. Everyone had done their part. Everyone but me.

I heard the basement door open. Lucas lifted his head in the next cell over. I pushed myself up until I was sitting, suddenly alert. How much time had passed? Had it been an hour already? Were they coming for Lucas? He met my gaze and I read pure terror in his eyes. We weren't the only ones harboring this thought.

"Get behind me, Lucas." Dad stood, moving to the door of his cell, grim faced. If they were coming for Lucas, they'd have to contend with Murphy first.

I rose to my feet and found my dizziness had subsided. Surprised, I pulled back the collar of my shirt. The wound had scabbed over. I stretched out my arm and hissed as a twinge of pain shot through my shoulder. But that was it... just a twinge of pain, not the ripping agony I'd felt when the wound was fresh. I wasn't completely healed, but I was well on the way. I looked up, through the bars. Lucas met my gaze. I opened my mouth... but what could I say? After raking him over the coals, what comfort could I offer?

"It's okay." He flashed me the briefest smile before turning toward the basement stairs, steeling himself for whatever was coming.

The steps descending the basement stairs reached the bottom. I expected Clay, or maybe Sutherland. I didn't expect Father Jerome. Lucas let out a breath, equally surprised.

Simon straightened, gripping his daggers. "You can't be here, sir. You need to turn around and go back upstairs."

"He's here at my request." Thane emerged from the stairwell behind Father Jerome, eyeing Simon with disdain. I felt my breath catch. I stared at the men. My head may not have understood what I was seeing, but my heart began to beat a little faster, sensing the presence of hope.

"Clay gave specific orders." But Simon licked his lips, betraying some of the nervousness he felt. "No outsiders are permitted down here."

"Stand aside," Thane growled. "I don't have the time for intra-Guard politics right now."

Thane brushed past the soldiers, drawing Father Jerome with him. The priest was holding the acolyte book in his hands. He read my astonishment and shrugged.

"When you failed to return with the book, I decided to come looking for you." He inclined his head to Thane. "It was fortunate that I arrived when I did. It seems Thane was on his way to find me. A few moments later and we would have missed one another entirely."

I turned to Thane. He still looked conflicted, but he met my gaze. "I agree with Clay that Lilith must be stopped." He spoke slowly, his words measured, as though it were painful to utter them out loud. "But I cannot see the logic in killing three young women who could be saved by other means." His eyes shifted to the priest. "Beyond that, it seems your priest has some additional concerns."

Jerome nodded. "I had a chance to leaf through a few more pages of that horrible copy while we were waiting for you." He glanced down at the book in his hands. "It seems that death itself is not guaranteed to release the souls from Lilith's grip. If we want to deny Lilith her vessels, this incantation is our best bet."

"Have you told Clay?" Dad's voice drew Thane's attention.

Thane shook his head no. "I don't think Clay is seeing things clearly at the moment. Under the circumstances, we decided it would be prudent to handle this matter without involving him." Thane turned away from Dad to face the soldiers. He rested a hand on his daggers. I saw the Guardsmen take note of this. They edged back, tense. "I'm going to open these cell doors. If you have a problem with that, you're welcome to try and stop me."

Simon drew his daggers, then glanced at his compatriot. The other Guardsman hesitated, then lifted his hands and stepped back even farther. He saw Simon's incredulous look and shrugged.

"They're right, Simon. Clay's…" His eyes found mine. "He's lost the mission."

Simon turned back to Thane. But then his eyes slid past the old archivist and settled on me. I watched him, unable to suppress the surge of hope swelling under my heart. Simon considered me for a long moment, then lowered his dagger. He reached into his pocket and pulled out a set of keys. Wordlessly, he tossed them to Thane.

Thane caught the keys and turned to open the door to my cell. I met him at the bars, awed. Thane caught sight of the expression on my face. His lips tightened with irritation.

"I told you," he said. "My loyalty is and has always been to the cause." He turned the key in the lock and it sprang open with a soft metallic click.

"Royal's in his car, waiting out back." Jerome frowned as he studied us. "But it won't fit everyone."

"You go." I faced Jerome, ignoring Dad's anxious look. "You're the one who needs to be there to perform the ritual. We'll follow as soon as we get out of here."

Jerome nodded. He slipped the acolyte book in the pocket of his coat, then headed up the stairs.

"We need to get you and Lucas out of here now," Dad growled.

"Let me go first," Thane said. "I'll distract Clay and the other Guardsmen so you can escape. Give me three minutes, then move." He didn't wait for our response before following Jerome up the stairs to the main house.

Dad's hands drifted to his side, where he usually kept his daggers sheathed beneath his coat. "I feel naked."

"Sir?" Simon flinched when Dad spun on him, pulling back reflexively. He was holding his daggers by the intertwined blades, offering the hilt to Dad. Dad looked from the offered daggers to

Simon's face. "Take them. It's not like Clay's going to let me keep them after this, anyway." He gave Dad a humorless smile.

Dad took the offered daggers and nodded his thanks.

The other Guardsman let out a sigh, then offered his daggers to Gretchen. "Good luck," he said. She nodded, springing the interlocking daggers apart and handing one to Lucas.

Whatever distraction Thane had planned, it sounded like it was working. We heard running boots in the hallway upstairs. After a few moments of silence, Dad nodded. It was time to move.

We crept quickly up the stairs, alert for any sounds that might indicate danger. When we reached the landing at the top of the stairs, Dad signaled for us to stop. He leaned his ear against the door, listening. It suddenly moved, yanked open from the outside. Dad recoiled, gripping his daggers, prepared to fight.

The spotter Marla stood in the hallway before us. She eyed Dad with an exasperated look, then jerked her head toward the front door. "Go. You don't have much time."

And just like that we were racing out of the Guard's house onto the front porch. When I saw the sky I missed a step, catching myself on the railing. The sun was perched like the fat yolk of an egg hovering just above the horizon. It was official: we were running out of time.

20

The Firebird was still parked on the curb. Clay's men had taken my cell phone, but they'd missed the car key I'd shoved deep into the front pocket of my jeans. I fished it out and unlocked the doors, moving aside for Lucas and Gretchen to climb into the back seat while Dad walked around to the passenger side.

"Wait." I stopped Gretchen before she climbed into the back of the car. "Someone still needs to pick up Emma... She won't fit in the car, not with all of us crammed inside."

Dad and Gretchen traded a look. "I'll drive," Gretchen said. She hadn't been searched, she was still carrying her car keys. "You guys get to Lookout Point. You should be there for Cassie."

I nodded, full of gratitude. I rooted through my glove compartment for the scrap of paper with Emma's address on it, the one I'd gotten from her manager. I handed it over to Gretchen.

"Go," Dad said. "Don't wait for us."

Lucas and I didn't need to be told twice. We slid into the car and I turned the key in the ignition. The Firebird roared to life. I shifted the car into first and pulled away from the curb, leaving the Guard's house—and Clay—behind in a cloud of grit and dust.

"There's still time," Lucas said. It sounded as if he was trying to will himself to believe it.

I forced myself to nod in response, then refocused my attention on the road. I wasn't going to breathe easy until I knew Cassie was okay. We sped past the outskirts of town, making a beeline for Lookout Point. The low sun cast warm shadows across our path, filling the desert evening with a rosy glow.

It was beautiful out here, the kind of desolate beauty only a desert can convey. Patches of bare sand seemed to pick up the colors of the sunset, making it look like a watercolor painting done in hues of rose and orange and gold.

The scale of the desert can play tricks on your mind. I had the pedal floored. The scrub brush and prairie grasses lining the road whipped by in a blur, but the mountains towering above seemed to move at a glacial pace. At the horizon before us, like a ticking time bomb, the sun dropped lower and lower.

When we pulled off the road at Lookout Point, I killed the engine and leapt out of the car. Cassie spotted me first, face shining with relief. But her expression changed when she caught sight of the blood still drenching my shirt. "Braedyn, you're hurt."

"It looks worse than it is." I looped my good arm around her shoulders, trying an awkward side-hug.

"That's not exactly true," Lucas murmured.

I shot a look at him, then shrugged, caught. "I'll heal."

Cassie eyed Lucas, surprised, then drew me in close, hugging me gingerly. Even though she was being careful, I could tell there was something wrong. Her grip felt... feeble. I pulled back, concerned. Cassie's skin looked pale in the rich glow of the setting sun. She smiled up at me, but her cheeks had a sunken appearance and her eyes seemed almost hollow.

Someone moved behind us. Karayan. At first I could only stare at her, but then the relief that flooded through me almost knocked me over. I released Cassie and stumbled toward Karayan, throwing my arms around her. If I hadn't cried myself dry already today, I would have lost it again. I gripped her tightly and felt her surprise, but then she hugged me back.

I pushed her away, searching her face for answers. "How...? He sent men... I thought... I thought they were going to kill you and I couldn't reach you, I couldn't warn you."

Karayan's expression shifted to one of sick understanding. "Vyla came for Emlyn." Her eyes looked troubled. "When they left with Ben, they left everything behind." She looked down at her hands, which held a small stuffed rabbit. "I thought she was over reacting, but..." Karayan's eyes raked over my blood-soaked shirt. "When Royal came for Cassie, there was nothing left for me to protect. What happened?"

There was too much to explain. For a moment, I grappled with how to answer her. Lucas spoke first.

"Clay." His voice was solemn. Karayan nodded, then ran her fingers over my shoulder gingerly.

"You made it out. Good." Father Jerome approached, holding the open book. He must have beaten us here by just a few minutes. He bent to check a collection of items laid out on a cloth on the desert floor. The oils and tinctures we'd collected had joined a handful of fresh flowering herbs and a silver bowl.

Royal hovered at his side, ready to help. He eyed my shirt with a sick look on his face, then met my eyes. I flashed him what I hoped was a reassuring smile. Royal nodded in response, but he didn't return the smile. Every muscle in his body looked taut, and I knew exactly why.

"We should get started," I said, turning to Father Jerome.

"Agreed." Jerome finished his examination and straightened. He began assembling the anointment, mixing ingredients in the silver bowl as we watched in silence.

A car pulled off the road behind us and Karayan and I turned as one. It was Missy's car, but I wasn't expecting all four doors to open at once. Missy, Ally, Carrie, and Amber emerged. I shot a questioning look at Royal. He spotted Amber, too.

"She must have been with Carrie," he murmured. "Or… maybe they called her. It's not like she's not a part of this."

We turned back to watch as Amber and Missy helped Carrie out of the back seat. I heard Karayan hiss quietly at my side, but I couldn't take my eyes off Carrie. As bad as Cassie looked, it was clear now how much worse she could have been. Carrie leaned against Missy and Ally, clinging to them with the last of her strength. She looked like a living skeleton.

"Do you see it?" Karayan spoke quietly into my ear. Her eyes tracked Carrie across the dirt toward where Father Jerome stood waiting. Even he looked shaken by her appearance, though he flashed her a reassuring smile.

"What?" I hadn't been able to look away from Carrie, but it wasn't until she crossed the setting sun that I saw what Karayan had already spotted. An oily taint seemed to hover around Carrie, like a greasy shadow that never quite resolved into focus. "Oh…"

"What is it?" Karayan breathed the question into the air, like she didn't expect an answer. But I knew what it was. I knew as surely as I'd known what the miasma in Cassie's dream had been.

"Lilith." I battled a swell of nausea, then met Karayan's eyes. "We're running out of time."

We collected around Jerome at the edge of the cliff, where we had the best view of the western horizon. The sun had contacted the horizon. It glowed with a dull red fire, painting the mountains a dusty pink.

"Who's first?" He looked at me. I turned toward Cassie, but she was looking at Carrie.

Before I could stop her, Cassie answered Jerome. "Start with Carrie." Missy shot Cassie a look of unadulterated gratitude, then helped Carrie stand to face Jerome. I fought a grimace. Lucas met my gaze, concerned. But it had been decided; Carrie would be first.

"Help her take off her shoes. She needs to be barefoot." Jerome thumbed open the acolyte book as the girls helped Carrie take off her shoes.

Cassie let out a breath of relief beside me. I glanced at her, curious. She shrugged, embarrassed. "For a minute, I thought he was going to say we needed to be naked." She blushed, and I saw some of the old Cassie in the twinkle of her eye.

"Royal?" Jerome beckoned Royal forward. Royal clasped the silver bowl and held it by Jerome's side. Jerome hovered his hand over the bowl and read the incantation written in the margins of the acolyte book. His voice was rich and strong, and the Latin sounded majestic against the backdrop. I let the words wash over me, focusing on Carrie's face. When he finished reciting the words, Jerome dipped his finger into the silver bowl. He dotted oil on the top of Carrie's head, on each of her hands, and on each of her feet. Then he straightened.

"Is that it?" I eyed Carrie, unsure. "How will we know if...?" Carrie suddenly doubled over, dropping to her hands and knees. She gagged, coughing up a sick glob of oily residue. Missy cried out and moved to comfort her sister.

"Stop!" Jerome caught Missy's arm, holding her back. "Let it do its work."

Missy looked up at Jerome, terrified. Carrie made another wet coughing sound, then sat back, wiping her mouth with the back of one shaking hand. Then she hissed with pain, reaching toward her face. She blinked and something fell from the surface of her eyes.

"What...?" Carrie looked up. Two grey, semi-transparent husks, smaller than rose-petals but larger than contacts, rested in the palms of her hands.

"Scales," Father Jerome murmured.

Carrie dropped the scales onto the ground. They—and the oily substance she'd vomited out—seemed to disintegrate into a fine black mist that dissipated in the fading light of the sun. Jerome released Missy. She knelt beside her sister, grabbing her in a tight embrace. When they finally stood, Carrie's smile was as bright as the sun.

Lucas let out a breath, awed. "I think it worked."

Royal looked up, catching my eyes. I saw something like pride flicker in his eyes. "One down, two to go."

Carrie took a deep breath and let it out, then turned to Father Jerome. "Thank you." Her voice was choked with emotion. I felt a stinging in the bridge of my nose.

"Celebrate later," Royal said. "It's Cassie's turn."

"Yes." Jerome nodded, flipping the book open to the right page to begin the ritual a second time. He glanced up at Cassie. "Shoes."

"Right." Cassie kicked off her shoes and moved to stand before Father Jerome at the edge of the cliff. He held his hand over the bowl and began reciting the words once more.

The sun was sinking into the horizon now, dipping lower with each heartbeat. Emma needed to get here. I bit my lip and turned away from the scene at the cliff's edge to scan the road behind us. I heard a vehicle approaching. They were cutting it close, but there was still time. I turned back to watch Jerome reading the incantation. Cassie waited impatiently, fidgeting, eager to be freed from Lilith's taint.

I heard the approaching vehicle pull onto the turn out behind us. Followed by a second vehicle, then a third.

I looked back, surprised. I didn't see Gretchen's car among the new arrivals. But there was one vehicle I recognized. The van's passenger side door opened. Clay stepped out into the glow of the setting sun. All around him, soldiers were emerging from the vehicles.

The Guard had arrived.

I spun back to Cassie and Jerome. "Finish it," I hissed. Jerome lowered the book, eyeing the approaching Clay with consternation.

Missy pulled Carrie back, away from Clay and his men, but we were standing on the edge of a cliff—there was only so far they could go. Amber and Ally joined them in a close huddle.

Clay's eyes caught on something over my shoulder. He slid his daggers out of their sheath with a deliberate malice that set my teeth on edge. "Karayan. I was wondering when you'd turn up." He didn't take his eyes off Karayan as he called to the soldiers flanking him. "I want her alive."

Clay's men sprang forward, daggers in hand. I moved, stepping between the advancing Guard and Karayan. They hesitated. Facing two Lilitu, even at the edge of a cliff, seemed to complicate things. Fine. I wasn't about to make it easy for them. But then Karayan spoke at my shoulder.

"Don't, Braedyn." Her voice was thin with fear. I turned. Karayan stood at the edge of the cliff, frozen. I'd never seen this expression on her face before. The terror filling her eyes was shot through with... acceptance. It was like she'd known this moment would come. She stepped forward to meet the approaching soldiers. She made no move to run, just lifted her hands out in a sort of resigned plea.

"Karayan." I started to move toward her but she stopped me with a look.

"Help Jerome. He needs to finish the ritual. *Right now.*" Karayan inclined her head toward the horizon. I followed her gaze. The sun was almost gone.

I only pulled my eyes away for a heartbeat, but the Guard saw their opportunity. They sprang on Karayan, surrounding her. Someone drove a fist into her stomach, dropping her to her knees. She let out a grunt of pain.

"Stop!" I took a step toward them. One of Clay's men spun on me, daggers flashing with the last gleam of the setting sun. I hesitated, acutely aware that I had no weapons, and no powers.

"Braedyn, don't!" Karayan looked up at me through the legs of the men surrounding her. Then her eyes shifted and her expression changed. Shame washed over her. She dropped her head, keeping her gaze on the ground even after the soldiers had hauled her back to her feet.

I turned. Thane approached, his face hard. I couldn't read the emotions playing through his eyes. But when the soldiers dragged Karayan back to the waiting van, he looked away.

When the guards opened the side of the van, Dad and Gretchen spilled out. They had their hands bound behind their backs like Karayan.

Dad searched the faces before him, eyes wild with an urgent fear. "Braedyn?!"

"I'm here!" My throat closed around the words, seized by another wave of emotion. We'd come so close…

Dad's eyes found me and some of the tension eased from his shoulders. Soldiers caught him and Gretchen by the arms, keeping them from moving. The Guards started to muscle Dad back into the van, but Clay held up a hand.

"Hold on." Clay's eyes slid to my face. "I think they've earned the right to see this."

I took a step back, suddenly cold. Clay walked out onto the precipice of Lookout Point, hands clasped behind his back as if nothing here could threaten him. I watched him with bated breath.

Clay stopped in front of Jerome, eying the book in Jerome's hands and the bowl in Royal's. "I'm surprised, Father. I would have thought a man of the cloth wouldn't be so easily manipulated by a demon."

Father Jerome studied Clay, startled. "Demon?"

Thane stepped forward. "Let him finish his work, Clay. We can sort through the details after."

Clay ignored Thane, keeping his gaze fixed on Jerome. "She didn't tell you? Braedyn is Lilitu." Clay turned back to face me. His smile could have been carved from ice. "And you've been playing right into her hands." I saw the doubt enter Jerome's eyes.

"Wait." I stepped forward, struggling to keep my voice calm. "It worked. Jerome, tell him."

Jerome looked down at the book in his hands, still open to the page inscribed with the incantation. But a new suspicion had entered his eyes. Cassie saw it, too.

"Father Jerome?" She licked her lips, unsure. She turned to look at the horizon. It had to be now—only the topmost edge of the sun still peeked over the horizon.

Jerome's eyes seemed to refocus. "Demon or no, I think she's right. We need to finish the ritual."

Clay's smile faded. He ripped the bowl from Royal's hands. In one motion he turned and pitched the bowl—and its contents—over the edge of the cliff. For one horrible moment, I saw the oil drops glimmering like golden gems against the sky. Then they were gone, falling to the desert floor hundreds of feet below us.

Royal and Jerome stared at Clay, too stunned to move. But Cassie let out a sound that chilled me to the core. It was a soft, hitching sigh, the sound of hope disintegrating. She took a step toward the edge of the cliff, then dropped to her knees. The red-gold sunlight edged her features in a beautiful halo, but her eyes… her eyes were empty.

Carrie screamed, pushing her way past Missy and the other girls. "Why did you do that?! He cured me, he could have cured her, too!"

Clay ignored Carrie. He gestured back at the crowd. Sandra approached Jerome, jaw tight with anger. She gripped the acolyte book and drew it out of Jerome's hands. Jerome, still stunned, didn't resist.

Clay nodded at Sandra, then looked around, studying Missy, Ally, and Amber closely. "Which of you is the third acolyte?"

Carrie glared murder at Clay, refusing to answer. Clay tilted he head to one side, considering them. "Someone should answer my question before I lose my patience." His eyes settled on Missy and I saw his body coil, ready to strike.

"We sent Dad and Gretchen to get her. Ask them." My words sounded flat, devoid of emotion.

Clay turned to Dad, curious. "Do you have her?"

Dad's eyes simmered with undisguised fury. He shook his head no.

"Unfortunate." Clay turned to Sutherland, calm. "Put the children in one of the vans. We'll deal with them after." Soldiers moved toward the girls still huddled at the edge of the cliff. Missy gave a wail of fear as one of the men grabbed her arm, trying to separate her from Carrie. The sisters clung to one another, fighting to keep from being parted. Another soldier stepped up to help.

"Braedyn?"

I heard Cassie's breathy fear over the din and turned. Cassie's dark eyes were wide and staring. As I watched, the fiery light edging her face dimmed. The sun was almost completely swallowed by the horizon. Cassie turned toward me, lips parted. Terror shone from her face.

"I can feel something—" Cassie's voice broke. Her body spasmed unnaturally. It looked like someone had grabbed her by the forehead and pulled her backwards, arching her slender frame across the desert floor. She hit the dusty earth and pitched sideways, convulsing.

"Cassie!" Royal moved first, rushing toward Cassie.

Clay bellowed out orders. "Move, move, move! Kill the girl before Lilith can assume control of her body!"

I spun on Clay, horrified.

Time seemed to slow. A soldier caught Royal around the neck, hauling him back from Cassie. At the edge of the turnout, I could see Missy and Ally fighting the soldiers trying to shove them into the back of the van. Murphy struggled to free himself from the three soldiers holding him back. Gretchen had dropped to her knees, screaming for Lucas. My eyes sought him out, it felt like minutes stretched by with every breath.

Lucas crouched in front of Cassie, one dagger in his hand, trying to defend her from the soldier drawing closer. They threw themselves at each other, crashing together like fighting rams, locked in a contest as much of wills as of physical strength. Cassie's body thrashed on the ground behind them, her fingers digging into the dirt with enough force to claw deep lines in the earth.

Clay shifted his weight behind me, his daggers glinting against the dusk. He charged forward, eyes locked on Cassie's helpless form. He dropped beside her, gripping her shoulder and flipping her on her back. She stared up at him, uncomprehending. He raised the dagger above his head, ready to plunge it down into her heart—

I hit him at a full run. We tumbled past Cassie, rolling together toward the edge of the cliff. Time resumed its frantic pace, sending me skidding toward the sheer drop ahead. I flung out my hands, scrabbling at the dirt to slow myself. My toes slipped off the edge of the cliff, raining gravel down into the steep ravine below. Clay's daggers skipped past me, sailing over the edge unimpeded.

My heartbeat thundered in my ears. I scrambled back from the edge of the cliff. Clay let out a heavy growl a few feet away. I looked up into his eyes, twin pools of hatred, and saw rage etched into every line of his face. He turned back toward Cassie.

Cassie was pushing herself up on her elbows. Her long black hair draped over her face, hiding her features. For half a second, I felt a stab of fear. I didn't know who occupied the slender body before us. Was it Cassie? Or was it something… else? She didn't seem strong enough to sit up yet. Clay moved behind me. He rose to his feet, gripping a fist-sized rock in his hand. If I stopped him, who would I be protecting? Friend or foe? I had a split second to decide.

I threw myself in Clay's path, blocking him from his target. Clay's eyes glittered. He shifted his weight, then swung out. He caught me across the jaw with a stinging blow. I hadn't had time to block him, but I wasn't expecting the blow to flatten me. I hit the dirt hard, stunned. It struck me, dimly, that I had never fought without my Lilitu powers fueling my body. I shoved the shock to the back of my mind and pushed myself back onto my knees.

Clay was already turning back toward Cassie. I saw his grip tighten on the stone. Cassie, still prone on the ground, would never see him coming.

And then the sun set.

Something like a distant sonic boom rocketed across the landscape. A blast of air struck us, powerful enough to knock Clay backwards several steps. He froze, then turned to stare back at his men, stricken. Some part of me knew what he must be thinking, but it was drowned out by another explosion. Only, this one was in my head. Even though I had been cut off from the Lilitu part of myself, I could feel the dreamscape churning in turmoil. It was more powerful than an earthquake, more devastating than a tsunami.

Nausea swelled in my throat. I choked it back, gasping for every breath. Around us, the shockwave died leaving an unnatural stillness in its wake. No one spoke. No one needed to—we all knew what had happened. We had failed.

Lilith had returned to the earth.

21

I don't know how long we stayed frozen on the edge of that mountain. I don't know what we were waiting for. Fiery hail to descend from the sky? Rivers of lava to open across the valley below? More unnerving than any visible symbol of Lilith's presence in our world, was the silence that followed. It was as though the natural world sensed the presence of a new predator and knew better than to draw attention to itself.

But then... life continued. I heard a sound and turned. A meadowlark chirped and leapt from its perch to dart away into the gathering dark.

The rock dropped from Clay's hand. He staggered back.

Everyone stared at Cassie. She hadn't moved a muscle—not to stand, not even to lift her head.

I forced my body up, struggling to my feet. But as I passed Clay, his hand shot out. He grabbed a fistful of hair at the base of my scalp. I hissed at the pain. Clay tightened his grip. He spun me around, steering me back to the waiting soldiers. I stumbled, my knees hitting the ground, but he didn't stop.

As he dragged me forward, I clawed at his hands. It was all I could do to hang onto his fist, to keep him from pulling me forward by my the roots of my hair. He stopped at the edge of the waiting men and thrust out his hand.

"Give me a dagger." Clay waited, but no one moved. I heard the incredulity creeping into his voice. "You saw what she did! She paved the way for Lilith's return!"

"Clay!" Dad's shock cut across the eerie silence. "Clay, look."

Clay turned, which is when I saw Cassie getting to her knees. She heaved, ejecting an oily mass from her mouth. Cassie straightened, shuddering. Then she hissed as two shadowy scales fell from her eyes. For a moment no one moved. Cassie looked up, stunned. Even in the blue of twilight, I could see a healthy flush spreading back into Cassie's face.

Father Jerome let out a victorious shout. "Did you see…?"

Royal broke away from the soldier holding him and ran to Cassie, dropping beside her and pulling her to his chest. After a minute, Royal pushed her back, holding her at arm's length to examine her face. "Are you okay?"

"You mean, after vomiting out the pure evil and watching my eyes shed a layer of grey snakeskin? Yeah, I'm feeling a little better." Cassie gave him a watery smile. I could hear the people around us shifting their weight. Cassie and Royal looked up, suddenly aware they were the center of attention. Royal's arms tightened around Cassie again, as though there were some way he could protect her from the united power of the Guard.

"But…" Clay's voice hardened. "You didn't finish…?"

Father Jerome shook his head in wonder. "Perhaps the partial ritual offered some protection even though I was unable to complete it. Or perhaps we had help from some unseen hand. Regardless, it appears you have emerged from this ordeal whole." Father Jerome studied Cassie with a warmth that surprised me. Clay did not look convinced.

"No." Cassie looked up at Father Jerome. "It wasn't the ritual. I… I felt her. I felt her trying to break into my mind. I don't know what kept her out. Maybe if she'd had more time… but she passed me over." Cassie's eyes shifted to mine and I could see the question in her mind. Had it been the shield? Had it thrown just enough of an obstacle in her path that she abandoned Cassie as a vessel? But then Cassie dropped her voice, sick. "She… she chose someone else."

"The third acolyte." Clay turned back to Dad and Gretchen.

"We were on our way to bring her here." Murphy glared at Clay. He no longer struggled in the arms of his captors. "We could have saved her life. We could have stopped Lilith. But then your men attacked us and she bolted. They overpowered us before we could find her."

Another silence descended around us.

"Then it's happened. Lilith has returned." I felt Clay's fist tighten in my hair and sucked in a sharp breath.

"This is on you, Clay." Karayan glared at Clay from where she knelt on the ground. Two Guardsmen stood over her, daggers drawn, but they didn't move to silence her. "Braedyn could've stopped it. You didn't have to help her. You didn't even have to listen to her. All you had to do was stay out of her way."

"You." Clay's voice dropped to a dangerous level. "You should have run when you had the chance."

"I'm done running." Karayan shifted her gaze to me. "It's time to pick a side." The Guards standing over Karayan exchanged a veiled look. Something was happening, but I couldn't see quite what. Before I had a chance to work it out, Clay hauled me to my feet, still gripping the hair at the nape of my neck.

"A dagger!" He held his hand out once more. Again, no one moved. "Guardsmen! I gave you an order!" Clay's voice swelled with rage.

I saw a few of the men jerk back. No one offered Clay a weapon. Clay let out a disgusted grunt and dragged me forward, toward the closest Guardsman. But when he reached for the daggers still strapped to the man's leg, the soldier recoiled, stepping back.

Clay threw me to the ground and advanced on the soldier. The soldier faced Clay down, angling his dagger-side away from the older man. Clay stared at him, astonished. "What the hell do you think you're doing?"

I didn't have to see Karayan's face to know she was grinning. I could hear the triumph in her voice. "I think the technical term," she purred, "is 'reconsidering his allegiance.'"

Clay faced Karayan with a look of utter outrage. "His allegiance? His allegiance is to me!"

"His allegiance is to the Guard." I pushed myself to my feet, ignoring the throbbing pain along the back of my scalp.

Clay's eyes narrowed, but he allowed himself a small smile. "I *am* the Guard."

"Are you?" I straightened, facing Clay eye to eye. "The Guard exists to protect humankind."

"I don't need a demon half-breed to lecture me on why the Guard exists," Clay spat.

"Then explain why you turned your back on three girls whose lives you could have saved." I walked toward Clay, feeling stronger with each step.

Clay edged back, keeping a healthy distance between us. "They chose this path for themselves."

"They're just kids."

"None of that mitigates their crimes." It was Clay's turn to stand his ground. "The wages of sin are death, even for children."

Something stirred in the group behind us. I wouldn't win this argument by defending my friends. It was clear that while I knew what had motivated Cassie, Clay—maybe most of the Guard—would only see the fact that she had voluntarily walked through Idris's initiation. I nodded slowly.

"Maybe you're right." I relaxed my hands, unclenching the fists I'd unconsciously made as I faced Clay down. "But did you even stop to consider how freeing them from Lilith's grasp might prevent Lilith from returning? That by saving those children you are so ready to condemn to death, you might have saved the world?"

The group of watching Guardsmen behind us reacted. I heard more than one murmur as soldier turned to soldier. Clay heard them, too. He eyed the crowd uneasily, then shifted his eyes back to me. He licked his lips, suddenly unsure.

"Monday morning quarterbacking." Clay turned to the crowd, shaking his head. "There's no telling what might have happened if we'd done things differently. Maybe I should have clamped down on our excesses earlier. We could be standing here because I was too lenient with the rules of our order. The Guard depends on discipline and obedience. Who knows?" He turned back to me, spreading his hands in an almost friendly gesture. "If I'd executed you the day I arrived, we might be celebrating our victory over the darkness at this very moment."

I shook my head. "The Guard's been clinging to discipline and obedience for centuries. Maybe it's time to try something different."

Clay scoffed. "It's a little late in the game to change leadership." He eyed the crowd, looking for allies. But the men watching us gave nothing away. They simply waited, listening.

"Too late?" I glared at Clay, acutely aware of the listening soldiers. "Or is now the perfect time to stop and really think about who we're going to be moving into the future? The world has changed. Forget the last few centuries, look at the last few *decades*. If we want to survive? Then the Guard has to change, too." I searched the faces of the watching Guardsmen, willing them to listen to me. "We have a choice to make. We can remain an unbendable, militarized organization, too slow and rigid to respond to the crisis at hand..." I glanced back at Cassie and Jerome, my meaning clear, "or we can evolve into a fluid, responsive, compassionate organization focused more on surviving this war than on exacting petty revenge."

"'We?'" Clay folded his arms over his chest. He addressed the men with open hostility. "Am I the only one here who remembers what she is? For all we know, this demon is enthralling us right now. She's Lilitu, it's what they do!"

"How?" Lucas stepped forward, shaking off the soldier who'd pulled him away from Cassie. He marched over to me, grabbed the collar of my shirt, and pulled it down, exposing the wound on my chest. "You stabbed her with a Guardsman's blade. She's powerless until the wound heals."

I felt the eyes of the watching crowd zeroing in on the scab above my heart. Lucas released my shirt and I adjusted it, covering the wound. One by one the watching soldiers turned back to Clay, waiting for his response. Clay studied the soldiers, his eyes calculating.

After a long moment, he spread his hands. "All right. She's made some valid points. But none of them changes the fact that Lilith has returned." Clay's voice grew grim. "We're on the doorstep of the end times. The Guard needs a strong hand at the helm."

I felt a sick realization wash through me. This is what Clay had to offer the Guard, years of experience leading soldiers into battle. I searched my thoughts, struggling for a way to hang onto the hearts and minds I may have reached just moments ago, before their allegiance returned to Clay.

But before I could formulate an argument, Thane stepped forward.

"Clay is correct." Thane nodded at Clay, then addressed the assembled. "I've served the Guard since I was a teenager. I've seen how we function in different situations enough to know that we need strong leadership, especially in crisis." I felt my heart sink.

Clay shot a veiled look my way. Though he tried to hide it, I could read the smug satisfaction in every line of his face. I swallowed. Thane glanced at me, catching my gaze for the space of a heartbeat.

"In the tradition of our forefathers, I put forth the name of Braedyn Murphy to take over as the head of the Guard. Will any second my nomination?"

"What?" I stared at Thane, numb.

"I second it." Matthew stepped out of the crowd. His voice was clear and strong.

"I third it." Gretchen clambered to her feet, flipping her short hair back from her face. She joined Matthew, giving him a smile.

He bent close to her ear, but his voice carried, "I don't think that's a thing." Gretchen sniffed and shrugged.

"The nomination stands," Thane continued. "I call for a vote of…"

"I object!" Clay strode toward Thane, furious. "These… these people lived with the Lilitu long before we arrived. She's had time to work on their minds. They may not even know…"

"Then I'll second the nomination." Marla stepped out of the crowd, crossing her arms over her chest. Clay stared at her, speechless. Marla gave Thane a matter-of-fact shrug. "Does that cover it?"

"I believe it does." Thane drew a line in the sand between Clay and me. "Guardsmen, choose." He moved to stand beside me. I looked up at him, but he was studying the crowd. Waiting.

Dad, Lucas, Gretchen, and Matthew moved first, lining up behind Thane and me on my side of the line.

Karayan called to Dad as he passed her, still kneeling on the ground under guard. "Mind giving a girl a hand?"

Dad reached down and helped her up. The soldiers standing guard over her traded a look. Then they sheathed their daggers and followed Dad and Karayan to my side of the line.

The soldiers all chose—one by one at first, then in groups of three, four, six—until every single Guardsman stood shoulder to shoulder at my back.

Clay faced us, alone on his side of the line. After a long moment, he stepped forward, crossing the line in silence. A tension seemed to break among the assembled. But as I met Dad's eyes, I saw I wasn't the only one who wasn't relieved. But Clay was a problem for another time. My thoughts turned to finding Emma.

"Braedyn." Thane spoke at my shoulder. I faced him, distracted. He dropped to one knee before me and drew his daggers, resting them across his open palms and earning my full attention. "I, Robert Thane, make this oath: I dedicate my life and my strength to the Guard, to our mission, and to our leader."

For a moment, I was too stunned to do anything but stare. Thane glanced up at me, expectantly.

"I don't believe it," I murmured.

Thane actually smiled. In that moment, I saw the man he might have been, if his life hadn't been tainted by the deep bitterness born of suffering and loss. "How many times am I going to have to say it? My loyalty is and has always been to the cause."

I cleared my throat, then reached out and closed his hands over the dagger. "In that case, I hear and accept your oath. Rise, brother of the Guard."

Thane stood, sheathing his daggers. Then he gripped my hand tightly and gave me a solemn nod.

"So. Robert, huh? Does this mean I can call you Bob now?" I asked.

"No." As he turned away, Lucas stepped up to take his place, hiding a smile from Thane. One by one, the Guardsmen approached to pledge their lives and loyalty to the cause and to me. With each oath, I felt the weight of an unlooked for responsibility grow heavier on my shoulders.

Someone must have released my friends from the van, because as the last of the Guardsmen finished his oath, I saw them standing at the edge of the clearing, watching me, mystified. Then Karayan was standing before me. She grinned, eyes brimming.

"Look who grew up to be a rock star."

"I don't know about that," I started, choking the words off as Karayan dropped to one knee and lifted her hands, palms up.

"I, Karayan Thane, make this oath: I dedicate my life and my strength to the Guard, to our mission, and to our leader." She glanced up at me, looking almost vulnerable.

I clasped her hands in mine. She didn't need weapons, she was the weapon. "I hear and accept your oath. Rise, sister of the Guard."

Karayan stood and embraced me tightly. My eyes found Dad in the crowd. He was watching someone, and there was unmistakable tension around his eyes.

Clay stepped forward. The Guardsmen around us fell silent. I felt the skin along the backs of my arms start to tingle, like it did before a fight. Clay drew his daggers. It took all my willpower to face him without moving to defend myself.

Clay dropped to one knee and offered up the daggers in his open palms. "I, Terrance Clay, make this oath: I dedicate my life and my strength to the Guard, to our mission…" He swallowed, and for a moment, I thought he might not be able to finish. But then he drew a fresh breath. "And to our leader."

I folded his hands over the blade of his dagger, feeling beyond self-conscious. "I hear and accept your oath. Rise, brother of the Guard." I finished the acceptance in a rush and pulled my hands away.

Clay straightened and stepped back into the ranks of the soldiers facing me. I looked out over the Guard. This was the force that would face down Lilith. These were the brave souls who'd give everything to try and prevent her from reclaiming this world. And now, they looked to me for leadership.

It was something I'd never sought, and as I looked over the crowd, a tiny seed of doubt wormed its way into my mind. What if I wasn't up to the task? But even as I acknowledged this doubt, another part of me hummed with an eager anticipation. It was as though something within me was shifting into alignment. Like this was exactly where I needed to be right now, this was exactly what I needed to be doing.

I took a deep breath and let it out. And then my gaze caught on one face in the crowd. Clay. His eyes were as hard and cold as steel. A shiver passed over me.

He was not going to forgive me for this.

Not ever.

EPILOGUE

"It's so weird." Royal slapped a copy of the town's newspaper down on the dining table. We'd spent the morning taking our history midterm. The afternoon would be dedicated to AP Biology. To say it was jarring, going from that night on the cliff back to something as banal as school exams, was putting it mildly.

I glanced at the newspaper. Cassie's face covered the front page, alight with joyful tears, wrapped in her parents' arms. The headline read, MISSING GIRL FOUND SAFE. The cover story was that Cassie had been driven ill with the stress of senior year and fell into some kind of fugue state, wandering off into the desert. It read as an almost romantic tale, which credited a group of dedicated friends, chiefly among them Royal, for going out and finding her before she could die from exposure.

I exchanged a look with Lucas, but it was Cassie who answered first, shrugging. "People see what they want to see."

She looked healthier than she had since the summer, but a new shadow hovered over her. This shadow wasn't supernatural, and it wasn't confined to Cassie. Looking around the table, I could see it hovering behind the eyes of all my friends. Royal, Lucas, Missy... even Amber and Ally—we all carried the knowledge that something terrible had been let loose into our world.

It hadn't taken long to ascertain that Emma was missing. The police—acting on an anonymous tip—had gone to her apartment building and questioned her roommate. The roommate described Emma leaving with a handsome young man. His description fit Seth to a T.

Lilith was now in possession of her vessel. The final battle had begun.

It didn't feel like there was much to celebrate, but on Christmas morning, I came downstairs to find Dad putting the final touches on a Christmas tree. Karayan watched him from the couch.

It felt good to have our house back. One of my first acts as head of the Guard was to let people live where they chose, with the caveat that Karayan got her old room back. Gretchen had happily moved back next door to be with Matthew and Lucas. Sandra had decided on taking one of the rooms next door as well, to be close to Thane and the last remaining Guard Archive. But most of the new Guardsmen had spread out in small groups, renting a few houses in the neighborhood. No one was too far away, but we weren't crammed on top of each other, either. It seemed like a small enough change, but it had improved some of the tension within the Guard overnight.

Karayan looked up as I entered and raised a mug in salute. "Hot cocoa? I left some on the stove."

"What's...?" I moved into the room, feeling sluggish.

"Merry Christmas, kiddo." Dad reached under the tree and retrieved a small package. "One of your friends left this for you." He handed me a little present, wrapped in delicate white and silver paper.

I turned the tag over, but all it said was: *To Braedyn*. I opened the present, curious. Inside I found a beautiful turquoise pendant, hanging from a soft leather necklace. There was a note tucked beside the necklace. It was from Missy.

Turquoise is supposed to be a symbol of protection, it read. *When I saw this necklace, I thought of you. I'm starting to realize more of us owe you thanks than even realize it... so on behalf of the clueless people lucky enough to have no idea what you do for them, thank you. And thank you for saving my sister. You'll have our gratitude for the rest of our lives.*

With a full heart, I set the note back in the box. My eyes stung, but the pain was welcome. It felt good to feel something other than grief. Dad must have been watching me. He threw an arm over my shoulders and drew me in for a warm hug. I let him hold me for several long moments, then straightened.

"I think I'll get some of that hot cocoa," I said. I made my way to the kitchen, rubbing the moisture out of my eyes. The cocoa had filled the kitchen with a warm, earthly sweetness. I found a mug in the cupboard and was turning back to the stove when something caught my attention.

I set the mug down and rushed out the kitchen's back door. He was standing in the fresh snow, examining the long icicles that hung from the branches of one of the backyard trees.

"Sansenoy." I gripped the back porch rail. Fury boiled up inside me. "Where the hell have you been? We needed you. We needed your help. And now… Lilith… she's returned."

Sansenoy faced me. Something moved across his face, something that almost looked like surprise. "I'm afraid you've misunderstood my intentions," he said. "My mission was never to stop Lilith's return. My mission is to fight the last battle with all the strength given to me and—if possible—win."

The door opened behind me. "Braedyn, the cocoa is boil…" Dad's voice broke off. "Sansenoy." The angel inclined his head toward Dad, acknowledging him silently.

I felt my teeth grating and forced myself to relax. "So why come back now?" I couldn't keep the hostility out of my voice.

Sansenoy turned back to me. If I didn't know better, I'd say he looked exasperated. "You made a request of me, did you not?"

For a moment, I had no idea what he was talking about. Then the realization hit me. I felt my mouth drop open. "Emlyn…?"

"What better day to bestow a gift?" Sansenoy's voice sounded strangely gentle.

I turned to Dad. He stared at Sansenoy, transfixed. "Dad?" I had to touch his arm to draw his attention. He looked at me, then came back to his senses.

"Right." He shot one more look at Sansenoy, then disappeared into the house.

"She's not here," I said. "I need to call her." I fished my cell phone out of my pocket. Vyla had given Karayan the number to a disposable phone. It was meant to be used for emergencies, but I had no doubt she'd want to take this call. Vyla picked up on the third ring.

By the time Dad returned with Karayan, I was a mess. Vyla's joyful sobs had triggered my own tears. Karayan saw my face and broke into a watery smile.

"Crap. Now I'm going to cry." Karayan held a small stuffed rabbit in one hand, the rabbit Emlyn had left behind when Vyla came for her.

"Why are we crying?" The door behind us opened and Lucas emerged. He held a small present in his hand and he was smiling. But when he saw Sansenoy, his smile faded. "Whoa."

A bolt of unease shot through me, dispelling the joy of the previous moment.

"Hey, Lucas." Dad tried to usher Lucas back inside. "Why don't you wait for us in the living room. This won't take long."

The Lilitu gate opened behind us on the lawn, shattering the air with a kaleidoscope of light. Vyla stepped through, carrying Emlyn in her arms. The gate shimmered shut behind them and Vyla set Emlyn down. When she straightened, Lucas got a clear look at her face.

"*You!*" Lucas moved, but Dad was prepared. He caught Lucas's arms, keeping him from charging Vyla.

Vyla straightened, terrified. She shoved Emlyn behind her back. I saw the terror lighting Emlyn's eyes.

"Stop!" I planted a hand on Lucas's chest. "Lucas. Stop."

Lucas struggled in Dad's grip. His eyes sought my face. "What's going on? What is she doing here?"

I glanced at Dad, hesitant. Dad read the question in my eyes. "If you think it's a good idea," he murmured. Lucas eyed me, unnerved.

I turned back to Vyla. "He should meet her."

Vyla's eyes shifted to Lucas. She bit her lip. Emlyn peered out from behind her legs, staring at Lucas with frightened curiosity. I heard Lucas's sharp intake of breath.

"That's...?" Pain edged into his eyes, but it was accompanied by a dawning realization.

"Your niece." I turned back to Emlyn. She looked up at her mom. Vyla knelt and drew Emlyn into her arms. Emlyn studied Lucas. Her hazel eyes mirrored his so perfectly it was clear they shared a family connection. Both sets reflected the same cool greens, flecked through with the same golden highlights.

Then Emlyn saw Karayan. Karayan held up the rabbit and Emlyn's face lit up. "Bunny!" She raced forward, breaking out of Vyla's grasp. Karayan held out her arms, bracing herself for the hug. She caught Emlyn and swung her around. The little girl laughed, her fear forgotten.

"That's Eric's laugh," Lucas breathed, his face a strange mix of grief and wonder. The fight seemed to go out of him. I met Dad's eyes and nodded. Dad released Lucas. Vyla and Lucas eyed each other for one tense moment. Karayan, noticing this, didn't set Emlyn down.

Sansenoy was the one who broke the tension. "Bring the child to me." He knelt, waiting. Karayan set Emlyn down and Vyla took her hand, leading her toward Sansenoy.

Emlyn eyed him skeptically, then glanced up at Vyla. "This is the angel?"

Sansenoy smiled. He laid a hand on her head, resting his thumb on the center of her forehead. Dad and Murphy didn't react, but Karayan, Vyla, and I stepped back as one—we were the only ones who could see the power radiating from Sansenoy's touch. Like the dawning of a thousand suns, it speared out fingers of brilliant fire, putting the morning light to shame. I squinted, lifting a hand to shield my eyes, but the light wasn't physical. As my Lilitu sight adjusted, I saw the golden fire cascading over Emlyn, filling her until she was nothing more than a gleaming silhouette.

Emlyn sighed—a sound of perfect contentment. The light subsided.

Vyla dropped beside her daughter, searching her face. "Baby? Are you all right?"

"It's... nice." Emlyn looked down at her body. "It feels warm." Vyla caught Emlyn up, crushing her to her chest. The girl laughed, startled. "Mommy, too squeezy!"

"Thank you," Vyla said, turning to Sansenoy. He dipped his head in response.

Dad let out a ragged breath behind me. I turned. A small smile played at the corners of his mouth, and his eyes were brimming. He shifted his gaze from Emlyn to me. A tear slid from one of his eyes, snaking its way down his cheek, unnoticed. I held his gaze, swallowing against the lump rising in my own throat. We didn't need to say anything; it was clear we shared the same hope in this moment.

Lucas let out a breath. "What... was that what I think it was? Did he just...?" He swallowed. "Is she human now?"

"It's why they came to Puerto Escondido." I caught Lucas's hand. His eyes flicked to my face, but it was hard to tell exactly what he was feeling. "I didn't know how to tell you," I floundered for the right words. Lucas squeezed my hand, stopping me.

"But she's human?"

I nodded. Lucas's face split into a beatific smile. He turned back to Emlyn. She gave him a shy smile, pulling her bunny closer like a shield.

Vyla looked up, torn. "We should be moving on. We don't want to risk the rest of the Guard seeing us."

"Where are you going?" Karayan's eyes shifted to Emlyn. With a pang, I realized how attached Karayan must have grown to Emlyn during their time together.

"Don't worry, Karayan." Vyla gave Karayan a warm look. "We won't lose touch."

We watched as Vyla summoned the strength to open a new gate. She and Emlyn stepped through. Lucas's eyes followed them until the gate closed behind them. He dropped his eyes, lost for several moments in deep reflection. He didn't release my hand.

Sansenoy straightened, rising to his feet and taking a breath of the icy December air. He studied me with a look of unmistakable satisfaction. "I see your Guard has finally recognized what was apparent to me upon our first meeting."

I looked at him blankly.

"You have a warrior's heart, it is only fitting that you should lead the Guard." Sansenoy approached. "Please accept my help in this fight."

It was hard to push the last dregs of resentment completely out of my heart. He'd ignored us for months, leaving us at the mercy of Clay's megalomania, risking Cassie's life, and doing nothing to prevent Lilith's return. But I nodded. Not accepting his help wasn't an option.

"This is it then." I heard Dad's murmur over my shoulder, but I didn't take my eyes of the angel.

Sansenoy shivered in undisguised anticipation. "I can feel Lilith in the world." His eyes shifted. There was a sort of eagerness in him I'd never seen before. "After eons, the final contest is at hand. Whoever wins this battle, they shall be the victors of this war."

A NOTE FROM THE AUTHOR

Thank you. Thank you. Thank you.

Thank you to the readers who've reached out to let me know you enjoyed the story. You have no idea how much it means to me. I can't help but feel the amazing friendship of this growing community.

Thank you for taking a risk on an indie author. The publishing world is changing—I feel it, and I'm willing to bet you feel it, too. The gates are coming down, and more and more writers are able to get their stories out into the world. This leaves readers with a wealth of options, and I'm honored and grateful that you've chosen to read this series.

Just by reading, you've already done more than enough, but if you have a spare moment, I'd be grateful if you'd consider leaving a review online, be it on Goodreads or Amazon or wherever you bought the book. Don't worry, it doesn't have to be long or involved, but every honest review helps spread the word.

Thanks again for reading. I can't wait to share the next of Braedyn's adventures with you.

- Jenn

ABOUT THE AUTHOR

Originally from New Mexico (and still suffering from Hatch green chile withdrawal), Jenn is the author of the award-winning *Daughters of Lilith* paranormal thriller YA novels.

Outside of writing books, Jenn has penned projects for TV, comic books, and film, most recently being tapped to adapt Erica O'Rourke's novel *Dissonance* for the big screen. She created *The Bond Of Saint Marcel* (a vampire comic book mini-series published by Archaia Studios Press), and her produced television credits include Twentieth Television's *Wicked, Wicked Games* and *American Heiress*.

Jenn currently lives in California with her husband and sons, and is realizing a life-long dream of growing actual real live avocados in her backyard. No guacamole yet--but she lives in hope.

Sign up for Jenn's Newsletter to get a free copy of "Stolen Child (Daughters Of Lilith: 3.5)," a short story bridging books 3 and 4.

Books by Jennifer Quintenz:
The Daughters of Lilith series:
Thrall (Daughters Of Lilith: Book 1)
Incubus (Daughters Of Lilith: Book 2)
Sacrifice (Daughters Of Lilith: Book 3)
Guardian (Daughters Of Lilith: Book 4)

Follow her on Twitter: @jennq
Visit her blog: JenniferQuintenz.com

Made in the USA
Charleston, SC
16 September 2016